Downtown Perryburg   Winter 1926   (c) George McFeeney

PERRYBURG

An Autobiography of a City

by

Randy Becker

Published by Perryburg Press

www.PerryburgPress.com

Copyright 2025, Randolph Becker

OTHER WORKS BY RANDOLPH "Randy" BECKER:

Fiction:

The Venice Stories (2001)

It's Always the Little Things (2017)

It's Always One Thing or Another (2020)

Non-Fiction:

Reclaiming the Soul of Your Faith:
Finding the Vital Elements of Your Own Beliefs

Travels in Venice, I and II

This work is dedicated to
the people of Perryburg
- past, present, and future –
whose stories are the stuff of history

and to my wife
Jane Leff
stalwart and encouraging partner
in the research and creation
of this narrative.

CONTENTS

FOREWORD

Margarita Gonsalvez, Ph.D.

Farnsworth Professor of Urban Studies

Mohawk University

In her ground-breaking work, "Many Histories," Karen Magnusson writes:

> We often mistake the word "history" for a single concept, and that mistake usually defines history to be the recitation of dates, events, and facts. However, there are many histories of any given place, person, city, culture, or nation. When we open ourselves to this multiplicity of histories, we begin to craft the mosaic which is the real fabric of reality passed through time.

G. Harold Pimsmith, in "Counting the Peoples" writes:

> The distinctive line between history and urban history is that the former is concerned with political, religious, cultural, and ethnic records of what has been deemed worthy of remembering by some subsegment of the people while the latter is concerned with the people, all the people, who happen – for good or ill, in freedom or bondage, akin or diverse – to inhabit a place on the surface of the earth.

When Randy Becker turns his eyes on Perryburg, and invites us to see through his eyes, he melds these two understandings of history into one, a new formulation which might be called Urban Mosaic History. We look at the whole through the lives of individuals, we look at the lives of individuals through the larger perspective of the community, and we try to see both the individual pieces and the overall pattern of the revealed shared memory.

If you have ever been to Ravenna, Italia, and toured the Basilica of Sant' Apollinare, you will have probably been dazzled by the mosaic images spread throughout the church. Standing back, you will see the vivid visages of saints; moving closer you will begin to see the small, almost tiny individual tiles which make up the portraits. Solely seeing the portraits gives you only a portion of the magic and meaning of the portrayals; see only the individual tiles and you miss the larger message.

Today, several large metropolitan hospitals use similar efforts by creating large images of patients, successfully treated, with those large images composed of many much smaller photos of the massive teams of people who made their treatment successful.

Becker is in the tradition of Ravenna and this modern image-mosaic tradition. He places real people, carefully researched and represented after painstaking interviews and historical documentation, onto the canvas of Perryburg's more familiar history of dates, changes, and luminaries. In the process, he gives us a narrative history of a city which is both the city, and some of its inhabitants, AND a larger picture which reaches beyond Perryburg. Because these individual people realistically live out the struggles of life familiar to so many of us, and the composite image of all their lives brought together in one place seems so known to us, whether we have ever been to Perryburg or not is irrelevant. He invites us to say, "I know that person," or "I've been to that place."

"Perryburg: An Autobiography of a City" is probably the most accessible entry to Urban Mosaic History available so far. Its stories will engage you, the settings will feel strangely nostalgic, and the people, oh the people, they are you, they are me, they are us.

This is history written anew.

PREFACE

An admission: I grew up in Perryburg. I left Perryburg for a long time. Then I moved back.

The Perryburg of my youth is filled with nostalgia, the Perryburg I left seemed outmoded and archaic, the Perryburg I have returned to struggles to find its new identity.

Perryburg shares much of its story with many other cities and towns in the so-called "Rust Belt." It also has its own peculiar and quirky problems. Like other city pairs with similar names (for example Ithaca and Utica), Perryburg is often confused with Perrysburg not only in its own state but in other states. Mail is often mis-routed, delaying its ultimate but untimely arrival. Like other communities that developed using First Nation names for places, it often has unique spelling for streets (e.g., Kanastota Avenue).

The larger question has always been how those things — peculiar, quirky, and unique — bind more than separate Perryburg to/from other communities; what are the patterns of similarities by which a person who has never been to Perryburg will find familiarity and connection?

As an urban historian, I have studied communities around the world, looking to find the various strands of their history by which we can understand them as vibrant, moribund, or dead. One of the questions I have asked repeatedly is, "Can a city that seems on its last legs revive and stride into the future, not as a recreation of its former glory, but manifesting something newer and grander?"

My political history colleagues will argue that the only way to answer such a question is to examine both historic and contemporary institutions of governance. How are decisions made? Who makes them?

My philosophical colleagues will ask: what were and what are the values which inform the existence of the community?

My sociologist colleagues insist that I look at the overall trends of the masses and their collective institutions, looking for the social forces and impediments that have shaped both past and present, and preordain the future.

My economist colleagues ask me to look at the forces of resources and production as indicators of the health of a community, noting when either of those forces is out of balance with the other there will be a terminality to the community.

My Rock n Roll colleagues will argue, "We built this city on rock n roll" and so the most accurate measure of any community is the vitality, decline, or absence of live music. Extrapolated, this becomes the arts argument that: a community is only as healthy as its diverse artistic expressions.

As I began to think about the city of my birth, the city I had rejected, I tried applying these many techniques. Each one of them provided a picture of Perryburg, but each of those pictures seemed overly constrained. Something was missing.

I then remembered a trip I took to Norway.

Before I left on my trip, I studied the various travel guides for Norway. I also looked at various maps of the cities I would visit. I felt I was ready.

But what I had not taken into account was that travel guides are for what usually is true, and maps portray a flat world. On my first day in Oslo, wanting to get back to my hotel from the harbor area, I got on the appropriate tram that would take me to a transfer point to a second tram line that ran right behind my hotel. Easy, except at the transfer point it was evident the connecting tram line was not operating. Many signs, all in Norwegian, looked ominous. At this point no guide or map was of much use.

What was helpful were the people on the street. Several, seeing me looking at the signs and consulting a map, asked if I needed help. And they asked in English! Soon I was on my way again, on foot, around the work on the tram line to where service resumed. I was also told about the least steep path to get there, and even about a great place for coffee and perhaps a sweet along the way.

In any community, it will be the people who tell the real story.

When I returned to Perryburg after years of absence, I vowed to understand the city not only by its history, not only by its institutions, not only by its government officials, not only by its economic rise and decline, not only by its educational systems, not only by its arts offerings, but through the stories of its people. People at its founding, people in its development, people who moved there, people who moved away.

My research was as much about collecting stories as about scouring records. As much about reading letters and snippets of correspondence between residents as about official reports. Often the pictures that accompanied newspaper articles gave more of a story than the words.

That is why I have subtitled this collection about Perryburg, "An Autobiography of a City," because it is really the history of the people, real people, of the city. Their collective biographies, spanning hundreds of years, are the real history of the city.

In the process of assembling this autobiography of Perryburg, I have come to appreciate, much more than I ever did when I lived here earlier in my life, how much my story is a piece of that larger story. Now, as I write my own new chapters here, I am joined by others who find Perryburg to be where they wish to write their life stories.

I hope their stories will give you a more complete understanding of this city and many other cities like it that comprise the rust belt of our nation. Along the way, you might begin to understand how some of those lives are polishing off the rust from the hidden treasures underneath.

Randy Becker
January 20, 2025

INTRODUCTION

PERRYBURG: An Autobiography of a City is a modernist attempt to capture the character and essence of an urban area through a series of what, at first glance, appear to be short stories. In each of these stories there is a combination of history and lived personal experience. The intertwining of the historical with the personal narratives provides the reader with a deeper, more insightful understanding of Perryburg than any prosaic counting and accounting of events and buildings.

Of course, as with any biography and especially autobiography, a reader is tempted to ask, "Is this true?" One cannot vouch for a perfection of truth when dealing with the stories people tell, especially about themselves. But one can ascertain the underlying validity of those accounts by seeing if the surrounding history bears witness to the stories' claims.

In encountering Perryburg in this manner, one needs only to drive around the city and its suburbs and talk with its residents. One will quickly discover that the stories, as shared, were truly the cause of effects that can be seen today beyond the original stories. The buildings are there, the streets are there. Class reunions still recount prior events. Individual stories are included in the collective memory of the city. In other words, if anyone were to go to Perryburg today, they would find ample evidence that what is shared here is its history, told from a new perspective.

In the preparation of this book, especially in the interview phases, permission to use real names was universally obtained. For those who have died since recent events, permission to use the real names was obtained from the surviving next-of-kin. More historically, the names used are those contained in various, reliable public records.

A simple invitation: read these stories individually but understand them as individual but interconnected parts of a whole. No one chapter contains Perryburg but taken together they all do.

1. EXODUS

Perryburg, as most of the country knows, was famous for its precision tool and die works as well as the textile mills which lined both sides of the river. The foundries would expel the dark smoke of their forges while the sluiceways would mix the streams rolling out of the mountains with their brown effluent flowing into part of the canal system.

However, to recall either of these industries as dirtier or cleaner than the other would be to miss how many chemicals went with textiles and how relatively little smoke a foundry might produce. The thoroughbred steam trains roaring through town, taking the passengers and products of the Northeast to the Midwest, gave off much more smoke and noise.

Perryburg was not Pittsburgh nor Gary, nor was it a Love Canal.

It was Perryburg.

In its birth, the city had arisen because of its location and the abundance of natural resources. At first, those resources included trees and water. Its location in the essential valley of westward expansion brought with it first the canals, then the railroad, and later the Interstate highways. The proximity to hydro-electric plants added electricity to the list. Along the way, the steady if varied stream of immigrants was a key factor as well.

Perryburg should have been the epitome of the industrial age. It was. That is until the industrial age was over, and in that same moment, many would say, Perryburg was over.

Down by the old canal warehouses, buildings long since abandoned or repurposed (despite the regular spring flooding), there is that sort-of paved parking lot. Not covered by asphalt but by cinders

1

from the old coal-fired steam plant for Union Station, the lot sits pretty empty and bleak these days.

Back about 75 years ago, it was home to a giant fleet of rental trucks. Orange, black, and white conveyances of many varied sizes, from petite trailers to large trucks. People were moving then. Moving to Perryburg, moving in Perryburg, moving out to the suburbs of Perryburg. Nobody seemed to be leaving Perryburg except for an eternal rest at Shadyside Cemetery. Almost any weekend, and especially around the first of any month, the lot would be empty because every mode of self-haul was needed.

I remember when my parents moved up from the capital in one of those rental trucks. Or at least I have heard the story of the move as I was just a growing presence inside my mother at that point. They had to pay a surcharge on the move to Perryburg because so many people were moving there but few were moving out. Except on weekends, there was a glut of trucks that had been driven there.

However, later, on weekends when I needed to get things to college, I learned to make my reservation early to ensure a vehicle, any vehicle would be available. The tide had turned, and the supply in that lot was limited.

These days, the lot is usually empty. Why?

To understand that, let me tell you a story.

Hugh Griffith had met Laura Lloyd at Perryburg High. It may not have been love at first sight, but over the four years they shared in high school a relationship grew, one of mutual respect and support and finally love.

After graduation, Hugh entered the apprenticeship program with the tool and die works while Laura went to the local community college to become an LPN. By the following June, the two were married in the Welsh Anglican Church down by the old Civil War monument. The next weekend they began the ritual of moving.

Between the households of their two sets of parents, they had scarfed together enough to furnish the one-bedroom apartment they had rented over on the west side of town. It filled one of the smaller trucks, a truck they first took empty to the house he had called home for most of his life, and then to the house she had called home for about half of her life. Filled with the longings and belongings of two lives now intricately entwined, they drove across town, down the tree-lined side street, and up in front of what would be their new, shared home.

The house had been a single-family residence for the Mitchells, a home into which seven children had been born and six of them had grown up. Little Sarah, the middle child, had known it as home for only four years before polio ended her residency. Forever after it would be a lively place that was also filled with deep sorrow. The three children's bedrooms were assigned first based on age, then later gender. By the time the older ones were in high school, the desire for more privacy, more space, and more quiet, led the parents to reserve one of the biggest trucks for a move to the suburbs.

The house – that of love, of hope, of memories, of grief, of joy – was then sold to the Grzywacz family, immigrants from Poland, all three generations of them. They arrived a couple of days after the Mitchells moved out, another rental truck bringing large, dark furniture.

The house was modified to create a one-bedroom apartment downstairs for Róża Woida, Mrs. Grzywacz's mother. Róża would soon become a fixture on the street, sitting out on the front porch, talking with any passers-by, waving to passing cars. After school, as the kids would walk home, she would often have warm cookies for them.

The other members of the family lived in the rest of the downstairs and the upstairs. On weekends especially, the sound of an accordion and dancing could often be heard inside the house, and friends would drop over without invitation.

Then the ambulance came, then the black bow was on the door and a steady stream of people silently filed through the house, then the little casket for the old woman was carried out to the waiting hearse, and Róża was no longer at home.

About two weeks later, a medium-sized trailer was attached to Walter Grzywacz' pickup truck, and the contents of the apartment were loaded up, to be driven to over to where new arrivals from Poland were renting a place for their family. It was like that, back then, one household dealing with their loss by helping another.

No one in the family could stand the thought of anyone other than Babcia living in the apartment, so the rooms sat empty, echoey, unused. Occasionally a box of this or that would be stored in there, but not for long. No one liked to go into those rooms. It was filled with too much grief.

Finally, that empty space in their lives was too much for them. They found and bought a nice little Cape Cod house up in the Windwood area, one with no empty rooms. On a snowy January Saturday, a small rental truck would make four trips between the two houses until one was filled with the future and the other emptied of the past.

The new owner of the house was simply in it for the money – she saw a single lot that had two rental properties on it. The one-bedroom apartment, which had been Babcia's, was where the Griffith's moved into.

As they moved their goods into their new home, Hugh and Laura both felt and then spoke about how it felt like a place that known lots of love. "Just like us."

(Right about now you may be wondering why I am telling you about a house when I started to tell you about moving trucks. Trust me, this is about those trailers and trucks, with the house being simply a vehicle to move the story along.)

The Griffiths loved living in their little apartment. It was just the right size for them, or it was until two years later they were three in the same space. Their daughter, Margaret, quickly grew from a nice addition to the little household to a demanding presence in the by-then too small space.

They began the search for a house that would hold their growing family, with space to spare. By then Laura had enhanced her LPN credentials with more education and was now an RN. Between the two of them they had financial stability they had never known before. In late Fall, they found what they sought: one of the older, larger, stately homes on one of the side streets off Mohawk Street, the main thoroughfare of the city. Built in the 1920s, the red brick house offered space, privacy, and a solid sense of being "at home."

They gave notice, and on the last Saturday of November (right after Thanksgiving), they were joined by their extended families for the move into that new home. Yes, the usual rental truck was there, outside the two-family conversion, ready to be loaded.

With the apartment vacant, the landlady tried to minimize any investment in the property and avoided repainting and repairs. The house was at the start of its downward spiral. By this time, the supply of apartments was greater than the demand, and fewer people were interested in the cobbled-together apartment in what was once a single-family home. It sat vacant into the new year. Mid-winter, when an interested family finally asked for a look, the damage from the frozen waterline was discovered. A patch-up job of repair was completed, but before the next prospective renter saw the apartment the prior water damage had seeped further into the structure.

5

The owner now faced what was facing so many landlords in the city. Costs were beginning to outpace returns. The only solution seemed to be to try to reduce costs to the level they matched rental income. The die was then cast. Within three years, the empty, now nearly abandoned, apartment decayed within the larger house until one day a rental truck pulled up to remove the detritus of the renters of the other portion of the house. They had given up. They had skipped out on the last month's rent. What was carted out was treated as junk, not goods.

With windows boarded up, the once-proud house stood for a year before a Halloween fire took its toll. Reduced to rubble, and a large tax write-off, it would take the city to clear the lot. No more trucks came to bring or take away the households of anyone.

But, had anyone tried to get a trailer or a truck, they would have been hard pressed to find one. Perryburg had changed from a moving city to a move-out city. Over the preceding few years, first one by one, then more by more, people were leaving. Leaving not just for the suburbs. Leaving leaving. Getting out of town. Saying goodbye forever.

Remember the Griffiths, who had started this story? In their new home, in addition to Margaret they welcomed Gareth and Elizabeth. But, soon after Elizabeth's birth, the senior Griffiths, Hugh's parents, announced they were leaving, moving to Savannah. As Hugh helped them load and then drive the rental truck one-way to their new home, he felt like something was breaking in him. He turned in the truck in Savannah and that truck would never see Perryburg again. Taking Amtrak back to Perryburg, he had hours to think about what was happening.

A year later, it was the Lloyds who made a journey, this time to Arizona. Ever the frugal couple, they were planning to do the driving themselves, but again Hugh stepped in and drove. Their truck would never see Perryburg again either.

Then Margaret loaded up a trailer and went off to college in New England. Both Margaret and the trailer would never again spend real time in Perryburg.

And so, it went. Gareth off to the Northwest. Little Elizabeth, suddenly and embarrassingly pregnant, married and moving with as much furniture as the family could give her, to follow her Army husband. That truck would take up residence at Fort Sill.

With the old house now an empty, echoey survivor of livelier times, the Griffith began to feel the strain of their years and of life in Perryburg. Much which had been familiar was gone. You could not shop "downtown" because all the stores had gone. You could not walk to the movies, all replaced by cineplexes off in the suburbs. The Welsh Anglican congregation, shrinking like so many other places of worship, merged with another congregation, which then merged with another congregation, barely sustained by the few dozen members left.

In the end, one October day, the Griffiths held a giants yard sale on the lawn of the great house. Much of their shared life went for pennies on the dollar and loss on the memories. What was left fit into the largest of the rental trucks. Margaret and Gareth came back to help in the process (Elizabeth was now with her husband, stationed in Europe) and they would drive the truck for their parents down to Pensacola before scattering to their own new hometowns. The truck they drove would never go north again.

As the Griffith handed over the keys and a lengthy instruction manual to the new owners, the Masouds, immigrants to the city about ten years prior, they wished them well. The Masouds thanked them for the negotiated lower price on the house and then began to unload one of many, many trips in the family's minivan. There were no trucks to be had.

If one could have had a time-lapse camera pointed out to the Interstate, one would have seen month by month the sad reality. Rental trucks and pulled trailers, all orange-black-white, moving down the extension of Mohawk Street and turning onto an entrance ramp in one direction or another. One rarely if ever saw one coming down the exit ramps into the city.

And then, it was as if the Mitchells and the Grzywacz and the Griffiths had never been there, all their goods and deeds and hopes and losses and memories had been loaded onto a truck of forgetfulness. Perryburg was losing itself.

Back in Biblical times, when time seem to both expand and contract inexplicably, the exodus of the Israelites from Egypt was a sudden, abrupt event, carried out over a matter of hours. In Perryburg, where time sometimes seemed to stand still, the exodus was so gradual, so normative, over a matter of years not hours, that few noticed. However, the effect was the same. Where once there had been craftsmen raising up the great city, now there were empty forges and lathes. Where once bakers produced bread for hungry families, now there were cold hearths and fewer families. Where once one could hear the voices of praise raised in churches and synagogues, now a less-sanctified quiet emptied the air.

That cindered parking lot is empty. No trucks stand ready to help those moving anywhere. No trailers await a hitch to change. They have left, and Perryburg with them.

The millennium closed, and Perryburg with it.

2. REUNION

Perryburg was just another of those northern rust-belt cities that was once a bustling place, full of mills, factories, banks, stores, and all the signs of economic vitality. That was 50 years ago. Time, and a changing world, had not been kind to Perryburg.

First the mills went south in search of cheaper, non-union labor. The global electronic industries soon followed suit as the full impact of transistor technology and the digital world took hold. Without those mainstays for the workforce, the population began to dwindle. Some people fled to the suburbs; others just left. One by one downtown stores closed, replaced for about three decades by the new mall outside of town, it to be replaced by a bevy of big box stores. The banks consolidated and then were bought out by interests from afar.

The population count at the 2000 census registered a 57% drop since the 1960 census. In the interim, petty crimes had risen while major crime (if you count capitalist asset raiding) soared. Corruption probes of city officials became commonplace.

In 2002, a new administration was sworn in and one of its first activities was to replace the old city slogan ("A City with a Future") with a new appeal. It would be emblazoned on the many signs at the city's entrances and on a massive sign out by the Interstate, the very road that had siphoned away through traffic passing through downtown and out some five miles. The new slogan was selected from many entries in a public contest (the prize of which was, ironically, a fully-paid trip to somewhere else). Among the suggestions were such gems as "A Questionable Past, A Dubious Future," and "Perryburg – At Least We Are Not Detroit".

In the end, what was chosen was "Perryburg – The Place To Do Business."

By the time that Dorothy was driving into town, the big sign out by the Interstate had been modified by someone (Police never determine who it was) to read "Perryburg – The Place To Do *Your* Business." Many residents sort of agreed with the amendment.

Dorothy was driving to her 50th high school reunion. Sitting next to her was Stan, a younger man. Stan and Dorothy Engelbart. Dorothy had not been back in Perryburg in those 50 years; Stan had never been there.

Seeing the big new, but modified, sign from the Interstate exit, all she could do was snort a laugh, "Ain't that the truth."

Most of her class still lived in Perryburg or the suburbs. She had no one to stay with, her family either long dead or dead to her. The Best Western was probably the best choice for the night considering that she did not want to risk any B&B, Air or otherwise, where she might meet someone she knew.

Until the reunion, she wanted to stay under the radar. They had eaten on the road, at the town up the road, Florence, so they would not be eating in town. She had packed some breakfast things so they would not have to go down to breakfast in the all-too-open breakfast room.

The reunion was scheduled as a brunch, out at the old Twin Pines Country Club and Event Hall. She remembered how, 50 years before, that place had already looked and felt dated, like it was unlikely to survive any cultural change of modernity. But, against all odds, it was still around when almost all the institutions of the city had fled. She wondered what people now had to celebrate in the Formica-surfaced splendor of yesterday.

The online flyer had stated the times as 11am to 3pm, but she doubted anything would really start until at least 11:30, and she wanted to be among the last, not the first, to arrive.

Driving into town and toward the Event Hall, she was struck by how stuck in time the city was. Fifty years had not graced any of it. Empty lots stood as markers of the fiery demise of many of the old houses, alongside unkempt properties in which people still lived. The storefronts had more than their share of emptiness as well. To say the city was living up to its modified motto would be an understatement.

The parking lot was nearly full, causing them to park at the edge, down by the stumps of two, once-majestic, pines. The stumps had been carefully refashioned into benches, but time had transformed the benches into splintery, slimy places on which no one would wish to sit.

As Stan and Dorothy walked toward the entry, they could see others only just now arriving, and a train of walkers slowly wheeling their way, of couples who looked so old. So worn down.

There was a small line at the check-in table and while waiting for their turn, Stan asked Dorothy to remember the last time she had been in that space. "It was for my Senior Prom," she replied, looking a bit wistful but also troubled. "I went with Danny Pataki, the football quarterback. He and I didn't really date, but when he asked me, I said 'Yes' because I wanted to be seen with him. I wanted to be seen as someone special."

Stan wanted to follow up on what she said, but the person behind the table said "Next."

"Hi, we are Dorothy and Stan Engelbart."

The greeter was looking down at her registration list and only looked up at hearing the name. A look of surprise covered her face. In front of her were a couple with a very attractive woman impressively dressed by big-city standards and a handsome, distinguished, somewhat younger man equally dressed for an important occasion. She didn't recognize either of them, but she did

11

note that the old proverb was proving true – after a couple lived together for years, they begin to look like each other. But, oh, he was a good looker indeed. "Good for her," Muriel thought.

"Dorothy," Muriel said, "Janice, our chair has a note here that she wanted to talk with you when you arrived. Just give me a minute so I can get her." Looking over to the next table where all the swag was being given out, Muriel called out, "Janice, oh Janice dear, could you come here please?"

Janice, ah Janice, the Prom Queen, Janice Albright, voted most likely to become a Hollywood star, Janice Albright, the fashion-queen of the class, looked over, ended her conversation about this nicknack versus that, and walked over.

Dorothy could see the nametag now, "**JANICE** (Albright) **PATAKI**, *Class of 1974.*"

"Yes, Muriel?"

"These are the Engelbarts."

"Oh," Janice said, as if startled, "Hi, I'm Janice Pataki, Reunion Chair. When we got your registration and payment online, we were curious. None of us on the committee could recall anyone in our class named Dorothy or Stanley. We looked at the yearbook and didn't match you up with anyone. So, we were wondering, which of you is the class member, or are you both?"

She looked over at Stan, and realized what a handsome face he had, how virile he looked, in much better shape than all the other men in the room. Somehow, he also looked familiar.

Now Dorothy was ready. She knew this moment was coming and she was cherishing every minute of it. "Dorothy was my middle name, which I never used in high school," she said slowly. "You probably knew me as Patty Osborne." She let that name drop with all its weight.

For a moment, all one could hear was Muriel dropping her pen.

"Well, ah, uh, Patty, er, Dorothy," Janice stammered, "Welcome back to Perryburg High School Class of 1964."

Dorothy could hear, behind her, a murmur of whispers filtering through the reception area.

"And, this is my dear Stan. He did not go to Perryburg."

"Well, welcome Stan. It is good, and brave of you to join us today for a reunion that is not yours."

"Thank you, I have been looking forward to it for a long time."

"Where did you go to school?"

"Out in the Hamptons, Southampton High to be precise. The Engelbarts have lived out there for many generations. Class of 1992."

"Welcome, then, to both of you," Muriel chimed in, "I have made new nametags for both of you."

"Thank you, Muriel, and especially thank you, Janice for making us feel welcomed," Dorothy said. She looked down at the nametag Muriel had made for her: "**DOROTHY** (Patty Osborne) **ENGELHART,** *Class of 1974.*"

As she and Stan clipped on their nametags, they turned to face the reception room, and found they were being stared at by nearly everyone. Pulling herself together, Dorothy took Stan's arm and confidently walked across the room, into the dining area, and looked for open seats at one of the back tables. One table was totally empty, the six seats awaiting them.

They could hear, after they left the reception room, conversation resuming among the others, even highly animated conversation.

"Be a dear," Dorothy said to Stan, "and get us drinks. And be on your best behavior," with a wink.

"My pleasure," Stan replied, with a wink of his own.

Stan noticed (and Dorothy could also, even from back there at the table) that when he walked up to the bar the conversation in the reception room slowed and quieted down. While he was waiting to place their drink order, an over-made-up woman of a certain age approached him. "**SHIRLEY** (Montgomery) **HALPERN**" was all he could catch from the nametag, and he had to assume she was one of the alumni.

"Stan, or is it Stanley?"

"Just Stan. Shirley, it is good to meet you."

"Oh, don't call me Shirley. Everyone knew me, knows me, as Cookie. My mom was the cook at school, so I became Cookie."

"Interesting name derivation, Cookie."

"Huh? So, where did you meet Patty, er, Dorothy?"

"I met her in Huntington, out on Long Island. Long, long ago. And it was love at first sight. She often talks about it, how from the moment she laid eyes on me she was in love. It took me a little longer, but in the end we were inseparable."

"Ah, I love a good love story."

Turning to the bartender, Stan ordered two Bellini's. Hearing that, Cookie gushed "Ew, how cosmopolitan."

"I hope these will be as good as the ones we had at Harry's in Venice last year when we were celebrating our time together."

Gathering up the two drinks, he left an amazed Cookie behind, with her Miller Lite and lots to run to tell the others.

Dorothy welcomed Stan back with both thanks for the drink and a question, "Did Cookie want to know everything about you?"

"Why, yes."

"Just like the little gossip she was back in high school. She never really fit in because she was the daughter of the cook, but they let her hang out with them all because she had the best items on everyone and everything. You would be amazed what a cook hears when she silently listens in on everyone in the cafeteria line. And did you tell her everything she asked about?"

"Yes, just as we had talked about."

"Good."

Very soon the insufferable huffing and puffing into the microphone, to assure that it was turned on, summoned everyone to sit and quiet down. As soon as they were all seated, the Class President, Craig Williams, said "Please rise for the Pledge of Allegiance."

"Ugh," Stan grunted, but he joined Dorothy in standing. Neither of them said a word of the Pledge, but no one noticed them, way back there.

Then came the litany of all reunions: invocation, singing of the Alma Mater, words of welcome, recognition of the faculty who were there (three very decrepit women), a short humorous reflection by one of the other class officers (which often fell flat), and then the blessing of the meal followed by the slowly moving buffet line.

The food wasn't half bad. Their table had remained their own until just before the program began. At long last, two other couples joined them, but introductions waited until the brunch break. Something felt different with these two couples. They smiled, looked pleased to be at the table with them.

While other tables were being invited to the buffet, Dorothy looked across the table and said, "Irene and Amy and Jimmy and Juan. It is so good to see you all again."

Looking at nametags, Stan quickly determined that it was Irene and Jimmy, and Amy and Juan. He also noted that while Irene, Jimmy, and Amy were all Class of 1974, Juan was Class of 1975. The four of them seemed like a team. However, he soon discovered it was a team of five, not of four.

"Back together again," Amy responded, "the Five Troublemakers!" Everyone but Stan laughed. This was some inside joke, apparently.

Taking pity on him, Dorothy said to Stan, "Stan, you've got to know, back in the day, we five, well actually six until Bob Flixen moved away in 10th grade, were known for pulling pranks, usually at the expense of those who thought themselves too important to relate to the likes of us. But, we were careful, and we never did anything to the teachers, or administration, or the staff. In fact, we were really tight with most of the staff, especially the janitors, who would look the other way whenever we had something going on. They all – teachers, staff, and the administration – seemed to like to see the entitled get put in their place."

"I get the picture, and I now see how much practice you had for the rest of your life," Stan replied.

"What does Stan mean?" Irene asked.

"Yeah, tell us about your life since back then. We know you were not allowed to participate in Graduation because that last stunt of yours, and then you just disappeared. Is the warrant still active?" Amy probed, with a sly chuckle.

"I hear a story I need to know," Stan jumped in immediately.

"Stan, you heard the story, but long ago. (He is getting forgetful!) It was the day after finals were over and the day before graduation. I was finally fed up with how badly we five had been treated, how we were looked down on, or ignored, or abused. So, it was the day when everyone would report to homeroom, then go clear out their lockers, and then go home. With the celebration of graduation in the air, I came into school very early, even before the doors were opened. Remember, we had friends in low places. I came in and found the lockers of the "in crowd" members. One by one I superglued their doors shut – didn't need the combination to do that – and you know those little vents up by the top, I put a nozzle of spray foam insulation in each one, quickly filling the innards full. I then popped the last locker, the one belonging to big-shot Danny Pataki, and I put all the evidence inside – glue, canisters, nozzles, all – and then I sealed it shut but did not fill it."

"Man, you should have heard the commotion that morning," Juan quickly inserted, "yelling, pounding, cursing, and more. Seems that a number of them had important things in their lockers, including a diamond ring one of them was going to give out at the end of the graduation, on bended knee up on stage. Eventually, the janitors were summoned, thinking that all they had to do was pry open the lockers and all would be OK. But when they opened the first one and found it filled with hard foam, they knew it was worse. That damned foam would penetrate nearly anything in there, seeping into things and swelling.

"Then, they got around to Pataki's locker. Crowbar, chisel, hammer, and creeeeeeaaaak, like the Mummy's tomb, it opened. At first, Danny was relieved to not see any foam. But then he saw what was in there. A hand took hold of his shoulder, the hand of Mr. Best, the Assistant Principal. 'Son, I think we are going to the office.'

"They got him almost to the office when my father, Juan Senior, one of the good old janitors, stepped in. He had always looked the other way before, especially since I was involved (I did hear warnings at home, however). But this time, he told me later, he had

17

to speak up because more than ego had been damaged. Lockers were destroyed, contents ruined.

"So, Pops told Mr. Best that he had seen Patty Osborne in the school before hours, and she was carrying a large bag. Later, when he saw her leave, she didn't have that bag."

"Yep, ratted out. Hey, Juan, just so you know, I was never sore at your dad. He was a stand-up guy. And I had it coming. And, as to the warrant, which no one was ever able to serve on me because I was gone to the wind, it lapsed seven years after that great day. I have always wished I could have seen Pataki's face as he, the golden boy, was marched down the hall by Mr. Best."

Dorothy paused, and then added, "Maybe someday I will have my wish come true."

"That was some day, all right," was Irene's reaction. "But what happened to you?"

"Long story – I'll share more some other time, but here is the short version. I left town that morning, thumbed a ride as far as Long Island. There I quickly found a job waiting tables. I enrolled in CCNY, the old City College. No real application process. If you were a high school graduate (I was, just without a graduation) and still breathing, you were in. I waited tables, went to school, got my law degree, passed the bar, started working in family law, especially around domestic abuse, sexual exploitation, and child rights.

"It was some years into my life in court that I caught the eye of a scion of wealth but also an icon of equality. Nothing about my life – my past, my age, etc. – bothered him. So, we were married, and I became Mrs. Engelhart. Eventually we moved out to the Hamptons."

It was just then that more huffing and puffing into the microphone alerted folks that the program was about to continue. After a pitch for class T-shirts and hoodies, the speaker, a former School Board chair, delivered the remarks: "Blah, honor, blah, loud blah, integrity, blah, forever, thank you."

Class President Craig Williams resumed his position at the microphone. "Now is that special time where we all bring each other up to date on class happenings."

He began with an In Memoriam reading of the names of those had died since the 40th reunion. Too many names, most meaningless to Dorothy, but one brought regret to her heart.

Then, the open mic (Muriel will bring around a microphone to each table for those who want to speak. And, please, stand up, so we can see you.)

The painfully slow litany began: grandchildren, even a few great-grandchildren, partners ill or dead, a few retirements, second and even third marriages, and the like. The microphone finally arrived at Dorothy's table. She gestured for the other two couples to go first, which they did with quick sharing of simple things.

Taking the microphone into her hands, Dorothy started in story-telling mode, noting her sudden departure from the class. She remembered the locker incident matter-of-factly. But then, in an almost prosecutorial manner, she said, "Do you ever wonder why I did all that?" A murmur of both interest and judgment ran through the room.

"OK – I'll tell you. None of you, not even my best friends here at this table, ever really knew me. You didn't know the violence and abuse of my home. School was my refuge, but most all of you refused to welcome me. You only saw some one who seemed broken and desperately needy. You saw someone who first suffered from the sexual abuse by my father, and then someone whose father abandoned her, leaving her both confused and wanting."

19

At this point, Muriel tried to reach in for the microphone, but Dorothy was stalwart.

"No, Muriel, I've come here to say this, and even if you take the microphone, I will get it said, and I assure you, I can be heard without it. So, back off." Back off, she did.

"I didn't know how to relate to males, I didn't know how to be the woman I was becoming, I didn't have anyone to turn to because my mother always defended my dad.

"Now, I know most of you remember Prom Night. How grown up we thought we looked. I thought I looked amazing. And I was so proud, and so excited that Danny Pataki wanted to be there with me.

"But, do you remember what you called me? I seem to remember 'Easy Patty' was one." Dorothy heard more than one gasp in the room.

"Or was your choice word 'Slut,' or maybe 'Whore.'" Now she heard more gasps, and she saw tears forming around her girlfriends' eyes.

"Yes, I will admit, because of all that had happened to me, I was a little more willing to go where you boys – didn't think I would leave you out of this, did you? – wanted to go. I didn't do anything that any of you women in here haven't done, I just did it a little earlier than most of you did, but I know not earlier than some of you who called me those names behind my back. You felt you could foist your own feelings of shame and worthlessness off on poor, old me.

"But, from all of that, I made a life. I got out of here. I became an attorney, a very good attorney."

She was beginning to sound more and more like a lawyer in court.

"As you know, I came here today with Stan Englehart. Englehart is my married name. Stan, would you please stand up." Stan, with a slight smile, stood beside her.

"Back to that Prom Night. Right here at Twin Pines, when the pines were still standing. Danny, so suave, so loving. Toward the end of the evening, he invited me to walk out under the stars, under that full moon, out onto the golf course. Down along the number one fairway. I remember how it felt to have his arm around me. I felt loved. I felt protected. No one was going to hurt me with Danny around. We got down by the second green, that soft, smooth green, and he took off his black tux jacket, and laid it on the grass. He invited me to lie down on the jacket."

The room was hushed now, but looking around the class, Dorothy could see more than one face looking pale, both men and women looking pale.

"Yes, he asked me to lie down on his jacket, and when I did ...." she paused with just a little quaver in her voice, "he came on top of me and pinned me down. Suddenly there was another pair of hands holding my ankles, and another holding my hands. Hands I knew too-often had handled the football.

"And then, without a word more than 'you slut, I know what you want,' he had his way with me. And when done, he, ever the team player, invited others to follow his lead."

By now, she could hear sobbing among the others in the room.

"Wait, I'm not done yet. It wasn't just boys out there on that green. I heard girls' voices, I felt more than one female hand fondle me. One even reached down there and tried to bring me off while her boyfriend was pumping away.

"And finally, as I sobbed and sobbed, and pleaded for them to stop, as I said 'No, No,' more times than I could count, I suddenly felt all

21

weight off me. I saw that moon above, unobscured by some horny boy pounding away. At last, he said 'Do you mind?' and peeled the tux jacket out from under me. He walked away, along with a great crowd of all of you, and in the distance I heard laughing.

"That night I had no one to go home to who would listen. I knew no one of authority would believe me. I was all alone. YOU all knew, but you would choose to either not remember or not pay attention to the rumors.

"I then vowed my revenge. That was found in superglue and spray foam. But, when I was found out, I never looked back. I moved on, but you all were condemned to stay here and try to forget the Prom you wanted to remember forever.

"Here we are, in the same place, once again. I asked Stan to stand with me, because he knows this whole story, he was the one who wanted me to come here and open the past."

Tension held the whole room.

Stan now spoke, "I'm Stan Engelbart, I was born on March 13, 1975. I became the adopted son of Clarence Engelbart, the man my mother met, fell in love with, and married. But, who am I the son of really?"

Stan searched the room with his eyes, and then with pointed finger, began his inquiring accusation: "You? You? You? You?"

"Maybe my mother cannot tell which of you, from that night, fathered me. But there is one way to know which of you did not. Simple."

Taking a small case from his coat pocket, he opened a display of several specimen tubes.

"A little swab, some DNA, a quick lab test, and we can know the truth. I'll be behind the registration desk for those sure that they are not my father. See you there."

With that Dorothy and Stan strode out of the dining room, and Stan sat down behind the registration table, while bedlam broke out in the reunion. The noise, the accusations, the denials, the cries, the sobs, and more, were sweet sounds to Dorothy's ears and she knew she would never attend another reunion of her class.

3. UNION STATION

Perryburg, while its own sub-species of city, is like so many towns of the Industrial Age. One of the more common quirks of such communities is that Main Street is not the main street of the city. That honor goes to Mohawk Street, but more about it elsewhere. Main Street is a stubby little street that fronts Union Station.

On that stub of a street, stories have unfolded like an old-time road map, opening up to reveal life's direction but then hard to fold back into how it had been. Before I get to some of those stories, I need to get you more acquainted with Union Station and its environs. Nothing happens in a vacuum, and the setting is so important, be it the road to Damascus or Maine Street in Perryburg.

To add to the irony of Main Street being a secondary street, Railroad Street is not down by that great hulk of a building called Union Station. Railroad Street is about a half mile away, fronting a vast empty lot.

The empty lot once held a sprawling public housing complex, "The Projects," but time and doctrine had doomed those ghettoized apartments to the wrecking ball. Before the housing was there, the space had been home to a collection of old, wooden buildings that served as the depot and the freight house of one of the railroads that served Perryburg. Hence, that was where Railroad Street was.

You ought to know a bit more about the geography of Perryburg. One of the great coordinates of directions ran just about straight down the main street (no, not Main Street), while the perpendicular axis almost perfectly followed the path of the main railroad through town. But it was not the only railroad to serve Perryburg.

No, not by a long shot.

What many would now call "the railroad" was, in fact, the combined remnant of two, once-mighty railroad empires. Born in competition, by now they were not competing with anyone other than their own failures. Like ornery branches sticking out at odd angles from that iron spine, was a series of other railroads, most of them poor imitations of the big time. They hauled goods out of mines and forests to be interchanged at Perryburg enroute to their final destinations. They picked up milk, cream, and butter at rural stations deep in the rich farm country of the valleys and consolidated them heading for the bigger cities. They offered transportation to the people, and their needs, who sought recreation and escape from those bigger cities. More than one of them had been built to satisfy the ego of a magnate of another industry.

While "the railroad" had followed the natural valley with its pre-existing river, then trails, then roads, then canal, most of the other lines were limited to less rational choices. One railroad founder bought up the name and rights to an unbuilt canal, not recognizing that the reason it had not been built was that it had no business being there. Another great Baron of industry unrolled a flat map onto his desk and circled the cities of modest size that did not yet have a railroad. Then, playing connect-the-dots, he created the plans for his rail system, ignoring all the geological and topographical constraints that he would encounter.

Later some would quip that rather than the given, hyperbolic names adopted by these minor tributaries to the great river of steel, they should be known as "The Road of Shame," or "Iron Rails into Idiocy." The old T & P, "The Tinertown and Perryburg," was commonly called "The Tired and Puny."

Of course, back when railroads were coming to Perryburg, Perryburg wanted as much railroad action as possible. Corrupt politicians, the mainstay of mid-level cities in those days, worked land deals and civic concessions to ensure that anyone with a railroad ambition could find a place in town to build a depot.

What with various railroad mergers and bankruptcies, in the end Perryburg had four different and separate train stations, each of its own style and grandeur (or lack of it). In the space between the four stations was a tangled maze of connecting tracks often cluttered with freight cars in transit or in storage.

This would not pose much of a problem except that the maze of tracks and the clutter of cars was right at the heart of the developing city. To get from one side of downtown to another was an exercise in frustration.

So it was, in 1899, that the City Council appointed a Railway Commission, with the sole objective of straightening out this mess. With all due speed, by 1905 the Commission had proposed a Union Station, to be just beyond the developing main street, Mohawk Street. All railroads would be required to use the new station for passenger trains and no car, engine, or other piece of railway equipment was to "linger or dwell for more than 10 minutes other than in the Union Station and its associated freight yard, nor shall any train, stopped or running, block the Mohawk Street crossing for more than 5 minutes."

The solution was quickly and easily accepted until the question of cost was raised. The city, citing the profit-making nature of the railroads, offered only to build the local roadways and utilities. A "Railway Compromise Committee" was then appointed in 1906, a committee which work diligently for three years to hammer out the financing. The end result was simple: the total cost would be delegated to the participating railroads based on the reported profits of each involved railroad for the year 1910. What this meant was that "the railroad" basically paid for the whole thing, as the smaller lines were either essentially insolvent or just squeaking by.

In 1915, the new Union Station was opened with great fanfare. Each line ran special trains to Perryburg and on opening day, at the same hour, after (too) many speeches and an attempt to bust a ribbon with a locomotive (which only resulted in tearing down two telegraph poles used to suspend the celebratory ribbon), trains on each line whistled twice and began their journeys out of Perryburg.

It was a grand station, with separate men's and women's lounges, both a station restaurant and lunch counter, a barber shop, and more. Finished in polished limestone from nearby quarries, it virtually gleams itself into being.

Over the years, famous trains ran through or stopped in the station. You may remember the Centennial Limited, with its distinct rear drumhead glowing in green (changed to red after the unfortunate collision from behind when a following Mail and Express train mistook the decoration for a clear signal). Lesser trains, like the McKeever, the Fast Mail, the East Shore Limited, and TaCumSeh also appeared daily.

The smaller lines generally just used train numbers except in the summer months when both The Clear Aire and the Vacation Special would appear at the platforms, pulled by smaller locomotives of diminutive railroads.

Outside the station there was always a scene of bustle and hustle. Local street cars looped by. Taxis lined up for customers. People often came down to the station just to watch the comings and goings.

All that excitement peaked in the 1940s with the demands of the War.

After the war it was still a happening place, but then when Eisenhower proposed the Interstate Highway system, and the State began its portion, first as the AllState tollway and then as part of the Interstate system, the handwriting was on the wall.

By the mid-1960s. the station had fallen into disrepair. Fewer than half the number of trains now ran daily, and only two of the railroads were left. By the early 1970s, federally imposed consolidation had reduced that number to one. There was nothing to unite in a Union Station.

If you drive by today, with the grace of state funding and private grants, you will see a once-proud building looking good again but robbed (for the most part) of its function as a railroad station.

Now, why am I boring you with all this railroad talk? Because Union Station is where three stories connect, even if only a few of the characters in the three stories ever knew each other. Only Union Station knew them all.

. . .

Early 1944, a Sunday afternoon. and Union Station is bustling with activity. People coming and going in every direction. Out on the mainline platform an eager crowd awaits the arrival of the train from Dunkirk, heading for the big city. This route is so important, so busy, that within an hour two different trains will stop at this platform. Soon in the distance the shrill whistle of the steam engine announces the imminent arrival of the first train.

Among those waiting on the platform is a man known to many others also waiting. He is the Superintendent of School, the former Principal of the high school where most of the others waiting had been students or parents of students.

As usual, he is dressed in a vested suit, a blue tie, a heavy overcoat, and a grey fedora with black band. He was not the type to add a feather to the hat, but he was the type to sport a patriotic lapel pin.

He is awaiting the arrival of his daughter, a nurse, from Dryden, where she worked in the emergency room of the teaching hospital. After a long ten-day shift, she is coming home for two days off. He knows that she will be bringing two suitcases, one simply filled with dirty clothes from those 10 days. His wife is back home, dutifully over-roasting the precious beef that saved ration coupons had allowed them to buy. Their son, an aviator in the Pacific campaign, would only be present by the periodic letters he could send home.

With a huff, and a puff, and a steamy groan, the train pulled to a stop. He was about halfway between two stairways down from the cars and the eager crowd of travelers seeking a chance at a seat on the crowded train had already massed around both those stairways. With an eager eye, and much head turning, he scanned both places for a sight of his daughter.

He was startled to see her descend from the train with a young man in tow. What stood out was a young man, much less a young man out of uniform. The young man was toting his daughter's two suitcases, as nimbly as anyone could. He was a clean-cut looking man, dark hair, whose caring eyes seemed only to look at his daughter.

As the crowd surged toward the train after the last arrivals in Perryburg had alighted, his daughter and this young man walked over. Putting the bags down, the young man said, "Sir, here is her luggage," and to her, "glad I could be of help." "Thank you," echoed two replies.

"You better get back on board, young man, unless you plan to call Perryburg your home."

"Don't think that is likely, but with all that mail up front I probably have plenty of time. Good day to you both," he said, adding to the young woman, "It was swell meeting you."

He was about halfway back to the stairs when an abrupt "All Aboard" was called, causing him to quicken his steps, step up on the first step, turn, and wave to them. A sudden double toot of whistle and the noisy release of brakes announced the train's immediate departure.

Before the last car had cleared the end of the platform, the father turned to his daughter and asked, "So, Gladys, who was that young man?"

"Oh," she said, "that was Bill, just someone I met on the train. Probably never see him again."

Had she been able to see how he had looked at her from the rear window of the train, she might have answered differently.

. . .

The Vietnam War was raging. A divisive draft policy meant that, while all young men were subject to its demands, the majority of white boys who had access to college were not called up. Roosevelt Jones, Jr., was neither white nor college bound.

He had grown up in "the projects," only a short walk from Union Station. He remembered how the whole apartment would shake as one of the crack limiteds or a long coal drag would pass by, just yards away from his bedroom The nearby Lincoln Street crossing meant every train would whistle the warning long, long, short, long like it was warning him personally.

Many nights he wondered and worried. He wondered if he would ever travel on one of those trains far, far away, to one of those places he read about in history class. He worried that the answer would be "no," and he would live out his life, stuck in this decaying hulk of a city.

Upon graduation from Perryburg High and turning 18, he had gone down to the Selective Service office on Mohawk Street and dutifully registered. Then, he walked over to the paving company office to respond to what his father, Roosevelt Jones, Sr., had told him.

"Son," he had said, "I've been working for Mr. Matera now for longer than you have been alive. And he told me, once he saw how you played on the football team, that he would always have a position open for you, if you didn't mind hard work, dirty work, sweaty work anymore than I didn't mind. I told him, 'No, sir, that boy of mine be a good worker.' I played the good, Black worker for him just fine. Now, get your black ass over there and get that job."

He was immediately hired, assigned the lowest level work on a scale that went from boss to low-level, to lower-level, to lowest-level. All summer long, he had stood, shirt off in the blazing sun, coaxing scalding asphalt onto the streets needing paving. It was brutal work, but at least he was earning money, unlike many of the young men in the projects. He was also toning his body far more than any preparation for football had ever done.

Around about the end of October, with the hot paving season about to come to a close, he got the letter. "You are hereby ordered to report …" it read. Report he did. First, for a physical that found him physically, intellectually, and mentally more than fit. Then, in a few weeks, to an assembly point at the local armory (the old one, down on South Street), before being marched to Union Station, where he and many he had known from high school boarded old coaches serving as troop transport, for his trip to New Jersey and basic training.

At the station, his father stood proudly by while his mother quietly wept. As he marched up the platform, a very subdued round of applause rippled through the mainly African-American crowd that had gathered. The train loaded with little fanfare as those on the platform watched their hopes and dreams, one by one, ascend the steps to their destiny. Two short toots of the horn on the diesel and the train was underway. Few left behind had the strength of the moment to wave.

Jones, as he was now called by superiors, or Junior, as he was now called by his fellow draftees, looked out the window, and hearing the warning horn for the Lincoln Street crossing scanned the brick façade for one last glimpse of his bedroom window. It was soon gone, and he was looking at a world he had never seen before, of a deep valley, little towns with foreign names, another mid-size city, the great river, and finally the big city. He was still not sure if he was filled with wonder or worry.

. . .

The days of the crowded World War II trains were long gone, as were the days of the tired and worn troop cars of the 1960s. By 1975, the Amtrak trains passing through Perryburg had shiny new Amfleet cars, tubes of stainless steel that were as modern on the inside as they were impressive on the outside. Each day three trains in both directions stopped in Perryburg, but the passenger count for the city was always depressing. More people boarded than disembarked. The long exodus from the city continued.

However, on this one day, the numbers would be reversed. The train, from the big city, was running about 40 minutes late. A small contingent of local residents had assembled on the platform to meet the train, not take the train.

After the predicted delay, the approaching train's horn was heard and soon its headlight bore around the slight curve into the station. Coming to a halt right where the old entrances to the passenger tunnel to now-abandoned tracks had channeled all those people back in the 1940s, two adjacent traps were opened and stairways dropped. A small trickle of passengers started to step off. But then, in brightly colored garb of another world, a large contingent of people alighted, most without suitcases but carrying great cloth bags of possessions. The waiting delegation surrounded them with shouts of "welcome to Perryburg."

These were refugees from Africa, the displaced people of famine, war, and more. They had come to America in search of life, liberty, and at least a small possibility of happiness. Arriving in the big cities of the East Coast, they were temporarily housed in large shelters. Within weeks it became apparent this arrangement was not good for either the refugees or the cities. Political eyes turned toward other regions with the hope of resettling these people.

Somewhere in the chain of political command someone remembered Perryburg. While it had an official and several unofficial nicknames and slogans, one that held historical truth was "City of Immigrants." (No one in the establishment, once they were a generation away from immigration, wanted to promote that phrase. The old "raise the drawbridge after my people got here" dictum was in play.)

So, the local charity organizations that had, in the past, welcomed the Irish, then the Italians, then the Poles, then the Eastern Europeans, then the Hungarians, then the Hmung, were contacted. The welcoming delegation on Union Station's platform was from a coalition of those organizations and agencies.

Imagine, if you will, people familiar with deserts, hot weather, donkey carts, and all the other accoutrement of Somalia experiencing the new, comfortable, speedy train that brought them up a great river, into a long valley, and finally to Perryburg. All their senses were overloaded. They were living in shock.

Jamilah stood tall among the group now gathering on the platform in this very foreign place. In her home community, she had been a teacher of girls, a well-educated woman by their standards. She was a faithful Muslim, whose speech, garb, mannerisms, and customs reflected all the cultural attributes of that devotion. Right then, all she wanted to do was stop moving, and see if the world around her would stop moving as well.

But those shouting welcome were now beckoning all of them toward the walkway to the parking area, across what had once been more tracks of the station. There, sitting in the parking area, was a large bus, its uniformed driver waiting by the opened cargo doors on the underside of the bus. Upon seeing this sight, many of the arrivees shuddered and hesitated. Back home, being told to get on a bus (true, not a nice, new bus like this) meant that you were about to be "disappeared." The driver looked too much like police and giving their meager possessions over for him to stow under the bus felt too much like confiscation.

The welcoming committee tried to reassure them all, less with words and more with gentleness, smiles, and a willingness to put their own handbags in the luggage area and board the bus.

Jamilah looked at these nice people, looked into their eyes, looked into their souls, said a quick prayer to Allah, and strode over to the driver, gave him her bag, and then walked to the door and boarded the bus. Then she turned to the others, and in a commanding voice in their native tongue told them that it was OK. A murmur among the rest followed, long looks at each other, many shoulder shrugs, but soon they all followed her lead. She was, after all, the teacher.

Jamilah had learned English as part of her education, so she understood what those greeting them were saying. She was the only one among the refugees who did. But she kept this hidden in most public situations in this new country. Understanding but not known as understanding had made her privy to many a conversation the speakers had thought were private.

It would be weeks before the re-settlement committee knew of her proficiency in English, and a formal British English at that. Once her skills were known, both as a teacher and an English-speaker, she was in great demand. Less than six months later, she was hired by Perryburg Public Schools to teach the English as a Second Language classes to the growing number of immigrants from her home country and even elsewhere. She was so very good at it, probably because she remembered well how it was for her to have learned English as her second language.

. . .

So, now I have told you the three stories I promised. Three times, out of the millions, that Union Station was witness to a coming or a going. These three stories. But now I will tell you the story of these stories.

Yes, Gladys drove off toward home with her father, and Bill rode on, on the train, to the Capital. There he worked for the railroad, the big one. He was heading back to his office after a weekend at home in Dryden with his family. Right out of college, he had been eagerly hired by the railroad as a civil engineer and was quickly declared an "essential worker" at the outbreak of the war. That was why he was not in uniform.

When Gladys returned to her Nurses' Residence in Dryden the following Tuesday night, a letter was already waiting for her from Bill. He had carefully listened to what she had told him on the train when they met, figured out the address for the Nurses' Residence, and sent a note "hoping you will remember me as the boy from the train."

Remember she did, and even as late as it was when she read the letter, she penned Bill a response, assuring him he was remembered. Soon letters flew back and forth between them, as fast as the mail in those days could deliver.

Less than a year after that meeting on the train and their short goodbyes on the Union Station platform, they were wed. As one of his letters had said, "in times like these, when I know how I feel for you, I know we can't wait for some time later." On their wedding day, they were back together, husband and wife, boarding another train for their Honeymoon trip. A week later, they would return by train, but not back to Perryburg. They settled, together, in the Capital, in a shared rented apartment, housing being so scarce.

Before long, Bill was offered a promotion. "Any chance you would be willing to move to Perryburg and staff our engineering office there?" had been the follow-up. Bill remembered his words on the platform at Union Station on that fateful day several years before when he had deemed such a move unlikely. This time he eagerly accepted the chance to take his bride, and now his small son, back to her hometown.

Over the years after that move, Bill worked out of Union Station, up in the office hidden from view, way above the transiting masses below. His family (growing with the birth of several more sons) would often meet him at Union Station to catch the Friday evening train to Dryden and visits with his family.

One day, looking down from his office window, onto the platforms of Union Station, now greatly diminished in number and use, he spotted a passenger train arriving, one of the strange mix of cars that came with the start of Amtrak. He watched as the slim column of passengers got off, such a change from the scenes he had known before. However, he saw one young man, a tall Black man, in full uniform, come down the steps, pause for a moment to look at Union Station, shake his head, and then with both feet on the crumbling asphalt of the platform, stride off with no one to greet him.

Roosevelt Jones, Jr., now Sergeant Jones, was coming home. Unlike too many of his army buddies, he was actually coming home. Well, almost. He was physically back in Perryburg, but a part of his mind and his spirit was lost somewhere in the Mekong delta. There he had seen things he wished he had never seen and wished he could forget. The scars you can't see run much deeper than the scars of healing you can see. He knew this only too well. The Army had continued to deem him fit for service, even rewarded him for his leadership, as others fell behind him. He had ridden out his recruitment, re-upped twice, been promoted based mainly on survival. Enough was enough. He dared not continue in such a path that was destroying his soul even as it built up his body and his reputation. He was coming home "honorably discharged."

It was true – when he stepped down the train's stairs, he saw a place he never thought he would see again. He knew no one would be there to greet him. While he was away, death had taken all those he loved here. But, where else could he go? Perryburg was home. At least somebody in Perryburg might remember him, the him even he was having a hard time remembering.

On the next Monday morning, he showed up at the paving plant office. When Savio Matera looked up from behind his desk, his face brightened. "Roosevelt, you're back."

"Yes, sir," Roosevelt responded, "back and looking for work."

"Always glad to have you working with us. But I've got to tell you, the last several years have been tough. The Perryburg you've returned to is not the Perryburg you left. City shrinking, city budgeting shrinking, city contracts shrinking, work shrinking."

"Mr. Matera," he started.

"Savio, please."

"Mr. Matera, I'll take any work you've got."

"OK, be back here tomorrow at 7am, but all I got for you is what you were doing back then."

"Sir, thank you, sir," preceded a firm handshake.

Seven in the morning came that Tuesday and a return to work for Roosevelt. The very menial nature of the work helped to slowly allow Roosevelt to replace Sergeant Jones, then to replace Junior.

He was starting to heal in ways that the Army would never understand.

About six months after Roosevelt had hired on, Mr. Matera placed a call over to Union Station. He was looking for Bill. Bill had been his go-between on many paving jobs for the railroad. Savio knew Bill was a straight-shooter and someone who saw people as people. He also remembered how Bill's father-in-law had helped his family when they were young immigrants from Italy, making sure they were encouraged to get a good education.

"Bill, I've got a favor to ask," he began, "I've got a young man here, a decorated vet, from Perryburg, who is working way below his pay grade, but he never complains, always shows up, and works. I've got nothing more for him here, so I'm wondering if the railroad might be looking for some workers."

Bill assured him that, even with smaller track gangs, the railroad was always looking for reliable workers. "Back in the day, a people would see a railroad trackworker job as a great opportunity for advancement, but now they see it simply as work. I'll see what I can do."

What Bill could do was what he had done many times before for people who really wanted work. He called various department heads until he found someone with an unfilled position. Bill's referral was all the reference those hiring needed to know.

In three weeks, Roosevelt Jones, Jr., now just Roosevelt Jones, started work for the railroad. He was a track worker. He was surprised to see how much that job had changed since he had watched the track workers out on the track he could see from his window in the projects. Few if any spike hammers were being heaved. No teams of many men were lifting, with rail tongs, new rails replacing worn rails. No ballast rakes were encouraging the small stones back into place. No tamping rods were being repeatedly shoved under the ties.

Mechanization had come to the railroad. Large, noisy machines replaced the chanting gangs. Instead of men, pneumatics pulled worn ties, inserted new ties, spiked them in place, and lined and surfaced the tracks. Even the ballast was swept up by wire brushes, not to be tended by any human.

Roosevelt proved an adept student of the work and was soon operating a tamping machine unsupervised.

One of the things Bill loved about his job was that much of his work was outside the office, away from the desk. He would need to go do some surveying work along the main line or one of the secondaries. This was before the introduction of digital technologies that would revolutionize the work. So, he would always need an assistant to hold the level rod, hold the end of the measuring tape, etc. Such an assistant's job was what Bill had started at, but by this time the railroad had eliminated the position. Bill's only choice was to go find a track gang, see if anyone was available to help.

Looking on the daily work sheets for the division, he saw that a lining and surfacing gang was working in the same direction as today's project that needed surveying. Driving down the old state route 5, he found the gang tied up in the little town of Frost (so aptly named).

Bill knew the foreman of the gang, a burly old-time railroad full of curse words and a kind heart. "Stan," Bill began, "I need one of your gang for about two hours. Got anyone you can spare,"

"Well, look what the damn head office sent down here. Bill, how are you?"

"Can't complain. You working hard?"

"Right now, we are hardly working. Those shitheads down in the city give us production numbers, and then they fucking tell us to lock down here for hours until the hotshot, or is that hotshit, freights go by. Today, we were told we could rest for about an hour but now the freight has gone in the hole, and it will be hours before we getting a fuckin' thing done."

"So, you've got men to spare."

"Some I'd like to spare for more than an hour or two. But I'll tell you what, Bill, go ask the tamping machine operator if he'd like to do the job. He's sharp and polite, not like me."

"Thanks, Stan."

"And tell that beautiful wife of yours I look forward to a dance with her at the next retirement shindig at Club Regency."

"She'll look forward to that," Bill answered, knowing all too well what Gladys would say when he told her about what Stan had said.

Bill then walked down the ballast to the tamping machine, where he found a tall, strong Black man sitting in the shade of the operator's stand, gazing up at the sky.

"Hey, there, I'm Bill, a civil engineer from the Perryburg office, and I need an assistant for a couple of hours to help with a surveying job down the line. Stan said you might be interested."

"You mean be interested in doing something other than sitting here for hours with nothing to do? I'm your man."

Grabbing a shirt to cover his undershirt, Roosevelt came down off the machine, sort of shook himself out, and then followed Bill toward the car that was parked where the old fourth track had been.

"Bill Packer."

"Roosevelt Jones."

"You aren't related to a Roosevelt Jones who worked for Matera, are you?"

"Which one – my pop was Roosevelt Senior and until he died, I was Junior."

Bill stopped and looked at the younger man. "Yes, I can see it. I knew your father when he would do paving work for the railroad. A nice, smart man who loved his family. I would sometimes hire him out to help shovel out switches after snowstorms."

"I remember that – you would come to the house and ask if he would like to earn some extra cash. Many a holiday was much brighter because of that cash."

"I also remember him talking about a son he was very proud of. Football, Army, everything."

Roosevelt's mind raced – here was this white man not just remembering his father but remembering what his father had said about him. And a white man who could see his father in his face. A white man for whom all black faces did not look alike.

As they drove to the job site, Bill asked Roosevelt about his life away from Perryburg. He asked about the war, and something in Roosevelt told him this man was someone he could safely tell about what it had truly been like.

In the end, the simple job that required just a second pair of hands and two more eyes took no more than 30 minutes. However, they did not return to the track gang for four hours. Bill had kept track of the stalled freight and knew the gang was going nowhere anytime soon. Instead of being stuck on a hot machine in the sun waiting, Roosevelt was sitting in the shade trackside, enjoying a long, rambling, thoughtful conversation with a man who seemed as different from himself as could be, but who revealed himself as much like him as he could admit.

They discussed clouds, worries, ideas, religion, and so much more. On the way back to the gang, Bill pulled into a service station for gas and offered to get Roosevelt a cold drink. Roosevelt offered to run in and get it, but Bill said, "No, just sit. I'll get it. I know the owner here, and he wouldn't treat you the same way he would me."

This left Roosevelt speechless until he uttered a "Thank you, sir," when the cold bottle was passed to him.

He said the same thing again when Bill dropped him back to the gang, which was still just waiting there on the siding.

As Bill drove away, Roosevelt thought, "something just happened that I have no words for."

That night, over dinner, Bill told his family about the afternoon with as much amazement for the encounter as Roosevelt had. He talked about knowing Roosevelt Senior and now could put together a name and face with the person that Savio Matera had sought to help. Bill also shared about the long talk the two of them had about life and its meaning.

Roosevelt felt the lightest he had felt in years, like a giant burden had been lifted from his body and his spirit. Someone had let him be himself – not just a soldier, a worker, but his whole self.

Over the next few months, whenever Bill needed an assistant, he would track down the gang and see if Stan could assign Roosevelt to help.

"Bill," Stan would say, "I see you coming for another of your goddamn asks, and I know what you want – my best worker. But, if I want that dance, I better do it."

By the next production season, Bill would lose Roosevelt as an assistant and have to settle for someone else. But Bill's openness to conversation about all manner of things, always treating the assistant as an equal, would impress many a worker. Roosevelt was not available because he had bid on and won an assistant supervisor position.

A few years later, promoted to heading up inspection work and often working alone or with just one other person on a HiRail vehicle that could shift from highway to riding the rails, he was passing through Perryburg Union Station on the other platform track. He went into the station itself to use the bathroom and check in with the dispatcher about what tracks were clear ahead.

Inside the station, he was surprised and delighted to run into Bill. They had not seen each other in a long time, but they remained friends whenever they did meet. It was never a short conversation, with much catching-up for both of them. When an arriving Amtrak train was announced, Bill said "Let step out and see how they are doing today."

The train had come to a halt and Roosevelt saw a large group of obvious refugees assembling on the platform, newly arrived in Perryburg. Bill said, "Reminds me of the great migration back in my youth – when we were welcoming so many people of color who came here for work. Things seem to happen in cycles."

Roosevelt had never thought about it that way, but then he realized that his father had once been one of those earlier migrants standing on a platform here at Union Station, not sure what he had gotten himself into but feeling like a refugee from Jim Crow Land.

What caught his eye this day on the Platform was a tall, stately young woman, about the same shade of skin as he, who suddenly emerged from the group and appeared as a leader to the rest. He watched as she gave her parcels over to the bus driver and entered the bus, leading all the others to follow. What strength, what dignity in what is certainly a stressful situation.

As the bus drove away, he asked Bill, "Any idea what group that was and who was picking them up."

"I imagine it was the Perryburg Refugee Center. They are in charge of welcoming people to town who have been displaced from their own homelands." And then he added quietly, "She caught your eye too, didn't she?"

Blushing, Roosevelt had to admit, "Yes, there was something about her."

Back home that night, in the one-bedroom he shared only with a few cacti and a large library of books, Roosevelt did some phoning around to find out more about the Refugee Center. Depending on who he talked to, it was a godsend to people in need and a goddamn nuisance of busybodies who were trying to change Perryburg. He went away from his conversations with some reappraisals of who his friends really were.

He tried calling the Center, but his attempt to find out more about the young woman at Union Station was fruitless. All such information was confidential and thinking back to some of the telephone conversations he had he painfully understood why.

Days stretched into weeks, weeks into months, and the seasons changed twice. Union Station had been blanketed with fallen leaves carried by autumn breezes, then by heavy snow out of leaden skies. At long last, the first breath of spring was in the air, and Roosevelt was again in Union Station. Bill, who now not only worked for the railroad but was kind of a mayor to Union Station, was doing his usual morning break walk around. He would pop his head into the barbershop to say hi to Danny, then a wave to the ticket agent, assist a puzzled-looking passenger, before heading back to his office.

"Roosevelt," Bill called, "I've got something in the office to show you that I think will interest you."

"Oh, what?"

"You'll see."

They took the creaking and creepy elevator upstairs and then walked the circuitous hallways that followed the path of the lower ceilings in the main waiting room. In his office, Bill picked up a weekly paper from one of Perryburg's neighborhoods. "Take a look at page 8."

Roosevelt thumbed his way to page 8 and saw an article about a community action council meeting for a part of town that was foreign to him. He was about to put down the paper and ask Bill what he thought was so important when he saw it – the picture. It was she. The young woman from Union Station, those many months ago. He quickly scanned the caption: "Jamilah Ahmed, ESL teacher for the Perryburg schools, will present a workshop on living in a new culture at the Refugee Center on May 15."

May 15 would find Roosevelt Jones in attendance at the workshop. He sat toward the back, feeling anxious with anticipation. Would his memory from that day be matched during this evening?

Jamilah entered the room and took her place at the front. Again, Roosevelt was struck by her almost-regal look. After some opening remarks, she was introduced. She then stood but did not stand at the lectern. Instead, she took the microphone and moved in front of the table, leaving nothing between herself and the audience. She looked out over the large, half-full auditorium, slowly looking into each face. "It is never easy to move into a new culture, a new place and way of living. Sometimes this happens because we have become physically uprooted, and sometimes it is because we have changed while the world around us has not, and sometimes it is because the world around us has changed but we have not."

As she looked around the audience, looking deeply at each person as his solidly cadenced words were clearly enunciated, her haze finally fell to the back of the room and onto Roosevelt. She paused just a moment and then went on.

"Change is never easy, even when we have sought it, wanted it, been delivered by it, been rescued by it." Roosevelt heard these words reverberating somewhere within him, deeper than thought.

The workshop then developed into small group sharing and whole group reflection. Three parts: leaving home; being adrift in uncharted waters; finding home again. Roosevelt was surprised how much of the discussion resonated with him even though he was living where he had always called home. It was a transformative evening for him.

When the workshop had ended and the many thanks had been given, he rose to leave. There was a long line out the single front door of the room and so he lingered rather than push his way out. At last, he was face to face with the face he had thought of so often.

"I'm glad you were here tonight," Jamila said, in the same tone of voice he had heard her use with others in the line before him. But then she looked straight at him and said, "I have this feeling I have seen you before."

While Roosevelt was struggling to say something, anything, she continued, "Do you work for the railway?"

"Yes, yes, I do."

"Were you at Union Station on the day we arrived?

"I was. But how did you …"

"I remember a kindly face, looking at me as if I belonged here, not like some washed up piece of trash from somewhere unfortunate.

Your look gave me the courage to help my people move ahead to their better future. I have several times gone down to Union Station to see if you were there again, but no, never again."

"I have been looking for you too. I tried the refugee center, but they would not give out information."

"Good for them, keeping us safe."

"I kept looking, hoping, that somehow our paths would cross."

"And, Allah be Praised, they did."

"Let me introduce myself. I'm Roosevelt Jones. I grew up here in Perryburg."

"And I'm Jamilah Ahmed, and I did not grow up here in Perryburg," she said lightly with a slight laugh. "But now I am growing here in Perryburg."

"Does Miss Jamilah Ahmed drink coffee?"

"Is Allah merciful?"

When Roosevelt looked puzzled, Jamila quickly added, "Of course."

The two of them walked down to the Perryburg Roasting Company. The warmish evening inspired her to suggest they sit outside. "I like being outdoors whenever I can."

"Me, too."

There, under an early Spring sky of stars and a brilliant crescent moon, the two of them began a relationship born in conversation; that conversation would be the first of many, many more.

Early on in this growing relationship, Jamila and Roosevelt found themselves often talking about what mattered to them, the things they valued. For most people, when they speak of values, they speak in terms of religion.

"I am Muslim," Jamilah said.

"And I am Black Baptist," Roosevelt said.

Both admitted they had little idea of what that meant for the other, their respective religions foreign territory. Slowly, carefully, they began to explore what each meant by such simple labels.

"A man I worked with," Roosevelt said, "suggested to me that most religions are like cups, cups filled with what gives life meaning. But, we have to be careful not to think the cup is what matters. It is what is in the cup."

Jamilah looked thoughtful and then said, "I think that man was very wise. And what a gift to have discussions like that at work."

"Yes, Bill is quite a guy. He never talks down to me, and he encouraged me to look deeper into life at a time when that was hard to do."

"Bill? I have met a Bill who also works at the railway. He stops by the Refugee Center with items his church has donated to us. Wait. I just remembered. He was standing with you at Union Station when I first saw you, yes?"

"Yes, that will be Bill. He noticed you then, too."

"That explains why he seemed so friendly the first time he came in. He did something no one else does. He came up to me and introduced himself. Me, a woman, a foreign woman, a Black woman, as if I were a regular person."

"That's the way Bill is. He accepts everyone for who they are. Have you met his wife, Gladys?"

"She is a wonder. She offered to help me negotiate the channels of government here, so I could help my people better."

"See, there is good out there, even if that good is held in a different cup. They are neither Muslim nor Baptist, but they respect me, and they respect you."

In the end, the two of them agreed to find out more about their different faiths, looking for points in common more than differences. With that seeming impediment to their relationship dissolved in the waters of love and acceptance, the following months were times of learning more about each other, getting to know customs, and trying new foods.

Month by month they not only felt more comfortable in each other's world, together they felt like they were both growing as individuals and growing closer together.

About a year after that meeting, when Roosevelt was finally able to speak to Jamilah, and after having a very private meeting with her uncle, Roosevelt invited her to again have some coffee with him at the Perryburg Roasting Company. When the coffees had been brought to their table, he suddenly dropped to one knee.

"Jamilah Ahmed, daughter of Ibrahim Ahmed, would you do the honor of becoming my wife."

"Roosevelt Jones, Junior, son of Roosevelt Jones, Senior, the honor would be mine."

The whole coffee house patio broke into loud applause as the two hugged fiercely.

The next year was consumed with getting to know each other better, meeting more of the extended families (even if remotely), and planning a wedding. Every day confirmed for each of them that they were more complete together than either would have imagined alone. They often spoke of how thankful they were that they had seen each other, met each other, been open to each other despite all the seeming differences.

On a bright, slightly warm day, with permission from the Union Station management, a large marquee was erected out in the parking lot. Inside the tent, the tables circled a center space, which was centered on the exact spot Jamilah had stood when they first saw each other. In a very interfaith ceremony that honored Muslim and Christian teachings, Roosevelt invited Jamilah to share life with him, and Jamilah invited Roosevelt to share life with her. Then together they pledged to be husband and wife, life-partners. The culminating kiss brought loud applause, amens, and ululation.

After a great meal, many speeches, and much dancing, Jamilah and Roosevelt retreated to a private room in the station to change out of their wedding finery. In clothes more suitable for travel, they emerged to the assembled wedding guests waiting to shower them with fragrant flower petals.

Just beyond the tent, Roosevelt's car had been parked. While the couple had been changing, mischief had been underway. The car had been festooned with the traditional cans strung from the rear bumper, as well as wax on the windows proclaiming, "Just Married." The couple began to make their way toward the car. Bill was carrying their two bags, with a sly smile on his face.

Just then, in the distance, a train horn could be heard. The couple, with Bill and the bags following behind, changed direction, and by the time the train had screeched to a halt they were all on the platform right by the door of one of the sleeping cars. The crowd then realized that they were not using Roosevelt's car to leave, but the shiny train now stopped in Perryburg. Imagine the startled looks of passengers already on the train when the large wedding party gathered on the platform to watch the two lovers embark on the journey of their married lives. From the vestibule, Jamilah and Roosevelt waved to everyone. Two short horn blasts were heard, and the train began to move. Camera flashes flashed. Family members cried.

Off to the side, Bill and Gladys stood, watching the young couple leaving on a fast train, just as they had done those many years before. Bill turned to Gladys and said, "I hope they will be as happy as we have been." Gladys, gently kissing his cheek, replied, "I doubt any couple could be as happy as we have been." They then turned as one to see the marker lights of the receding train take the future off to its fulfillment.

A few years later, the restaurant in Union Station was packed to the gills. It was Bill's retirement party. Forty-one years with the railroad. The party that night was different from most other retirement parties of people in management: there were more workers there than bosses. And almost all of the speakers were people who knew Bill out of the office, out where he had invited them into discussion, into thinking about life, into seeing how they could become better people.

Bill had also specified one thing about the party. There was to be no dancing. He had promised Gladys that Stan would not have his promised dance.

. . .

Getting to Perryburg is not as easy as it once was. The old regional pattern of air flights is now gone. The nearest airport is 60 miles away. The old cross-state bus system is now gone, a victim of the pandemic and of corporate mismanagement. One bus a day gets to Perryburg, but that bus doesn't connect to any of the towns up and down the valley. However, Amtrak still stops there eight times a day, with connections into Canada and out into all of the United States.

So, maybe you will travel to Perryburg in a shiny stainless steel, modern railroad car. Maybe you will step off onto the well-worn platforms, and stroll into the majestic passenger hall. Maybe the day you arrive there will be immigrants from elsewhere – Somalia,

Ukraine, Southeast Asia – hoping Perryburg will welcome them. Maybe a young man will be helping a girl he just met on the train down with her luggage. Maybe another young man will be boarding, heading for the start of his career and his ticket out of Perryburg.

Or, just maybe, you will be writing your own story of arrival, a story Union Station is waiting to witness, and to bless.

ALL ABOARD.

4. WISTERIA GARDENS

In many ways, Perryburg is no different from any other city born in the wilderness and raised in the Industrial Age. Remnants of every era of its existence coexist, like the layers of the sedimentary rock upon which it rises.

At one time, the simple log cabins were dull, dark places, heated by wood fires and lit by flickering candles. In time, those who were prospering could afford finished interior walls, larger windows of real glass, and lighting from oil lamps.

The great Barons of industry, not content with the opulence of prior generations, began to build a procession of mansions on both sides of Mohawk Street, beginning far enough away from the river to avoid its riffraff and its summer cloud of mosquitos and rankness. These monuments to wealth (most with a Mansard Roof design so that the shorter top level servant quarters would not be counted a story for tax reasons) were built of brick and stone, built to withstand the rigors of time and decay.

Most of these mansions still exist, although some have been broken into apartments, others into offices. If one were to have a chance to visit one of the intact houses and walk through the grand first floor rooms, one would see ornate ceiling lamps hung from equally ornate ceiling rings of plaster. Looking more closely at the chandeliers, at the little prisms of light now illuminated by the most modern LED bulbs, one could then trace each arm down toward the individual stems and there, just below the socket, one would spot a small valve, a little piece of brass usually with its own handle. Look again at the numerous sconces on the wall and see that each of them also has such a valve.

Those valves tell us that once, long before Mr. Edison and the light-at-a-flick-of-a-switch era, these were gas lamps. Great gas mains had been laid under Mohawk Street, a branching smaller main into each of the mansions, allowing for the great rooms and halls to be brilliantly lit without the need to replenish the oil, trim a wick, or find a new candle.

But where did this gas come from? We now know that just south of Perryburg, up along the Oneidan Escarpment, one of the immense gas pipelines, that keep New England warm, channels natural gas from its source to its consumption. But these mansions were from before that pipeline, before natural gas.

Again, like most industrial cities of that age, Perryburg had a coke plant. Note, I did not say a Coke plant, for this was not about soft drinks. No, a coke plant heated coal in the absence of air to drive out the natural gases contained in the coal. The process produced the gas that would flow into those lamps and coke, a highly concentrated form of carbon that was useful not only in heating but essential in the making of iron and steel.

The coke plants were variously called coke plants or gas plants depending on whether the community was more in need of the fuel byproduct or the gas byproduct.

Perryburg's coke plant (because the forge and tool industry required the high-grade fuel) was out to the west of town, along one of the secondary railroads. Daily, long strings of coal cars would arrive (financially sustaining a railroad with little other commerce) and a portion of them would be reloaded with the hot coke remnants to be taken by rail to smaller communities without their own coke plant, communities where oil lamps and candles still sufficed.

A coke plant is a dirty, smelly thing. The fumes, containing amounts of sulfur, induce contemplations of hell. The residue is toxic. By day a grubby structure of blackened metal, by night a glowing furnace, the coke plant was unwanted by any neighborhood, but its products were desired by many. Few lived close to the plant except for those who were too poor or without other options.

With the arrival of natural gas and the closure of the various hearths that required the coke, the plant was shut down for good right after World War II. Its hulking presence stood there for several decades, a source of a common admonition of parents on that side of town, "Stay away from the coke plant!"

It was finally razed during one of the fits of attempting to make Perryburg an attractive city for the new times. That would have been a good goal had not the soil sampled during the demolition shown contamination worthy of being a Super Fund site. Like all government initiatives, while the area was deemed uninhabitable and fenced off, it was not remediated for decades.

Finally, the ground was cleared deep enough and refilled to render the site acceptable to the EPA and Perryburg got back a huge block of its territory. What to do with it? It might have been scientifically ready for anything but culturally Perryburg had only known it as a place to stay away from.

That was until the CMD corporation proposed the purchase of the whole parcel as the site of a new Retirement Care Community, which would offer Perryburg its first taste of comfortable living for its elderly. Independent living villas, assisted living cottages, long-term care buildings all on a well-manicured campus with lawn bowling, nature trails, a pond with fountains and, of course, most importantly, a grand entry archway proclaiming it to be the place where life is rewarded.

This proposal was immediately accepted by the city because it offered a three-way benefit: the useless land would be sold, the tax rolls would be enhanced, and the target population would be unlikely to pose any objection.

That is how the old coke plant site became Wisteria Gardens: Where Long Life is Rewarded.

All of my snarkiness aside, Wisteria Gardens is a beautiful development, with well-constructed facilities, pastoral grounds, great staff, decent enough food, excellent care, and ironically not a single bit of wisteria anywhere on the grounds.

Viewed from above, the campus appears like an eight-spoked wheel. The Community Center holds the dining room, the activities center, the chapel, the gym, and more, and is the hub. It is built around an all-season, retractable roof atrium, home to social hours, concerts, and more. Covered walkways connect outward to the various other buildings.

Half the circle, at the end of four of the spokes, are clusters of the independent living villas. A quarter of the circle, at the end of two of the spokes, are the assisted living apartments, while the final quarter houses the long-term care facility.

Between the spokes are a mix of lawns and gardens. Beyond the larger circle of buildings is a circular roadway lined on the outer edge by individual garages and maintenance garages. Beyond them newly planted evergreen woods replace the old, rusted security fence. Viewed from above, one might think it was some Buddhist retreat center.

I have often said that Perryburg is not that different from any other similarly sized and developed city in the country and therefore Wisteria Gardens is not that different from any other Retirement Care Community in the country. They are all like upscale college dorms for seniors: social events, dining halls, activities, and inviting grounds.

However, the demographics of the residents are skewed, and I don't mean by age. Everyone there is 65+ (unless they are the younger spouse of someone 65+). However, the population tilts heavily female. Many couples move in together, but higher male mortality leaves many widows. As for singles, more unmarried women move in, not wanting to live alone at that time of life. Men, at the same age, often assert their rugged individualistic independence. They also, sometimes, make disparaging remarks about not wanting to go to a place so dominated by women.

Wisteria Garden's about 300 independent and assisted-living residents break down this way: 77 couples; 12 single men, 127 single women. I quickly add that if you ask any of the 127 single women about those 12 single men, the most common comment is: "If you met them, you'd know why they are single." Many of those same women would add, "Don't need a man, anyway." But there are a goodly number of women who might, at least inwardly, feel differently.

It was late April, with spring finally in the air and the roof over the atrium opened for the first time in the year, that a man was seen peeking his head into the various rooms in the Community Center. Later that afternoon, he was seen in the company of the Residence Director who was showing him around the property. Before dinner time, he mingled in the social hour, awkward at first but more comfortable after one Manhattan. It being Thursday, the residents' trio started up some familiar songs from "back when." He turned to one of the women near him and asked, very politely, "Care to dance?" By the time the dinner chime sounded, he had made the evening for several of the women, all of whom would have memories of a graceful partner, so both gentle and forceful in his leading.

At dinner, the Residence Director introduced him to a table with two couples and two single women already seated. "Folks, this Bob. He is thinking about joining us here at Wisteria."

Bob now seemed somewhat reserved and more interested in asking questions of the others than sharing much about himself. His questions covered the whole range of life at Wisteria. At the end of the meal, he excused himself, thanking everyone for an enjoyable time.

As he walked out of the Dining Room, more than one of the single women turned their heads to watch the retreat of the tall, thin, silver-haired man. Once he was gone, several of them wandered (actually more like stampeded) over to the table where he had been seated and talked to (actually more interrogated) their neighbors about him.

The next few days there was a buzz in the community. A possible new arrival. A man. A handsome man, a dancer, whose clothes showed great taste and not a little wealth.

But Bob's expected quick return did not happen. Some of the more inquisitive (should I say nosy) residents sought out the Residence Director, who claimed all such matters were strictly confidential.

At the end of June, it was as if an encore performance had been ordered, this time with a substitute for Bob. This other man was also tall, well-dressed, shaved head with mustache and goatee, looking to be of mixed racial background. He carried himself so well, and his unexpected blue eyes were piercing to all who met him.

At dinner, the Residence Director again brought the visitor to a table with an empty chair, and introduced him, "Hello everyone, I'd like you to meet Kenneth, who is thinking about becoming part of our community."

"Well, Ken," one of the men at the table started.

"It's Kenneth," was a quick reply. But that misstep did not sour the conversation. Kenneth was quick on repartee, loved a good joke, and was good company. He just said, when asked more about himself, "O, let's leave all that for when I am really here."

The buzz from April now returned, all the louder for the earlier spark of possibilities.

Alas, Kenneth was not seen again.

October first was an auspicious day for Wisteria Gardens, especially for its female residents who had felt a spark of hope arise when Bob, and then Kenneth, had been in their midst. It was at lunch that Kenneth reappeared, looking as healthily debonair as before. He found a table with a couple empty seats, otherwise filled with single women. Sitting down, he introduced himself to all. Just then, Shirley came toward the table and Kenneth rose to welcome her, even pulling her chair back. More than one intake of breath could have been heard if hearing loss was not so prevalent.

"Yes, my dears," Kenneth said, "I'm moving in. Today's the day. Of course there is still some painting to be done, and all that. But thank God, I'm home with you all."

The welcomes rang out around the table, and the word of his coming to Wisteria Gardens spread like wildfire through the whole Dining Room.

At the end of the meal, he rose and said, "This is a delight I hope we can repeat often. Now, duties call." With that, and a slight touch of his fingers to his forehead as if a salute to all, he strode out of the Dining Room.

That afternoon the conversations were all about Kenneth. Would he be at Social Hour? Why did he choose lunch to make his appearance? Must be a widower because he is still wearing a wedding band.

He was not at Social Hour and a disappointment ran through the room.

Since only one meal a day is included in the independent living villas rentals, few from lunch were at dinner, only the handful of assisted-living residents with all meals included in their rentals who still feel they can stay up that late. Just at the start of dinner, Bob walked into the room, and many heads turned to look at the new arrival. One table beckoned him over, pointing to an empty chair.

"Good evening. Thanks for the invitation to join you."

"Glad to have you here. Back for another look?"

"No, not really. But you can call me neighbor starting today. I was busy directing the movers all day, and now I am famished. Hope that tonight's dinner is as good as it the other time."

"Where did you move into?"

"Villa B-4, an end unit, with lots of light."

"Ah, the McHenry's old unit. We do miss them. After Fred died, Martha went to live with their kids. He was a Rotarian. You a Rotarian?"

"No, and not a vegetarian. Please pass the meatloaf."

And so, the meal progressed. Bob was as gregarious this time as he was reserved before. He made no mention of a wife, and more than one woman noted the well-worn wedding band on his finger. Ah, another widower. And he, the dancer.

After dinner, he lingered for a time, even joining in the communal watching of Jeopardy. Finally, he said "time to get home. Boy, that sounds so good. Thank you all for making me feel so welcomed."

And then he was gone, but his presence lingered in the form of many comments and many questions.

The next day at lunch, many eyes scanned the door with hopes that one might see Kenneth entering. No, no Kenneth. In fact, no one had seen him since the day before.

It would only be about 30 minutes into the Social Hour that Kenneth would appear. He came striding into the room, marched up to the bar, and ordered a Manhattan, up please. While waiting for his drink, he scanned the room and smiled at several of the residents who smiled back. Three of the single women took the initiative and went to him, engaging him in conversation. He seemed interested in what they had to say, but he also seemed just a little distracted. At long last, he gave out a small laugh, and said, "Ah, there's the one I have been waiting for. Excuse me."

Kenneth turned, put down his now-empty glass, and walked toward the door, where he greeted Bob with a great hug and kiss.

To say you could have heard a pin drop would be misleading, since practically no one in the room could have heard pain drop. But, if you had been there, you would have seen many jaws drop.

Together, the two of them walked to the center of the room and Bob gave a short whistle, followed by Kenneth saying "Hello Evvvvverybody. I'm Kenneth and this gorgeous man with me is my husband Bob, and we are here to reap the rewards of our long lives! Thanks for making us so welcome. Come see us in Villa B-4, tomorrow night at 5pm, for our own little social hour and see what wonderful things we have done with the place."

Needless to say, Wisteria Gardens has never been the same since.

5. EMMET'S

In late September they were in their own Septembers, each being in their late 70s. Married just a little over two years. Two very good years. Bob Fogle and Ellen Goff.

Every year, about this time, for as long as Bob could remember, he would plan his annual trip to the cabin (in Perryburg they call it a "camp.") up by the lake in the woods. The cabin had been in his family for generations (and Ellen often said it looked it).

The half-hour drive up to the lake was precipitous, rising up about 1500 feet above the valley. Best taken before ice and snow began to accumulate. After most of the leaves and the temperature had fallen, Bob (and his father before him, and his grandfather before that) would set aside a day to rake the leaves and drain all the water systems.

The year they had gotten married, Ellen had a family event late October which made for a perfect day for Bob's annual outing. The next year, Bob's broken ankle precluded his trip, so his brother Ralph followed the detailed checklist provided by Bob. The old practice of putting out mothballs to keep away the mice had been replaced by more modern, less odious and toxic options.

But this year it was finally Ellen's turn to participate in the annual ritual of "closing up camp."

In preparation for that day, Bob told Ellen he needed to head to the home improvement store. You know, one of those big box affairs that line the edges of Perryburg. There's one out by Interstate, another across town just over the city line, and, of course, New Hamburg (the swankiest suburb) has its own. Three different companies, three similar inventories.

It was on a Tuesday in early October that Bob told Ellen about the trip to the home improvement store, and Ellen immediately invited herself along. This made Bob happy. None of his previous wives had ever wanted anything to do with such a store.

Together, the two of them went off to Rapp's Home Center (you know, the one with the bright yellow and brown logo of a saw cutting through a roof). The parking lot was less than about a quarter full, which pleased Bob – he hated to deal with weekend DYI clowns, as he called them.

Parking nearer the exit ("why do those fools park by the entrance?"), Bob opened Ellen's door for her and said, "M'Lady, hardware awaits."

As had been their way since courtship, they made shopping play more than task. Down one aisle, looking for new things, wondering about what this or that was for, cracking jokes about the badly worded signs.

Each of them had several items to the cart when Bob said, "Well, I'm just about done. How about you?"

"Yes, I think so."

"Just one more thing."

Bob started their cart toward the electric tool section, but he had checked before going so he knew his destination. Just beyond the electric circular saws was the automotive area, and there, the app had said, he would find his needed RV antifreeze, the stuff that kept the toilets and the traps from freezing up and cracking over the winter.

Yes, the app had said they had 968 gallons of the stuff. But the shelf where the app had said he would find it was 968 gallons short. Looking down aisle after aisle, he finally found one of the employees with their brown shirts and yellow aprons and asked about where the RV antifreeze might be.

"I think I saw it on an end cap down by kitchens," was the reply, and the employee moved in that direction.

"Nope, not here," was the comment a minute later and farther afield from the original site. The employee pulled out his inventory device and saw the big 968 with no trouble, but the only place listed was the already-checked empty shelf. This information seemed to shake the employee, who said "wait here." Off he went, toward another employee in the far distance. Bob and Ellen waited, and waited, and waited.

After several minutes, the two employees returned with the announcement, "Chris here thought they were out by gardens, but not there either. Why don't you try Customer Service."

Ellen and Bob, a little wearily, tramped off to the far corner of the front of the store to the Customer Service desk. A very young person was finishing up a return and then turned to them. "How may I help you?"

Bob asked again where he might find the RV antifreeze. The Customer Service Representative (Hi, My Name is Pat) went into the large computer on the counter and after a few keystrokes proudly announced that they had 968 gallons of it, all on Aisle 23.

"Nope. Not there."

"Do you mean the pink stuff?"

"Yep."

"Well, that is where it should be."

"True, but should and is are two different things."

"Let me make a call."

The Customer Service Representative got on the phone and spoke with someone. "Someone will be here in a minute."

"Thank you."

The minute was more like five. At long last another employee, this time with a more permanent name badge, appeared. "Looking for the RV antifreeze?"

"Yes, two gallons."

"Well, we've got plenty. I'll go get you two."

And off they went.

At this point, the search for the antifreeze had taken about 25 minutes, and the wait was not over. In about 10 minutes, the second Customer Service Representative returned, empty-handed.

"Not there." ("Could have told you that," Bob thought.)

Then a more frantic search on the computer. Ellen had begun to hum the main theme from the 1812 Overture, tapping her feet to the required cannon blasts. Pat had stepped aside trying not to make eye contact with customers and superiors alike.

"Yep, 968 gallons," was the pronouncement. "But they are all up."

"Up?"

"Yes, up!" gesturing toward the ceiling.

"Up?"

"Not available at the moment. If you've got about an hour or so to do more shopping, we can have them down by them, probably."

"You know what," Bob said peevishly, "I think you can keep your 968 gallons of RV antifreeze, and these other items in our cart." He was pissed. "You know, when we had Emmet's, we never had this kind of run-around."

With that, he took Ellen's hand and stormed out of Rapp's ("Where Every Customer is Treated Like a Neighbor").

Once in the parking lot, he quickly felt foolish for storming out, and for not consulting Ellen about her desires. "Look, Ellie, I just had it with that stupidity."

"Bob, I was surprised you lasted that long. I would have been out of there about 30 minutes earlier, leaving our cart somewhere in some aisle. If I got the drift of that place, if we had left our cart out in Aisle 23, we could probably go back in a day, or even a week, and find it sitting there waiting for us. Glad to have walked out on them."

"You sure?"

"Yes, more than sure. But just one thing."

("Here it comes," thought Bob.)

"Yes?"

"Who or what is Emmet's?"

"Ah, Emmet's. Let's just get home and over dinner I will tell you all about Emmet's. OK?"

"Yes, it's a deal."

- - -

Over a meal of shrimp stir-fry, Bob began.

"Emmet's. Where to start?"

And this is the story Bob told Ellen.

Back about 150 years ago, just after the Civil War, a newcomer to Perryburg arrived on the late afternoon train from back east. His name: Geoffrey Emmet. He was a tinker, a hawker, a tradesman, a salesman, a jack-of-all-trades. He was also sharp, ambitious, and inventive.

Stepping out of the old train shed down by the river, he surveyed Perryburg with the knowing eye not of predator but of prey. He didn't want to be the one seeking but the one sought. Now all he had to do was figure out what was so needed that people would seek him out.

The following week he made a series of appointments in the various factories in town, followed by appointments with several of the contractors, and last (but not least) appointments with elected officials. To each of these "pillars of the community" he asked a simple question: "what's your biggest problem doing business?"

The answers were universally common: getting supplies. Sufficient supplies. Quality supplies.

But what kind of supplies? He was told that the new railroads were bringing good quantities of cheap coal. The forests to the north provided ample wood. But hardware, all kinds of hardware, was hard to come by. Either they needed to order larger quantities than they needed, or the goods that arrived were of shoddy quality, or shipping cost more than the cost of the smaller quantities they desired.

Geoffrey Emmet had his answer. Hardware!

Being a shrewd businessman, Emmet realized that where he placed his new business was crucial. Too far from the railroads, and he would eat up much of the profit by simply getting the goods from the rails to his store. He also recognized that almost all the businesses he had contacted, all the contractors he had consulted, all the elected officials he had met with on a nearly daily basis sent workers down to the railroad. If he located his business in that same area, he could have his customers pick up their goods rather than his having to deliver them.

He could buy quality merchandise in bulk, have it readily available to be examined by the local buyers, and sell it at a mark up that was handsome. As long as his marked-up price was less than what similar items bought in small quantity directly from the manufacturer would cost when transportation was included, his hardware would appear to be a bargain. He was also counting on the competitive and secretive nature of business, construction, and government to keep any of the individual buyers from thinking about forming any cooperative agreements that would provide the same products at an even lower price, at a price not affording him a profit.

A warehouse, rendered redundant by the end of the War, just across from the railroad station was available. With only modest modifications, it was transformed in a few short weeks into "Emmet's Hardware Emporium – Parts and Tools for Every Craft and Industry." Supplies arrived daily from north, south, east, and west, and the quantity arriving surpassed what had ever been ordered by a single company. Of course, no one knew most of it had been purchased on credit. Emmet was risking everything on making this work.

The opening day of Emmet's was the cause for celebration in Perryburg. Not just the big buyers but also the homeowners came by to see the diverse items available for sale. People could see and touch items they could only vaguely describe. People even began to imagine uses for things they did not know existed.

Before a year had passed, Emmet's had become one of the most profitable businesses in all of Perryburg. He was respected from his modest markup on items ("couldn't get it for much less in the City") and his willingness to order anything that was needed. To have his warehouse of merchandise at hand meant that many a business and many a project did not have to suffer hours or days of down-time waiting for the required item to arrive.

Geoffrey Emmet also had a unique quality: he could visualize nearly anything a person could want. He had other salespeople on the floor, but when a mill operator would bring in a broken part or a farmer would arrive with a simple sketch, the cry would arise, "BOSS!" He almost always knew what was needed.

All the loans for the initial stock were repaid early, and more than one banker rued the decision to offer credit instead of seeking a piece of the business.

Before long the official name was forgotten. It was simply "Emmet's," as in "go on over to Emmet's and get me that a dozen of those ¼ inch by 4 bolts."

Hardware was not the only thing that was flourishing for Geoffrey. He was soon the catch of the year, the bachelor with the greatest promise in the whole area around Perryburg. At various socials during the year his dance card was filled with many a hopeful. To each and all he was polite, complimentary, and kind. By none was he taken. The fluttering eyelashes, the elaborate gowns, the fancy fan waving, the glittery jewelry all seemed fashioned to hide, not reveal.

But then, in about the fourth year of his residence in Perryburg, Geoffrey Emmet looked out across his sales floor one bright morning to see something he had never seen before, at least not in Emmet's Hardware Emporium. A young woman, with her hair tied up for work, a rough cotton shirt and a hard cotton skirt over high boots that had seen much work in their days, was slowly assembling a sizable basket of items from his wares, the startled salesclerk relegated to carrying the basket instead of locating desired merchandise.

At the moment he spotted her, she looked up and spotted him, and the edges of her smooth mouth turned ever so slightly upward, to hint at a smile. Geoffrey remembered having seen such a smile

72

once before, in a book about art. With a slight nod of his head, he acknowledged her presence. And then their eyes met, just for an instant.

Geoffrey tried to get to the cashiers' cage before she did, but he was stopped in his tracks by the Mayor and the Commissioner of Public Works who needed to consult with him on supplies for a new project. By the time he could escape their civic demands, she was gone.

"Who was that customer?" he inquired of his chief clerk.

"Oh, that was Maggie Fenwick, from up the Onandagus Creek a piece. Farms the most fertile land in that valley. Farms it herself after old Douglas Fenwick, her dad, was lost an Antietam. Well, actually she has several farm hands, but she is in charge up there. No questions about that. Rides the branch line down into town every couple of weeks to get supplies and the like."

"Well, when she comes in again, please tell her that the owner of this Emporium would like a word with her."

With a slightly raised right eyebrow, the clerk quickly responded, "Yes, boss."

It would be three weeks before there would be a knock at his office door and his chief clerk would poke his head in to say "Miss Fenwick" is here to see you." Taken aback is an apt description of that moment.

Geoffrey rose to his feet, pulled himself together, and walked toward the door to welcome his visitor. His clerk opened the door and with a courteous wave of a hand, showed Maggie into the office. They met at the threshold, moving toward each other, almost colliding. Both looked down for a moment, then took a step back. Geoffrey extended his hand and said "Geoffrey Emmet, welcome to my Emporium."

Extending her hand, she said "Maggie Fenwick, who deeply appreciates your fine establishment."

As their two hands met, he was impressed with the firmness and strength of the hand in his, and she was impressed with the gentleness yet steadiness of the hand in hers.

Their courtship was the talk of the town because it did not occur at soirees nor at balls nor at socials. Rather, it was carried out perusing the merchandise at the Emporium and walking the fields of the Fenwick Farm. Dirty hands and muddy feet were more common to their relationship than lavender and lace.

Ten months later Maggie Fenwick became Mrs. Geoffrey Emmet, but to the two of them she would always be Maggie Fenwick. He called her such whenever he spoke of her. Only the stodgy old keepers of society ever called her Mrs. Emmet.

And then, as the years passed, their family grew: three daughters evenly interspersed with two sons. Against all conventions, Maggie and Geoffrey referred to the daughters as Fenwicks and the sons as Emmets. Yes, they all had legal names, but with two such successful people local wisdom deferred to their preferences.

One of the daughters would die of rheumatic fever when not yet ten years old. The scar of that loss would be a reminder to the two of them for all the rest of their years.

Of the other four, one son and one daughter would marry people with visions of new lands, pioneers fields, and more. The other two, the elder son and the youngest daughter, would often be found running in the rows of merchandise at the Emporium, or helping to unload new shipments. By the time they each were of age, they had integrated themselves into the life of the Emporium to such an extent that they were indispensable. Perry, the son, (named with a bit of localized pride) was adept at all matters of commerce, especially in the procurement of the best products at the most advantageous prices. Little Agnes (Aggie Fenwick as it said on her nametag) inherited her father's gift of envisioning items based on the slightest of description or the smallest remnant of a device.

Early in 1890, the property to the side of the Emporium suffered a catastrophic fire, leaving a large barren lot once the charred remnants had been cleared. Here, Perry proposed that a new Emmet's Hardware should be built, on a scale no one in Perryburg had ever seen much less imagined. Agnes envisioned the design from the street entry to the many-storied lofts of merchandise. It would be a substantial building, built more in the mode of a mill than a store, so no weight of merchandise would ever threaten its integrity. The most modern freight elevators would allow access to the upper floors.

When Emmet's Hardware was finished in 1896, the Times reported that it was the only store of its size and quality between the City and the frontier. Oddly enough, for an Emporium that sought to avoid delivering items to customers, Emmet's Hardware now, in the manner of other great stores a whole nation, began to ship to people far away. It was as likely that a person in Omaha, or even San Francisco, might seek out something from Emmet's as for someone from New Hamburg.

First Perry and then Agnes found life partners and had families. Joy and sorrows intertwined with stock market panics, World Wars, Flu Pandemics, and so much more. A third generation, and then a fourth generation, and then a fifth generation of Emmets and Fenwicks (mixed in with Prentices and Eliots and LaPierres and Savinos) played among the merchandise and rode the freight elevator and watched as one of their parents would respond to a customer, "I know what you mean, I think it is up on the third floor" before taking the customer on an always-fruitful search and discover mission for some needed part, piece, item.

Every generation would produce at least one new member of the extended Emmet's family who would find her or his calling in the business.

Fancy houses, good educations, generous benevolence, extensive travels, comfortable retirements would all come to the descendants of Geoffrey and Maggie. And no one in Perryburg would begrudge them these things. No, no one would because they had always served Perryburg so well. Generations had known that to go to Emmet's was to be successful in getting what one wanted or needed. Outside the area, mentioning the name of Emmet's would always elicit a recognition "Oh, that's the place in Perryburg."

Good things don't necessarily last. It was sometime in the 1980s that Allen Eliot, as the current President of Emmet's and Isabella Savino, the visionary part of the team, sat down at the well-worn work bench that was behind the front offices. This was the work bench where many an item had been examined by Isabella as she sought to imagine the hardware item needed to restore its function. This was the same workbench where, almost a century before, her great grandmother had done the same.

Allen just sat there and looked at Isabella. Isabella looked at the small piece of machinery that Henry Macpherson had brought in that morning. Isabella looked up and said "I just can't do it. I can't fix it for Henry for less than a new, knock-off version would cost."

"I know, coz, we just can't do it anymore. Our whole model was based on our ability to buy in bulk to make the profit compared to what small lots would cost people. But the mills are gone, the construction industry has its own supply chain, and everyone else is rushing out to those damned home centers where no one knows how anything works and their small packets of screws cost twice what we sell screws for but without the fancy little bags. I think we are screwed."

"We provided service, and quality, and attention to detail. We knew the little things people were describing or what would work in a certain situation. You know, they've got kids just out of high school trying to tell people how to do their own roofing. I can't stand it," Isabella added.

"Maybe it is time to get out while we are still above water."

"Yes, I can see that is the only path ahead. But what will you do?"

"I've been offered more than one position over the years to head up purchasing for the state. And you?"

"The new branch of the state university, the one planned to deal with emergent technologies, has twice now sounded me out about being on the faculty. I guess that degree from MIT will be used as intended."

"Oh, come on Isabella, it's not your degree they want. It's your imaginative envisioning of the world they want. That's what has always powered your success here."

"Success, ha! But, yes, success. Over a century of serving this community, and the larger world. Over a century of integrity. Over a century of providing for our families. Now it is time to see success as turning out the lights and moving on. But, heaven help Perryburg and heaven every other community that has to rely on Rapp's and its ilk to meet their needs."

"Yes, a quick prayer for all those who will never know a place like this."

- - -

"So, was that the end of Emmet's?" Ellen asked.

"Yes and no," Bob replied. "The store was closed, the Emporium ended. The merchandise was auctioned off, the building cleaned out. The doors closed and locked. The family scattered to new pursuits and other places.

"The old hulk stood opposite Union Station, opposite a building it had helped to build a century ago, waiting for its future. About five years ago, with the slow rebirth of Perryburg and the Union Station area, the doors were opened again and the thick floors renewed as the basis for new loft apartments. Luxury living where once there had been nails, bolts, wires, and so much more."

"So, not all is lost. Emmet's rises as a place for people to live," Ellen commented.

"Yes, but heaven help them if they ever need to buy RV Antifreeze. I hope, on some autumn night, when someone is thinking about closing up their camp up in the mountains, they will hear a voice echo through their apartment 'I know where it is, come on, it's up on four. Ride up with me.' and they will know what a real hardware store was."

"Bob," Ellen said, raising her glass high, "let's raise up a toast. To Emmet's."

"To Emmet's"

6.   TIP-TOP HOUSE

There's a spot along Mohawk Street where you begin to get a sense that downtown is behind you but uptown is still far away.

You are not yet up to Mohawk Square. That it was called a square is ironic because it is really a circle, a large embolism of the main artery of the town, with various side streets bursting from its center, each arm striving and wishing to be as important and grand as Mohawk Street, but none succeeding. It was there at the square that the street cars would circle around a large granite monument to the "War Dead" with no clear delineation of which conflict.

But, before you get that far along Mohawk Street, before the library on the other side and after the telephone company building, there is a squat brick building, painted stark white, with a strange black logo over the door, a top hat on top of an outline of the building's roof peak. Below the logo, in stark black letters, "TIP-TOP HOUSE."

Tip-Top House was a luncheonette, an urban diner if you will. Open 24 hours a day, its long counter and several booths were always important to Perryburg. Or, at least from 1923 until today.

Now, no one ever raved about the food there. No one complained either. It was not the food that drew people. It was something more, a something more that morphed with the many changes in the city over a century.

Back on Tuesday, September 4, 1923, with the Labor Day parades and speeches and picnics and fireworks over but before school had resumed, Tip-Top House opened its doors at 8am. That event had been heralded for several weeks with advertisements in the local *Times-Dispatch*. An impressive guest list had been invited, including all the many civic, religious, fraternal, and business leaders.

Patriotic bunting had been draped from the roofline and a large banner proclaimed the opening.

The opening came and went with barely a notice. At 8am that day, the line out the door had been scant (OK, nonexistent). By noon, only 14 orders had been placed. If Tip-Top House had been a patient in hospital, the chaplain would have been called.

It was only at sunset that things began to pick up. Just after the many lunch counters in the store downtown closed for the day – Woolworth's, Kresge's, Neisner's, and WT Grant – the door began swinging open again and again. In poured a wide cross-section of Perryburg: shop clerks not wanting to eat alone, janitors at the end of their shifts, taxi drivers just off work, newspaper pressmen headed to work, and many more. With every other simple eatery in downtown Perryburg closed and only the fancy restaurants still open, where was an ordinary person supposed to eat?

In the other parts of town, across the river, or up in uptown, or out in the suburbs, people were expected to eat at home. Only the core of the city had eateries, and after about 6pm you had better plan to spend good money or you were out of luck. That is until Tip-Top House opened.

By Wednesday, September 5, 1923, the word of mouth had begun to spread. No, not so much for lunch as there were other places to get that meal, or even a mid-morning or mid-afternoon snack. But, if you waited until the stores with lunch counters were open to serve breakfast, you were already running late for your day.

Tip-Top's breakfast business took off like a rocket, and it never looked back. Likewise, after sundown it was always a bustling place, up until about midnight. What I want to tell you about are the times of the day between those two busy periods.

The breakfast crowd began thinning out about 10am. During most of that opening September you could always find an open booth midday. Right about the middle of October, something changed. One by one the booths began to fill for lunch and late lunch and early dinner. Who were these people?

It was on October 10th that Oliver Skinner (that's Attorney Oliver Skinner) said to Ernest Franz (that's as in Franz and Walpole Insurance), "How about we get a bite to eat over at that new place, say about 11, and maybe we can straighten out this mess with the fire insurance claim at the old Musgrave Factory?" Seated in a booth, a discrete distance from anyone who cared and far from the front doors of the Court House (and its adjacent Restaurants and Men's Clubs), Skinner and Franz had both a decent meal and a productive conversation. No interruptions.

About a week later, Father Edmond Fitzsimmons (of St. Anne's Episcopal Church) and Deacon Harold Aldrich (of First Congregational Church) were in another booth, working out plans for a shared holiday appeal.

And so it went. Business and civil and fraternal and religious leaders began to see Tip-Top House as a comfortable alternative place to meet across the many lines that usually separated the community.

When the Courthouse opened again at 2pm, Tip-Top house moved into a small slump period, but then about 3pm the crowd became more female with many domestic workers stopping in after the day's work. No one ever noticed, or at least said anything about it, but this was a very racially mixed crowd. Maybe because it was almost all women, no one was bothered. Maybe because these hard workers recognized other hard workers, their tips were generous.

Dinnertime and into the evening, as I said, was soon very busy when people needing to be downtown after the other lunch counters closed but who did not want to spend a fortune made their way to Tip-Top House. After the last after-movie crowd went home, on about midnight, things got slower. More lingering over a late dinner or an early breakfast. Still, the place was usually full most of the time, filled with cab drivers, night-shift people, police, firefighters, and others for whom the deep nighttime was their time to be out.

Now what you probably don't know is that practically no one knew who owned the Tip-Top House. Sure, people knew the various chefs on duty, and the cashiers and wait staff. Suppliers knew who signed the invoices and the checks. But no one ever answered to the call of "Boss!" A rumor had always been that the daytime head chef, Roscoe, was the owner. Roscoe was a shy man, happy to be in the back of the house. Roscoe signed for all those deliveries during the day.

Another rumor was that the owner was the cashier, Ruthie Talmadge, because she was so careful with all the finances. It was her name on the checks.

Still, there were many other guesses. The fact that Tip-Top House never served liquor meant that there was no license displayed with a proprietor's name on it. All the filings with the City of Perryburg were in the name of the restaurant with two lawyers shown as agents. The place had never been incorporated so there were no records in the Capital to reveal ownership.

One day, in November 1973, the city was shocked to find that the outside of the Tip-Top House had been draped with black crepe. Against the stark white brickwork, it was a startling sight. The Logo and name had been covered with a large black wreath. It was evident that a death had occurred. But whose?

The regulars didn't notice anyone missing on any shift. To their questions about "why the crepe?" the answer was simply "he died."

"He died." Who died last night?

Silence was the general response, but Ruthie added, "the man of my life for 50 years." Everyone knew that Ruthie was a lesbian although no one ever uttered that word.

Now the search was on for the mystery man who had died, a man apparently connected to the Tip-Top House so intimately that the house would mourn his passing. The newspaper was scanned for possibilities, all recent deaths noted. No one made sense. The former alderman? No, he hated to eat out. The Sunday School Superintendent from the Methodist Church? No, Tip-Top House was open on Sundays. Mr. Waggerhorn, the retired physics teacher at PHS? His moth-eaten jackets seemed too poor for the owner of such a place. Abe Sugarman, one of the pillars of Temple ben Shalom? No, Tip-Top House served bacon. How about Percival Channing, the power behind the operation of the palatial Crown House just off Mohawk Street on Court Street?

Soon the search for who had died, died down. The everyday citizens of Perryburg, relegated to single paragraph notices of the deaths, were rarely scanned. On Sunday, November 26, the *Times-Dispatch* had its monthly listing for recent, non-obituary or notice deaths; in other words, people neither famous nor rich enough to warrant more than passing mention.

Take a look at the list:

Anna Bishop, 75, October 27, Perryburg
Aaron Costello, 62, November 3, New Hamburg
Thomas K. Duncan, 83, October 30, Hurtzboro
Dorothy Elders, 47, November 5, Perryburg
Mary Heiss, 56, November 18, Perryburg
Joseph Lemke, 77, November 9, Smithfield
Mary McMahon, 82, November 18, Perryburg
Opal Olmsted, 63, October 31, New Hamburg
Phillip Pappadoulous, 83, November 11, Perryburg

Ralph Randolph, 32, November 12, Perryburg
Susan A. Smith, 67, November 20, Hurtzboro
Susan S. Smith, 71, November 14, Perryburg
Timothy Threadborne, 84, October 27, Perryburg
Ulysses S. Upchurch, 91, November 18, Perryburg
Hector Vincent, 59, November 4, West Windgate
Willilam Wiliams, 66, November 3, Perryburg
Zylpha Young, 71, October 29, Perryburg
Howard Zahn, 64, November 15, New Hamburg

You might not see it right away, and few people in Perryburg noticed it either.

There's Mary McMahon. The name mean anything to you? Probably not. Mary came to Perryburg in 1898, a child, along with her parents and two sisters, immigrants from Ireland. Her two older sisters joined their father in working in the mills. One by one, the mills caught them out, maiming and then killing. By 1908, Mary and mother Margaret were alone. Margaret was working as a domestic and Mary wanted to help her. She had completed High School with a very respectful record which might have opened other doors to her had she not been Irish. Slowly the many losses Margaret had known – loss of homeland, loss of husband, loss of two daughters – weighed too heavily on her. Today we would say she was developing depression but in those days, she was labeled as "mad." She was shipped off to the State Hospital in Mercy, never to see the outside world again.

Mary, at age 19, was then all alone, having to make her way in the world. It was 1910 and the best she could imagine was as some lower-level domestic worker. Spending all of her days inside houses and her nights in the windowless room she could afford soon left her ill and ill-at-ease. The social worker who called on the rooming house once a month suggested that, for Mary's health, she ought to spend as much time as she could outside.

Mary took to walking. Walking the streets of Perryburg, observing many things. She observed the street vendors, hawking various wares. She observed the women of the street who hawked other wares. She observed the young boys who stood on the corners and sold newspapers. Of the three options for work outside, the first two did not appeal to her, but selling newspapers strangely tempted her. It would mean she could read the news every day and even make some money at it. But, would it be enough?

She was surprised how quickly she was sought out for the several daily newspapers she sold. Most of the boys only sold one, but she had started with three and then expanded. Apparently buying a newspaper from a comely lass was a businessman's choice as opposed to street urchins.

Within three months, Mary had added a couple of magazines to her offerings and her sales grew. Adding some women's magazines grew those sales even further. Soon, she was offering a full news and magazine store from the pushcart she had made for herself. Making sure she was always clean and neat, and that the cart looked top-rate, Mary became a fixture down by the corner of Mohawk Street and Commercial Avenue. She was tucked into the corner, in a dead-end alleyway that afforded easy access not only to passersby but also to the road traffic.

Mary was on that corner for nearly 50 years. Had you lived in Perryburg, even if you didn't know her name, you knew who she was. You would pass her a thousand times a year. Mary, always with a smile and a wave.

Mary was one of the nighthawks in the Tip-Top House. After the shows let out, she would pack up her things, head to the Tip-Top House, and have her second real meal of the day. Her first would have been a very early breakfast there every morning before getting to her corner before the offices and stores opened.

The day the black crepe went up, when everyone was asking who had died, Mary had let on to a very few of her nightly friends that she knew but would go to her grave keeping that secret secret. She made good on that pledge by dying less than a week after the crepe had been hung.

When the Probate Court for Westing County listed her estate, it was finally known she was worth over a million dollars. Apparently in the earliest days of her business she had saved a decent sum, and with the coming of the Great Depression, while her sales were down, she was still not only making enough to live on but a bit more as well. Putting all of that together, and using her astute mind, she began to invest in blue-chip stocks and government-backed bonds. Through the War years, into the prosperity of the 1950s, her investments grew, and grew, and grew.

Many people were surprised to find that Mary had a will, a very simple will. She left all her estate to create a Foundation. As stated in her will, "This Foundation shall seek to promote and support such places, institutions, and events as give equal access to all the inhabitants of Perryburg."

More surprising was that her estate also included a 50% interest in the building and the business of the Tip-Top House, an interest that had been purchased in 1930. It was a very peculiar ownership, a shared ownership with the right of survivorship. In other words, whoever of the owners of shares in the building and business survived, owned it all.

You can imagine the frenzy that revelation caused. Of the other 50%, had it been held by one person, or by several others? If several others, how many of them remained alive? If only one person, who was that person? Was it the one for whom the crepe had been draped?

There was another 50% ownership deal in her will, a small row house down by the tracks. A shotgun style affair whose front door opened onto Kay Street and whose back door opened onto an unnamed alley. Again, people wondered who now owned that decrepit-appearing house in the wrong part of town, and why would she own any part of it? Mary had been a woman of mystery for all the time she spent in the very public eye.

Let's go back to that list of deaths. Take another look. Any other name stand out? Probably not. But the person whose story I am telling now was not known by that name to most people. He was a Greek immigrant who arrived about a year before Mary. He quickly learned that immigrants in general, and immigrants with strange names, did not fare well. So, he took his name and shortened it.

I bet, if you were to talk to your grandparents and ask them about Phil Papp you would hear stories. "Phil Papp never had any schooling but he sure was streetwise." "Phil Papp had that old vegetable cart with the two horses. You could hear him coming for blocks." "Phil Papp would come around on Mondays and Thursdays when we were kids, and he had everything, like a grocery store on wheels."

Yes, Phillip Pappadoulous became Phil Papp: Green grocery, general grocer, street merchant, the original home-delivery guy of Perryburg.

He had arrived in Perryburg alone, coming from Greece by ship to Baltimore, and then up to Perryburg by train, getting off in Perryburg because he liked the looks of the hills.

Having been raised in the countryside of Greece, he had no taste for factory work. He wanted the fresh air and the feeling of freedom that came with it. With the small fortune he had brought with him (it was a fortune in Greece, not so much in America), he scouted out the farms about an hour outside of Perryburg and offered to buy produce on a regular basis from farmers if they gave him a good price. Using a handcart at first, he would roll his goods back the two to three miles back into town and start to sell them on the residential streets. His thick accented voice would ring out the day's best buys, and soon, hearing his voice enticed both housewives and domestic cooks out to the curb to see what he had.

Toward dusk, he would walk back out of town toward one of his farm suppliers, the one who offered to let him keep his cart there overnight. Phil would use the cart as his tent overnight, cleaning up with the hand-pumped well water both evening and morning. He figured this way he could get the fresh produce into the city earlier than many of the markets would have it. He would be calling out his wares an hour before most stores opened, before the stores could get to the farmers' market, haggle, buy, and bring it back to the stores.

Business grew quickly and soon he negotiated with that farmer for a horse, then two horses, and a very old rig which he converted into his store on wheels. He paid the farmer for feed and livery, and everyone was happy. He was now sleeping in the barn with his horses and he could get the produce to town even earlier.

But Phillip Pappadoulous was an astute observer of people and patterns. While his Phil persona would serve, Phillip would watch, notice, and then act. Phillip knew his little business would soon rankle the store owners, so he approached various greengrocers near his route. What if he brought them produce directly from the farms, early each morning, saving them (and the farmers) the bother of the farmers' market trips. Everyone saw savings and benefits. In only a few months Phillip changed from a solely retail endeavor into both a wholesale as well as a retail one. Before long, he added in several of the best restaurants in town.

So, if you had seen his wagon leaving the farms, you would have seen it loaded with two or three times as much produce as would be on it as when he started down the residential streets. By the time he got to those streets, the hard work for two horses was over for the day. That is why they always seemed so content clopping down the tree-lined streets filled with houses.

When he retired from his route, no one threw him a retirement party. No civic award was offered. All that happened was that the ordinary people of Perryburg relegated him to stories of "back then." "Whatever happened to that Phil who would come by?" was often met with "I don't know, maybe he died."

The stores switched to commercial sources, reinforcing people's memories of how it had been better when Phil had come by the house, better produce back then. The restaurants found other suppliers and tried to cover up the inferior quality of older and poorer produce with more sauces.

Now Phil Papp always seemed a quiet, self-effacing man, belonging to the old world more than the emerging new world of Perryburg. Like so many of those who serve our wants and needs, he was always there but often invisible. He was never invited to any social events, never involved in any political party, never considered for any roles in the community other than as a slightly eccentric greengrocer. No housewife or domestic cook ever invited him in for a cup of coffee. No chef, after paying for his delivery, ever suggested that Phil have dinner in the restaurant. No store owner ever offered Phil a discount on purchases. Phil was simply there to serve others, not be a part of the community.

His businesses had grown. His stream of income assured. His strongbox, hidden in the hay, was filled. But, that nest egg in hay was not going to grow on its own.

It was Phillip, not Phil, who observed that while the rich and the pretending-to-be-rich could get a good meal any noon or night of the week, the common folk, people like he, had to squeeze shoulder to shoulder at a counter in a frenzied five and dime for mediocre fare at lunch and slouch home for dinner. In this fact he saw opportunity.

Seeing an old, ramshackle building on Mohawk Street, up away from the business district along the route home for many, Phillip purchased it in his legal name. Then, through a series of young, ambitious, crafty lawyers, he changed the deed to show "Tip-Top House." His relationship with the property was then erased. Next, the entity of Tip-Top House had designed and built what would have been called a diner if it stood alone, but standing as it did along Mohawk Street in what appeared to be a white brick house, it was something other. All along Phillip had dreamt of the place where people of all stations in life could feel they were home.

Having seen too many kitchens of fancy restaurants and seen what had been done to his fine produce by too many chefs, he designed a practical kitchen that could be kept open 24 hours a day and be kept clean. He designed a menu for each meal period that was long on quality and low on profit, believing that with the extended hours and good food the volume of business would generate reasonable profits. Unlike many of the others he met in the trade, he only sought to make a little more than what the prevailing interest rates might be.

This model, after the first fitful emptiness on that morning in 1923, succeeded. Slowly at first, then steadily, his income from Tip-Top House came in. Phillip was pleased. He had created the kind of place where he would like to eat, and it was providing him with a good income.

Things sailed along until October 1929. When the whole world seemed to go crazy, he saw his business rise not decline. Soon people who would never deign to darken the door of Tip-Top House were eating the lowest priced meals there. But that was a problem. He had always had several low-priced meals on the menu as a gesture to his idea of hospitality. He never wanted anyone to feel excluded from Tip-Top House because it was too expensive. Struggling businessmen could arrange meetings with those who were still successful, order one of those house specials, and not appear on the brink of failure.

(Now, you might ask, did Phillip ever eat there? The answer to that is simply "No." But Phil would periodically be seen sitting at the counter, alone, toward the end of the day, his now-empty produce wagon and horses parked out front. He would always be enjoying one of those specials. He tried to appear humble in his station in life and very much a loner.)

By mid-1930, his plans began to go awry as those specials were losing him more and more money. The business had gone from a deep black to a pale shade of grey with tinges of pink: red was on the horizon.

It was in those months that the loner Phil was seated at the lunch counter about 11pm when the news stand lady, Mary, came in. Looking up and down the counter and seeing several groupings of the pretending-to-be well-to-do, she sidled up to Phil and asked if he minded company. After getting his quiet consent to the stool next to him, she turned to Phil and said, "I can't, for the life of me, figure how this place can keep going in times like these."

"What do you mean?"

"Hell, doesn't take a genius to know this food we are eating is costing the owner more than we are paying."

"How do you think they can do it?"

"Well, I figure they are short on cash right about now, but the business is a good one. If it can only be kept going until things pick up, it'll be all right. I mean, you and your produce – you only have to finance a day at a time, right?"

"Right."

"Just like me – if I don't sell as many papers tomorrow, I'll cut my order for the next day. Rather sell out than be left with papers I can't sell. You must be the same. Too many cucumbers one day would mean you would buy fewer the next day. Right?"

Phil looked at her and quickly realized he had met his mate in life's appraisal. Here was someone who thought like he did, saw things that others did not see, and kept her own counsel.

"Yep, that's how I see it too. But this here restaurant doesn't have the luxury of cutting back even one day."

"So, if you and I want to be able to have this place survive, what can we do?"

"Don't know."

"Sure you do. This place needs the security of enough money in the bank to weather the storm."

"But how?"

"We would need to talk with the owner, whoever that is, and arrange a little financing."

"You got a bank in your handbag?"

"Let's just say that I do. And let's say that I'm in the market to find a way to put my money to work toward that time when me and you won't be of working age anymore. And let's just say that I have a suspicion you know the owner of this place pretty well."

"I'm listening."

"Phil," she said with a wink, "I'd like to talk with Phillip."

"That can be arranged."

"When?"

"How about tomorrow, at your stand, about 8:15pm, when the few who are still rich are off to dinner or the theatre or the church social or whatever."

"Tell Phillip to bring some fresh carrots. Haven't tasted a good one, other than here at the old Top-Top, in way too long."

The next night, clomping down the street, Phil's cart rolled to a stop in front of Mary's news stand. He gave each horse a nice, thick carrot to chew and then walked over to Mary and said, "I think you ordered these," handing her a bag of small and sweet carrots.

There, on that quiet night, with few if any customers coming by, Phillip and Mary had their conversation. No one would have noticed the two of them, because neither was anybody. She sold papers, he sold produce. Nope, nobodies.

The deal they worked out at first was that Mary would provide a much-needed infusion of cash to the Tip-Top House provided it could be done without her name being mentioned. In return, she would get a 50% interest in the business and property with a survivor clause. Deal. Handshake. Done.

And then, surprising to them both, they hugged.

"One more thing," Mary added.

"What would that be?"

"I got me a little house down by the tracks."

"I always wondered where you lived. You always seemed to be here.'

"Well, I got this simple place down there which is easy to walk to, practically nothing in taxes, and is all I need. Practically all I need."

"What else?"

"It gets lonely there. All day long I am with people, but none of them ever really relates to me. 'Mary, give me *The Register*,' and 'How about a copy of *House and Home*,' but nothing about me. After a day of being the wallpaper to life, I would like to have someone, just someone, who might care, really care about me,"

"I can relate to that."

"So, here is what I want to propose. That house will become part of the deal. You can find someplace uptown to house your horses, not way out in the boonies, and then make your way back down there each night. Maybe stop by the Tip-Top on the way."

"I like the sound of this."

"The place has two bedrooms, so I am not suggesting anything, .. ah"

"No, I understand."

"I'd ask you to use the front door, as I always use the alley door. Deal?"

"Deal."

Within a month Phillip had helped Phil find livery closer to the heart of the city. With that obstacle overcome, Phillip moved into the house down by the tracks,

That first night, as he entered through the front door, he had a strange sense of homecoming. The house was empty but on the kitchen table was a simple note: "Welcome." He had never felt so loved in his whole life.

About half an hour later, Mary arrived, coming into through the alley door into a kitchen, warmly lit. Phillip sat that the table, some fresh carrots peeled and cleaned on a plate before the empty chair. Mary never felt so loved in her whole life.

They sat there, on opposite sides of the table, for more than an hour, sharing about their days, listening to the sweet anecdotes of the other. In that time, the old ramshackle house became a home.

Before you get to speculating and surmising and projecting, Phillip and Mary never shared a bed. The arrangement they had started with was maintained. Sure, they hugged often, but never kissed. Yet, they were a more intimate couple than most in Perryburg. Every night they brought home their lives of obscurity in the public eye to be enriched in each other's eyes.

Their home became the one place they were together except for the rare occasions when their meals at Tip-Top House overlapped. On most of those occasions they would sit apart from each other, knowing they would have plenty of time to talk later; such separation allowed each to be much more observant of people and events around them and prevented anyone from guessing their relationship.

When November 11, 1973, arrived as a cold, wet Veterans' Day, Phillip awoke to trouble breathing. It had been coming on for several weeks with coughing. But that day it was much worse. He had trouble even calling Mary's name to summon her to his room. It was she who insisted that he needed to be in hospital and it was she who helped get him up and dressed, out onto the street to wait for a taxi to take him there. She would never see him again. He would die just about at the time when, for so many years, he had entered through the front door after completing rounds with his wagon and then his truck.

The one thing Mary could do in his honor was, on that November 12th, go to the Tip-Top House, order the Special Dinner, and sit all alone with all of her memories of that special man. Going home after that meal, she entered a house that felt emptier than it ever had, even in the years when she had lived there alone. Once she had known companionship with Phillip, the space had been transformed. It had meant life, and warmth, and belonging, and love.

Mary's heart, taxed by all of those years outside in all times and seasons, worn by so much loss and loneliness, tired by the end of the relationship that had redeemed life itself for her, slowed. Then slowed some more. Then it stopped.

On November 18th, when her news stand was unattended, one of her early morning regulars, Sgt. Joe Polini of the Perryburg Police Department, made it his business to find out why Mary was absent from her line of duty. With the help of several friends, he tracked her down to that old house down by the tracks. Not getting an answer to his knocks, he went to break down the door only to find it opened to his touch, as if Mary had been expecting someone. Inside he found her slumped over the kitchen table. In her hand was a very yellowed note which simply read, "Welcome."

No foul play, just a death of an old person, at home alone. But Sgt. Polini was perplexed by something. The second bedroom was neatly made up as if waiting for someone who lived there. There were some simple clothes in the closet and a few personal items in the dresser. Not much. Nothing to identify who might be there other than it was an older man. Sgt. Polini decided, once the Medical Examiner had ruled it death by natural causes, that there was no point in reporting the observations about another resident.

Mary's attorney was quick to respond when Sgt. Polini called him, and within a day he was at the Court House filing the paperwork with the Probate Court. It was this filing that caused that stir in the community.

Phillip's attorney, off on a trip to the Poconos with his new, much younger wife (Mount Airy Lodge, you know), only filed the paperwork relating to Phillip's death about two weeks after his demise.

Phillip, too, had a Will. When the court watchers caught sight of its contents, many a gasp was heard. He left all his estate to create a Foundation. As stated in his Will, "This Foundation shall seek to promote and support such places, institutions, and events as give equal access to all the inhabitants of Perryburg."

It also outlined various investment holdings in excess of two million dollars, a 50% interest with survivorship in a house in Perryburg, and a 50% interest with survivorship in the building and business of Tip-Top House.

The news of this revelation spread like wildfire throughout Perryburg and its environs. At long last, everyone knew who owned the Tip-Top. Two of the most unlikely people in town. They owned it, and then after Phillip's death, Mary owned it all. The Court was called upon to verify this timeline of ownership and the consistency of Phillip's wishes with the terms of Mary's Will.

After much wrangling, and objections from more than one "civically minded individual" about the establishment of the desired Foundation, and the collection of legal fees, The Mary McMahon and Phillip Pappapoulous Foundation was established. Its assets were extensive and almost immediately people who would never have given either of the named benefactors the time of day sought to access those funds. The trustees held firm.

Over time grants were made to the Perryburg Library, to projects in several of the parks in Perryburg, to the Boys and Girls Club, and a few other groups that were truly inclusive and welcoming.

About twenty years later when the Tip-Top House, facing less business and aging equipment and structure was close to insolvency and building condemnation, this asset of the Foundation was about to dissolve. When word of that possibility reached the community, there was an uproar.

Downtown was just a shadow of its former self. Fewer people went there for any reason. However, nearly everyone had a story to tell, a good story, about a time at Tip-Top House. It felt like the soul of Perryburg was going to be lost. A new group, the Tip-Toppers was formed as a community organization, with the sole mission to save the Tip-Top House and keep it in operation. At the first meeting of the group, the Rev. Maya Holiday of the AME Zion congregation told the packed meeting in her congregation's sanctuary, "In all of Perryburg, there was never any place that was as welcoming to all of us – rich and poor, black and white, in town and from the country, old line or new immigrant, up early or out late, young or old, wanting a warm cup of something or a full meal, coming from a factory or coming from a prom – like Tip-Top House. It has opened its doors to all of us, and now we need to open our hearts to keep it open."

When the application from the Tip-Toppers, by then a 501(c)3 non-profit, reached the Foundation, it was a done deal. For one dollar and other consideration, the ownership of the Tip-Top House was transferred to the Tip-Toppers, along with a sizable grant for needed repair, upgrades, and all.

Last November, on the 100th anniversary of the opening of Tip-Top House, the renewed luncheonette officially reopened (although it had never actually closed), returned to its 24-hour operation that had been curtailed during reconstruction, ready to greet customers in a city that was having its own rebirth.

Speeches were made, ribbons were cut, and crowds waited in line to eat there once more.

The day shift people show up for breakfast, the office workers for lunch, the lawyers and other wheeler-dealers after lunch but before court reopens, the kids from Perryburg High School late afternoon, and a steady stream of dinner diners who value good food at reasonable prices. Evenings and overnights one will hear so many accents, for Croats, Hmung, Karens, Bahamians, and more, all the other night and graveyard shifts people that kept the city running.

If you were to walk up Mohawk Street, just passed where the commercial blocks end, there you will find the white brick building with the black logo of the top hat on the peak of a roof with the words "Top-Top House" in stark black. And below it, in equally black but smaller italic type: *Where Everyone is Welcome!*

Going inside, you might decide to walk past the busy booths and the early counter seats. Then, coming to the last two stools, you might sit down. Looking down at the counter you would see two plaques, each in front of those two stools:

PHIL

Just order one of the specials

Mary

They're made with love

7. NEIGHBORHOODS

"Where do you live?"

It's a simple question, but its answer will reveal so much.

And what it reveals depends on when the answer is given.

This is true in almost every place in the United States, and no more so than in Perryburg.

Let's remember back for a time.

Let's remember back to the founding of Perryburg, when all there was consisted of a river and some First Nation trails. Some miles off, a solitary log cabin stood. Downstream a ways was Old Fort MacKenzie. Upstream was a poor stockade known as Fort Erie, though the appellation of Fort was on the level of what kids today build in the woods.

The first permanent settlers (honoring the fact that there had always been transient First Nation folk who spent a night at the spot on their journeys by water or land) had been merchants and traders who sensed that the confluence of routes and needs was perfect for their business. The first neighborhood had been down by the river, and it had no name. It just was.

Soon, surrounding those initial places of commerce, other buildings arose, both commercial (livery and blacksmith) and residential as families of traders and merchants appeared. If someone wanted to refer to the place, they simply said riverside (never capitalized because it was a description not a name). This differentiated the place from those who lived out-country. And with that, neighborhoods were born.

Even at this prototypical level, the two neighborhoods were not equal. The riverside folk almost never went out-country, but the out-country folk would often come down by the riverside. The power dynamic of status and appeal was powerfully established, a reality of neighborhoods reaching right up to the present.

Those from out-country were considered quaint (for their speech patterns and dress), primitive (for their assumed hygiene), stupid (for their lack of formal education), and therefore not equal. I mean, they didn't even dress up to come down by the riverside; even the First Nations people had the sense to do that once the white men had arrived.

(Of course, what the white men thought were ceremonial dress-up items were in fact signs of enmity. Over time, they would be corrected on that thought painfully.)

Those from out-country thought the riverside folk to be snobbish (acting like they didn't understand ordinary language), sneaky (trying to pull fast deals all the time), deceitful (couldn't take them at their word), and therefore not equal. I mean, they had no sense of the earth, of hard work, of the seasons, of honor.

More than once, after an out-country person left a place of business down by the riverside, the merchant and assistant would share a gale of laughter at the country person's expense. Not as often, but equally true, after a riverside person's wagon had become disabled by something that could be simply repaired and that person chose instead to walk back to the riverside along the muddy trail, the country folk would guffaw at the ineptitude.

Location implied standing in the world, but it was never clear which location implied the higher standing. Let's just agree – different standings.

Settlements and the towns and then cities grow in a pattern. The countryside also.

In the population centers, from the aboriginal natural elements that dictated the appeal of a place, a center would form around some sort of common ground. Once that common area had been surrounded by settlement, people would begin to look elsewhere. In what would become Perryburg, the natural inclination was up, up away from the river. This meant an approach toward the country, a fate worse than death. Something had to be done to clearly show that the newly developed area was not country. This meant a central road kept from mud, and much bigger houses, not those hovels of the country. It meant a schoolhouse (not like those uneducated louts) and a church. The first neighborhood had been riverside, the newer neighborhood was upland.

Out in the country, development was just as certain but not as defined. The earliest settlers would be content with their own cleared lot and simple house. By a generation or two, and many children, the house would become houses, and the clearing would annex much more land. If the in-town model was one of expansion with a continuing centrality, the country model was one of expansion without needing a center. Activities focused on home, not on business.

The pattern in-town repeated itself over and over, with each successive expansion of the center defined by the intended neighborhood inhabitants. The pattern in the country repeated itself over and over, with each successive expansion defined by how much acreage was needed to sustain the family. Two very different models.

But we are seekers of Perryburg. We   will leave the country for another chronicler of tales.

About a generation after the first mansions (or at least mansions compared with the rudimentary housing down by the riverside) were erected upland, they stood in the way of commercial expansion. Some came down and some were so modified as to be unrecognizable (more than one commercial structure, being demolished centuries later, would disclose its domestic origins). Soon, the old riverside area became, because of its proximity to the seasonally flooding and then noxious river, less desirable. The more desirable place for commerce was Downtown.

Downtown displaced upland and so the mansions moved further along the road, creating Uptown.

So much for the wealthy merchants and traders. But, what about for the rest of the community's residents?

Like branches of a tree, new, rutted, muddy tracks led off Mohawk Street in search of places to build housing. At first it was single households who bought, built, and resided. With the creation of Perryburg, individual initiative in creating such housing passed to speculators, both small and large, who would build. Much of that speculation, which required buyers for what was built, had to have an intended market in mind.

To the one side of the main spine, streets began to have larger but modest houses which could house large families, families of certain ethnicities. On the other side of the main spine, the houses were a bit grander but obviously created for smaller families, of a more perceived gentility. Those were the sentiment used in the marketing of the respective houses: "where your whole family can call home," versus "Where everyone can have a bedroom."

If you were newly arrived into Perryburg, coming off the railroad down by the riverside, you would probably be met by promoters of hotels for your temporary lodging (unless you had family here already) and then in the hotel lobbies by promoters of the new housing. To which hotel you were steered depended greatly on your perceived social (read that racial, ethnic, religious, class) status. Therefore, the promotions made to you in those hotels would be to an already-selected audience.

(Lest you find a rise of anger at this history of an unnatural selection process of neighborhoods, let me suggest that you take a look at which timeshares are touted in which hotel chains in resort areas. Times may change, but the prejudices of commerce do not.)

So, the directors went to one neighborhood, the managers to another, the workers to another, the laborers to another. There they would find people like themselves: similar ethnicity, similar education, similar religion, similar economic status, similar lifestyles. If nothing else, being in one's own neighborhood made one feel safe, connected, included. You also knew that your kids would be playing with, learning with, falling in love with, and marrying people just like you.

The developers doubled down on their plans in simple ways. Land was set aside for places of worship with careful deed covenants that restricted which faiths would grow where. The Presbyterians there, the Catholics there, the Baptists over there, the Episcopalians over there, the Lutherans here, the Methodists there. Back when transportation meant feet and horses, no one wanted to have a faith that was worshipped too far from their house.

Of course, there were those whose upward desires took them into neighborhoods "above their station," often assisted by convenient religious conversion. Faith can be a malleable thing in the search for social recognition.

The Jews in town had already purchased a lot just off the main road and erected a synagogue. Their reasoning was that on the Sabbath they would be walking anyway, so what's another mile or so. They didn't know the same restrictive covenants that prescribed which churches would be placed where also would keep most of the Jews out of these developing neighborhoods.

Even as the new neighborhoods were born with class distinctions, soon they were subdivided by ethnicity. In the melting pot that was the growing United States, ingredients in the pot often refused to blend.

For example, down on Joseph Street, that ran perpendicular to Mohawk Street, it was all laborers, but the various ethnicities of laborers enjoyed different foods. That meant different markets, and one would want to live as close as possible to the market of one's palette so bringing home the groceries was not a problem. Proceeding along Joseph Street, at nearly every corner there would be a grocery and back in those days a grocer was also a butcher and sometimes a fishmonger. If the grocer contracted with Phil Papp for the freshest produce to be delivered, all the better.

To cross busy Joseph Street was unwise, especially for children sent to the store for something. So, the placement of one's ethnic food source dictated on which side of the Joseph Street divide you were likely to look for housing.

The elementary schools were each placed in one of the neighborhoods which meant that education was segregated by social or economic class. It would only be at the level of Perryburg High School that the classes would mix. By then, parents hoped, the years of inculcated identity along class, ethnic, and religious lines would be enough to prevent too much mixing.

Of course, like any other northern industrial city, Perryburg was the recipient of a portion of the Great Migration, and faces of color began to appear. They came as laborers, and workers, and even managers. It was not easy to immediately put them into a "proper" neighborhood. And they worshipped in places like AME and AME Zion and Missionary Baptist, which had no local affiliates. A new neighborhood then developed, down on the land by the railroad. "The Flats" was where it was expected these people would live, no matter what their class. A new elementary school was cobbled together down there. The city fathers hoped, just as with the class distinctions, the races would know better than to mix once they were in High School.

(The Flats would be the first section of town leveled after World War II as part of the new concept of Urban Renewal, replaced with "The Projects." The old school was never replaced, much less renewed. It's still there if you take a look.)

With each economic expansion, Perryburg grew its neighborhoods as growth spoked outward from the center core. The same old principal streets ran, but ran a little further out into the country. The same linear patterns of commerce and travel prevailed, just a little longer for the later arrivals.

Of course, the 1950s and 1960s were a time of change in many cities. With Urban Renewal, and its promise of new vitality in Perryburg's core, nothing was mentioned about the neighborhoods except for The Flats.

The Green Necklace, as the string of parks from the 1900s that ringed the city's core at the edge of the first neighborhood expansion was called, had been overcome by time, nature, neglect, and city growth.

Houses once proudly single-family homes were subdivided into apartments. Owners, first trying to keep the nature of their neighborhoods intact, soon gave in to economic reality and rented to anyone with the right money and references. The old neighborhood lines were crumbling.

By the 1980s, with the commercial core victim to the new malls out in the suburbs and the neighborhood groceries driven out by the supermarkets, there was no pattern that would tell anyone who anyone was based on where they lived. Schools once known as the province of the college-bound elementary kids became equally filled with those thinking of trades. Churches, in decline in Perryburg as elsewhere, were consolidating, closing, or moving in almost every neighborhood. Once The Projects were torn down and the residents able to buy or rent anywhere in the city, racial identity was not as matched with residential address.

It was only with the arrival of various refugees from around the world that Perryburg re-established some neighborhoods. The historic draws of markets, places of worship, and people of common language once again drew boundaries and offered enticements.

Where, you ask, in all of this socio-economic history of Perryburg are the people?

I am getting to that.

For with any city, and especially for Perryburg, its history may be told in many ways, but to tell the story of its people is to get to the heart of any city. I've already hinted where those stories take place. Can you guess?

If you guessed Perryburg High School, you are right.

The year was 1935. Perryburg High School was so crowded that it was on split sessions. Juniors and Seniors in the mornings (so they could get to jobs after school) and First- and Second-year students in the afternoons. Gladys, a lively girl who had grown up in one of the middle-class neighborhoods that led up toward the upper-class one, was active in the Methodist Church, and was the daughter of the principal of the High School, began her classes there. About a fifth of the 1000 First Year students were from the same elementary school she attended, boys and girls she had known all through grade school. Like Gladys, they all had Anglo-Saxon names, fair complexions, and were Protestant.

Her first two years at Perryburg High went smoothly and she enjoyed the larger world that it represented. By her Junior year, her younger brother, Ray, had joined her at PHS. Ray was into music and their home jumped with the beat most of the time he was home. Soon, on many a Saturday night, their mother would let them roll up the living room rug for dancing, and a small combo of some sort would play the latest tunes, with Ray on the trumpet. These gatherings brought a wide range of music lovers into their home.

It was in October 1937, that a new face appeared, a talented piano player, who gave the dancers (which included an enthusiastic Gladys) a bigger sound to propel their feet. Gladys had never met him before, but she was intrigued by how skilled, and how handsome, he was. At the first break, as the nominal hostess for these occasions (Her mother stayed away from "that kind of music."), Gladys passed out the beverages and made sure to approach the piano player first.

"Hi, I'm Gladys, Ray's sister."

"I know."

He knew? He had noticed her.

"I really enjoy your playing."

"You have any requests for songs."

"Anything you like."

Ah, the words of young people trying to connect: tentative, hopeful, sweet.

"Where are my manners? I'm Remo. Remo Bonafacio."

"Remo, that's a nice name."

And so, Gladys and Remo would share Saturday evenings in the living room as he played piano, and she danced. After a few weeks, Saturday night dance parties were supplemented with Friday evening movies. The two of them, both class of '39, would then see each other in the hallways of the High School.

Gladys' mother was descended from English stock, and her cooking favored the well-done beef roast. No tomato gravy nor pasta had ever been served from her kitchen. Now, she and her educator husband were entertaining someone who was "Eye-talian." But they both found him respectful, conversant, and kind to their daughter.

Most of Gladys' friends thought that, upon graduation, she and Remo would likely get engaged and later married. They were wrong, and it was in a chance meeting on a train several years later that Gladys would find her life's partner.

But, what neighborhoods had kept separate, connections in the High School had rendered moot. In fact, that connection would open Gladys' world to the many different people in life, a recognition that would inform her work as a nurse and then as an agent for social equality.

And Remo? While he would not marry Gladys, he would remember those days when her house was as open to him as his own, and someday even more. He would remember Gladys' mother's awkward attempts at Italian cuisine, experiments that ended when Remo told her that he preferred her, as he called it, English cooking. His professional life took him away from Perryburg but as often as he was home to visit family, he always made sure to stop by that house up on Netherlands Avenue where he had played piano, met a delightful girl, and found a whole world outside his own neighborhood.

His was not the only story of this transition from neighborhoods to community.

The year was 1965, and Rhonda Smith had been a student at PHS for only a month, after her family had moved from Louisiana. Her father, Abraham, the new Maître d' at a downtown restaurant, was a Veteran who had served as a cook in World War II in Europe, where he met a beautiful Swiss girl there. Yes, her name really was Heidi. They were married soon after the war and settled in New Orleans so Abraham could follow his culinary career.

They chose New Orleans for several reasons. Even if the Army was not the best place to learn haute cuisine, it was a good place to learn techniques, especially technique under pressure. The next step would be to meld those techniques with appreciation for fine dining.

The other reason that Heidi and Abraham chose New Orleans was that Heidi was white, and Abraham was black. New Orleans had shown some openness to mixed race families, and they thoroughly intended to have that family no matter what skin color they produced.

Produce they did, and over the next five years, five little Smith's had entered the world. Abraham Jr., Alexandra, Robert, Darnell, and Rhonda. Their children presented a spectrum of color none of which was as dark as Abraham nor as light as Heidi.

Abraham was a quick learner and soon mastered not only the back of the house routines of preparation, cooking, plating, and presentation, he also began to observe and learn the duties of the front of the house. He watched the Maître d' of the several restaurants in which he worked in his first years back in the States. At home, he would practice those skills with his growing family. None of the babies were ever that impressed. However, Heidi was. She encouraged him to think about that work as a career.

In New Orleans he luckily found an opening at a well-regarded restaurant just off Bourbon Street and for eight years he was the face of the restaurant to its clientele. He was good. No, he was superb. From the line cooks in the back to the reviewers of what was served in the front, he succeeded.

Heidi, as supportive as she had been of Abe, was never really comfortable in the steamy climate of Louisiana. Her heart longed for a place more reminiscent of home. While Abe was making a name for himself in the Big Easy, Heidi was scanning the trade publications for opportunities that might speak to her heart.

One day she saw it, a listing for a Maître d' at a "continental cuisine" restaurant in Perryburg. She got out her old Rand-McNally road map book and looked for Perryburg. There it was, up north, in a valley between hills and mountains. Her heart skipped a beat.

Abraham was more than willing to apply, with little hope that this Black boy from the south would ever get a job "up north." His references, however, never mentioned race, only style and competence. He was flown up to Perryburg, the final leg on that regional airline, "Algonquin," which knew how to make any flight a memory (not necessarily a good memory). In a bumpy ride from New York that touched down and took off from two other airports before Perryburg, Abraham decided he hoped he would be offered the job because he didn't want to be subjected to many more interview trips like this.

After the interview, the restaurant owner and its manager asked Abraham to wait outside in the restaurant's lobby. Too nervous to sit, he stood and waited. Surprisingly, several customers entering the restaurant for lunch spoke to him, offering greetings and naming the number of people in their party. No one seemed to have any trouble with seeing him, a black man, as the Maître d'. He had to quickly say "just a moment," step over to the hostess stand, and relay the information. By the fourth time he did this, the hostess, Bea, looked at him and said, "So, did they give you the job already?" He just laughed and said, "Not yet.

At one point, while he waited, Bea left her post for a minute and ducked into the office. About five minutes later the Manager stepped out and gestured for Abe to come back into the office. The owner stretched out his hand and said, "Bea, our hostess, confirmed what we had seen. The position is yours if you want it." A salary and benefits package was mentioned which almost took Abe's breath away.

Reaching out his own hand, Abraham said, "Sir, it would be an honor."

That was how it came to be that in 1965, fifteen-year-old Rhonda, a rising Junior, first strode down the hallways of Perryburg High School. Tall, thin, mocha-toned, with straightened dark hair that reached below her collar. When she spoke, her drawl seemed like sweet molasses. And when she spoke, one knew immediately that she was extremely intelligent and worldly.

Her schedule card showed the usual cluster of core classes: English 3, World History, Algebra 2, Chemistry. It also included German 2, as well as the required PE and Chemistry lab. Ending her day was Orchestra – Rhonda was an excellent cellist.

That first day Rhonda was the object of some attention. Over the summer the English students had been assigned reading, but Rhonda did not know this. When the teacher, Mr. Rapperty, opened class with "Today we will see how well you did with you summer assignments," Rhonda's heart sank. She had so wanted to be on-pace with her new classmates.

"So, can anyone tell me about a secondary theme, not the main theme, of 'To Kill a Mockingbird'?"

Rhonda felt her whole body relax. She knew that book. She knew the characters as if they were old friends. She raised her hand and was surprised that hers was only one of two hands raised. She looked over to her right and back a row to see a boy as eagerly seeking to answer as she was.

"Yes, Mr. Gander."

The boy began, "One could consider Boo Radley and whole subject of mental illness as a subtheme. But, in another sense, one could argue that Boo Radley is the glue that holds the whole story together."

"Wow," thought Rhonda, "I was going to say something about that, but he said it so well."

"Yes, Mr. Gander, good observations."

Rhonda, with her hand raised again, was racing through her memories of the book for something cogent to say.

"Yes, Miss …. I don't think I know your name yet."

"I'm Rhonda, Rhonda Smith, sir." She saw Mr. Rapperty look startled at the word "sir."

"I was thinking of two characters, Calpurnia and Miss Maudie. Both figured significantly in the lives of both children and especially Scout."

"True."

But before Mr. Rapperty could continue, Rhonda tried to finish her thought, "but from the start there is the difference between the two, with one addressed with her name, as if either a servant or someone of no consequence, and the other with the honorific of 'Miss'. That tension underlines the racism in all the narratives in the story."

A quiet hung in the room for a moment before Mr. Gander started a slow but steady tapping of approval with his pen against the desk.

"I see we are in for a good year," Mr. Rapperty responded, "and for once Mr. Gander will have some real competition."

Rhonda knew she blushed but probably no one in class could tell under the darker skin.

After the class was over, after no one else in class said anything memorable about the book (which she suspected had not been really read by most of the class), after she had gathered her books together and prepared to find Room 228 for her German class, she looked up to see Mr. Gander standing by her desk.

"Hi, I'm Geoffrey, Geoff," he sort-of stuttered, "but, for obvious reasons everyone calls me 'Goose'. It sure is going to be good to have an intelligent person in this class. I loved your comments."

"I *surely* love your compliment," Rhonda drawled, laying it on thickly.

"What's next on your schedule?"

"German – and you?"

"French. Maybe I'll see you in a later class."

"I hope so." (Did I really say that?")

After finding Room 228, Rhonda had taken a seat at the back of the classroom. The teacher, a Mrs. Weiss, a stern and solid woman, stood behind the teacher's desk and at the stroke of the class start said, "Achtung! Wie heissen sie, bitte?" pointing to the person in the first seat in the first row.

"Ich heissen Eric?"

"Nein!" and she pointed to the next student.

"Ich heissen Carol?"

"Nein! Niemand?"

Rhonda slowly raised her hand.

"Ja. Wie heissen sie, bitte?"

"Ich heise Rhonda."

"Zehr Gut. Heise, kein heissen. Wie heisst deine Mutter?"

"Meine Mutter heißt Heidi. Sie ist von Schweiz."

By this point the room had become very quiet, all the white faces turned to watch this dark girl have a real conversation with Mrs. Weiss. Mrs. Weiss had a slight smile on her face which no one in the class had seen before. Mrs. Weiss then broke the spell by saying to Rhonda, in English, my mother was Swiss. She was from Bern. She paused a moment, and then began a new drill about where the library was.

Rhonda had felt very self-conscious in the exchange while at the same time feeling very relieved to be able to speak a language which her mother had shared.

As class let out, Mrs. Weiss said to Rhonda, "I'm so glad we will get to share this year together."

"Ich auch."

The rest of the day was similar: in Algebra she was able to solve one of the problems the teacher had previously posted on the blackboards. In World History, she was able to identify the most countries in Europe.

It was in Chemistry that the biggest surprise happened. As she entered the room she realized that the classroom and the laboratory were the same space. Tall lab tables, each equipped with gas outlets for Bunsen Burners, small sinks with with tall faucets, and a hard rubberized surface, stood before pairs of lab stools. As she looked over the sea of tables, she heard her name being called. "Rhonda, over there."

There stood Geoffrey, or Geoff, or Goose (which name should she use?) pointing to an empty stool mid-way back. The welcome startled her, and that startle also startled her.

"Let's get this straight – you can call me Geoff or Goose, but never Geoffrey. Only my mother calls me Geoffrey and then only when I'm in trouble."

"OK, … err, Goose, your offer of lab partner is accepted!" she replied with a smile.

After the two-period class and lab, Goose and Rhonda seemed to go their separate ways but in the Orchestra Room they startled each other by emerging from the instrument storage rooms, each with a cello.

"Really?"

"Really!"

"After you."

"No, after you!"

Taking two chairs in the section to the right of the conductor, they awaited this first rehearsal. But first there was the decision about who would play first chair, etc. The conductor, the kindly but proper Dr. Schindle, worked his way through the orchestra, challenging players in different instrument groupings to play passages, and then assigned the seating. After the violins and the violas, he came to the cellos.

"Ach, a new face. Let me hear a short passage from the Bach Suites for Solo Cello."

Geoff made a gesture for Rhonda to start first. With a long intake of breath, Rhonda launched methodically and lyrically into the first Suite, with a tone and precision that brought silence to the whole room. When Dr. Schindle signaled she had played enough, Rhonda reciprocated the gesture toward Geoff.

With a smile on his face, Geoff began the second Suite, as fully competent and musical as what Rhonda had done. Dr. Schindle kept listening for a time and then signaled for Geoff to stop.

"Such a problem to have such talents. Two equally good cellists. I am blessed. I welcome our newest member and invite you to introduce yourself."

"Thank you. I'm Rhonda Smith," she drawled, "and I just moved here from New Orleans."

"Well, Miss Smith, I welcome you to our little ensemble. I hope you will not be disappointed but today I offer the first chair to Geoffrey." (Rhonda could see Geoff cringe.) "He has seniority in the orchestra. But, in a month, when the first seat challenges are open, I hope you will be challenging him. In fact, I hope you will challenge each other all year."

"Thank you, sir, I will prepare for the challenge."

She could see Dr. Schindle straighten just a little at the word "sir." She could also see Geoff's warm smile when he turned to look at her. As second chair, first section of the cellos, she would be turning pages for him until she won that coveted first seat.

After school was over, Rhonda looked for Geoff, but it appeared his exit from PHS was on the opposite side of the building. She headed downtown, not because she wanted to shop but because the only house her parents could buy in Perryburg was one of the single-family Capes that had been built after World War II, not quite at the projects but in that direction.

The sad truth was that while Perryburg, like so many northern cities, had no racist laws on the books that were so common under Jim Crow, the practices of real estate brokers, banks, and neighborhood covenants kept many a neighborhood closed, especially to newly arrived people of color, especially those from the south.

As Rhonda burst through the door full of excitement about her first day at the High School, her father was just preparing to leave for the restaurant's dinner service. Not letting him go, she sat with her father and her mother at the kitchen table and regaled them. "It was the best day of my life! I loved my teachers. I think I showed them all that we from the south are not stupid or uneducated. And I met this guy, Goose, who is so smart, and so polite, and so good at cello."

"Slow down, Rhonda. You'll have plenty of time to tell us the details."

"But, Daddy, I am so happy we moved to Perryburg!"

"Well," said her mother, "isn't that a nice change from the pouting I heard back in New Orleans."

Looking a little sheepish, Rhonda replied, "I'm sorry for that. Not knowing anywhere else, and hearing all those stories about people up here and how they treat people like me, I just didn't know how wrong I could be."

Abraham looked at the shining face of his daughter and said, "I am so happy for you! But, as a father, I am obligated by the laws of the state to ask just one question: who is this Goose?"

"Oh, Daddy. His name is Geoff. And he treated me like I was some newly met long-lost friend."

"I want to hear more, but I must get to work right now. Later?"

"Yes, Daddy, later."

Who is this Goose? Geoffrey Chandler Gander, middle child and only son of Helen and Leonard Gander. The Gander family came to Perryburg in the mid-1800s from Virginia. They had been strict Abolitionists so continued residence there was nearly impractical and ethically impossible. Mrs. Gander, the former Helen Loudon, had come to the Perryburg area as an elementary teacher from her home in North Carolina.

Helen and Leonard were social liberals, often in the leadership of community activities for social justice. They had raised their three children to look to a future world in which all people were not just welcomed but also included in the wealth of the world.

They lived in a comfortable Dutch Colonial house in one of the neighborhoods uptown that had been developed in the 1920s. It was one of those neighborhoods that had its own elementary school drawing only from that area. While the streets all had sidewalks, almost no one walked on them once their children were of school age. The students would walk to and from the neighborhood school but otherwise the sidewalks would only see the daily postman and an occasional salesperson.

This neighborhood was built and designed as an automobile neighborhood. There were no corner stores to walk to, no shops just down the street, no places for people of any age to congregate. That was what the city was for, not the neighborhood. The demographics of the neighborhood were thoroughly middle-class, white, Protestant.

As they had watched Geoffrey grow, they had delighted at his eagerness to make new friends outside the boundaries of where they lived. His Little League team reached beyond their neighborhood. His Boy Scout troop, hosted by the Jewish Temple, included boys from all over the city. When he entered PHS, his world widened even more as the diversity of the whole city was present in its hallways. However, they had been dismayed to find out how lacking in diversity most of the classrooms were in his College Prep set of classes.

Dinnertime at the Gander household was always a lively affair, especially when all three children were at home. The topics around the table would begin with personal experiences from the day, followed by comments about current events, and finally whatever idea someone wanted to bring up.

When the older daughter, Sandra, was in her Junior Year at PHS, one evening she brought home a boy from her class. Karl was a bright, engaging young man with polite table manners. However, he fell silent at the intellectual free-for-all that was a Gander dinner. Later he told Sandra he had never experienced anything like it. In his household, you either agreed to the ideas of his parents, his father especially, or you better keep quiet. He had never comfortably watched children and parents have such open discussions.

Sandra had told him that in the Gander household, only three rules applied: never say anything that is derogatory about any person or group; never insult another person at the table or their argument; and keep whatever was said around the table in that place and time.

"You mean, your parents can't later bring up what you said as a way to provoke you or punish you?"

"No. We try to engage in ideas, not in personalities"

Karl had just shaken his head with disbelief.

By now, the older daughter, Sandra, was off at university and the dinner circle was smaller by one person. Geoff had tried his best to step into Sandra's shoes as the chief provocateur at the table.

That night, after the first day of school, Geoff went on and on about this new student in his grade. He complimented her for being as smart as he was. He also made a passing mention of how nice she looked as well as her southern drawl. He then proceeded to try to engage the whole family in a continuation of the class discussion about "To Kill a Mockingbird."

Over the next few weeks, Rhonda and Geoff enjoyed each other's company in classes with comfortable intellectual competitions in several of them, much to the delight of teachers but the moans of classmates.

In late October, when they were settling into their chairs in Orchestra (Rhonda had challenged Geoff earlier in the month, but Geoff had kept his first chair), and Rhonda was smoothing out the music for *Finlandia* that they were to start rehearsing that day, Geoff, in almost a whisper, said, "Would you like to be my date for the Fall Dance?"

"Excuse me. I couldn't hear what you said."

Slightly over-reaching in volume on a second attempt, Geoff repeated his question, "Would you like to be my date for the Fall Dance?"

His words were loud enough for the whole cello section and the basses to hear.

"Aaawwwww," was the common response.

Unfazed by her fellow string players reaction, Rhonda, summoning her full New Orleans self, replied, "Why, Sir, it would surely be my decided honor to accompany you to such an occasion." She then smiled a smile that melted an already softened heart in Geoff.

When Geoff told his family that night that he had asked Rhonda to the Fall Dance, his family was more supportive than the orchestra members had been. They had been hearing about Rhonda nearly nightly and had assumed it would only be a matter of time before he asked her out.

Leonard simply reached over and patted his son on the shoulder and then reminisced about the first time he had asked Helen out.

Helen, turned to her son, and said, "Geoffrey, I am so happy you have found someone your equal that you are thinking about in other ways as well. Why don't you invite Rhonda here for dinner the night of the dance?"

Geoff, excited by the positive response from his family but reluctant to go as far as subjecting Rhonda to a Gander dinner, said, "Thanks, Mom, but let's not make this such a big deal. I will need a ride, though."

It was then set that Leonard would drive Geoff to the Smiths to pick up Rhonda and meet the Smiths, then drive them both back over to the dance. Rhonda had said that while her father would be working when she was picked up, he had offered to pick them up from the dance.

Somehow, in all the excitement of telling their families about each other, they had failed to include some information. The Ganders did not know where the Smiths lived, but assumed it was probably in the area down the hill before you got to midtown. They also had assumed that if Mr. Smith would not be around when Rhonda was being picked up, he must be employed in some shift or commercial position.

On the other hand, the Smiths had no idea where the Ganders lived and, since they knew that Geoff had walked their Rhonda home several times, it must be close by, either in their neighborhood or the projects.

The Smiths knew the Ganders were from Virginia and North Carolina. The Ganders knew the Smiths were from New Orleans. Many assumptions were made both ways.

You see, while Geoff and Rhonda had seen each other daily for nearly two months, neither the Smiths nor the Ganders had seen the others' child. What they heard from the two of them was about ideas, thoughts, math problems, chemistry labs gone wrong, cello passages, and much more, but little more.

On that Friday night, Geoff had taken an extra long time in the bathroom. He willingly wore the sport coat his mother had insisted he needed as a young man. His father helped him pick out and tie a necktie. Even his little sister, Eve, gave an approving whistle when she saw him. Helen simply wiped away a small tear at seeing her little boy off on his first, real date.

At the Smith household, Rhonda was taking even longer in the bathroom. She had opted for clothes that were much different than her usual school attire, dressing as she had seen teen girls do for soirees in New Orleans. "Looking mighty fine," was what her mother said when she walked downstairs from the children's upstairs bedrooms.

Geoff had set the schedule for his father and even though he thought Geoff was over-estimating the time it would take to pick Rhonda up, he went with his son's timing. They walked out to the car and once inside Leonard said, "Where to?"

"109 MacArthur Street."

Leonard paused and looked at his son. "You sure you've got that right?"

"Yes, Dad, I've walked her home several times."

"Hmmmmm," was all Leonard could offer, and he was wondering if there was a way he could find a phone booth and call Helen to let her know what they were doing.

Leonard guided the car over through the maze of streets and onto Mohawk Street. Down they went, past all the neighborhoods Leonard had thought he was headed for, down around the circular square, down past the Tip-Top House, down through the commercial district, then left onto Berkeley Boulevard, and finally right onto MacArthur Street. Stopping in front of the very-well maintained house at 109, Leonard turned on the inside light, looked at Geoff, straightened his tie, and said, "Go get her."

With a bounce in his step, and small corsage in his hand (which neither his mother nor his father knew he had bought), he walked up to the front door of 109 and rang the bell. He could hear some young voices inside sort-of teasing someone and then he heard Rhonda say "behave."

A very blond woman answered the door and curiously looked at Geoff. Geoff looked at her.

"Yes, may I help you?"

"Maybe I have the wrong house?"

Then he heard what he wanted to hear, Rhonda's voice. "Mama, it's Geoff, invite him in."

Now, as often as he had walked Rhonda home, he had never been inside. He had never seen any other members of her family. When Heidi opened the door wide for Geoff to enter, he found himself in a beautifully decorated living room, even fancier than his own home. Rising from the couch were two young men who looked like they could be twins except their skin was not the same color.

"These are two of my sons, Robert and Darnell. My older two children are off at college, one at Howard and the other at Cornell," Heidi said by way of introductions. "Girl, where are you?"

The two boys reached out their hands in greetings, but with something Geoff could not quite fathom. "Hi, I'm Bob," one said, while the other offered, "I'm Darnell."

"Geoff."

"So, you're the famous Geoff, or Goose we hear so much about."

"I guess that would be I."

"Oooo, 'I', he knows his English."

"Hush up now, Robert. Robert, you see, is studying English here at the local college. He likes to correct all our grammar, and some of our grammar is a bit patois."

As Heidi said "patois," he could hear Rhonda's voice as well. It sounded so nice.

At that point, Rhonda came down the stairs, this time in a more dramatic fashion for its full effect on her date. Robert and Darnell stood slack-jawed. "Sister, I have never seen you look so fine," was Darnell's comment.

"She does look fine," Geoff added, "so maybe this is gilding the lily, but I think you deserve it."

With that he presented the corsage to Rhonda, who immediately blushed a bit and begged her mother to help pin it in.

Looking at her now, all Geoff could do was smile as broadly as Rhonda was smiling.

But then Darnell jumped in, "Little sister, was there, perhaps, just a little something you forgot to mention about Geoff?"

"What do you mean," Rhonda retorted. "This is Geoff. What you see is what you get, but if you engage him in discussion, you will get so much more. O, wait, were you, perhaps making an oblique reference to his pigmentation?" Rhonda had moved from graciousness to a fierce attitude of indignation. "In this house I would think we would all be way beyond that!"

"Sorry, sis. Not an objection, just a surprise."

"Apology accepted. Geoff, shall we go and welcome in Fall in the elegant gymnasium?"

"Mrs. Smith, Bob, Darnell, very pleased to meet you all. I look forward to meeting Mr. Smith later this evening. I promise, I will treat Rhonda as the delightful young woman she is."

As Rhonda turned to say goodbye to her family, assured that Geoff could not see her face, she stuck out her tongue at her brothers. Then, she kissed her mother goodbye and accepted Geoff's arm for the walk to the car.

Leonard had been waiting in the car, wondering what was taking so long in the house. Then, he remembered himself being a young man waiting for a date, nervously sitting on a sofa while seemingly hours passed before she came downstairs. He understood.

But he still did not understand about this house, in this neighborhood. Who were these people? He had seen a very blond woman answer the door and invite Geoff in. Did white people actually live down here?

Finally, the door was opened again by the same blond woman and out came Geoff helping a young woman over the threshold. She was stylishly dressed, maybe more dressed than a PHS dance called for, and she was gracious, and …. she was a person of color.

Leonard tried to wipe the shocked look from his face. Rather than sit in the driver's seat, he opened the door, stepped out, and greeted the couple. "Why, you must be the Rhonda we have heard so much about. Welcome."

"Thank you, sir," she drawled. Geoff winked at his father.

Geoff opened the back door of the car for Rhonda, telling her he would go to the other side to get in. After seeing her safely in her seat, Geoff closed the door. Looking at his father, he saw his father's eyebrows arch just a little, but didn't know what that meant. Going around the other side, Geoff got into own seat, closed the door, and they were off.

Almost immediately, Geoff and Rhonda were deep into a discussion about the book *Invisible Man*, a book Leonard remembered discussing with Helen many years before. Hearing their back and forth, he could only smile.

At the High School the driveway past the gym entrance, usually closed off during school hours, was open for cars, and Leonard drove the couple right up to the doors. He wished them a great evening. Rhonda assured him that her father would get them home. "But," she added, "if you have any concerns about that, you can reach him at this number." She handed Leonard a small business card with her father's name on it.

Leonard thanked her for that but did not look at the card. He was too eager to get home to Helen and share all the evening's revelations.

At about the same time, Heidi was on the phone trying to reach Abraham. When he came to the phone, he explained that several emergencies were all converging at once at the restaurant and unless this is an emergency, can't it just wait until he was home.

"Not an emergency, but if you get a chance before picking up the kids at school, give me a call."

"Okay. Got to run. Love you."

Before she could respond, he was gone.

Inside the school's gym, Rhonda and Goose saw many people they knew from classes and activities. The girls all admired Rhonda's dress and gave eye-glances toward Geoff in an approving way. The guys complimented Goose for being with such a worldly-looking young woman in a guy kind of way, with backslaps and rib-pokes.

As the evening wore on, it became more and more apparent that while they were there, there was no place for them. The cluster of Black students all seemed to close up their circle when Rhonda and Geoff came toward them. The larger community of white couples seemed to dissipate when the two of them came over. Nonetheless, they enjoyed many a dance and lots more talking.

However, the real truth came out in the bathrooms. The couple separated to go to separate restrooms, familiar areas of the gym where they each had PE twice a week.

When Geoff walked into the "BOYS" area, a small group of white students, none of whom had classes with Geoff, noticed him and one crooned out, "Oh, the Goose and the Nigger Girl."

"What did you say?" Geoff shouted back.

"I said it looks like the Goose likes dark meat."

Just then several of the Black students entered the sink area from the toilet area and, looking at the person who had just said that, one of them quietly said, "I think you want to be leaving right about now."

The white students straightened up, pulling their shirt sleeves back, but then assessed the odds and thought better of anything other than to leave. As they left, one started up "Honk, honk" and the others joined in.

After they had cleared the room, one of the Black students, one Geoff knew from his French class, ambled over to Geoff. "Now, don't get me wrong, mon amie. Nothing those honkies were doing was right, but not all of us like you with one of our most beautiful girls. We get slim enough pickings, and you just decreased our odds."

Geoff was shocked and stood speechless.

"Not saying it's not right in the big scope of things, but it's not OK here in Perryburg for us."

"Look, guys, look ….," Geoff stammered, "I didn't mean any disrespect, or competition, or whatever. I just relate to her, and to me her color doesn't matter."

"Well maybe her color doesn't trouble you, but my skin color causes me too much trouble."

At that point, little Jimmy Jeffers, one of the school's track team nicknamed *Black Lightning*, added, "If any of us ever get even a hint that you or any of your white friends are treating her with anything less than respect, we will come looking for you. Got it?"

"Got it," Geoff responded.

"OK"

"OK!"

With that the group left the room and Geoff could finally carry on with the business that had brought him there, now more urgent than ever.

Over in the rooms marked "GIRLS," Rhonda was fairing no better. She, too, had a circle of white girls who found some creative racial slurs to sling her way. Then a group of Black girls came in and the tension mounted. Rhonda turned to them and asked, "So, what's your beef in this?"

"Uppity, southern-belle Uncle Tom, that's what."

"Say what?"

"You act all superior, with cello playing, and your smart ways, and that accent. And you treat us all like dirt and take up with that pale hunk of meat. None of our boys good enough for you? Who do you think you are? When the sun goes down, and people start dividing up, you are too light to be colored and too colored to be white."

"Well, I am sorry if I don't fit your mold of conduct ..."

"Eweee, there she goes again."

"Look, I just want to be me, Rhonda, not this or that. Can we leave it at that?"

"Oh, we leave it, but just for now. But don't be trying to say you are one of us when the other side starts doing this rejecting shit. Come on, girls, let's go."

And with that, Rhonda was alone. Shaking, more furious than afraid. Nobody in New Orleans had ever treated her like this.

When Geoff and Rhonda met again on the dance floor, they noticed that everyone was giving them space. Rhonda told Geoff, "We've got to talk."

"And how!"

Making sure they were not observed, they used the backstage passageway down to the Orchestra Room. There they sat, in darkness, not speaking at first.

"Geoff, I have to tell you what happened in the Girls room."

"And I need to tell you what happened in the Boys room. You first."

Rhonda then told him all the things that had been said about her, about him, about them. Geoff listened with a mixture of anger and sorrow. When it was his turn, he told her about the parallel things said to him. Rhonda now felt her own deep pain of loss and yet determination.

When Geoff was finished, and a long silence followed, they held each other close. There were tears for both of them, as much for the other as for themselves.

"You know," Rhonda began softly, slowly, "sitting here in this dark room, I can't tell if you are white, or black, or something in between."

"I was thinking the same thing. I was thinking about how until those things were said, I never thought about my color, or your color. I just know that we can be open with each other, we challenge each other, we can support each other."

"And race doesn't come into the relationship."

"Unless someone tries to force it in."

The silence deepened.

"Rhonda, I love you," Geoff then whispered in her ear. He immediately felt her sobbing and wasn't sure what caused it.

When she had composed herself a little, Rhonda said, "Geoff, I love you too. I feel for you something I have never felt before. And now these people want to tarnish all of this, I'll be damned if I am going to let them."

"Me too! Let's get back up there, let's dance as two people who like each other, love each other, accept each other, care for each other. Come on, let's dance."

After a long hug, and a long kiss (which neither of them had expected) Geoff offered Rhonda his hand and together they retraced their steps into the gym. A slow song was just starting, and they took each other into their arms and let everyone see them for what they were.

There was no more trouble at the dance. They had made a statement of strength and solidarity.

While they were dancing away, Leonard was home with Helen, clutching the card that Rhonda had given him. He had told Helen about where Rhonda lived and what Rhonda looked like. Helen, bless her, only wanted details of Rhonda's outfit, shoes included! She had heard too much divisive racial talk in her life, and she was not going to allow it in her household. Leonard was less composed about this. He was musing about what this all might mean for his son.

Would all the racism and hatred in the world infect the sweet, caring boy he knew? Would violence knock at their door, threaten their lives?

Helen counseled him to believe that their parenting had raised a son whose values would see him through whatever was to come. This was just a Fall Dance, not the end, nor the beginning, of the world.

Finally, Leonard turned the card over. There was Rhonda's father's name, Maître d' at the city's most treasured restaurant. The Ganders had eaten there on several occasions. In fact, just two weeks ago they had been there for a celebration of a friend's birthday. They recalled a suave, polite, worldly Maître d' who had welcomed them, who had seated them, who had checked on them during the meal making sure that everything was perfect. A man who was, yes, Black, but so much more than that. Thinking back to that very professional man, he could see the resemblance to the suave, polite young woman who had sat in the back seat with their son earlier in the evening. Some of the anxiety left his spirit, and he reached over to Helen and said, "I think this will all be more all right than we can know."

It was just about 11:45pm that Abraham Smith turned the key and activated the alarm system at the restaurant. He would be on time at the school to pick up his daughter and her date. He remembered that he had not called his wife back to find out what she wanted to discuss with him. Oh, well, home soon enough.

Outside the school, in the line of cars waiting for the couples to leave the dance, Abe looked around and saw very few faces that looked like his. Then he remembered his own high school days and how none of his friends would ever expect, much less allow parents to pick them up. It was a cultural thing, maybe even a racial thing, but this was a different world in which he was sitting in a car waiting to pick up his daughter. He was also thinking about how nice it had been of Geoff's father to take them there. Perryburg was a great place he had chosen for them, where families like his would meet families like Geoff's.

At the stroke of midnight, with one of the church bells nearby ringing the hour, he saw his beautiful daughter come out of the gym, dressed so well, with – is that a corsage? Nice guy to do that! – and then he saw her holding hands with a white kid. And the way they were looking at each other, he knew this had to be Geoff.

Ah, that was what Heidi wanted him to know.

As they approached the car, he got out to greet them.

"Daddy," Rhonda said, "we have so much to tell you about tonight … the good, the less-than-good, and the marvelous. Daddy, this is Geoffrey, Geoff.

Geoff offered his hand to Mr. Smith and slowly said, "Sir, thank you for letting your daughter be a part of one of the most meaningful nights of my young life." He looked Abraham in the eye for the whole time.

("Wow," thought Abe, "He sounds like her.")

"Thank you, son, for treating my little girl as the princess she is. Now, let's get us all home. Where to?"

"2882 Glenmont Drive, sir."

("Wow, that's uptown a piece. It's a neighborhood a world away from ours.")

Abe watched Geoff reach over to the car door handle, open the door, help Rhonda into the car, and then go around to his own door – no asking her to slide across the seat!

The car was soon filled with lively conversation among the three of them. Rhonda and Geoff would keep some pieces of it to be shared in their respective homes. But there was plenty else to keep the talk going, much of the time with Abe just listening to two well-matched young people take on the world.

It would take some time for the two households to thoroughly assimilate what had occurred that night. In a world so built on class and race, divided into neighborhoods by those same lines, it took a dance at Perryburg High School to both reveal and heal some of those lines of division.

I'll bet you wonder what happened to Rhonda and Geoff. I'll let their son, Michael, tell the rest of the story:

> "Mom and Dad continued as best friends and dating partners throughout high school. They were named Valedictorian and Salutatorian, and I will let you guess who was which.
>
> "It wasn't always easy because of the way they were treated by many other students, but they had a small but loyal cadre

of students who only saw two people very much in synch and very much in love.

"Of course, they won many prizes in their time at PHS. Perhaps some of how others treated them was from jealousy more than racism. I think I know the answer, but that is for later.

"April 15, 1967, Rhonda and Geoff eagerly awaited the thick envelopes of acceptance. Mom had applied to Curtis in Philly (the cello had won her heart), Eastman in Rochester, Julliard in New York, and Boston Conservatory. Dad had applied to the University of Pennsylvania, University of Rochester, Columbia University, and Harvard. His talents and desires had encouraged him towards the sciences.

"Their great worry was that they would only have acceptances from places that did not match. They asked their parents to intercept the mail that day and bring it over to PHS, so they could open the letters together.

"Sitting on the bench out in front of the High School, they waited for two cars to drive up, with two sets of parents bearing envelopes. At about 3:30pm, first the Smiths and then the Ganders had driven up.

"I should mention that by that time the two families had become good friends. They had figured if the kids could deal with any negativity, they could too. Now, at least once a month, everyone was over at 109 or up at 2882, sharing meals, games, ideas, and dreams.

"Dad and Mom tried to read the faces of their parents for clues, but too many games and too many years raising children had made them poker-face experts. In a strange twist, Grandma Heidi handed Dad his mail while Grandpa Abe shook his hand with words of wisdom: 'It will all be good.' At the same time, Grandma Helen handed Mom her mail while Grandpa Leonard gave her a soft kiss on the cheek with the quiet words, 'All good things come to those who wait.'

"Taking their mail in hand, Dad and Mom divided the fat envelopes from the skinny ones. In Mom's pile Boston and Julliard were skinny. In Dad's pile, Rochester and Harvard were skinny.

"Suddenly a smile broke on both their faces. As quick as they each were with math and logic, they had figured it out. There would be thick envelopes of acceptance from Curtis and U Penn. Life, or rather their abilities, had given them a match.

"Four years passed, and their relationship only deepened as they matured into adulthood. Of course, it was not always easy. Just as there had been neighborhoods back in Perryburg, in Philadelphia theirs were schools that tried to separate people into pigeonholes based on majors and perceived value of the schools. Mom and Dad continued to cross some of those lines. As much as Pennsylvania is a northern state, it was far from being free of prejudice and more than once, as they walked downtown, someone would yell a slur at them. As they learned years before in PHS, they held their heads up and looked at each other.

"I don't want to sugar coat all of this. Sure, they had their spats. Becoming an adult, pursuing a career, juggling academic and social demands is hard work, and sometimes one, or the other, or both would get it wrong. The one thing I admire most about Mom and Dad is how, when a distance has come between them, either by their own actions or the actions of others, they have a way of owning their own actions and placing the actions of others in perspective. So many times, when I thought an impasse of feelings had been reached, I would look over and see their two hands slowly inching toward each other and I knew everything will be OK.

"They each graduated *Magna cum Laude*. Dad was in the front row at Mom's senior recital. Mom was in the front row at Dad's Phi Beta Kappa installation. That June weekend, when both graduated, thankfully on different days, the Ganders and the Smiths were all there in full force.

"After graduation, again seeking invitations to employment in the same area, they were relieved when offers for work came from Cleveland. They were on their way in their careers. Mom was last chair cello in the Orchestra and Dad was a very junior researcher for a tech firm.

"Life was good there, they tell me. They lived in Shaker Heights, where they found many people welcoming them. It was there that I was born in 1975. My first school years were there and if you think Mom was mixed race, think about me. I soon learned to tell school friends who noticed my different skin tone that I was a prototype model of the future when all colors would blend to a soft brown. I am not sure they believed me.

"Then, about 1980, life back in Perryburg started to take a slow turn. Grandpa Abe had bought the restaurant but with the general downturn in the city, he was under stress to keep it not only profitable enough to support him and Grandma but also to avoid bankruptcy. The pressure was too much for him and, like many Black man with high blood pressure, he suffered a stroke. Not a totally debilitating stroke, just one that robbed him of some of his strength and words. Fortunately, Antonio, the Sous Chef, was ready and able to step in and save the day.

"And almost at the same time Grandma Helen fell, broke her hip, and endured a long rehab.

"Soon either Mom or Dad, and sometimes both of them, often with me, would journey back to Perryburg to clean houses, prepare a week's worth of meals, run errands, and be company to the fallen and the weak as well the not-yet fallen and the slightly stronger. Age was taking its toll.

"Of course, Aunts and Uncles, and the many cousins, supplemented our family's efforts. The task of scheduling all these helpers was monumental in itself.

"As a child, I was kept out of the loop about my parents' reactions to all of this, so it came as a surprise when, in June 1981, they announced we were moving, moving to Perryburg. To me Perryburg had meant grandparents, and holidays, and reminiscent drives around town to see what was no longer there. For my parents, Perryburg was 'home.'

"Mom had gotten first chair cello in the Perryburg Symphonic Society, a premier outfit in the minor symphonic leagues, and also been offered a teaching position in the local college's music department. Dad had found a promising research position at the new IT company located in New Hamburg.

"I started second grade in the same school my dad had attended. There were still some teachers there who had taught him. When I began to excel in math and science, he was often remembered, and I would be embarrassed by their memories.

"Soon after arriving in Perryburg, my parents apparently thought I was not enough trouble, and my sister Gwen was born. As much as we two are now the closest of siblings, when I was eight or nine and she was one or two, what a

139

pain I was thinking what a pain she was. The mix of races played a trick on us. Where I had that summer-tan to the extreme all year long, Gwen looked like Grandma Heidi. People would often ask which of us had been adopted. We always pointed at the other, and in time came to giggle at it.

"What I am trying to share with you is my view, a child becoming a young adult view, of my parents, and in a sense of my grandparents. I was lucky. I grew up with loving people who doted on respect and served large helpings of welcome. I can remember my mother, seeing my Dad walk into a room where she was, breaking into her special smile. I can remember my Dad scrupulously remembering every event in their relationship with some gift for her. The grandparents had, even with their infirmities, remained close and supportive friends.

"Until I was older, I didn't recognize the importance of one change for the Grandparents. Together they had joined the Methodist Church downtown, reacting to inclusionary votes taken by the larger denomination. As Grandma Heidi would say, 'I'm a Christian first, and a whatever second' affirming the larger, more inclusive, more welcoming understandings she found in the Bible.

"When I was in tenth grade, I tested those wells of acceptance and welcome. About halfway through the year we were alerted that several newcomers would be arriving at PHS (yes, I was back in the same school where my parents had met). One day I was summoned to the Assistant Principal's Office. With more than a little fear I went to Mr. Adler's office. He was the disciplinary side of the leadership and being summoned to his office usually meant you were in trouble.

"When I arrived, Mr. Adler said, "Mr. Gander, please sit down," and he gestured to the known hot seat that faced his desk.

"As you have heard, there will be several new students this semester, and all of them are refugees from Bosnia. As one of our outstanding students, I am asking you to be an ambassador of Perryburg High School to these new students. Show them around, invite them to club events, explain the city to them, and all that. Are you game?"

"I felt I had no choice for two reasons. One, no one dared say 'no' to Mr. Adler, and two, I had been brought up to be like that to strangers. So, of course, I said 'yes.'

"Within the week, I joined seven other PHS students, divided equally between the grades, for an after-school welcome session. There were, as I remember, 17 of the Bosnians that afternoon. I agreed to welcome the tenth graders and along with Silvio Assesi, we invited those in our grade to come over to one corner of the room. There were three of them, two boys and one girl.

"I immediately noticed one thing. The girl wore what I now know is a Hijab. I had seen women dressed this way on the news, but I had never encountered one of my age, in my school. Silvio nervously spoke quietly to me, saying he would talk with the boys. I nodded.

"'Hello,' I said, 'I'm Michael Gander, also in tenth grade, and I want to welcome you to Perryburg High School.'

"The young woman, at first, did not look at me, but then turned her eyes toward me and said, in crisp English with a moderate accent 'I am Medina Alić, and I am pleased to meet you.'

"I told her some about the school and then asked what classes she would be taking. It turned out that she would be in three of my classes. I told her more about the teachers, and about the clubs associated with those subjects, and about life at PHS in general. She smiled at each new disclosure, and for some she made notes in a little notebook. Finally, I asked if she had any questions.

"She immediately looked away, and then asked, 'Why is your skin closer to the color of my skin than to the others in this school?'

"I hesitated a moment and then gave her the Reader's Digest version of my family. When I was sharing the part about my parents and the challenges they faced, I could see Medina relaxing.

"After I had shared my background, she inquired, 'Do you have any questions for me?'

"Spurred on by her respect for me as I told my story, I suddenly felt comfortable to ask, 'What is this head covering you wear?'

"Medina then told me that her family was Muslim and one of the commandments of her faith was of modesty for women. The Hijab is one garment many of her fellow Bosniak women wear to honor that commandment. The grace with which she told me this struck some inner place I didn't know was inside me.

"OK – cut to the chase. If you thought my parent's story was amazing, our story was an equal. I found Medina to be intellectually curious and mentally adept. I also found her to be one of the most caring people I have ever met. Unlike some of my fellow students who saw only in black and

142

white, she detected so many shades of gray, not to mention beautiful hues of the rainbow.

"But, here's the story. My parents, in returning to Perryburg, has joined their parents as members of the Methodist Church. As more and more people left the core of the city for other neighborhoods or the suburbs, that downtown church, despite the influx of all the Smiths and Ganders, was dwindling. A preacher can't preach the Word to the masses if there are no masses there to listen. Not to mention tithes to pay for heat and light and repairs and staff.

"It was in 1987, that the downtown Methodist congregation, with some vigorous prodding from the Bishop, voted to merge with the New Hamburg United Methodist Church. The old ark of a building was closed, to sit idle for two years. It was then that the growing Muslim community in Perryburg, seeking a central place to draw from all the dispersed neighborhoods where Muslims had found refuge, offered to buy the building.

"While this seemed a good thing for all concerned, at least on an intellectual level, on a gut level it was hard to see the cross removed from the steeple and a crescent placed there. It was hard to see the battleship grey of the exterior bloom into floral palette catching to the eye. It was hard to watch the new signboard 'Perryburg Islamic Center' cover the 'Central Methodist Church' carved in stone over the door.

"By the time I asked Medina to the join me at the Spring Festival at the Art Museum, we had become good friends. I had certainly mentioned her name at home enough, but I was always leaving out pieces of information. Mom and Dad knew she was from Bosnia, but they did not know she was Muslim. They did not know she wore a Hijab.

143

"It was at the Spring Festival, at the Art Museum, and Medina and I were strolling along the long outdoor gallery of juried paintings that I suddenly heard my name called out. Looking up, there, leaning on his cane, was Grandpa Abe holding Heidi's hand. The moment of truth had come.

"Medina and I walked over to them, and I introduced her to them. Somewhere from her depths of understanding me, with a thick Bosnia accent, she said, 'It is my pleasure to meet you, Sir and Madam.' I didn't have to look to know they had been won over.

"That night I knew the phones would be ringing. If Grandma or Grandpa had some information that no one else had, they would be eager to share it. About nine o'clock I heard Dad calling me, asking me to come down to the living room. Imagine my surprise when I found the room filled with my parents and all of my grandparents (at least I was spared my sister's presence!)

"My mother started what I thought was going to be an inquisition. 'Michael, Heidi and Abe were telling us about meeting you at the Art Show today, and you were not alone.'

"I hesitated to gather my thoughts. 'Ah,' was the best that came out.'

"'They said you were with Medina.'

"Again, 'Ah….'

"'That she seemed like a nice, polite young woman.'

"'Ahhh….'

"'Who is Muslim, yes?'

144

"I summoned all my strength, and my feelings for Medina, and replied, 'Yes, I was with Medina and she is a nice, polite young woman who is Muslim.'

"'Then why haven't we all met her? Are you ashamed of her?'

"And that is when I felt ashamed. I thought that they would not understand that I might have feelings for someone from another country, for someone who was Muslim, for someone whose community had moved in where their congregation had left. 'No, I am not ashamed of her, I think I am ashamed of myself, for assuming you would think it wrong.'

"'What?' Grandma Helen said, 'You know the story of this wonderful family, you know how we feel about welcoming all who hold love and truth and honesty in their hearts and show them in their actions.'

"Grandpa Abe jumped in, 'Look, if growing up in this strange family taught you nothing else it surely has taught you that we don't look for differences, we look for connections.'

"Then it was Grandma Helen's turn again, 'Now, look, see if that nice young lady will join us for dinner on Sunday night. And don't worry, I've already located a Halal butcher out in the east end and I know the supermarket has a Bosnian section now. We won't embarrass you.'

"By then, I was in tears. Thank goodness that was the moment when Gwen, my little sister, made her entrance, complete with tutu and tiara, thanking everyone for coming to see her latest dance creation. The laughter in the room confused Gwen, who left in a pout.

"I don't remember if it was Dad or Grandpa Leonard who suggested it, but soon we were in a great big group hug, hanging on for dear life to the people who always surprised me by how much love they had to give.

"Now, as for Medina and me, I will save that story for another day, only to say that we hope our children will find new ways to break down the old walls of assumptions so we can accept the ones they love into the greater neighborhood we have created over these many generations."

Yes, in Perryburg there are neighborhoods, there will always be neighborhoods. But the only closed ones now are the ones held in memory of days gone by when some measure of strict definition implied a measure of security and familiarity. Perryburg, through all of its changes, has grown beyond many of those limitations.

People in Perryburg, as elsewhere, have learned that neighbors of the heart, neighbors of one's values, neighbors of shared vision, create the real neighborhoods.

It was Helen and Heidi who had encouraged Abe and Leonard to find a place where their large, diverse family could be buried, where they could all be buried together.

In looking into the existing neighborhoods of memory, there was no such place for them all. The existing cemeteries in town still kept to the old patterns of the old neighborhoods: this one for Catholics, this one for Protestants, this one for Jews, this one for the Irish, this one for the Poles, and so forth.

Now, outside of town, up on one of the rolling hillsides above one of the creeks, there is a new neighborhood. It is a quiet place. Simple roads and tree-lined paths link the departed in the inclusive community of death. It is Perryburg Memorial Garden, created at the end of the last century by families who had embraced a wider future.

Up there, you will find bronze memorial plaques sunk into the ground so no one marker of remembrance rises above another, all equal in death.

Up there you will see plaques with the names of Abraham and Heidi, of Leonard and Helen.

There is a new plaque, too new to be weathered with the patina of age, with the name Geoffrey and a small image of a goose.

There is also another relatively new plaque of Ibrahim, son of Michael and Medina, who died much too young from the COVID pandemic.

You will also see plaques, some of the first to be installed, long before the Ganders and the Smiths were interred. The resting place of pioneers who embraced this welcoming vision of such a place.

Over there, next to each other, are the memorials to Bill and Gladys, and not too far away also one for Remo, all who looked beyond what had been to what might be.

You look out over the rolling hills of grass and trees, across the gentle valley with its gentle stream, and feel a peace "you did not make and cannot mar." This is a neighborhood that would welcome you, and anyone, and everyone.

8. MATTERS OF FAITH

The old sacred stone of the First Nations had been close to the confluence of the Oneida and the many creeks, about where Union Station stands today. Here the tribe and its many confederates would gather for ceremonies of thanks and entreaties. By custom and belief, the land where the stone was, and the distance a person could walk in an hour, was considered sacred. No one would even consider any acts of hostility in that space.

The origin of such a concept was simple. The origin myth of the people talked of the earth as a great turtle upon which all arises – plants, animals, waters, and people. Where that turtle's shell juts through, surprisingly, unexpectedly, is where the divine meets the ordinary. The stone was such a place, sitting as it did away from any mountain, hill, rocky outcropping, or any other stone. Surely this was a special place.

While at times there were hostilities between neighboring and more distant tribes, no would ever violate that sanctity.

The first act of hostility came with the arrival of Palatinate German immigrants in 1720, who decided, soon after the small settlement was established, that the town needed a Lutheran, a German Lutheran, Church. The simple frame structure with steeple was erected within sight of the sacred stone.

Old Tinsdale, out at his remote trading post, outside the understood circle of sacredness, simply shook his head and said, "Now they put their foot in it." At the time he was staring at a deposit his old cow had left in the back lot.

Yes, they had put their foot in it, indeed. The First Nations agreed that since White Man had broken the circle, they were no longer bound by it either. The new settlement was fair game, not just for periodic attacks but also for more devious means of subversion.

However, even with the occasional arrowhead stuck in the clapboard siding, the church stood and withstood the assault of the local tribes. It did not fare as well from other assaults.

With the second wave of immigration flowing from the east, English started to arrive. What both the natives and the German settlers did not understand was that the English didn't seem to like each other. Again, Tinsdale shook his head and said simply said, "Where there are two English, there is likely to be a war."

Those who professed the Church of England were not disposed to accept the Puritans who swept in from Massachusetts. The Puritans were not likely to abide the separatists from Plymouth Colony. They all despised the Baptists of Rhode Island. Sprinkle in a few free-thinkers and the English were just 99 years short of a hundred year's spat.

As the settlement grew, each of the traditions felt the need to worship in their own style, with their brethren. First in homes and then in larger quarters, the factions of faith established themselves. Each, in turn, somewhere along Mohawk Street, bought land and built a church. Within a few short years, steeples of every kind reach skyward toward the divine that the natives knew was resident below, in the earth itself.

More suspect were the few Jews who arrived. They found no welcome in any of the other places of worship. When enough had arrived and a Minyan was possible, they followed the same pattern: house worship, store-front worship, and then their own place of worship. Some in their community wanted it to be called a Temple, but the more strictly religious members said the only Temple would be in the rebuilt Temple in Jerusalem. Some in their community wanted it to be called a Congregation, but the more conservative

150

members argued this sounded too much like some of the Massachusetts folk. Someone suggested it be called a Shul, which was met with "So, now we are running a school?" A small minority objected to it being called anything of a religious nature, being secular Jews who thought it outside their faith and also bad for their businesses to look too Jewish. In the end it was called a Synagogue. It would be built just off Mohawk Street and look much like one of the churches.

The First Nations had long since moved on or were moved on to be more accurate. The great sacred stone was even dug up to make way for the first railway. Religious matters became established as each faith community claimed their space, their theology, and even their idolatry. One year there was a fight in town when two different churches painted their front doors red. Each said the other was trying to confuse people who might be told that the Episcopal Church was the one with the red door and then find themselves in the Baptist Church.

But none of those fights was even close to what happened when the first sizable Roman Catholic group of immigrants arrived, first to build the canal and then the railroad. Suddenly, out of nowhere, a Jesuit appeared and made himself available to the Catholic community. That he had been sent by the church to convert the heathens, as well as the Protestants, was not acknowledged until much later.

In this way, the gauntlet of holiness that was a portion of Mohawk Street became part of Perryburg's identity. Competing adherents would all be taking their carriages or walking along the same part of the street, politely acknowledging each other while, under their breath uttering "heathen!"

Why, you might ask, should matters of faith raise such fierce feelings? Were these churchgoers all theologians, some measure of it might be understood. But, based on the way they actually understood what was being preached each Sunday, it was clear they were not theologians.

Some of it was a matter of prejudice, usually a prejudice that had sailed over to the new land from the old world of religious wars, inquisitions, and more. Some of it was class warfare, as certain churches attracted certain classes in the new, allegedly "all men are created equal" democracy. Most was simply ignorance, with many suppositions made about what happened behind the open doors of foreign sanctuaries. More than one tradition either said or implied that setting foot in another place of worship was a form of sin.

But under all of that, the real reason for the antipathy between faiths was commercial. As much as religious institutions like to portray themselves as above the fray of everyday life, there is probably no more competitive business in the world than the fight for souls. The number of souls in the pews was directly related to how well-financed a congregation might be, and therefore how magnificent their edifice would be.

If there is such a thing as guilt by association, there is also status by association. If one were to be known as a member of say, the dark-stone, tall-steepled Episcopal Church, one would have more social capital than someone attending the clapboarded sided, un-steepled Baptist congregation. Like the three little pigs with their houses of spurious materials, the ephemeral business of religion was more often decided most certainly by the quality of the building materials more than the tenets of faith.

Reading the accounts of those congregations back in the day, one would often find mention of Reverend Whoever leaving his congregation (always "his" never "her") with details of how many new members they had attracted or what successful building program had been undertaken in his pastorate. (If they had been so successful, why were they leaving?")

Such written history was often supplemented by the folk wisdom of memory in which various members of the clergy were recalled more for what they had done for the church than what they had done for anyone's faith. "His leadership brought the largest pipe organ west of the Hudson to Perryburg," or "The expansion of the sanctuary to double the seating capacity was a hallmark of his ministry."

I hesitate to also mention the ones less fondly recalled, the various clergy who had failed to increase the standing of a congregation by their ministry. "He never really related to the people of Perryburg, more content to share from the Bible than in the issues of the community," or worse "His family never lived up to the image that members of the congregation had hoped for."

Religion was as big a business in Perryburg as any other. It was competitive. It was very worldly, not other-worldly. It was as much about power and influence as it was about anything else.

As Perryburg grew, one could sense the intense competition for new members, especially while the town remained in a linear, limited area. But, with the coming of new neighborhoods one could only imagine the competition growing even fiercer. However, the growth of Perryburg's neighborhoods was far from linear and was intentionally classist and then racist. The size of lots, the size of houses, and other factors were used to basically segregate people into enclaves of their ilk (or, if you prefer, into clusters of like-minds and like-stations-in-life).

The main line religions on the main street in town did not have to reach out to all the neighborhoods. Their only need was to first establish a mission, then a simple church, then a more elaborate edifice in one or two of the nascent neighborhoods. The simple rules were these: build where your kind would likely be living; don't worry about the other neighborhoods; and never, ever build something in the neighborhoods that would rival the main, "real," church in Downtown.

This patchwork of churches, defined much more by ethnicity than theology, helped create the modern Perryburg. And, as we will see, a different fabric of faith was woven into post-modern Perryburg.

The parochialism of religion in Perryburg was strong and persistent. Various attempts to cross the divides of faith were attempted, usually about every twenty years. Once the several Baptist churches tried to unite but there was enough difference between them to result in a shoving match. Later, the several Methodist congregations attempted to find common ground, operating as they did under a common book of discipline; common discipline did not apply to common appreciation of the meals served in the neighborhoods. While the arrival of the Catholic Bishop always brought all the parishes together, it was also always noted that he only ever said mass at the Downtown Cathedral. The wave of humanism that spread through several traditions in the early twentieth century was cause for a short-lived unity by others in the neo-orthodox response until they tried to out-orthodox each other.

The rise of the National Council of Christian Churches inspired an attempt at a local Council of Churches. At one of their earliest meetings, the Rev. Dietrich of the German Lutheran Church up on the westside, proposed that there needed to be a doctrinal test for membership or else he would not support the effort. Trying to keep the Lutherans in the flock, the Council amended the proposed bylaws to require any member congregation to "affirm the supremacy of Jesus Christ as the only Lord and Savior of Mankind." That meant the Jews were surely not welcomed, and the Universalist Unitarians neither. A few of the Congregationalists squirmed in their seats and acted with their feet by not attending future meetings while still remaining on the membership lists. Of course, it was tacitly understood that such a requirement would exclude the Roman and other Catholics because its wording was slightly divergent from dogma.

When the Vatican Council II met and announced an era of openness to ecumenicism, new battle lines were drawn: all Christians in, everyone else out.

At about the same time as this "radical" notion of ecumenical relationships was exciting various church leaders, local congregations were deeply struggling with a declining city, the growth of secularism, and too many aging properties. Fewer souls in seats, less money in the collection plates, more bills in the inbox, and seriously eroded influence in the matters of the city.

In the same era that saw first one, then both of the Downtown department stores close, soon afterwards by the closure of the several Five and Dimes, several of the houses of worship in town closed their doors.

The Orthodox Synagogue out on Joseph Street, which had faithfully served the mainly Ashkenazi Jews in that neighborhood for the previous century, merged with the House of David, a Conservative Congregation that was being led by an Orthodox rabbi. St. Margaret's Catholic Church and School closed, by direction of the Bishop, and the parish and school were absorbed into the larger but equally declining St. Patrick's. Plymouth Congregational toward Uptown sold its building to the local poverty agency and merged with First Congregational, only to have the new First Plymouth Congregational merge with the Second Congregational out in New Hamburg to become All Souls Congregational Church.

It was a time of cascading religious decline as measured by the congregations of Perryburg. One was startled to see "For Sale" signs up in front of several of the church buildings along Mohawk Street.

At the same time, from store fronts to reclaimed houses of worship to new structures, vital signs of religious fervor could be seen and heard. On many a street away from the more affluent parts of town, Sunday mornings and Wednesday evenings would be filled with jubilant singing, often accompanied by guitars, drums, and more. One these emergent congregations rented the old "Showcase" night club in Downtown, changing its neon sign to read "Show Love," and offered music as good as it had ever been offered as a club, only this time with a spiritual message.

These days, one is as likely to hear a Call to Prayer over the loudspeakers on a modern minaret of a new Muslim community center as any steeple bells. Elsewhere, subtle changes can be heard.

Statistically, there are about the same number of houses of worship in Perryburg now as there were a century ago. The difference is, with the exception of the New Beginnings Mega Church out on the Turnpike in Hurtzboro, these contemporary communities are smaller. Gone are the days of cathedrals, tabernacles, temples with hundreds if not thousands in worship each week. Religion has become both more personal and more exuberant.

At the same time, it has become no less competitive. Endemic to many faiths is the concept that there is a war on for souls, a struggle between good and evil. If you are not out trying to enlarge the number of people committed to your own version of the truth, you are failing that truth.

Such a spirit of competitive faith leaves little room for cooperation. Or at least cooperation between institutions.

But, like so much of Perryburg, the story of faith is really not about institutions. Any real summary of faith communities is only a reflection of the lives of people, individual lives connected to something larger than themselves, larger than their faith traditions, larger than their buildings.

History tries to say that the important things were the congregations and their buildings. People would tell us differently.

Down in the flats, down by the tracks, in the neighborhood most associated with people of color, there were three houses of worship. The largest was the AME Zion church, a handsome if modest building that had been erected by its founders. That was not to be confused with the AME church, an even more modest building that had once been two single-family houses, joined and converted over the years to house a sanctuary on the main floor, a social hall below, and an apartment for the preacher above. The front glass windows of a former shoe store proclaimed, in gold leaf letters:

LIVING WATERS BAPTIST CHURCH

All who profess faith in Baptism
WELCOME

You can do your own reading about the differences between the three faith communities, and you might discover some old lines of separation. All three, born out of the era of slavery in the south and racial separation in the north, sought to create a distinctly Black religious option. AME – African Methodist Episcopal – lays it all out there: this was a church for those with roots in Africa, which would be governed by a common set of principles and behaviors, with a governance structure that was Episcopal (hierarchical). It would operate like an Anglican congregation, followed the beliefs structures of the Methodists, and express the issues of African descent.

Then, what of the AME Zion churches. They were an offshoot of AME. The dividing line originally was the preparation for ministry. AME found its preachers, or they found the AME through their strong call to ministry and their familiarity with the Scriptures. However, some free Blacks from the Philadelphia area, wanting to find equality with the white faiths in their community, craved an educated clergy, with their ministers having been thoroughly trained. They needed to know not just Scripture but also Theology, not just great speaking but also Homiletics, not just the Commandments but also Christian Ethics. Congregations that moved to that more rigorous standard became known as AME Zion.

And the Baptists? They might share much of the theology of both types of AME, but they offered much more enthusiasm and much less hierarchy. No Bishops, no common book of expectations other than the Bible, and a fervent presence of the Spirit in every service. Some Black Baptist ministers were seminary-trained, other home grown. Unlike the two AME traditions in which ministers might be assigned to congregations, Baptist congregations made their own decisions about leadership.

If you have ever heard the Rev. Dr. Martin Luther King, Jr., speak, you would hear his seminary training, but you would also hear the Spirit alive in his words. You would also know that his ministry at his home church, Ebenezer Baptist Church in Atlanta, was a matter between him and that congregation. No outside power could ordain it or prevent it.

I tell you all this because you need to know it in order to understand what happened on a night in late October 1937. It was a Wednesday night, the Wednesday night before Halloween, and each of the congregations had held their mid-week Bible studies and services with a common concern: the idolatry of Halloween.

It was a calm, unseasonably warm evening. It was a last quarter moon, rising late, just on the horizon as the last of the congregants left their respective houses of worship.

Now, one thing my grandfather taught me was "the preacher may have the pulpit, but the person who really runs any church is the sexton."

That night, three different sextons, having checked their beloved properties thoroughly (remember this may have been long after the Civil War and far in the north, but it was not unheard of for Black churches in places like Perrybury to be vandalized or burned), turned the keys in the back doors securing their charges for the night. If one could hear steeple bells chiming on Mohawk Street, down here you would hear keys rattling.

Ezra Jenkins walked out from behind the AME building, took a look at the shrinking moon, and was about to walk home when he saw someone coming towards him. At once a bit frightened to be out alone when a stranger was approaching, his fear dwindled when moonlight passed where shadows had been.

"Why, Mr. Parker, it sure is good to see it is you on this night."

Stumpy Parker. Sexton at Living Waters. Given him nickname after an unfortunate accident as a child on the nearby train tracks. Missing a hand, he was not good for much work, but he was more than adequate for the Baptist Church.

"Ezra, likewise glad to see it is you and not some other no-good."

With a laugh, Ezra shot back, "other no-good? You mean like that rascal Rufus?"

Out of the shadows a voice rang out, "Who's calling me?"

"Rufus, git yourself over here right now."

In just a moment, the three sextons of the three churches, finished with their evening's duties, gathered under a streetlamp. They each pulled out a cigarette and Rufus lit them all from his lighter.

"So, boys, what did the preacher tell your crowd tonight?" asked Rufus.

"We got the word about the creeping devil found in Halloween."

159

"He preached to us about how all the costumes in the world couldn't hide the sinner from his God."

"And I heard about how the temptations of the world, like the candy handed out this coming weekend are like the coins tossed to us by the rich, white, folk." Rufus slowed down to pronounce those last three words very separately.

"Amen to that."

A hearty laugh engulfed the trio. Then an odd silence. Finally, Ezra spoke, "I've been thinking ..."

Before he could continue, Stumpy broke in, "Uh, Oh, here comes something we ain't never seen before, Ezra thinking."

"Stumpy, just be glad you ain't deaf because then if you tried to talk with your hands you would only make half sense. With your mouth, you make no sense."

"Let the man talk. We can cut each other up any time. I feel something important is coming."

"Thank you," Ezra replied, "just the thought that with our three congregations serving most all of the colored folk in Perryburg, we ought to have some power in this town. You know, there are already more than 1500 of us, which makes us as large as any of those big churches on Mohawk Street. Now, I'm not saying we see 1500 of us in church, but they sure ain't going anywhere else because nowhere else would welcome us."

"Amen,"

"Preach it, brother."

But when the people in power look at my church, and your church, and your church, they see 180 here and 150 there and 120 there. Ha, they say, don't need to pay them any mind."

"I hear where you are going."

"Together we add up to 450 people on a Sunday and we represent more than 1000 more. Come revival time, you know our tents are fuller than when the circus is in town."

"So?"

"So, this. What if we started a Negro Church League? A Negro Church League that could speak out on things that matter to us."

"Even act up."

"Yes, even act up!"

"I mean, picture a City Council meeting about to talk about some housing project and the League walks in. Not three little churches, but a whole bunch of us."

"Now, that is what I am talking about! We can't let a little religious talk keep us apart."

In the weeks that followed that late evening, moonlit meeting of sextons, more conversations occurred. By the beginning of 1938, the first meeting of the new Negro Church League had been called. With no one congregation big enough to hold the anticipated crowd, the old Opera House up on Mohawk Street had been rented. To keep a low profile in the community, it had been booked as an evening of entertainment and discussion peculiar to fellow people of color. That kept the whites away and made sure no one objected.

When the night arrived, with no billboard announcing it but with some fiery preaching from the three pulpits igniting the wildfire of whispers across the flats, the hall was filled with faces that ranged from pure black to lightly tanned, with accents from Bahamian to Creole. The listed capacity of the hall was 800 and if the Fire Marshall had dropped in that limit was evidently violated.

By the end of the evening, the Negro Church League, with equal representation from each of the congregations, had been formed, its mission articulated, and its first act of witness chosen. The Perryburg Theater was going to be challenged to remove its practice, if not real policy, of directing people of color to the balcony.

Local historians point to that night, Wednesday, January 12, 1938, as a turning point in Perryburg. It was the night that the first united front of people of color started to make demands about how life in Perryburg should be for all people. It was also the night that the barriers between individual churches and denominations had begun to fall.

Over the years, the Negro Church League morphed into the Black Church League and then into the Historic Black Congregations Association. It went from representing three congregations down on the flats to welcoming several other congregations spread out into other neighborhoods and congregations even less organized and more evangelical than the Baptists. The HBCA would, in time, sponsor college scholarships, health clinic, and more. When Dr. King was killed, they held a community-wide memorial service in the Civic Auditorium which now sits on what had been part of the flats. When George Floyd was killed, it was the HBCA that worked with the city and the police to keep the calm, and then later demanded accountability of the Perryburg Police Department for some of their actions.

The needs of people often dispossessed from the American Dream had found their champions on a deserted, moonlighted street when Ezra, Stumpy, and Rufus had had their own dream. Three sextons, three janitors in the Lord's House, saw clearer than any preacher had dared, something larger than denominations and congregations.

"Hello Verna, this is Gladys." That is how the phone call began.

With Verna one knew it would not be a short phone call. Gladys had waited until after dinner to call Verna, knowing it was better to call her at 8pm than at any time earlier than 2pm. You could even be safe calling her at 2am!

"Hello, Gladys, I'm glad you called, I have several things to talk about with you."

"Good, but let me tell you what I am calling about," Gladys got in before everything else that would take an hour or more to deal with.

"I was up much of the night, fretting about those poor Hungarian Refugees."

This was 1956, and the Hungarian struggle for freedom, the Hungarian Uprising, lasted just twelve days before being brutally put down by Soviet forces. In the wake of the uprising, hundreds of thousands of Hungarians had fled their country, an exodus of liberal, freedom-loving people which still ripples in the conduct of those who chose to stay under the thumb of totalitarianism.

"When I finally got to sleep, I had a dream. As refugees were arriving in Perryburg, down at Union Station, they were being met by a large group of local women who represented the many congregations in town. In my dream, there was not a minister, not a rabbi, not a priest in sight. In fact, no men at all. But there we all were, women, caring women, welcoming women, women who knew how to embrace frightened children, desperate mothers, shell-shocked men.

"This morning, I couldn't shake the dream, and I began to make a few phone calls to the women I know who are active in their churches and synagogues. So far, no one has turned me down.

"But I can't do this alone. You and I work so well together running the Sunday School, I am asking for your help."

Verna, uncharacteristically, paused a moment, and then responded, "This is the first hopeful and helpful thing I have heard since I knew those refugees were coming to Perryburg. I heard people say that they must be traitors to leave their homeland, that there may be Soviet agents among them, that they are not like us, and all that crap.

"Sure, sign me up. What do you want me to do?"

Over the next two hours, never getting to Verna's agenda at all, the two women brainstormed an Interfaith Women's Committee that would spearhead the efforts of welcoming, settling, including, and integrating these new Perryburgians.

Over the next week, by phone calls and visits, by letters and on-the-street conversations, a band of some thirty-four women had been recruited for various tasks. Housing, food, clothing, furniture, English-language lessons, school liaisons, and more each had their specific advocates.

When the refugees' train arrived in Perryburg, all seventy-seven of them, including thirty-three children, the welcoming party was more than a hundred, mostly women. Of course, the city officials had to be there, but Verna had been very skillful in making sure they had extremely limited speaking roles. She had also made sure the train would arrive late afternoon, when she would be awake.

Using her experience with Sunday Schools, Gladys had done three things.

She had contacted the relief agency in New York City that was sending the refugees to Perryburg and supplied each refugee household with the names and photos of the people who would be welcoming them at Union Station.

She made tags with photos and names of each of the arriving families, tags which the arriving welcoming committee members would wear so connection could be made.

And, she had a training session with the welcoming committee to not only explain the process but also teach the greeters some basic Hungarian. A language professor at the local college, herself from Hungary, eagerly accepted the request for this task.

The Interfaith Women's Committee had been actively preparing for this day. After Union Station, each household would be taken to their housing, appropriate to the size of their household. A warm meal would be waiting for them there. Beds with fresh linens would be ready. Food for several days would be in the kitchen and the refrigerator stocked. Pending registrations for classes for the children to start the next week were at the appropriate schools. So much had been done in such a short time.

The day arrived, the Committee and its supporters assembled, the headlight seen in the distance, the train screeched to a halt, and from the two rear coaches began a stream of people, some wide-eyed with wonder and excitement, some looking downward in fear. Children were either very quietly holding their parent's hand or anxiously giggling.

Up front, the long process of handling the mail and the baggage was underway, so the train had not yet left. Faces of the continuing passengers were pressed against the windows to see what was happening on the platform. Because the refugees had been in their own two cars on the rear of the train and had been boarded early at Grand Central Terminal, most of the other passengers had no idea what a momentous international event was unfolding in front of them.

The language professor called out to crowd in Hungarian, and a calm fell over everyone of the platform. She continued in their

165

native tongue, pointing to the tags on the welcoming committee members that held their names and images. Then she held up one of the information sheets they had been given to help identify their hosts. Chaos broke out on the platform as the two sides of the connections surged to meet each other.

Cries of "Isten hozott" and "üdvözlöm" filled the air, followed by handshakes, hugs, tears, and laughter. Slowly the mob dispersed into cars and taxis to go to the refugees' new homes. By the time the local train was ready to leave, the platform was empty but the hearts of most still on the train were full.

In time, most of those refugees would integrate into the life of Perryburg, adding to the cultural diversity, being skilled workers, excelling at school even in a new language. The all would become American citizens, one became President of the Common Council, another become the Valedictorian of Perryburg High School.

But something else happened. The Interfaith Women's Committee did not disband when this work was done. No. In working together, they had found a new unity which crossed so many lines which had previously divided them. Roman Catholics had worked with Jews, Lutherans had worked with Universalists, women from Black Churches had worked with every women from every white congregations. Gladys had even found a way for a few atheists and free-thinkers to be involved who worked alongside some evangelicals.

Verna and Gladys had not wanted these efforts to simply be fulfilled and then fade away. About three months after that day at Union Station, everyone involved in the Interfaith Women's Committee received an invitation to a celebratory dinner, which would be held in the social hall of Episcopal Cathedral in Downtown. Of course, an RSVP was requested. And there at the bottom of the invitation was this line: "If you know of any other women who might be interested in the kind of work we have done, invite them, please."

The thirty-four women who had been initially recruited had swollen to about sixty that day at the station. When the RSVPs were received, over one hundred women had answered the invitation. Something about the first experiences was contagious. Every faith barrier in the city had now become a path of connection, and women of faith were ready for it.

"You know, Gladys," Verna said about an hour into one of their evening phone calls, "I wanted to thank you for having that sleepless night and then that dream back when we first heard about those refugees."

"Thank you for hearing what I was saying. I have always felt that it should be our dreams, not our fears, which teach us."

Dreams. That reminds me of another story I heard out of Perryburg. My college roommate had become the Unitarian Universalist minister in Perryburg. The Unitarian Universalists are a far left-end-of-the-spectrum religious tradition that is welcoming and inclusive, and non-creedal. For all of those reasons, they often have not been welcomed nor included in communion with other churches in many communities. Perryburg had been no exception.

That friend (I'll call him Fred because if I mention his real name, you might know who I am talking about) was moving toward the end of his ministerial career, already 35 years in. He had served big congregations in big cities, mid-sized congregations in suburbs, and even a cluster of churches out east. He had grown up in a town like Perryburg, and it almost felt like coming home.

During his first week in Perryburg, while still unpacking, he received a letter inviting him to a meeting of clergy. That seemed like a good omen.

On the announced date, at the appointed hour, he entered into one of the congregations that had been down on the flats, now relocated to a westside neighborhood. Being the early-to-arrive sort that he is, Fred found a hall ready for a meeting, food ready on the side table, and no one else there. Having served in the ministry so long, he found even empty churches interesting, so he looked over the bulletin boards, leafed through the hymnal, and then sat himself down. In a few minutes others began to trickle in. Fred was glad to no longer be alone and quickly engaged others in conversation. They welcomed him as a newcomer to town.

It suddenly dawned on Fred that he was the only white person in the room. Had he been sent an invitation by mistake? Had he gone to the wrong place?

Then, to his relief, two other whites arrive, one a Rabbi and one a member of the Bahá'í community. Almost immediately, the pastor of the host congregation, the so-called Bishop Strange of the Sixth Baptist Church of Deliverance swept into the room and took charge. Opening prayer, getting lunch, introductions around the tables, and then,

"I want to tell you about why you are here. As you all know, Perryburg has been greatly divided in many ways. Last year, among us clergy, there were three distinct clergy groups. One was the Black clergy, one was the white clergy, and one was the white clergy that demanded scriptural adherence.

"About two weeks ago I had a dream. It was a simple dream. I dreamt that I sent out an invitation to every clergy person in town and to every religious institution I could find. I invited all the religious leaders in town to be here, today, at lunch. In my dream I heard a voice tell me that if I invite everyone, the right people will appear.

"Well, here you are, the right people. Give yourselves a big round of applause."

The room filled with applause. And the Interfaith Ministerial Alliance was born. Reaching across traditions, locations, styles, and other factors which had been divisive, the IMA quickly became a meaningful part of the religious life of Perryburg.

So, it would take several decades for the clergy in town to become as united and inclusive as their lay women were. The leaders came to know, especially in matters of faith made real, that they are often not as out in front as they think but running hard to catch up with dreams of their flocks.

Father Frank had a dream, too.

His was about music.

Serving in one of the Roman Catholic parishes in Perryburg, he was adept at conducting Mass. Sometimes maybe even a little too adept.

It was late one Sunday, as he was relaxing in the Rectory, that his assistant, who had been away mid-morning conducting Mass out at Wisteria Gardens, asked him about how things had gone at St. Patrick's 11am Mass. This was the most-attended Mass of the week except, of course, for the 4pm Saturday "Fisherman's Mass."

Frank thought for a moment and then realized he couldn't remember the 11am Mass as distinct from the 7:30am or the 9:30am one. Yes, he remembered that he had faithfully performed his function in the Mass at 11am, that he had said the right words in the right places, and done the right gestures at the right times, and read again the homily he had already read three times.

"It was OK," Father Frank replied, "and it was a good crowd. The choir sounded lovely." He decided not to add that once again, the choir master had chosen pieces that made the whole occasion feel like a funeral.

That night Father Frank had his own dream. In that dream, he was standing in the pulpit and the whole congregation was in front of him, but they were standing not sitting. He was not preaching; he was listening to them applauding and shouting "Amen."

In his dream, he remembered walking up the steps in the pulpit as the choir's anthem was finishing and it was not he, but the choir that had the people on their feet, cheering. A bit chagrined at this realization, the dreaming Father Frank turned around and saw the choir, in tie-dye robes standing around a four-piece band fronted by an electric guitar.

Father Frank woke up suddenly, both excited and frightened by what he had dreamt.

One of the hallmarks of faith traditions is that they represent what is considered enduring. Religions refer to time in millennia more than months, and patriarchs that lived long, long ago, not just a generation back. Continuity, not confrontation. That is why it is often hard for religious communities to deal with change.

As Father Frank was recovering the next morning over a good cup of coffee, he was thinking about this. What had happened to Luther when he advocated for change? What had happened to Dr. King when he preached change? What had happened to his own mentor, Monsignor Briscoe, when he had allowed a woman to read one of the lessons?

He found himself thinking about his own calling: "what had I felt inside me, what had I heard, that summoned me?"

He recalled having dreams about making the Scriptures alive for people. He recalled having dreams about preaching so forcefully that lives were changed. He recalled having dreams about being bedside in a time of crisis and having his words of comfort help entire families. He recalled having dreams about presenting the Catholic faith so positively in the larger community that his congregation would be considered a church for all the people of Perryburg.

He recalled that he never dreamt about keeping his head down so the Bishop wouldn't be upset. He recalled that he never dreamt about counting heads at Mass to see if his flock was declining. He recalled that he never dreamt of being so adept at saying Mass that he would forget how the experience had been and had felt to him personally and as Priest.

Out of his lips slipped, "Well, I'll be damned." And he felt damned.

Once upon a time, as a young Priest, he was not only aware of his dreams, he acted on them. Now, he realized, he was only going through the motions.

Fortuitously, or maybe in one of the strange ways in which God moves, he had recently accepted an invitation from the Rabbi at the Reform congregation to lunch. When he arrived at the restaurant, he had been shown into one of the small alcoves off the main dining room, one of those rooms that had a curtain across the doorway and the staff was well trained to receive a positive response to a knock on the door frame before entering. This was one of Perryburg's old-line Italian restaurants and those alcoves have held many a secret in the ethnic past.

In the alcove he found Rabbi Needleman, as well as Rev. David Mosher from First Presbyterian and Rev. Gwen Nusbaum of the Unitarian Universalist congregation. Ira Needleman was a late-to-the-Rabbinate leader, having been a community organizer previously. David Mosher had been a college sociology professor before getting tired of how humdrum the Presbyterianism of his youth had become, leading him to enter seminary. Gwen Nusbaum had a law degree, but the activism of the 60s led her to leadership in her free faith tradition. At first Father Frank wondered why he was invited, but then remembered he had once been an academic in a Catholic high school before he thought he heard a call to the Priesthood.

Ira welcomed him: "Frank, come on in. I think you know the others here."

"Yes, I do, from work with the Interfaith Ministerial Alliance. But, why this group?"

"Not to take away from the IMA," Ira replied, "but to go beyond it. I have noticed that IMA meetings have little room for personal sharing. We may be open about social action we want to share, but not as open about what is needling us from inside as religious leaders. If I am right, based on my observations of all of us here, each of us is wrestling with some important shit in our roles. Am I right?"

Father Frank was slightly taken aback hearing the "s" word in the company of clergy outside his own tradition. "I don't think you are wrong, but I wouldn't have chosen that word."

"Then, what word would you have chosen?"

"Hmmmm,… intransigence maybe," Father Frank offered. "But I think that is just part of being Catholic."

"Don't think you can claim that as your own," Gwen said.

"What?" Father Frank replied, "I thought your tradition was all about non-creedal stuff and not being bound to the past."

"You have not been to one of my board's meetings!"

172

With that start, a lively discussion began, interrupted only my discreet knocks of the server to take orders and deliver food.

Gwen expanded on her comments, sharing how nearly half of all new ideas she has tried to implement have been shot down: too costly, not the way we do things around here, we tried that once (twenty years ago), and more.

David jumped right in with his gripes about every move he makes gets some word down from the Presbytery that he is either moving too fast, moving outside his authority, moving contrary to doctrine, moving against the stated goals of his congregation, or just plain moving at all.

Ira was fast to share his recent frustrations with board members who, wanting to maintain the membership at Temple Beth Shalom, had started suggesting that getting a li more conservative would help provide a home for those Jews who had become disaffected at the Conservative congregation because their new Rabbi was Orthodox. All of a sudden he was being asked more about observing Kosher and Sabbath rules than about working on social justice issues.

Father Frank took all of this in. Finally, with a deep breath, he said, "I think this is the right group, and I am glad I am here." He then shared his recent revelation about how rote it all had become for him.

"The only real break from the tedium imposed by millennia of tradition and custom is my total frustration with the music in our services. It feels like we are holding Requiem Masses at every service. I want life! I want the Holy Spirit to be alive, not just words. I want to shake people up enough that they might be awake when we speak."

A round of "Amens" followed.

He then felt bold enough to share his recent dream, the one about the congregation on its feet, applauding an anthem that was backed up by lead and bass guitars.

He was speaking to caring and equally broken hearts. He thought he was alone on this, but he soon learned otherwise. Each of his colleagues admitted that they would love the same thing. Maybe not the same theology, but the same enthusiasm engendered by music that was alive.

It was then that an idea was hatched: The Perryburg Spirit Band and Choir.

A modern music ensemble, with a small choir that wanted to do dances more than dirges. Roles were assigned, under the strictest confidence. Father Frank was going to try to find a lead guitarist and a couple of singers; Gwen would work on the bass guitarist and some more singers; David was going to find someone for keyboard, and even more singers. Ira would get the drummer and some good singers too.

It took about a month for the group to be recruited, sworn to secrecy, and start rehearsing. But, before the first rhythm had been tapped out on the drumsticks, Ira addressed the group.

"Friends, you are part of a great experiment – to put life back into the most lively of all things, religion. This is going to be a test, to see if you can find the soul of the songs and not worry about the words. On some songs, you might say an 'Amen' to the words and on others you might say 'Wait a minute, I need to think about that.'"

"Don't do like all Unitarian Universalist do, read ahead to see if you can agree to ever word and nuance. Give yourself over to the music. Your understandings will come in some songs and not in others," Gwen added.

"You are not here to obey a catechism. You are here to catch whatever gives your spirit the shivers and makes you glad you got up this morning," was Father Frank's contribution.

"And please, please, look like you are having fun, because this is meant to be joyful work," David concluded.

With that the first song was attempted, and truth be told, it sounded awful. But then, they tried it again, and it was better. The third time something clicked. Patty, one of the singers from the Presbyterians said, "I get it, I think. We are trying to reach out of our own familiar zones, out of what we think worship is. Kind of scary, and kind of wonderful."

She got a round of applause for that.

Over the next two months, weekly rehearsals gave the group a repertoire of about eight songs, half "anthems" and half songs which invited congregational singing. At the eighth rehearsal, Sergio Ocasio, from St. Patrick's said, "I think we are ready. But ready for what?"

Father Frank looked at him with appreciative eyes, and said, "Ready for my dream." He felt comfortable enough now with all of them that he could share that dream, the one in which the music had been more uplifting to his congregation than his words or any traditional element of the Mass.

"So," Betty from UUs asked, "what does that mean?"

It was Ira who responded. "It means we are ready for the little experiment we have cooked up. Three weekends from now, on Saturday morning, we will all be over at the Temple where I am Rabbi, and we will bring the house down. Saturday afternoon, we hit the Fisherman's Mass at St. Patrick's. 9am Sunday we will be at First Presbyterian, and 11am at the Unitarian Universalists. Same music for all, and we will see what happens."

David added in, "And in each place, we four will be there, either leading or enjoying the service."

The result is legend in Perryburg.

The opening at the Temple started with scowling faces and at least one old-time member seeking out the President before the first notes were played. By the end of the morning, Jews who had only ever moved by davening during prayers were moving, clapping, singing along.

At St Patrick's, once the stunned silence after the first number faded and some of the younger members moved up front, things got even livelier.

The Presbyterians, true to their more somber reputation, took three songs, two of them participatory, before they got into the swing of it. But the usual 9am crowd at the service was surprised to find the church almost full of people they did not know.

By the time the group played the Unitarian Universalists, the movable wall at the back of the sanctuary had to be opened to allow the overflow crowd space to sit, stand, or even dance. As Gwen rose up to the pulpit, everyone was on their feet, clapping, shouting "Amen," and even "Hallelujah." With a lump in her throat, she looked over at Father Frank, whose eyes were brimming with tears. She knew, her colleagues knew, and in time the whole city came to know, that Father Frank's dream had fulfilled, not by him, but by everyone.

After all of this, you might wonder if there are still separate houses of worship in Perryburg. Of course there are. Different people have different needs and different understandings of how those needs will be met.

But every time events, circumstances, or forces push for more separation, every time one community of faith either tries to dominate or feels run down, every time the religions fail to notice the downtrodden and the strangers in their midst, someone will mention Ezra, or Rufus, or Stumpy; Gladys or Verna; Bishop Strange; Father Frank, Rabbi Ira, Pastor David, or Dr. Gwen.

And in some far-off sanctuary of dreams, where all faiths come together, is heard the closing phrase of a hymn, rocked out on a lead guitar with great bass and keyboard, supported by a strident drum and a final cymbal crash:

"what they dreamed be ours to do, hope their hopes, and seal them true."

9. SUBURBS

There were libertarians long before there were Libertarians, people who wanted to live outside the bonds of the social compact which is the foundation of a society and especially of communities.

There have always been those who came to this continent for reasons that propelled them to seek out such separation. Some were fleeing dire situations elsewhere, some were compelled to come here or face imprisonment, some were following greater dreams. Too many came here against their will, enslaved to a view of human life that denied humanity to some.

For those free people who had the choice, a notion of "rugged individualism" was rampant against the old-world notions of privilege, class, caste, and Calvinistic predestination. It would take Ralph Waldo Emerson to enshrine the sentiment in his essay "Self-Reliance," in which he wrote:

> Whoso would be a man, must be a nonconformist. He who would gather immortal palms must not be hindered by the name of goodness, but must explore it if it be goodness. Nothing is at last sacred but the integrity of your own mind. Absolve you to yourself, and you shall have the suffrage of the world.

(I would quickly add that such a concept was unknown to the native residents of this land, for whom all history, safety, lore, and promise rested on a communal sense of identity. Nothing one did could ever be understood outside of the context of the whole, and the whole did not truly exist without each and every person in it.)

Even before some of the European settlers had chosen the confluence of river and streams as the site for what would become Perryburg, there were those who, sensing the importance of that nexus of travel, chose to settle elsewhere. Like William Tinsdale, they carved out life away from others.

But, as history would show us, when settlement would slowly but surely move their way, these outliers would again resettle even more remotely. The usual accounts of the early days of the Great Canal would tell us that the packet boats were filled with immigrant families heading west. But, just as many if not more would be added mid-route, people who were finding the former wilderness insufficiently "wild" for them.

Other factors soon came into play in the development of what we, today, call "suburbs." Instead of being settled to avoid others, they were settled to be in contact with others. Especially to be settled with others who were the same.

While the origin of such new settlements might have been the drop in a stream that meant a source of power for milling, or the commercial imperative of goods and services less than an hour's ride away from many farmsteads, or some natural resource (forests, minerals, etc.), the real growth came from a cadre of people who felt they could be more "at home" there. In most cases, farms would be replaced with vegetable gardens, hundreds of acres with just an acre or even a fraction.

So, it was with New Hamburg. South of the slowly developing Perryburg, New Hamburg began as a simple settlement around a blacksmith and a lumber mill. The earliest settlers there being from Scotland and England, the first non-commercial or residential building erected was a Presbyterian Church. The third iteration of that congregation is still there.

The first church was lost to fire after less than a year, started from candles used to illuminate the sanctuary for a wintertime service. The regrettable lack of foresight in not creating a fire department added to the total loss. The second church, this time, built of stone, lasted for nearly 70 years until its steeple collapsed into the roof, the cause of the collapse being repeated displacement of stones by winter freezes of water not properly kept from the structure. The present church (you can still see it on the diminutive plot of green called "The Green," shared now with as many monuments as there have been wars) was built of brick with tuckpointing that is careful examined each year, the annual survey of which is in the congregation's bylaws!

Almost immediately after the establishment of that congregation, other Presbyterians looked southward and said (or at least thought), "that would be a good place for our family to live."

One of the earlier settlers, an Andrew Mackay, along with his wife Amelia, their daughters Amy and Anne, and their sons Andrew Jr., Arnold, and Archibald "Archie," move from in town to New Hamburg. In his journal, he wrote:

> I had undertaken the move with both excitement and hesitancy. That our new home would be called New Hamburg sounded too Teutonic for my liking, being the name chosen by the old blacksmith who had started the forge. He, a Hessian, had fled the military in his homeland to then serve under von Steuben in the War.
>
> That my household would be surrounded by God-fearing people of our own faith meant I knew I could deal honestly with the growing number of tradespeople. That we would be far away from the river meant we might be less prone to disease. That we would not be subject to decisions from alien factions meant we would not be subjects.

Mackay's sentiments were mirrored in many of the new residents in New Hamburg. Contrast his words with these of George Michelson:

> My family and I were so excited to be moving to New Hamburg. Out of our apartment into a real house. Away

from Perryburg with all that implies, into a town where we don't have to worry about crime, corruption, and mediocre schools. We can be with people more like us and not be ruled by "them."

Michelson was writing in the 1970s. in the midst of the great rush away from Perryburg into the suburbs.

Common to both accounts was a sense of escape from diversity into a world of familiarity. Reading dozens of accounts of relocations to New Hamburg, across two centuries, the most used phrases were: safety, people like us, God-fearing, good schools, and freedom.

In speaking of Perryburg in corresponding periods, the common phrases were: dirty, crowded, unsafe, poor schools, and corrupt.

Depending on whether one read the Perryburg or the New Hamburg newspaper, one was given contrasting sets of facts about, you guessed it, these same quality of life issues. Perryburg had more crime, but an almost identical rate of crime per thousand people. New Hamburg had schools of excellence, but Perryburg High School produced as many Merit Scholars AND also educated almost all of the tradespeople who would serve New Hamburg's households and businesses. Yes, the air quality in Perryburg was poorer than out in New Hamburg, but when one sought healthcare, the only hospitals were in Perryburg.

People in New Hamburg regularly argued for their superiority; leaders in Perryburg humored them.

But New Hamburg was not the only suburb of Perryburg. Out to the east was Hurtzboro, to the north, up on the hills, was Fronton, and to the west was Germantown. As New Hamburg grew, so did these other areas, these other suburbs. Hurtzboro, among these, was the first to really develop beyond their agrarian roots, but after World War II, Germantown and Fronton, because of their large tracts of GI Bill housing, soon caught up.

182

If we look at demographics of these suburbs in 1990, we can quickly see differences:

Community	Housing Avg Sq Ft	Size of Household	Education	Ethnicity
New Hamburg	2,800	4	College+	1*
Hurtzboro	2,100	5	some college	3*
Fronton	1,800	6	High School +	5*
Germantown	1,800	7	High School	5+*

* the number of ethnicities greater than 10%

source: 1990 Census

New Hamburg has consistently kept its homogeneous ethnicity, while Germantown is mixed with more than seven ethnicities at the 10% threshold. Household size may be misleading as more households in Germantown and Fronton show more than two generations in the same household; not all of the larger number children of the primary resident. Also, if education is modified to include training in trades, while New Hamburg would stand out with the largest percentage of post-secondary education, all the others would have similarly high education rates.

But, these statistics don't really tell the whole story; as often is the case, the whole story comes from real people living in these communities.

Svetlena's family had come from Hungary in the 1950s. Proud Hungarians, they had founded an ethnic neighborhood in Perryburg within two years of arrival. Svetlana had grown up in that setting, attending Perryburg High School but restricted from dating anyone not Hungarian. It was expected that after school each day she would help in the family's grocery store, so she had little time for clubs or sports. While her older brother was allowed to go to college, she was not encouraged to do the same. The local business school was her only option.

As a secretary at a local bank, she excelled in her work. She was popular but continued to be restrained in her social life by her family. She had been married to a fellow Hungarian when she was 22, a man found and promoted by her parents. That marriage would produce two children, Irene and Eric. That marriage would also produce much suffering because Svetlana's husband, Zoltan, carried many scars from his time in Hungary and the death of his father from the Communist regime. As many times as Svetlana had urged him to get help with his issues, he always refused, afraid of the social stigma for a man in his community.

At 30, Svetlana divorced Zoltan. That divorce drove a wedge into her extended family. To some, her actions were a betrayal of their heritage.

Irene and Eric would live with Svetlana, with Zoltan having only limited contact; his erratic and sometimes violent behavior was cited.

Svetlana, freed from Zoltan's fearful and controlling nature, began to widen her horizons. She progressed at the bank into a professional role. She joined a women's business group.

When Irene was old enough to begin high school, Svetlana was still living in the old house she and Zoltan had bought (with help from her family), still in the old neighborhood, one now shared with other refugee ethnicities. As Svetlana would write in her diary, "During each day I feel my world growing wider, but each night I come home to a world that feels smaller and smaller."

Each day she would interact with a variety of people, some of them men to whom she was attracted. However, she never acted on those feelings. "How could I bring a man, a non-Hungarian, into my tiny, old-world home, into my closed community?"

It was middle July in the summer before Irene would begin high school. Svetlana sat Irene and Eric down on the burgundy overstuffed sofa with its lacy arm covers for a talk.

"Mom, this better not be about sex," Irene quickly said.

Eric just looked really uncomfortable.

"No, dear," Svetlana began, "this is not about sex. This is about us. This is about making some changes."

"What kind of changes?" Eric jumped in.

"I am thinking of us moving."

Silence.

"I am thinking about you two, the schools you attend, the small world you live in here with me. Maybe we would be better where there are different people, where we don't look so much like a holdover from Europe. I want you both to get a better education than I got. I want you to have more choices than I had."

Silence.

Well, say something!"

Irene slowly opened her mouth, and word by word said, "You … are … not … talking … about … New Hamburg, I hope."

Eric quickly added, "what she said."

"No, no way New Hamburg. But I wonder why you say that."

Eric began, "because they all think they are better than we are. I would have to be in clubs and teams with them and they all have everything they want."

"I have never met anyone from New Hamburg that was like me," Irene said. "They don't dress like I do, they don't speak like I do, …," and her thoughts trailed off.

"Please, Mom," Eric implored, "we would be better off staying here."

"Not to worry. I was thinking of Fronton. We could get our own house there, nothing big, but our own. You would be going to their schools, which I hear are great."

"YES," was the unison shout.

Fronton welcomed them with open arms. The house they found was one Svetlana could easily afford. Irene and Eric quickly made new friends and dissolved into the world of school connections.

Sure, there were days that Svetlana missed the ease of the commute within Perryburg, and she also missed the deep resources of the Perryburg Public Library. Not everything was better in Fronton, but it was enough better to justify the move.

The first time she invited the extended family to Thanksgiving in her new home, she worried for weeks if any of them would show up. By that Thursday evening, she had fed nearly 30 people, and watched as old bonds were renewed. They complimented her on the various heritage items she had included in her new décor. They enjoyed hearing more about what Irene and Eric were doing.

The scab of her divorce seemed to be healed by the new life she created. Where once she had sealed herself away to avoid more hurt, now she was open to the future. She even heard that Zoltan, who had since moved to Cleveland, thought she had made the right choice for their kids.

The Silvestri family had grown in Perryburg across several generations. When Arturo Silvestri arrived from Torino, already a skilled signal worker for the Italian State Railways (FS), he was immediately hired, first on one of the minor railroads and then on the main line. Settling in the Italian section of Perryburg, he bought two lots. One for the house, the other for the garden.

His garden became famous. Melanzana, pomodoro, lattuga romana, zucchini, uva, and flowers for every season.

Generations grew up there. By the time Arturo retired, tending his garden full time, at least five descendants lived in the neighborhood and an equal number had left Perryburg for other cities. But, no one had ever moved to a suburb. Why?

"We are no-a wanted there," Arturo would say. He would quickly add, "And we no-a want to be there." There was a real sense of place and pride of continuity in the family.

His great grandson Anthony, an immigration lawyer in Perryburg, had married Teresa Lombardi, the great beauty of his high school class. They did not marry right out of high school. Teresa had said she would wait for him to finish college while she was doing the same. Anthony (never call him "Tony") was not too sure about this; he knew how attractive Teresa was.

Four years after high school graduation they married. She continued to work on her master's in education while he went to law school. The whole family made sure they could focus on their studies. They were given part of the big house as their apartment. Evening meals were always communal. Periodically, checks would arrive for both small and big amounts. Arturo's garden continued long after he had passed on, and some produce of the garden would come their way.

The day that Anthony and Teresa both graduated was probably the biggest celebration the street had known. It was a celebration of the two of them but also a celebration of the Silvestri heritage.

While Teresa began to make a name for herself in the Perryburg public school system, Anthony joined a law firm of two other descendants of Italy, Nopardo and Rossi. With the two original partners covering most of the local legal issues, Anthony noticed the growing immigration into Perryburg. Now more likely to be refugees than immigrants, the displaced people needed legal help. He thought of how someone had helped Arturo back when, and felt he owed others the same.

With each wave of new immigrants coming to Perryburg, he became their advocate. He steered them through the maze of technicalities, requirements, forms, hearings, appeals, and more.

At the time that their children were about halfway through elementary school, Teresa snuggled up to Anthony one winter's night and whispered in his ear, "We've got to talk."

Anthony immediately had a worried look on his face.

"No, dear, nothing bad," Teresa quickly added. "I've been offered the Superintendent's job for the Germantown schools."

Anthony shot up on bed, hugged Teresa with one of his bear hugs, and was full of excitement. "Wow, that is so great. You really deserve this. Wow, YES!"

"Anthony," Teresa interrupted his outburst, "but it would mean we would need to relocate to Germantown. The district is insistent the Superintendent live in the district."

Anthony stopped for a second, and then blurted out, "So, we'll move."

"But, ... the family?"

"Oh, I hadn't thought about that."

"Well, think about it. We can talk in the morning."

"You think I can sleep when I should be thinking about this?"

"Try."

The first thing he said in the morning was, "I've been thinking."

"O, dear."

"At least half of the people I have helped over the years now live in Germantown. The kids know many of them from events we have been to together. We wouldn't be strangers out there."

"I like your thinking. But, what about the families?"

"Let's see what they say."

In the weeks after that morning, and before the public announcement of Teresa's appointment was made, Anthony and Teresa had several family dinner parties. It was always good to get together with them all. With most of them living in Perryburg, and the few living at greater distance, willing to travel, they could talk with almost all of the family. They started with Teresa's side first, and then Anthony's. Knowing the news would spread in each family very quickly, they were careful not to mix the families.

Teresa's was shocked when old Mrs. Cosentino stopped her in the sausage store and said, "So, I hear you are leaving the old neighborhood." How had she heard that? News travels quickly and not linearly in Perryburg.

When all the dinners were done, there was a consensus: "Good for you!"

Several of the relatives pointed out that probably a few of the younger generations had totally left the Perryburg area because they thought they could not just move out to the suburbs. "They worried people would think them stuck-up if they left the neighborhood. Better Buffalo than Germantown? At least you'll be close by."

The transition, which had left Teresa and Anthony a bit anxious, went better than anticipated. The kids immediately saw other kids they knew. Family members helped them all move in. The first time in IGA in Germantown took most of the morning for Anthony and Teresa as people stopped them in the aisle to talk.

"You know, Anthony," Teresa said later that fall, "there have been some changes we didn't expect. I never realized how easy life in the old neighborhood was"

"Yes, those smaller lots were much easier to keep mowed. And I miss walking around the neighborhood. But, I love having a backyard big enough to have really big parties. And I love how happy you are in your new job."

"I am happy. I love how diverse this community is. I love how nobody in Germantown puts on airs. I love how well the kids have adjusted."

"You know, I think we might just stay here forever."

"Until our kids decide they don't need to stay in one place forever. Let's hope they are more open to change than we have been."

"And we need to remind them that their families will understand."

Being a minority is always a challenge. Being a visible minority even more so. Viola and Abraham Brown knew this, like many of their African American neighbors living down by the tracks in the projects in Perryburg. Stepping out from their neighborhood routinely meant being subjected to stares and the further they went from home, the more attention their presence drew.

Viola was the descendant of the Great Migration, that exodus from the deep south that followed the emancipation of formerly enslaved people seeking a non-agrarian future. Her great

190

grandfather had heard of opportunities in the north unheard of in the cotton fields of Georgia. Through grit and determination, Harold (or "Hey Boy" as he was known at Kitteridge) made his way steadily toward the Mason-Dixon line over the course of several years. Once in Pennsylvania, working a number of menial day-laborer jobs, he saved his money to go even further north.

Checking the train fares, he found that the main lines offered trains to Cleveland, Detroit, Chicago, and more, but the secondary railways offered much lower fares to other cities. In the end, his choice of route and destination was thoroughly economic – what was in his pocket.

Slowly, the mixed train inched its way north through towns now forgotten. No amenities were offered on board, and he was glad for the few food items he had brought from home. He was also glad to be north of Jim Crow cars.

When the Conductor finally pulled his seat check and announced, "Perryburg, next and final stop," he was one of only three people who had made the full journey. Alighting at the humble station of the minor railway that predated Perryburg's Union Station, he looked at the scrub side of a city trying to decide what it was going to become.

Within a day, Harold had found a janitorial job at one of the foundries to which he could easily walk from the boarding house for "People of Color." In short order, he made a name for himself, not just because he was so thorough in his cleaning without need of any supervision, but also as a man who knew how the machinery worked (or why it didn't work). Quickly he was elevated from his custodial role to a mechanic's role.

Harold's son, Roosevelt, inherited that gift of mechanical understanding, as did Roosevelt's son, George. When Viola was born, her family was one of the families of color in Perryburg with both a secure position and a superior income. Between George and Hazel, Viola's mother, a nurse, they could afford much more than they were spending.

However, truth be told, they were paying more per square foot in the ghettoized area of housing they called home than most were paying in the upscale parts of town.

Viola did not follow in her beloved mother's footsteps but instead inherited the mechanical understanding. As a black, as a woman, there was little opportunity to gainfully apply that gift. However, when the Community Technical College opened, she applied for a position on its faculty. Even without a formal degree, she exceeded the tested capabilities of other applicants. She couldn't be a professor because of her lack of degree so they made her an inaugural tenured lecturer in mechanical engineering. No one else would ever be offered such a position.

It was in that position that she met Abraham, Abraham Lincoln Brown. Abraham had grown up in Ohio with roots in Underground Railroad passengers who had fled the south during the time of enslavement. When Abraham was a teenager, he fell in with "the wrong crowd," and that earned him a juvenile record, one that would be expunged on his 18th birthday provided there were no more offenses.

On his 18th birthday, with that record cleared, he enlisted in the Air Force. The Air Force quickly recognized Abraham's intuitive skill at machinery, particularly jet engines. They trained him in all aspects of aircraft maintenance. He rose up the ranks as much as any enlisted man could.

When his original enlistment was over, he re-upped for another four years. By the time that commitment was over, Abraham had had enough of things military. He kept finding his mind racing beyond the bounds limiting him in his position.

His last posting was to the SAC base out beyond Perryburg. He had no desire to go back to Ohio, none of the other postings had been in places he wanted to call home, so he simply called a taxi and had it take him into Perryburg.

The local airline, based in Perryburg, Algonquin Airways, was delighted to hire Abraham. They rarely had the option of someone so skilled in both heritage and cutting-edge aircraft. Their fleet ranged from World War II era planes to the first regional jets.

Abraham was delighted with both the job and Perryburg, both big enough to engage him but neither big enough to overwhelm him.

It was at an NAACP dance that Viola spied Abraham sitting uncomfortably on the sidelines. She gathered her nerve and went up to him. "Want to dance?"

"Not much of a dancer," he lied, because, while he was a great dancer he would have much preferred to sit and talk with this beautiful stranger.

"OK," she said, "I'm Viola, and I want to get to know you better."

That began a series of conversations, at the dance, over coffee, after movies, over dinners out, and the like. They quickly recognized how similar they were in a love for the mechanical, their lack of degrees, and their dreams for the future.

Within six months, they were married and moved into one of the apartments in "the projects." Over the next six years, they grew in many ways. Both of their jobs expanded along with the income they produced, their family expanded by three children, and the apartment they rented grew by two additional bedrooms.

"You know," Viola said one night after the kids were tucked into bed, "this place is feeling too small for me."

"Know what you mean," Abraham responded.

With that simple meeting of their minds, their combined energies were focused on finding a larger, better place to live. With a very steady and sizable income, they knew they qualified for a mortgage on practically any house in the Greater Perryburg market. What they didn't know was that the banks had their own maps, maps annotated with red lines, areas being kept for only "the right people."

Their first attempt to buy a new home, in the Ridgecrest section of Perryburg, was rejected by several banks as "not of sufficient valuation to justify the requested mortgage." When they doubled the down-payment, the same response was sent.

Their attempt to buy a home in New Hamburg followed the same script.

Viola, more than a little angry about that response, researched the properties after those rejections and found that both the houses had eventually sold for what they had offered, with mortgages at the level and rate they had sought.

The next time, they sought out a real estate agent who was recommended by the NAACP, someone who could help them look for houses and financing more discreetly.

After several evening house tours, avoiding group showings, they fell in love with a home in Hurtzboro. A Dutch colonial with 5 bedrooms, 3½ baths, two car garage, and full basement, on a half-acre lot. Mature trees shaded both front and back yards. The kids would get bussed to their schools. Along the truck route were several strip malls with all manner of shopping.

One of the first things Viola and Abraham noticed was how quiet it was. It seemed like an immediate blessing not to have to hear neighbors, passing trains, industrial sounds, and even road noise.

After they closed on the house and moved in, they invited all their friends to a great backyard party. They also included their new neighbors. Abraham beamed by his new brick BBQ grill, looking at the umbrellaed tables of food and beverages. Viola, looking out through the picture window over the kitchen sink saw a picture-perfect representation of her dream life with the shady trees and the gardens of roses ready to welcome guests. Their kids had set up a series of lawn games in anticipation of meeting new children of their age.

First to show up were Abraham's co-workers from the airline, but almost immediately some of Viola's faculty members were arriving as well. Many of them brought their children with them and soon the backyard was a lively scene of eating, drinking, socializing, and playing games.

It was only as they were cleaning up later in the evening from what had seemed a very successful home-warming party that the family took stock of what had happened.

"Wow, the whole gang from the maintenance hanger and even some of the pilots were here, and they love this house."

"I know, and all my friends from the college said the same thing. I think a few of them were a little jealous of us out here in Hurtzboro."

It was the kids who brought them back to reality.

"Not a single one of my friends from back home came today."

"And I only met two kids from this neighborhood."

"But you were all playing with lots of kids," Viola challenged them.

"Yeah, kids of people you are friends with."

"I mean, they are the same ones we see at the company parties out at the airport or the ones we see at the college barbecues, but no one we ever played with every day, or every will in this new place."

Viola looked at Abraham and he looked back at her. "We need to talk."

After the kids were in bed that night, Vi and Abe did a little stocktaking. Who had actually come to their party?

From the old neighborhood, two single friends and one childless couple. From the new neighborhood, two households came, each with one child in tow. Of their co-workers, not one of them lived anywhere near them.

"Ouch."

"Yes," Abe responded, "ouch indeed. Maybe not all the red lines are on the banks' maps."

"What really hurts is that so few of our friends from most of our married life showed up. No one from the church, no one from the PTA."

This realization really struck home the next morning when the family, dressed in their Sunday best, all packed into the family car and drove to the United Methodist Church on Hurtzboro's downtown square. It was the anchor of the community not only religiously but also socially. Viola had assumed that since they had been African Methodist Episcopal in Perryburg, this new church would feel somewhat familiar. After parking on the square, the Brown family walked along one of the diagonals that led to the stairs up to the sanctuary.

As Abraham opened the old, heavy doors and ushered his family inside, he was immediately aware of how this church didn't sound like what he was familiar with. Very quiet inside. In the entry, a surprised usher greeted them, gave them bulletins (what do we need bulletins for – don't these people know their worship?), and ushered them to one of the pews towards the back of the sanctuary. The sanctuary was very white, not only in terms of its walls and furniture but also in terms of its occupants.

A soft organ prelude gathered the flock, but without much enthusiasm. The Browns awaited the lively Praise and Worship they expected would follow, stirring the whole congregation to song. Instead, they got a barely audible Call to Worship by a "Worship Associate." Looking at her, in her jeans and cotton top, they suddenly became aware of how over-dressed the Brown family was.

After a painful hour, including an awkward "passing of the peace," the service limped to a conclusion as lacking in energy as the beginning had been. And there was no indication that anyone had been saved that day. In fact, as Abraham whispered to Viola, "not sure some of these people are even alive."

The following weeks did not improve their outlook on Hurtzboro. School started and their kids were welcomed into their classes with what seemed like too much attention. Their eldest, Nygria, (named after their mother's roots in long ago in Nigeria) expressed what the others nodded to, "I just wanted to slip in, like any other kid, but that didn't happen."

Even trying their best to connect with others in the neighborhood, except for those two initial families that responded to the party's invitation they met no one beyond a passing greeting.

Even after repeated invitations to friends from the old neighborhood, now invited in clusters of two or three instead of large groups, only two families came out and then didn't stay that long. Gone were the easy interactions that would extend from the night into the early hours of the next day, while all manner of issues and relationships would be discussed.

When Veteran's Day rolled around, and Abraham saw mention of the town's annual commemoration of Veterans. There it was: "The committee has sent invitations to all veterans in town to be present, in uniform as possible, for the wreath laying." He had not received an invitation. and he never would.

By Christmas, which was the most sterile, empty-feeling Christmas any in the household could remember, Viola and Abraham had reached a decision. When they shared it with their children, the children had already arrived at the same place.

The house went on the market on the first day of spring, was quickly sold at a very handsome profit, and the Browns moved back to Perryburg. They were able to find a single-family house not far from "the projects," this time a four bedroom, two bath house on a quarter acre, with only one tree in the back yard and only bushes in the front yard.

The first night they stayed in that new house they heard the trains blowing for the crossing, they heard neighbors in animated discussions. Outside in their yard the next day, they were greeted with "Hello," "How ya doin'?" "Good to see you. Where you been?"

The simple open house they planned became a full house that commandeered both yards and spilled into the street. The first Sunday back at the Clothier AME Temple was like a homecoming, filled with energy and spirit.

That night, as they were drifting toward sleep in their new bedroom, Vi and Abe spoke to each other.

"You know, this was a wonderful weekend. I felt more at home than I have for a year."

"I gotcha – I found myself using some jargon I had kept hidden for a year, and it felt good."

"I know, I saw you jawing with several of those men, talking about nothing special but being friends in doing it."

"And you – I saw how you loved welcoming and feeding everyone. How did you cook all that food?"

"I didn't – most of it came with our guests. Here, in this neighborhood, in Perryburg, people want to connect and fit in, not stand out."

"What we have here is community."

"OUR community!"

And into a very contented sleep the whole household spent the night and many years thereafter.

At about the same time, uptown in Perryburg, Conrad Stinson, was thinking about having a similar talk with his family. Conrad, after graduating from the state college at Freeburg with a degree in business, had risen quickly in the Interstate Insurance Company. He had married Debbie, and now their family included their three kids, Carol, Robert, and Susan. Before the first child had arrived, he had been assigned to Scranton. Between Carol and Robert, he had been in the office at Pittsfield. Between Robert and Susan, he had become the assistant manager of the office in Erie. Soon after Susan was born he was appointed Manager of the Perryburg office.

In many ways, the move to Perryburg felt like a giant leap forward. He had a degree of authority, he would represent the company to the community, they could easily afford a decent house in a decent neighborhood.

But, in the five years since arriving in Perryburg, Conrad had begun to realize that Perryburg was a dead-end unless one could rise into the corporate ranks with an office out at the headquarters, about half an hour south in West Huntington. But he knew that no one who lived in Perryburg had ever made corporate. Why?

Much of the life of the corporate world centered on the great Onondaga Country Club, out on the Mohawk Turnpike, smack dab in the middle of New Hamburg. And everyone in Perryburg knew that with a Perryburg address they would never get accepted by the membership committee.

Conrad told Debbie that he had something serious to talk about. Debbie looked worried.

"It's not another woman, is it?"

"Relax, Debbie, you're the only woman for me. What I want to talk about is moving."

"Why? Where?"

"Unless you think what we have now is good enough, and you want me to settle for being a branch manager all my life, we need to go where I can interact with folks from corporate."

"And that would be?"

"New Hamburg."

"Connie, we can't afford that. It's too pricey out there, and we would need two cars because everything is miles away and there are no sidewalks. The kids there all go on ski vacations and go to Europe in the summer."

"Don't you want our kids to have ski vacations, to go to Europe, to have a better education? Don't you want them to associate with a better class of people than they do now?"

"My god, Conrad Stinson, you are sounding like a snob."

"Just sounding like someone who is thinking about the future of his family. If you are standing still in business, you are moving backwards. Let's move ahead."

"Don't give me that sales pitch talk! We are talking about our family, not some insurance prospect."

The discussion went on for weeks, and in the end Debbie softened. She began to realize that there were only three options for their future: Conrad could stay where he was and slowly become frustrated; they could move, giving Conrad contacts that would lead to a position in the corporate offices; Conrad could leave Interstate and find a position elsewhere, which would mean leaving the area and tearing up all the roots they had already planted.

Once Debbie was on board, they started house-hunting. The kids were both excited (it would mean more room for them) and disappointed (they would be losing friends). As a family they tried to approach it as an adventure.

By the following summer, after much anxiety about the cost of a new house, moving, and all, they moved into their new home at 44 Pleasant Valley Drive in New Hamburg. It was a great five bedroom, four bath house on a full acre. Yes, it came with a taxes much higher than in Perryburg, the mortgage was a multiple of what they had been paying, the old house didn't sell for as much as they hoped, but now they were New Hamburgers. The family was easily accepted into the Onondaga Country Club and the kids quickly made new friends over the summer.

By the end of the year, Connie had been invited to a vice-presidency at the corporate level, a position more rewarded with title and status than with money. Nonetheless, he felt he had arrived.

However, the next few years were hard for the family. Stretching to move to New Hamburg, finances were tight. The kids had to forego some of the luxuries others in town took for granted. Debbie felt more and more isolated, serving more as a taxi driver than anything else.

In talking with them about three years after the move, Conrad admitted, "It hasn't all worked out as we had imagined."

"Tell me more, please."

"Well, I found out that lower level corporate work is often about disappointing people. I also found out I really don't like golf, or tennis. I get to see many of my co-workers from the office at the Club, but that means I can't really get away from work."

Debbie then said, "And this is not the life I imagined it would be. I always thought the suburbs were more social, safer, and all that. I can tell you, there are more cliques here than ever in Perryburg. There your connections were based on what you did, in the community, for others. Here it matters who you are, how much money you have, and all that. And as for safer, there are more drugs in New Hamburg High School than there were in Perryburg High."

"You sound angry."

"I am, in a way. I feel like we were sold a bill of goods with lots of small print at the bottom. You are expected to always act like this town is a gift of God. You were expected to attend the old Presbyterian Church no matter what your beliefs are. You are expected to have extra money all the time for things like dance costumes, school trips, science projects."

Conrad then joined in, "The only saving grace that I have found, when I am away from the Club, is maybe hanging out with a few of the guys here in New Hamburg, down at one of our old bars on the edge of Perryburg. There most of us are not that different. We are all, except for the big dogs, struggling to be here, worried about money, trying to live in this isolating world."

Then it was Debbie's turn, "I see so much unhappiness, and I see it dealt with in so many different ways. I see rampant alcoholism, sexual affairs, depression, impressive spending of what people don't have. I will give you an example. My friend Mary, another ex-Perryburger, was excited to get a new car, a nice little Toyota Corolla. Before she even took delivery, she was told that her new car was not good enough. In the end, with social pressure, she went for a much more expensive brand, and every month, when it is not in the repair shop, she is sweating the payment."

"Sure," Conrad continued, "we've made a few friends here, but more we have made connections. Our kids will probably get a good education and then go to better schools. But, more than once Debbie and I have remembered fondly the old days when we could walk down our street and get engaged in conversations with nearly every neighbor in Perryburg.

There are some other statistics about the suburbs of Perryburg.

Almost no one ever moves from one of the suburbs to another; very few, until recently, ever move back to Perryburg.

The only ways out of one of the suburbs are moving away, moving into one of the retirement communities, or dying.

Once a family has moved to a suburb, the extended family and the descendants will continue to call that suburb home.

The governance of each suburb is now as complex, demanding, and limiting as in the city, and all together they are more dependent on the State than ever before. The libertarian dream from back when is long buried in the search for social status.

There is also intense rivalry between the four major suburbs, with much of it played out on the high school athletic fields. New Hamburg versus Hurtzboro will always be a sellout game. Fronton versus Germantown, likewise. The winners from those contests will compete for the County title. And the County winner will take on Perryburg.

If the suburban team beats Perryburg, the cry is always "See!." If Perryburg wins, "It was stolen." The social hierarchy requires that the suburbs are always seen as being at the top, but the top of what?

When the Mayor of Perryburg was interviewed recently, she was quick to point out a reality that was as contemporary as it was historical.

"Back when those towns split off, they claimed they went their separate ways. But you don't see a Union Station in any of them. You don't see the big regional hospital in any of them. You don't see a profusion of great, often ethnic, restaurants in any of them. The Art Museum, the great theater, and so much more are all located in the city. Economically, as Perryburg goes, so go the suburbs.

"Every time I hear about how much better one of the suburbs is than Perryburg, I am reminded of the old Greek tale called 'The Complaint Against the Stomach'. In it, the various parts of the body complain about the stomach. The feet say the stomach is lazy. The hands agree, pointing out all they do. The mouth, teeth, and tongue argue their essential role in the life of the body. Together they decide to go on strike, and not feed the stomach. No planting, no gathering, no cooking, no chewing, no swallowing. In the end, they all become weak. But when fed, the stomach shares its energy with all the rest. Those old Greeks were smart!

"By the way, there's a great Greek restaurant down on Union Street, the only one in the area, and I see lots of cars there every night with stickers from Germantown, Hurtzboro, Fronton, and even New Hamburg. Guess their stomachs know a good thing."

10. LOG CABIN MOTEL

When the junction of river and First Nation trails was only that, before any inkling of Perryburg existed, about 3 miles away there stood a simple log cabin. It was home to William Tinsdale.

Tinsdale had come from Dorset, England under circumstances rarely mentioned. His family had been mining tin in Wales for generations and since they lived down in a hollow not far from the mines, hence their name. They were a short lot, helpful in their calling. William stood just 5 foot, 1 inch tall.

Early in his life, as he watched his grandfather and father drag themselves home after dark, only to drag themselves to the mine before sunrise, he vowed such would not be his lot in life.

By the time he was thirteen, old enough to be apprenticed, indentured, or even gainfully employed, William had simply left family and home and town and Wales, striding off on his own for somewhere better, or at least somewhere other.

Sleeping rough most nights until wintry weather forced him to seek shelter, traveling without the aid of a map and frightened to ask much of those along the way, he scavenged food between the rare times when someone would shout "Boy, want to earn a farthing or so?" His slight size and youthful appearance made him an easy mark for those who wanted to exploit a laborer. His hunger made him an easy mark for agreeing to such bargains. However, more than one who had sought to exploit him paid him more than bargained for when they realized his height and youth belied a strong character and a tireless spirit.

The following spring, which would have been early May, 1653, he had reached Devonshire, a much more pleasant land than he had ever seen before. Yes, the land was as scarred by mining and its ilk as was Wales, but between the works the world was beautiful.

Coming down toward Ashburton, William saw what appeared to be an abandoned farmstead, actually no more than a unkempt hovel, a teetering barn, and a weedy field. Inquiries around, painfully undertaken, gave little information other than that the prior residents had left just before the interregnum. No one seemed to lay claim to it now. So, William laid claim.

Full of industry under the sun instead of inside the earth, William righted buildings and weeded fields. Chickens who considered him a usurper soon provided eats and even meat. He was getting by with a roof (albeit a bit patchy thatch at that) over his head. But by late August, it became painfully clear to him that this parcel of England would not sustain him through the winter. Not enough fuel, not enough food, not enough of the hard coin to buy what he might need.

It was on the 21st of August, as he watched a fine rake of horses led past his place, on their way to auction in Torquay, that an idea planted itself in his mind.

By the winter of 1654, his plan was in full operation. His father had always cautioned him not to "shite where ye eat." So off to Cornwall William went, in search of unguarded horses of good quality. With his own rake of them and riding one, he rode across Devonshire and on to Dorset, where he easily sold the mounts. Finding himself in Dorset, now riding a fine mount himself, he gathered up another rake of horses seemingly not so valued as to be protected, and guided them to their purchase back in Cornwall. Now, few like a horse thief but many liked a horse seller with goods at reasonable prices.

William had some rules to his trade. Never, ever, take a horse that appeared to be the only horse of a household. His appropriations were not about making people destitute but about evening out the playing fields of life. If this meant more taken from the affluent, the gentry, and more sold to the poor, the commoners, all the better.

Such was his commerce for several years, an annual trip to Cornwall, then to Dorset, then to Cornwall, before returning to Devonshire, well-rewarded in coin for his time and effort.

Until 1665, that is. Being scrupulous to not keep any records lest he leave some account of his doings (his inability to read and write also contributing to this), he had to rely on his memory of whence he had taken and where he had sold. However, he had not taken into account that some manner of peer or gentry might, quite possibly by either marriage or inheritance, be in a different Manor than several years before. In that spring, bringing a fine rake of horses into a paddock in Dorset, the Lord let up a great cry and summoned his Gillie with demands for arrest. The Sheriff was summoned and William found himself in chains, facing grave charges. He had tried to sell one horse once too often, to one who knew the horse too well.

The trial was swift and the verdict of guilt even swifter. Now, for the punishment. William could already feel a crick in his neck. The judge ("Yes, m' Lord") looked down at this wee man, and realizing that more than one of his prized horses had been bought from him without any questions, and said, "William Tinsdale, having been adjudged 'guilty' of horse thievery, I hereby pronounce sentence." At this point he paused, and an expectant hush filled the courtroom.

"You shall be taken this day …" more pause.

"To the docks at Plymouth …" more pause.

"Where you shall be placed upon one of his majesty's ships bound for the colonies. And if you ever allow your face to be seen in England, the gibbet will await you."

With that, the judge knew his own steeds were safe and he might never face this wretched little man again.

By Fall, 1665, William Tinsdale found himself unchained and cast off like some jetsam of an old world, tossed from shipboard into the shallow depths of Boston Harbor. Struggling to his feet in his new freedom, he did what he had done before. He started walking.

The onset of winter found him along the banks of the Connecticut River. There he became a curiosity of the local peoples, who found this little, round man strange indeed. He knew none of their language but seemed eager to learn. Had none of the skills of writing other white men had shown. He was a hard worker, unlike the other white men who seemed more skilled in bossing than in toiling. William became welcomed in the village and by spring they were sad to hear him say, in their own language, that he was leaving them. He pointed to the setting sun, and they understood. They presented him with several ceremonial gifts that might mark him as honorable to any other people of the First Nations he might encounter.

In the Spring of 1666, with the treasures bestowed upon him, he turned his face west and began the long trek over the mountains, following the setting sun.

May 21,1666, he reached a point about three miles from the confluence of many creeks into a greater river. Along the river he had seen (and hidden from) many of those for whom this land was ancestral. He did not want to be where everyone could find him. Now, a half mile from any flowing creek, not along any worn trail of other feet, he stopped. It felt right.

He quickly began to build himself shelter, a simple lean-to. It was in that lean-to one morning that summer that he awakened to find two bronze faces looking down at him. Not threatening, just puzzled. They began to speak, and he realized he could understand about half of what they were saying. He spoke in the language he had learned back along the big river, and they jumped back, not understanding how a wee man like he would know their words. Was he some apparition?

Then, remembering what his friends had told him, he took out a portion of the gifts they had given him, and his new guests were in awe. He picked up two of the pieces and held one out to each of them. After they had each received the tokens of respect, he raised his short little arms as wide as he could, pointed to all the land around him, all the immense forested land, and said (he hoped) in a language they would understand, "Mine, in peace with yours."

The two visitors looked at him, looked at the gifts, pointed more vastly than he could ever have done, and then smiled.

With that, William had bought his part of the earth from people who knew no such concept. In their minds, they honored him for honoring them, by accepting his presence in the wide circle of their gestures. Where no land deeds exist, acceptance matters greatly while where there is no acceptance deeds do not matter.

William Tinsdale, tin miner's son, wanderer, horse thief, convict, became the accepted resident of that area. Over the next few years, he built a small log cabin there. In time, he used the lower room as a general store selling to new settlers and First Nations alike. He used the loft as his residence.

He continued his rules of trade so long ago established. If someone less well-off than he were to ask the price of something, it would be sold at cost. If someone better-off than he were to ask the price, the profit would increase proportional to the differential in status.

One day, while bargaining over the value of a beaver pelt in relation to a bag of beans, a woman walked into Tinsdale's log cabin store. No woman had ever been in the store. Yes, sometimes he would glimpse a native family on the edge of his clearing from which the man would separate himself to come into the store. Likewise, the occasional settler's family would remain at a distance.

This was different. She walked right in, pointed to a hammer, a small cut of bacon, and a length of rope and asked, "Hoeveel voor dit alles?"

William had no clue. She repeated it, slower and louder.

It was then that one of the original two natives who had stumbled upon him years before spoke, in Oneidan, saying "She is one of the Dutch, she wants to know the price."

With a nod of thanks, William turned to the woman and held up five fingers. The woman shook her head and held up three fingers. Williams shook his head and held up five fingers. She held up three but then made a gesture to saw them off in the middle. In the end, when they both had four fingers in the air, a bargain was made.

William made a courteous nod and said "William."

"Wilhelm?"

He nodded again, and then discretely gestured in her direction.

"Katrine."

And then the two smiled at each other.

A whole book could be written about what followed, of his search to find where she had settled, to try to learn a little Dutch, of her search for reasons and the means to go back to the trading post, to try to learn a little English. In the end, by 1669, when William was 30 and Katrine was 25, they were married.

Soon the simple log cabin was supplemented with a much larger log cabin, just for the Tinsdale family. William had prudently built it large enough that the yearly arrival of another Tinsdale did not overly crowd the space. In the end, there were 3 boys and 5 girls, all of whom were, by the time they were ten years old, taller than their father. Of course, Katrine was taller than William, but as she said, "I will always look up to you," and then they both would break into laughter and their kids would roll their eyes and moan.

By the time of the Revolutionary War, the Log Cabin Store was in the hands of the third generation of Tinsdales. Each successive generation had acquired height and progeny. Some of the patriots cut off at Oriskany would find shelter at the Log Cabin. The history of the cabin grew and grew.

With the founding of Perryburg at the natural site of confluence of water and people, the Log Cabin Store became a less visited location. The intent of William Tinsdale to be a place sought out, not a place adjacent to other travels, determined a slow but sure decline in business. By the 1850s, little commerce was taking place and another generation of Tinsdales decided to transition to a new venture: lodging. First the canal south and then a branch railroad south followed the very path that William had taken from the river. People were now moving past the cabin, so why not erect more solidly to house them. For many travelers, the higher prices in Perryburg ("and getting higher ever year" was a rampant complaint) forced them to look elsewhere for accommodations, especially if the stay was for more than one night.

Almost a century later, Kemmons Wilson and his Holiday Inn idea would claim to revolutionize the travel industry. US route 20 motor courts would laugh at this notion, knowing they had done it in the 1910s. But Log Cabin Inn had the longer laugh with their small circle of little log cabins that offered travelers accommodations more private than a hotel or boarding house, supported by common facilities of a cookhouse and a for-the-times modern outhouse complex.

As with every endeavor of change, the revolutionary of one era becomes the ordinary of the another and then the outdated of another and then the abandoned of another.

By 1960, the Log Cabin Inn's several buildings were musty, worn-out, almost falling down relics of another era. The Interstate had consolidated lodging by its exit. Three miles out was a long way to go, and no one went there. That is until Mr. and Mrs. Vivek Patel arrived in Perryburg with their family of 5 children, looking to enter the motel business.

The Patels, emigrating from India, had researched their project well, but unfortunately their financial information had been terribly out of date. Arriving in New York City, they found everything well beyond their means. When they looked out from the city, scanning business opportunity listings, they found (again outdated) a small advertisement: Historic Rural Lodging Complex for Sale. Unseen, they made an offer well below the listed price (and well above what the Tinsdale heirs ever hoped to get). It was accepted immediately.

When the Patels got off the train at Perryburg and asked a taxi driver to take them to the address, the driver laughed and said, "that sorry old place - hope you aren't staying there." Mrs. Patel began to cry.

Standing in front of the ancient circle of log cabins, Mr. Patel started to cry too. Then his oldest son, Rajesh, hugging them both said, "I see promise here." His brothers and sisters stared at him." In response, he rolled up his sleeves and started pulling weeds.

That simple gesture, of hope and devotion, propelled the whole Patel family into action. No, not overnight but in a matter of months, what had been derelict became decent. The outsides were repaired and stained back into a consistent log cabin appearance. Inside, new plumbing, heating, electricity, wallboards, paint, beds, furniture, and more transformed empty spaces from another century into desirable accommodations.

It was little Layla Patel that thought of themes for the rooms. In contrast to the trend of every room looking the same, their new Inn would boast that every cabin was unique. They would feature people from the history of America.

The central buildings would offer a breakfast room (breakfast included!) and a gift shop of Americana.

With all this work complete, an opening date of June 1, 1961, was announced. A new sign was hung. A new name was introduced: Log Cabin Motel. After all, the only way to get there was by driving up.

Probably the smartest thing Mr. Patel did was to have the whole venture inspected by Triple A and Mobil. The arduous processes identified a few places for improvement but in the end earned them four stars from each, with praise for "the historic American accommodations brought to most modern specifications. You will drive up to history while staying in the modern world. A motel not like all the rest."

The Log Cabin Motel was an instant hit, but only with people coming to Perryburg from afar. No one in Perryburg thought about staying there or even having their company stay there.

Things at the motel rolled along well until about 1980, when the slow decline of Perryburg meant that fewer people were putting it on their travel plans. The Patels, by then having bought three other motels in the larger area, two of them licensed with major chains, saw the handwriting on the wall. Literally. One morning their cleaning staff entering a room occupied the prior night saw, scrawled on the large mural in the Washington crossing the Delaware, "The Man owned slaves!"

They had built their small empire, sent their children through university, and enjoyed a good life on the back of the Log Cabin Motel, but the income curve was obvious. Considering how little they had paid for the place, and how their thorough update of the property had meant they had no capital expenditures for over twenty years, they could offer it for sale at a very enticing price. That sale would end their tax liability on the property, and they could shift all their attention to their other properties.

This was when the mysterious Avedon Properties Group came on the scene. With an offer at the asking price, this privately held group of investors bought the Log Cabin Motel and installed all new management and staff. The rooms were stripped of their unique identities. The whole place became glitzy. Large mirrors were ordered and installed, often at places that baffled the installers. Soaking tubs replaced showers. When it re-opened as "The Log's Inn," the intent of the new owners was more than clear when the central building (once home to the family, then the breakfast room and gift shop) began an adult entertainment superstore.

Soon cars from other parts of the state and from other states began to arrive and business was brisk. Avedon had struck a below-the-belt blow to the community's hospitality market. Some came from the novelty, some for the naughtiness, but most for the implicit pleasure beyond the usual limits.

However, like all things that soar upon the scene, the "The Log's Inn" had initial success which slowly but surely faded with time. What seemed daring and risqué in 1985 seemed passe in 2005. Avedon then unloaded the property for about the price they had paid plus renovation to the DuBois brothers. The brothers put the nostalgic "Log Cabin Motel" sign back up, lowered prices, and did little else. By the passage of time, what had been salacious had become almost sordid. To match that decline, the DuBois offered overnight and less-than-overnight rates. They had a very transient clientele. Little checking of ID was done, and cash was king.

Now, if you went out to the Log Cabin Motel, you didn't want to be noticed AND you made sure you didn't notice anyone or anything else. That tacit understanding, however, did not always prevail.

Late one Friday night, actually more like very early on a Saturday morning in 2019, the residents of the various cabins were disturbed from their slumber (or more likely their passions) by loud shouting, crying, and a general ruckus out in the parking lot, aided and abetted by the fire alarm system. In several rooms, the tattered drapes were pulled back to reveal dirty mini blinds that were pried open a little so the couples being disturbed could see what was going on and spot any fire. The real fireworks were going on right there in the parking lot.

What they saw was a circle of eight people, all of whom were yelling, shoving, crying, and more. Let's see: 2 men, a woman, no 2 women, another woman, 2 more men, and another woman. But who were these people and what upset them?

It had been on Thursday evening that Drew McNamara's wife, Dara, told him that she was going to be joining her girlfriends for a hen party for Sasha Thurgood who was getting married on Saturday.

Earlier, on Tuesday, Hector dela Cruz had reminded his wife, Irene, of the company planning retreat he was to attend on the weekend, over in Copleman's Corner.

The Sugarmans, Edith and Ed, had long standing separate plans to attend alumni weekend at their respective colleges.

Robbie Robinson and his wife Nadine Minos had similar separate plans for the weekend, each to visit their parents.

Now, suddenly, Drew, Dara, Hector, Irene, Ed, Edith, Robbie, and Nadine were standing in the parking lot of the Log Cabin Motel, disturbing the peace of all the others who were there. To the casual observer from behind the drapes and blinds, it was just a large group that looked like it might be boiling to a fight.

However to two people peering out into the melee, there was something not quite right about what they were seeing. They saw people they knew from Perryburg, neighbors, fellow church members, scout leaders, friends. But they also saw that none of the couples was standing together. It was like all of the usual order was gone and new coupling was showing.

In fact, that is what was showing. New coupling. People who weren't normally together were together.

For example, Drew was standing with Nadine. Drew was fending off shouts from Dara while Nadine was hurling words at Robbie. Edith was crying between gestures at Ed and then at Robbie. Ed was reciprocating with a tirade towards Irene and Edith. Hector was turning his back on wife Irene while shouting at Edith.

(If you want to create a chart and pin down yarn strings between each of the people, that might help!)

What was happening? What had happened?

It had all unraveled like this. Everyone in the group had either known or had planned that they would be apart from their spouse that night. Every one of the reasons had been reasonable. In an age of cell phones, every one of them could have been contacted wherever they were and pretended to be where they claimed to be. Eight people, all in long-term marriages, finding themselves without the duty and restraints of their traditional coupling, had seized on the opportunity to act out desires.

Some of those desires had been acted upon before, some had only been glowing coals of passion longing to be fanned by such an opportunity, and some were more hidden drives given free rein by the circumstances to emerge out of the darkness. None of those desires would have been acted upon in Perryburg, at any of the homes, in any way in the motels out by the Interstate. The Log Cabin Motel, with its reputation, provided them each and them all with the venue. The partners had been provided with reason for freedom or the excuse for excess. Now they were all mixing it up in the parking lot of the most clandestine motel in the area, out there for all to see.

Everything had gone according to eight different plans. People drove off, ostensively, to hen parties, training weekends, reunions, visits with parents. The remaining folk drove off toward their rendezvouses with desire.

All were old enough to know what they were doing. The kids had already gone off to college, or armed forces, or distant cities, and the pets could tend themselves for several hours. Each arrived and parked "around back" as most cars did. (It was always interesting that while all the cabins might be full, from the road the main parking lot looked empty; there were spaces behind each cabin by the cabin back door. But, with the circle effect of the cabins, one could not see from behind any cabin what was parked behind any other cabin.)

It was about midnight that one by one the "couples" started to say, "good night," with lingering kisses, promises of future bliss, and pledges of secrecy. If only someone had not been enhancing the occasion with a little pot-smoking, all might have gone down without incident.

The old log cabins, as modernized as they had once been, were basically wooden cabins. Fire was a constant worry. The DuBois brothers had wanted to protect their investment (actually, they just wanted to keep any public inspectors as far away as possible) and had installed a state-of-the-art detection system, sensitive down the smallest errant insect.

The blaring horn sent the eight people, already in the act of getting ready to leave, to leave. In their sudden shift from passion and longing to distress, they all had forgotten that their cars were out back, and almost simultaneously they emerged out of cabin 1,2, 5, and 8 into the parking lot. The dim light of the parking lot still seemed glaring after hours in darkened rooms. Squinting around at the others emerging from cabins, people began to recognize their partners, but now with other partners. The sudden awareness of a transgression against them blinded them to the fact that they each were also transgressors. After a moment with just the fire alarm sounding, the noises began.

Accusations, hurts, notes of betrayal, shock, grief, anger … you name it. In about all of five minutes, all the stages of Kubler-Ross' Stages were felt and expressed with the exception of acceptance.

I suspect, by now, you are wondering who was with whom. I will spare you the need to untangle all your chart yarn.

Drew had ended up with Nadine. Dara was with Hector. Ed was with Robbie. Irene was with Edith. Every one of the couplings had worked together in some way – PTA, Republicans, Democrats, faith communities. Every one of the couplings had become intimate but not physical over time, sharing life interests and personal secrets. None of them had ever betrayed their spouses' confidences even as they had lusted outside of the promises made at marriage.

In the end, Drew and Dara found a way, through counseling, to return to their marriage, probably stronger in its capacity for love. Irene and Edith left their marriages, as did Ed and Robbie; the two women and the two men formed new partnerships that felt more authentic than anything they had known before. No, Hector and Nadine did not, as a consolation prize, find each other. They each accepted being single as a stage of their relational life. Eventually Nadine would marry a widower named Ralph and move away. The

220

others stayed in Perryburg, fed the gossip meter for some time and then became just other couples in the fabric of the city.

And the Log Cabin Motel?

The same gossip mill processed what had happened and not wanting to blame anyone's friend or neighbor assessed the motel to be at fault. Health and safety inspections, long overdue (Bill Kratz was fired for the discovered bribes from the DuBois brothers and the DuBois brothers escaped jail time barely) found so many defects that the motel was shut down fully and quickly. Within a year the land was sold to a developer for new housing. The cabins were going to be burned down as training exercises for local volunteer firefighters until the state DEP said "NO." Too much hazardous material. Instead, they were safely bulldozed and removed. The big building, the one that had been Tinsdale home, was in much better shape but stood in the way of the development. It was disassembled log by log, board by board. The elements were then sold to a reclamation firm for reuse.

In the last few years, young couples building their summer homes up in the hills wanting to give them the feel of permanence, had bought up all those remnants. Today, on many a lake in that region, people will point to a pillar here or a wall board there or a plank over there and "that was from the old Log Cabin Inn. Most visitors will humor them and say "Oh," but few if any will have any idea of that history.

11. THE ABLATATE

"Hey, Jorge, get over here. You gotta see this"

"Where are you?"

"In 507!"

Manuel was waiting for Jorge when Jorge ambled into what had been apartment 507 in the old Ablatate Building up on Mohawk Street.

Ah, the Ablatate Building, that massive limestone apartment house that rose up seven stories amid two story single homes. A monolith worthy of Pharoahs, or at least Ozymandias. Erected in the last decade of the 19th century, for its time it was the height of luxury for rental apartments.

It has been the dream of Morris Ablamon and Jonathan Tate, two well-healed developers in Perryburg, to move beyond the single- and two-family homes to something that spoke more of a real city. Having often traveled to New York and marveled at what was being built with brownstone there, they envisioned a gleaming monument of local limestone (of which there was more than an abundance) that would attract "the right kind of people."

Who were "the right kind of people?"

They were professionals, young couples without children but full of promise, and the rising crust of the new century.

Each of the 70 apartments would have multiple fireplaces finished in a variety of stone or tile. All would have a large living room facing Mohawk Street, with a semi-turret effect giving everyone a wider vista and alternating balconies. The view was towards the west, with impressive sunsets promised.

223

Elevators and stairs rose between couplets of apartments, a total of five such towers of access. On each floor there was a small landing outside the elevator and stairs, with the entrances to the individual apartments off those landings. One entered an apartment in a small reception area with a coat closet on one side and a telephone niche on the other. One then turned, entering the living room.

Of course, a formal dining room would be in the other direction. The kitchen and a bath separated the front of each apartment from the rear. Then the central hallway of each unit led to either one or two bedrooms. The one-bedroom units would have that one bath while the two-bedroom units would have two baths, one of them ensuite. The dining rooms were fitted with built-in china cabinets, the kitchen with a small pantry, and the bedrooms with walk-in closets. A rear entry opened onto a "servants" hallway and the back stairs.

Outside, like ancient Greek adornments, each of the ten "turrets" of the building bore, at the second-floor level, granite carvings of the seven virtues, supplemented on the ends by images of Moses and Abraham and toward the center of Lady Liberty.

The whole building seemed to glow from the electric lights inside, all lit at once on the night of the dedication. By then, 66 of the 77 apartments had been rented, all to upstanding citizens whose names were well known around town. Within a month the remaining eleven apartments were rented. The Ablatate was a resounding success. Living there was a mark of achievement.

In addition to the features of the apartments, what made it a success was its location, just beyond the commercial area and the original mansions uptown, but before the newer mansions of Uptown. A resident could easily walk to most of the offices in the city or catch a trolley down to Union Station.

Life in the Ablatate was glamorous. Parties among its residents became legendary. Visitors from out of town were amazed at the features of the building. Looking up at it from the street, before ascending the front stairs into any of the five lobbies, was like looking up at Parthenon. Descending from the building gave one a sense of being above the common fray.

The Ablatate continued to enjoy great favor for decades. It was always fully occupied, with a long waiting list. Then came October 1929. The financial hardship of renters would translate into financial hardship for the building's owners. But those rumored financial difficulties would pale in comparison to the effect of Jonathen Tate, Sr., leaping to his death from the roof. Money may have been a problem, but reputation was now a crisis.

Who would want to live there? Isn't the place jinxed? How do you erase the memory of that happening at the Ablatate?

By 1935, with the occupancy rate (diminished by both leases ending and evictions for non-payment) down to less than 50%, Morris Ablamon took the bold step of reducing rents substantially and requiring only a 6-month lease. People who had only dreamed of living there ever now might consider it. Teachers, small shop owners, municipal employees all found new homes in the old building. The Ablatate had been democratized.

Of course, with that change there was no future hope of restoring either the social standing nor the level of rents once enjoyed by the owners. Unknown to the new residents who became a majority of the renters, Morris Ablamon took other steps toward financial stability for the building.

Planned five- and ten-year maintenance and renewal was shifted to ten- and twenty-five schedules. Staff was cut to the bone. For example, midnight to 7am there were no elevator operators, so residents had to use the stairs overnight. Heat was cut back by five degrees, Lots of little things as well.

Then the war came. The changes in society in general were mirrored at the Ablatate. A greater number of females became residents. War supply needs rendered any plan for solid maintenance, much less any upgrades, moot. The large, flat, slightly sloping roof on the whole structure was over a rubber membrane, and with rubber essentially unavailable for domestic use, small holes in the membrane might get tarred, but never repaired. The roof, by then way past its life expectancy, was failing in many places.

VE day first, then VJ day, brought the hostilities to an end, but not the scarcity of many materials. At the same time, commitments to the masses of returning veterans made new housing a higher priority than aging hulks like the Ablatate. What had seemed state-of-the-art in 1897 was, by 1947, old, hard to repair, passe.

The downward spiral, started in 1929, hastened in 1935, not helped by the war demands, was accelerating. The apartments were not being renovated between tenants. The refrigerators that replaced the ice boxes back in the 1920s were not replaced. The gas stoves without pilot lights were not replaced. The wiring was not updated. Nothing about the building would have been considered up-to-code.

With new options opening every day and home ownership taking on a new social status, renting began to be seen as second-class. Renting a dated apartment in a run-down building more like third-class. To attract more residents, rents had to be slashed, but then if rents were slashed so were services and upkeep.

With the de-institutionalization of some of the state's wards held in mental hospitals and the growth of anti-poverty programs, the Ablatate became a residence of record for people displaced from the great American dream. Its halls became dirty and dim. The old elevators, replaced with automatic ones, were unreliable. Pipes banged. Lights dimmed. Strange odors wafted throughout the building.

When the last of the Ablamon family (Morris had long since passed over) gathered to hear the reading of the will of their patriarch, there were groans. They had each been given a percentage of the old building with no one branch of the family having enough shares to call any shots. Nor were they bequeathed enough for any of them to buy the others out. And no one had any clue about managing an apartment house.

In the papers reporting this outcome the story read: "Ablatate Become Albatross to Ablamons."

The extended family decided to put the building on the market, at "fire-sale" prices. That became a reality when apartment 206 was gutted by fire after a chimney blow-back in the fireplace. The new tenant had not realized that the fireplaces had been ordered inoperable in 1936, started a small fire, had the fumes going up 5 stories build into a pressurized bubble, and then blow back, blowing sparks out into the living room, starting a small fire. That the new resident was still unpacking and there were piles of packing paper about did not help.

While much of Perryburg had declined from its apex in the Industrial Age, the Perryburg Fire Department had not only maintained standards, but under Chief Bill Lennon it had invested in some of the most sophisticated fire-fighting equipment. Rumor had it that when the PFD budget was before the Council, some of the members of the Council would be personally contacted by Lennon with a simple admonition, "It would be a shame if we couldn't save one of your assets because we lacked the equipment."

A fire, even a substantial one, was no match for the PFD. Being on the second floor made it all the easier, with both fire suppression methods as well as traditional modes being used. In the end, except for a smoky smell throughout the central elevator shaft units (all the -05 and -06 apartments) the only units damaged substantially were 206 (gutted) and 106 (water damage). 106 was repaired quickly. It was decided that it was better to leave 206 cleaned out but unrepaired, take the insurance payout, and let the new owners deal with it.

Acorn International Properties bought the building at an undisclosed price. (City Clerk records show the transfer fees were paid on $100,000., a ridiculously low sum for a 70, no, a 69 unit apartment building.) But at least the family was out from under the rapidly rising costs with rapidly declining returns.

Acorn would be involved in a five-year court battle over taxes. The Assessor, claiming that Acorn's failure to make public its purchase price rendered any changes in assessment moot, kept the property on the roles at the listed valuation from 1975.

To make up for the court costs and the continuing tax bills at the inflated rate, Acorn accelerated the decline in maintenance and services.

By 2015, had the newspaper published obituaries for buildings, it would have included this:

> The Ablatate, once the proud Grand Dame of Mohawk Street, after a long period of decline and placement in Hospice care in 2014, succumbed to a panoply of ills on March 19, when the City Building Inspector declared the building unfit for human habitation. Former residents remembered the expensive features of the building while more recent residents remember vermin and decay. A wake of displaced residents was held outside the building on

Wednesday. No plans for disposal of the corpse have been announced.

The great, white building, its images of virtue and faith and liberty now soot-covered remnants, received a new decoration of plywood over all the windows and doors. Some of those, at the lower floors, received graffiti additions. Over time, somehow, the upper floors got the same treatment.

The residents were scattered, with the help of social service agencies, to other, empty apartments of which there were too many in Perryburg. The roaches, mice, rats, and more moved in, unhindered by human intervention. However, during the first winter, when the building went unheated and there were no more morsels of food to be found, even they relocated, much to the chagrin of neighboring properties.

And there she stood, the Miss Haversham of Mohawk Street, forsaken, fire-scarred, empty. Discussions were held by the city about disposition. As with many civic concerns in a declining city (as opposed to a community of growth where changes comes quickly and continually), the question of the Ablatate was referred to committees for further study and public comment. That's another way of saying, nothing was done.

Well, not nothing. Acorn defaulted on taxes for several years and the city took possession of the property after a public tax auction provided no bidders.

With the passage of the Bi-Partisan Infrastructure Bill, the most sweeping public-works support program since the Great Depression, a way forward for the empty hulk was found.

In the end it was simple. The city needed affordable housing and the least expensive way of meeting that need was rehabilitation of existing structures. The Ablatate was at the top of that list.

A comprehensive survey of the structure disclosed that, despite all the neglect and damage of many years, the basic structure was sound, very sound. It had been built beyond any standards and codes of its day. In fact, tearing it down would have presented some difficulties and bringing it back to life would be easier and cheaper.

Perryburg Housing Authority was the agency of record. They had, in recent years, been the force tearing down The Projects and building smaller public housing units spread around town. They had already been instrumental in a loft conversion Downtown.

With much fanfare, the old graffitied plywood came off The Ablatate, each of the five front and back stairway shafts reopened and repaired, and other renovations began. The roof was totally rebuilt. The exterior was surveyed and repaired as needed. Then, the workers began the long, slow process of renovating the old apartments into new, affordable ones.

For the most part, the old building would be cleared back to the basics. The Ablatate was built using industrial-strength floors/ceilings and solid stone walls rising up inside the structure, boxing in each column of apartments and each entry column. Inside, it was a really 10 structural units of housing and five columns of stairs, elevators, and utilities. Everything else was ornamentation, in a sense.

One of the earliest renovators had remarked that had a war started, she wanted to be in the central entry shaft, about third floor level, because nothing would ever destroy that.

With no structural repairs required, all the apartments could be cleared back to the bare floors and structural walls, with all the apartment walls, fixtures, and utilities removed.

It was in that process of clearing the building that Manuel had called over to Jorge. When Jorge got to 507, he saw Manuel prying loose some of the plaster and lath that had, for over a century, covered the stone walls of the building.

Walking toward the opposite wall, Manuel said, "This is what I wanted to show you." Manuel had started there first, making a small hole with the claw end of his hammer and then clawing away to open it up. The small hole revealed edges of plaster with many different paint layers, and then wallpaper layers. The whole history of 507 was revealed, generations of decorating choices from the first, slightly blue paint layer that had been applied to the fresh plaster more than a century before.

The hole was framed by rectangular section of wall which was darker than the surrounding area and, with a hook into the wall at the top of the area, it was evident that something hang hung for many years covering the place where the hole was.

But Jorge, looking closely, saw what Manuel had seen. About five layers back, back in the wallpaper eras, the wall covering had been neatly cut, cutting through the underlayers, down to the lath, and the lath had been neatly cut at that same line.

Jorge, seeing this, exclaimed, "Dios mío!"

The two of them slowly and carefully expanded the hole, working to keep the hidden flap intact. The many layers above it made that easy. The later layers came off as one. After a few minutes, they had revealed a 6 inch by 10 inch flap, still attached by old layers, that could be lifted up. Underneath the lath was cut to form a totally removable "window."

"Here goes," Manual said, removing the lath window from its long-hidden place. Behind the lath were the wall-supporting studs and behind that the stone walls. The opening was adjacent to one of the studs on the left side, and inside that opening was a small, metal box which appeared to have been screwed into the stud. The box, about three inches deep, had only a simple latch on its free side; no lock. Someone must have felt being hidden behind the wall was enough.

Reaching into the opening, Jorge opened the latch and the lid noisily swung open. Any hopes for hidden treasure were dashed when only letters were found inside. A packet of letters tied with a very old blue ribbon. Jorge took hold of the packet and pulled it out. It seemed to resist being brought into the light.

Manuel took the packet from Jorge and began to untie the ribbon. The ribbon almost fell apart in his hands.

There were about twenty letters, all in light blue envelopes which had been opened long ago. As he examined them, Manuel thought he detected an old, slight perfume scent. They had all been addressed simply to a post office box at the main station. No name, just PO Box 37, Perryburg 2.

"What should we do with the letters?"

"I'm going to take a look at one."

 "Should we?"

"It's not like it is money or jewelry or anything of value."

Manuel opened the one with the oldest postmark – it was dated in 1907.

> *Dearest*
>
> *I know our love must never be spoken in public, but I do long to speak your name to others, to let others know how loved I feel.*
>
> *Last Saturday's long walk in the country was a fulfillment of so much longing on my part. I had so often gazed at you and wondered if you had any feelings for me, any feelings as strong as I felt for you.*

Now I have my answer, and that answer is YES.

Please, may we not say our Saturday was a one-time meeting of our spirits, but rather just the start of a relationship of love which will hold us together for the rest of our lives.

Yours forever,

Ethel

"Wow, some stuff."

"Let's read another."

"Yes!"

The second oldest letter was similar from outward appearances, and it was dated about two weeks after the first.

Dearest,

Had I known the pleasures at Saratoga were not just to be the horses and the waters, but deeper and more passionate than my wildest dreams, I would have surely asked for two days there, not just the one night.

"¡Ay, caramba!" was all that Jorge could say.

Manuel read on, the note giving steamy details of a sexual encounter that sounded lurid even by 2021 standards. In an almost comic gesture, when he had finished reading the whole letter, Manuel used the letter to fan himself.

Jorge grabbed up the next letter, and began to read it. It had come about three weeks later. Apparently, the relationship was blossoming beyond all expectations. Jorge is known to use colorful language and, especially in his native Spanish, to be graphic about amorous things. Even he turned a deep red while reading it.

"So," wondered Manuel, "who was this Ethel?"

"No idea. But who lived in this apartment way back then?"

"He was some lover, apparently."

"Let's keep reading."

And read letters they did. Letter after letter. But after about twelve of the letters, things changed. Nine months had passed and the tone was different.

> *My dearest –*
>
> *It has been too long since we were last together. Too long since I could hold you close, feel your skin against mine. Hold you inside me.*

"Ow, wee, they are still at it."

"Wait, listen to this."

> *I know that your home life and the needs of your wife must come first, but I begin to feel neglected. Where I once thought I was the most important thing in your life, now you ask me to understand when our times together must be postponed. My heart still calls to yours and awaits you answering with the love you have pledged to me so often.*

"Trouble in paradise, eh?"

The rest of the letters chronicled a downhill relationship with pleas for more time together, questions about a promised divorce, two frantic letters about pregnancy, one almost threatening long letter about despair, and then a final one.

It began with no salutation:

> *I know you have loved me honestly and truly, but now I know you must make other choices. I do not fault you for that. I*

234

know, from what you told me last Thursday evening, that I will always be in your heart, that if circumstances of life were different, we would be together forever, making each other happier than we could ever imagine.

I have tonight, as I said I would, taken care of the troubling matter which arose out of our relationship. You do not need worry about that and any of its consequences.

The letter went on and on about what his love had meant for her, how she would remain available to him no matter what choices he made. She wrote about all the wonderful parts of his personality, his demeanor, and especially his lovemaking. She held nothing back. It was signed

Eternally yours, in undying love,

Ethel

That was it. No more letters in the box. Nothing else – or was there? Manuel reached into the box and found no other letters but then his fingers touched something – pulling it out he realized it was a strand of hair, tied with a piece of the same ribbon. On that ribbon was a simple word: Ethel.

At the end of the day, Jorge was ready to be done with the place. However, Manuel was still thinking about the letters they had found.

"Mind if I take these with me?"

"No problem. Just old stuff about people long dead."

Manuel took them home with him that night.

"Manny, is that you?" his wife asked, as he came in the door.

"Who else would it be?"

"I thought it might be Ricky. He should have been home by now, but he isn't."

Just then a second person walked through the door, a much younger version of Manuel. Father and son embrace, and then both went to kiss the cornerstone of their household, Momma, Thérèse.

As was their custom, the family assembled around their kitchen table at six. Manuel, Thérèse, Rickardo, Yolanda, and little Anna. After grace was said (they always held hands as they blessed the food), Manuel said, "I have to tell you about something we found today at work."

With that introduction, he gave an abridged version of the letters, making sure he did not get a disapproving eye from his wife.

When he was finished, he said, "I just wonder who those people were. It sounded so much like a Telenovela."

Ricky responded, "Papa, I have an idea. Your letters might help me with something."

"¿Qué?"

"In my history class at college, our assignment is to create a history project that requires us to research some local situation that is from at least a hundred years ago. I would like to find out who these people were."

"Before I let you read them, I think we need to have a little father and son talk."

"Not again!"

"Yes, again."

At that point, Anna asked, "Can I listen in?"

"No, muchacha. Not this time."

Anna produced her expected pout, but to no avail.

Later that evening, Ricky and his dad sat down together, and Manuel showed him the letters.

"Now I know why you didn't want my sister to see these. Wow!"

"Yes, wow. I know I always think of my great-grandparents, the ones who came to this country and then to Perryburg, as two people in old, dark clothing, without much of a spark of life. I thought all people from that time were like that. I was wrong. Please find out what you can about these people."

"I will, and I will show you what I find."

Manuel would periodically look at his son and say "So?" and his son would look back and say "Not yet."

Finally, one night about three weeks later, Ricky told his dad that he had some information. Manuel was eager to hear it.

What Ricky had found was that apartment 507 in the Ablatate had been rented, from the beginning and for thirty years, by Frank Matheson, President of the Perryburg Chamber of Commerce, President of Perryburg National Bank, Deacon of St. Stephen's Episcopal Church. He had been married to Evelyn Draper, daughter of Cecil Draper, the cotton magnate. The Mathesons were part of the social elite of the city. Their names were among the benefactors of almost all charitable activities in town. They were the mainstays of the Temperance Movement in Perryburg, as well as the Moral League of America. Mrs. Matheson, speaking at the time of Frank's death, said he had been a steadfast husband, and her only regret was that they had never had any children. Now the two of them are buried in Forest View Cemetery, in a prominent plot with a view of the Chapel.

The research on Ethel had taken longer. At first, Ricky thought he had reached a dead end. Then, in examining newspapers around the time of the last letter, he noted the death of an Ethel Comstock, unmarried, age 24. Delving deeper, he found her death certificate. It listed blood poisoning "subsequent to an abortion."

"It all fits together," Manuel said after sitting quietly with the information for a few minutes. "It explains why the letters stopped. It explains some of what Ethel wrote in the last letter. It explains why the affair had to be kept secret, and why he had slowly tried to extricate himself from her."

"But he kept her letters."

"Yes, he kept her letters, and even a lock of her hair, for years after that, safely behind the wall of apartment 507."

"Dad, one more thing. There was an article from about two years later that related a private dinner party the Mathesons had given for the Episcopal Bishop on his visit to St. Stephen's. In the account, the Bishop had remarked, with my appreciation, about a painting of the Savior and Mary Magdalene, which hung in the Mathesons' living room. Mrs. Matheson had told the Bishop that her husband had bought the painting about two years earlier because he said it reminded him of a forgiving spirit for the fallen among us. The description of where it had hung in the living room was "where the evening sunset light would fall upon it.""

"I know that spot – it is where my hammer claw caved in the plaster."

Apartment 507 was not the only place where there were surprises. Most were toys found behind baseboards, or the random coin fallen through a floor crack. Perhaps a random piece of antique clothing in a back recess of a closet or some spice tins a pantry from a company long since gone. But I need to tell you about Apartments 302 and 303.

302 and 303 were one-bedroom apartments. The two-bedroom apartments added their space by jutting out their greater width behind the rear access areas to be "L" shaped, while the one-bedroom units were more rectangular. If you can picture this, 303 was a mirror image of 302. Left-hand and right-hand of the same floor plan. Living room abutted living room, bathroom abutted bathroom (much easier to run the pipes that way), and the walk-in closet abutted the walk-in closet.

Ever since the building had been built, the assumption was that great interior stone walls were solid except where the piping for kitchens and bathrooms made their way to either side. The utilities ran up and the waste product ran down through a chase built into those walls, with openings into the chase at each floor to allow access to the pipes as needed. Everyone knew that behind the bathtubs there was a piece of the apartment wall that looked solid, but was a façade, giving access to all behind it.

But there was something more, which apparently only the people in Apartments 302 and 303 knew.

The demolition crew had been working their way down from the seventh floor, so the debris not placed in the demolition chute to the dumpsters could just fall down, and then down some more, as the workers worked their way down.

When the crew got to 302, they started at the front, stripping things back to the walls. Then, moving down the hallway, they removed not only the hallway walls but also the walls that created the dining room, the kitchen, the pantry, and the bathroom. Finally, they came to the bedroom.

Here they stripped the plaster, lath, and studs from the wall abutting 301. Then the wall to the rear exterior. Finally, the walk-in closet, which was formed with the same depth as the bathroom which adjoined it. That is where the surprise came.

As they started the demolition against the common wall with 303, one whole panel of the back of the closet came off as a unit, not nailed into the studs. Behind it was another opening, this one clear through the stone wall that separated the units. It was bigger than the utility chase located where the bathroom had been, about two studs wide, and about three feet tall. At the top of the opening, a solid iron beam supported by iron stanchions on either side of the opening started the wall upward again. The integrity of the wall was not compromised with the opening. Hinged into the stanchions was a double iron door, well rusted.

One half the iron door hinged to open into 302, and the other to hinged in the other direction. Neither halves opened, the hinges well-rusted. After a bit of old and good old fashion muscle was applied, the portion that opened into 302 squealed its way almost to open. Herman then went to work on the other half, its hinges not available for oiling. Drawing back his sledge, Herman gave it a solid whack, and it creaked open about an inch. He tried again, and this time the door moved hard against the inside of the closet wall of 303. One more hard strike on the door and the exposed back of the wall in 303 and door opened fully while a whole wall panel fell into 303's closet. Now they were looking at a passageway between the two units.

"What the?" was the best that Herman could utter. He quickly got on the phone with Earl, the site boss, who hot-footed it up to 302 to see for himself.

"Well, I'll be darn," was the best the local farmer turned construction supervisor could say. "Tell you what I need to do, I need to have you come along with me, and we are going to look to see if any of the other floors have anything similar."

"Look, Earl, Susie and me have worked our way down from seven and we never saw anything like this."

"OK, let contact the other crews, and have them check for the same."

They were working with 5 two-person crews, one assigned to each of the 5 seven-story sections which each were served by the same stair shafts. There were Hector and Isabel on the 9-10 units, Manny and Jorge on the 7-8 units, he was working with Iqbal on the 5-6 units, Tracy and Terry were handling the 3-4 units, Herman and Ted were in the 1-2 units.

Quick phone calls to the other three teams revealed that no one had seen anything like this. Two of the other teams were already at or below the third floor and nothing had been discovered like this.

Earl then went over to where Tracy and Terry were working the 3-4 units. They had just finished 304 and were about to start 303. Earl joined the two women to inspect apartment 303. Everything looked as usual for the decrepit place the Ablatate had become. In many places, ripping out the structure was more about picking up and discarding the pieces.

The bedroom seemed the most intact in 303, and looking into the closet they could see the panel lying on the floor. They also saw a great accumulation of dust on everything in the newly discovered passage. Herman, reaching through from 302, got a dusting on his sleeve.

Everyone just stared at each other for a moment until Tracy dared it, and walked through from 303 to 302, hunching down just a bit. (Tracy was one strong but short woman who knew how to tear apart nearly anything.)

"Man, if Nancy Drew were only here now," followed Tracy's whistle.

Soon everyone was trying out this discovered passage. It was Herman who finally asked the question that was lurking in everyone's mind, "Why do you think this is here?"

Manuel then shared with those observing this secret passage what he and Jorge had found in the wall in 507. He kept out the lurid details, but did say his son Ricky had done the research to fill out that story. "Maybe he can help with this, too."

Ricky was intrigued and took the question to his urban history professor. Professor Garcia had been fascinated with Ricky's project and the possibility of a follow-up exercise about the historic building was exciting. Instead of making it Ricky's project, he took it on as a class project. Fourteen students would try to find out what they could about the 302-303 opening.

The building had been totally gutted before the class project got answers. By then, the historic preservation society had gotten wind of the opening and went to court to prevent any changes to this historic and mysterious opening.

Research showed that from the opening of the building into the 1960s, apartment 302 was occupied by Francis Cash, an English teacher at Perryburg High School. Apartment 303 was occupied by Marion Medway, the librarian at PHS. Neither of the women ever married. Their estates both bequeathed their assets to the Perryburg Historical Society.

But, who were Miss Cash and Miss Medway. Neither of them came from Perryburg. They were from two different cities. They had not gone to the same college. However, they both had studied at Columbia for a Masters Degree, Cash in English and Medway in Library Science. graduating in 1897. Deep, deep dives into old records showed the two of them met when they shared an apartment in Washington Heights while attending Columbia Graduate Division (they would not have been welcome at the undergraduate college in those days!)

From that New York apartment, they had moved to Perryburg, starting their occupancy on the same day.

Now, here comes the stunning twist that the Urban History students were able to tweak using census records from 1890. Miss Cash was found in Ashtabula, Ohio, a teenager. Miss Medway was found in Paducah, Kentucky, also a teenager. But a Franklin L. Medway was found in Perryburg, with a listed occupation of construction foreman.

Checking the records of The Ablatate, the listed architect was none other than Lincoln Holmes, the famed designer of the Iroquois Hotel and the Palace Theater. The contractor was E. Parke Davies of New York. Local contractor, Phillip Hubbell and Sons. Site foreman, Franklin L. Medway.

Frank L. Medway!

Somewhere, in the bowels of Perryburg City hall, on brittle microfilm, one can see the details of construction. One can see all the purchase orders and all the change orders. And there on one change order, including changes to front step railing designs, was an order for a 32 X 36 reinforced opening to the the interior stone wall at the third-floor level, with accompanying addition of an iron beam, two iron supports for the opening, and a "reciprocating" hinged iron door. The change was initialed FLM on behalf of the contractor. By some slight of hand and figures, the total cost of the changes was zero. No accountant would ever see that it had been done.

But why?

One of the residents of Wisteria Gardens Continuum of Care Facility is Gertrude Medway, great granddaughter of Frank. Tracking her down was easy because Frank was well known around town, as was his son, as was his grandson, Frank L. Medway, III. Much of the construction of the boom of Perryburg had been supervised by their family firm. Mention "Medway" and people of a certain age will know who you are talking about. They will remember Frank, they might also remember the stern, hair-pinned-up librarian at the High School.

Gertrude remembered Miss Medway very well. As a little girl, she had often visited her great, great Aunt in her apartment in the Ablatate. Formal tea-parties were her favorites. And it always seemed like the apartment had a magical quality to it because suddenly Miss Cash would appear out of the bedroom, straightening this or that about herself, as if she had just used the wash room. But Gertrude never remembered seeing her enter through the front or back door.

Gertrude also remembered that while nothing was ever announced publicly, the postcards from Miss Medway's travels exactly matched the places Miss Cash had visited.

These days things are much easier. Two women who meet each other in graduate school and find themselves attracted to each other, can simply fall in love, move into together, get married, and have careers unthreatened by their affections. Back then, in the Victorian Age, one's reputation, one's career, one's welcome in a community meant that such love never be spoken, but less glimpsed.

Marion Medway had a doting brother. He always thought his sister found affection for women. But, so what? When she wrote Frank from New York about the love of her life, a love she could be more open about in New York but worried about anywhere else, he counseled her to come to Perryburg. The schools needed fine, career women who would not be tempted away by marriage. He knew just the right place for the two of them, where they could be as intimate as they wished and as discreet as society required.

It was Frank who made sure they could rent apartments 302 and 303, and that those two apartments would, in fact, be a single apartment, 302½.

For 65 years, two loving people, taking separate elevators or separate stairs up to seemingly unrelated apartments, would be coming home to the person they loved.

New tenants live in 302 and 303 now, probably not knowing anything about that history. They know nothing of the opening in the stone wall. The walls of their closets are now solid, not removable. But sometimes, they think they can hear people in the other closet, moving things, more than anywhere else in the apartments. Sometimes they think they can hear a woman's voice saying, "I love you," and then they hear another woman say "I love you, too."

The Ablatate's rehabilitation was completed on schedule, and just last year it opened as affordable housing. Most of the original touches were kept, the mechanicals all updated, the outside pressure-washed. Residents began to move in and the old lady came to life again. Lights shine once more from the turrets. Cooking smells rise up stairwells. Footsteps of the people who make Perryburg what it is today echo in the hallways. And the Virtues, the Patriarchs, and Liberty are there to inspire another generation, or two, or three, or more.

12. THE SEASONS OF PERRYBURG

WINTER

Even in the midst of deep winter the great Longhouse was warm. It was the warmth of many bodies, both human and animal, mixed with the smoky warmth of several fires. In the bitter cold outside the savage winds that blew the snow into drifts higher than the Longhouse rippled the layered skins of the house. These were times of survival, of communal care for one another. In the Longhouse, privacy was an unknown quality. The space, wide open from end to end, afforded no separations.

Just the previous winter the whole community had surrounded Kariwase the elder, one of the league of leaders who had helped the people of the Longhouse adjust to some of the new ways. As Kariwase lay dying, he gestured to Okwaho and Tyonajanegen. He had known the boy and the girl from their birth. Now they were man and woman, having come of age by both ceremony and maturity in the past year.

Okwaho and Tyonajanegen approached the old man they considered a spiritual Grandfather. Kneeling down beside the pallet where Kariwase lay, they sought to hear the words he was saying. Against the whistle of the wind, they could not hear his words. Sensing this, Kariwase reached out and took Tyonajanegen's hand and placed it in Okwaho's hand. He then cupped his hands around their joined hands and smiled. The two of them smiled as well. The elder had seen and understood their feelings for each other, and now he was ordaining and blessing their union.

Before the two could be joined in ceremony, Kariwase died. His death left a large hole in the fabric of the people, for his gentle but powerful spirit had guided them in so many ways. That grief held onto the people until the full Sugar Maple Moon rose bright and clear and Kariwase's pathway to the future was illuminated. At the next crescent of hope, the two, Okwaho and Tyonajanegen, were wed in a ceremony which remains to this day sacred and secret to the people.

In the following month, with the Field Maker moon in the night sky, the first crops of the new year were planted. Okwaho and Tyonajanegen planted their own seed in the promise of Spring. As grass and corn rose up, Tyonajanegen slowly grew. Now the couple counted not just the moons of planting and harvest, of hunting and fishing, but also the months of their child.

By the next time that the Moon announced the falling of branches amid the crushing ice of mid-winter, Tyonajanegen began to feel her body making its preparations for birth. A special place in the Longhouse was prepared for her, a little aside from others. Sitting in a small circle, the women elders, all who had known childbirth themselves, provided a living wall of privacy. Their chanting timed her breaths, their hands in hers shared strength, their herbal drinks eased the pain.

Outside the winds were fierce and the temperature was low. Snow did not just swirl outside but drove itself against the Longhouse like the roar of a waterfall. Its ferocity was met by the cries of Tyonajanegen as she labored to fulfill the dying prophecy of Kariwase the elder. Just before the dawn the wind suddenly fell silent, as did Tyonajanegen. A hushed silence filled the Longhouse, broken a few seconds later by joyous first cries of new lungs. Tyonajanegen wept tears of relief and joy.

Okwaho and Tyonajanegen had a son, a very healthy son. Given the direction and the blessing they had received, the elders named the boy Kariwase, "a new way of doing things." Onto his shoulders would fall the fate of the tribe to meet the future, but the future was already making its way towards him.

And this was in the Winter of 1624, very near where the city of Perryburg is today.

By the time he was fourteen, and so was a man, people would begin to arrive who did not belong to the tribe or any of its confederates. These people knew nothing of the old ways, understood none of their words, and seemed to disregard much of the wisdom of the earth.

It would be at the Council in the Longhouse the next winter that young Kariwase would sit quietly among the men, listening to their concerns, their fears, their plans in relation to these strangers in their midst. He would remain silent as the youngest of men in the tribal council. While he kept his mouth closed, his ears were open, and his mind was alive. The Council decided to follow a wait-and-see path, but he was actively thinking about options.

In his own life there was no wait-and-see path. He was wed to Kahsennenhawe who had caught his eye and heart. They pledged their common way forward before the tribe, the same community that would welcome their daughter Katsitsienhawi.

While he kept his silence in the Council, his mind constantly thought of what would be best for his family and the community.

Three winters would pass until Kariwase would finally speak in the Council. In that time more of the outsiders had found the tribe's land. Some of them would respect those who were already there, but others would treat them like savages. Kariwase's quietly and slowly said, "You know, when we hunt, we do not treat all those animals we hunt the same for, if we did, we would bring home nothing. And we do not plant all our crops in the same way for, if we did, we would have no foodstuffs for the long winters. If we don't get to know these people, for they are people just as much as we are people, like we have come to know our animals and our plants, we will not know how to wisely and safely relate to them.

And, if we treat all the outsiders the same, we then become no better than some of them are."

He then fell silent as did the others in the circle. Finally, the elder spoke. "What young Kariwase has said touches my spirit, but I do not know if it as truth or foolishness. Are these strange folk people like us, or some dark manifestation come to test us? If I were not wary, I would not be wise."

A great discussion followed, each one in the Council speaking while he held the pipe. In the end, despite Kariwase's plea, the tribe chose the way of wary distancing. They would not relate to the outsiders more than necessary, build their defenses, protect their lands, and, if needed, forcibly repel any who transgressed against the tribe's ways.

Kariwase's heart was heavy. He felt strongly that standing apart would allow the outsiders to treat them as "others," not as brothers.

When Spring came with its melting ice and greening buds, Kariwase would gather his household and bid his community farewell.

As Kariwase, Kahsennenhawe, and Katsitsienhawi prepared to leave, Kahsennenhawe's mother handed her a bundle wrapped in deer skin. "Open this when you reach you new home, and know you are always rooted in this place of your birth."

With many tears, the community unsealed the bonds of connections, and the three stood apart and then disappeared into the woods.

At their new place of dwelling, not that far from the Longhouse, but out of sight or hearing of it, while Kariwase set up their camp and Katsitsienhawi played along the edge of the stream whose winter's ice was beginning to melt, Kahsennenhawe opened the bundle her mother had given her. Inside were five cedar seedlings, giving off the smell she associated with ceremonial fires, warm summer nights, and home. The bundle also contained a smaller bundle which, when untied, disclosed earth she knew was from the garden at the Longhouse.

Facing the low sun on the southern horizon, she chose a place where the warming sun could nurture these gifts of connection. Spacing them apart, but not too far apart, she dug five holes. Into each hole she placed some of the dirt and then a seedling, pausing over each newcomer to the forest to bless it: "May life fill you and may you become the start of a new forest." Then, she sealed the ground around the holes and called to Katsitsienhawi, "Dear daughter, bring me some water."

Katsitsienhawi found an old gourd scoop and made five trips from the stream to where her mother knelt by five small trees. Each time, her mother thanked her and poured the water at the base of a newly planted seedling. Later in her life, when she would see those five trees, standing out in the otherwise barren whiteness of winter, she would remember that day when they made a new home.

SPRING

The passage from Massachusetts, over the Berkshires and into the valley of the Hudson was not easy. By 1724, many had already made the journey, sending back, as possible, advice and warnings for those who might travel the same way.

Ethan Wainwright, his wife Sarah, and their three children (William, Constance, and Margaret) set out in late March from the valley of the Great River, the Cannitticutt, because earlier travelers had said the passage over the mountains was better when the ground was still frozen. Waiting until the thaw had passed would mean battling mud and the many insects that Spring would bring.

Ethan was descended from some of the early stock in Massachusetts, but his branch of the family had broken away because of the required adherence to overly strict interpretations of religious doctrine and personal practice. In other words, they didn't like to be told by others how to live their lives. About 1680, his great grandfather, also named Ethan, had taken his family west into the wilderness along the Great River.

However, by 1724, a new orthodoxy was growing along the river, a sentiment of strict Calvinism which would find its fulfillment in the Rev. Jonathan Edwards and his vision of sinners hanging by a spider's thread over the fires of hell. Ethan was hellbent on avoiding anyone who talked of hell and especially those who wanted to make his life hell on earth for the way his family lived.

Not that his family were heathen. Far from it. But instead of being God-fearing people, they were God-loving people. They viewed the world as a place of possibility, other people as equals, and any afterlife as a home of fulfillment.

"If one approaches life with love," Ethan would often proclaim to his family as they avoided Sunday attendance at worship, "then whatever shall come will be a fulfillment of that love. If one sees life with fear, then whatever shall come will be a fulfillment of that fear. I, for one, choose love."

Such independent thinking, especially in the realm of religion, was increasingly unwelcome, punished even. Before his family could be formally shunned, expelled, or imprisoned, Ethan spent the winter of 1724 in conversation and then in planning.

"Like the Israelites in Egypt," Sarah had announced, "we shall choose the trials and tribulations of the great unknown rather than submit to faith that is not ours."

252

Did I mention this was a feisty household?

Up the Agawam River (we call it the Westfield River today), they journeyed by day and camped by night, their horses dragging the mighty sledges with their belongings. The higher they went, the easier it went, with great patches of ice on the river as smooth as glass. With small, careful steps, but without impediment, they quickly attained the top of the Berkshires with its flattened, swampy land. Here, too, the continuing chill of winter gave them footing against the many places that would otherwise have been mud and mire.

It was on the 12th day of April that they saw something they had been seeking. Until that day, all the slowly thawing winter's runoff was drawn behind them, downstream if only slightly, back toward where they had come. But, just before sunset, Margaret called them all over to the bank of the small creek whose path they were following (a path which bore the marks of prior settlers heading west).

"Look," Margaret called. "Look!"

There, under the thinning cover of ice, the bubbles of the moving water were now advancing ahead of them, flowing in a different direction. The Hudson Valley now lay ahead.

The way down, out of the mountains, was not as easy as the way up had been. The sun was higher in the sky and its warmth had begun the thaw. Smooth ice was replaced with slick mud. Travel beside the streams now took the place of travel on the streams. There were thickets and side-streams to navigate.

However, going downhill towards one's dream always seems easier than going uphill into the unknown.

Soon they could join the "road" which had been taken by others, a more regular path. What had started as a deer run, then become a

253

trail used by the natives, was now worn a little more into the ruts of both sledges and wheels.

On May 15, the mighty Hudson sat before them, an impasse to further travel. However, they had hardly stopped along its banks before they heard a lively "Yoleee," and a boatsman pulled alongside them. His was a strange craft, large enough for all of them and their horses, flat-bottomed to reach near the shore.

Through much dickering, and much misunderstood English and Dutch, the passage across the river was secured. It was the first time the Wainwright household had needed any money on their journey.

Landing on the western shore of the river, the boatman, as much as with gestures as with words, pointed them westward. After a thorough pantomime, Ethan understood that they would need to follow the hard path up the escarpment to reach the highlands. There another river would be found. Otherwise, the water route meant portages around waterfalls and rapids.

Once they had gathered all their belongings again, and harnessed the horses, they started the slow, steady, steep climb that had been predicted. Off in the distance, on the eastern shore of the river, they heard the yell, "Yoleee," and looking back across they saw their boatman approach another group of settlers who had found the barrier of the Hudson.

It would take two days to reach the higher plain where the great Oneida drained down toward the Hudson. Here the Oneida was placid, not filled with falls and rapids. Ethan remembered seeing paintings of ancient times, with tree-lined and peaceful rivers passing through idyllic landscapes. Here was such a river. It felt prophetic.

As with the Hudson, soon they encountered several boatmen who offered to take the family westward. They promised the river was deep enough ("Eeet eees Printemps, no?"). Choosing the offer made by Antoine, they loaded themselves on his flatboat. Their deal with him cost less because it had been agreed that least Ethan, and probably William, would aid in the poling of the boat upstream. In the end, everyone helped, which Antoine said shortened their journey by several days.

The scenery they passed amazed them. Once in a long while a settlement would be seen, perhaps European, perhaps First Nation. There seemed little difference between the appearance of any of them. Crude dwellings, smoke rising, some livestock corralled, small plots of land cultivated.

At the Palatine settlement just below the little falls of the Oneida, Antoine halted the boat and all of them began the short but steep portage. On the other side of the falls, a second boat similar to the first, was waiting. Antoine, ever the good businessman, made sure he kept his clients for the whole journey.

At long last, just about June 1, Antoine announced "C'est tout" and pointed to the small settlement by the river, where several creeks fed the river. The family looked at the rag-tag assortment of buildings and tents with both disappointment and excitement. It looked nothing like what they had left, and it looked nothing like what they had dreamt.

So far, no steeples to mar the skyline. No proclamations of "we know better." That initial optimism was soon squelched when the family discovered the social contract under which the community operated. "Some," know better than "others." Who the "some" were and therefore who the "others" were depended upon whom you were talking with.

It took less than a week for Ethan to tell his family that they were moving on. Heading out, they first came to the log cabin of Tinsdale, who welcomed them without a word of either qualification or censure. He introduced them to his few, scattered neighbors and to a large group of First Nations people who shared his area. There was respect among them all, which Sarah and Ethan could feel more than hear.

Tinsdale told the family to talk with a tribal leader, "well, actually a tribal outcast. Most of the first peoples have been either displaced, controlled, or killed, but this one's family long ago chose a different path." Tinsdale took Ethan and his family to meet Kariwase.

The handsome, middle-aged man they met had all the facial features of other native people they had seen, but his English was very good and his dress a mix of native and settler. He welcomed them to a table in his cabin.

"I see you are surprised to see me in a cabin, not a Longhouse. Long ago, my great, great, grandfather left the larger tribe. He believed that any path to the future should include change, change for both those who had been here and for those who would come.

"Beginning with his small family, he started a new group of my people, people who would invite the outsiders into our world even as we invited ourselves into theirs. We have lived here, in peace and plenty for nearly one hundred years. Many moons, many seasons, have passed, and with them have come changes. By being part of the change, we can make choices about what we want. We are not victims of change."

"Your ancestor was a wise person," Sarah said. "We have come from the east to find a place where we can live free from the demands of others."

"Then, welcome my daughter. I am called Kariwase, but some of the newcomers call me Karl."

"What would you like us to call you?" Ethan asked.

With a smile on his lips, Kariwase answered, "Kariwase."

"So it shall be." Ethan turned to his family, and looking at his children he said, "This is our friend, Kariwase. Always speak his name with respect." The children took turns practicing his name.

"You have come in the spring, a time in which we plant what will grow and flower," said Kariwase once he was satisfied with the children's pronunciation of his name. "Now, you must plant your family among us."

"What will that cost?" Ethan inquired.

"We do not speak of owning this land. You have met old Tinsdale, he who once bought land from us. We long ago paid him back for that, for no one can own this land other than by their respectful use of it."

"Then," began Ethan.

"I will take you to a place nearby where you may make your home. You may use the trees for a house, but no more than needed. You may clear the land for planting, but no more than needed. You may hunt and fish, but no more than needed. As long as you respect the earth and your neighbors, there will be no further demand on you."

Ethan and Sarah sat silently. They had been worried for months about how they could afford a new home, a place for the children to grow and thrive, a community that would welcome their beliefs more than impose them. Ethan looked over at Sarah and saw that she was crying. Any time that Sarah was crying, Ethan would soon follow.

"Your tears?" Kariwase asked.

Once composed, Sarah spoke for them all. "I cry for happiness. It has been a long journey. I have often feared for my husband and my children. Now all those fears pour out of me. I am ashamed to have been so emotional in front of you."

"Here," Kariwase, "tears are as welcomed as smiles, hugs as welcomed as handshakes."

Ethan and Sarah knew they had come home. The long spring of their journey was over. Now was the time to plant their hopes and dreams in the fertile soil of possibility, where, watered by the rains of communal care and nurture by the sunlight of friendship, they might see their children become good adults and their own later years blessed.

SUMMER

In the summer of 1824, most of the region around Perryburg was agog about the new canal. Beginning in 1817, this river of commerce would make the long, arduous journeys of a century before into smooth, predictable travel. Goods, people, livestock, and more, would, upon the canal's completion, link the Atlantic Ocean with the Great Lakes.

This was a modern miracle, a triumph of engineering. The 363-mile route would need to rise 565 vertical feet, pass by several obstacles of navigation and create a channel almost 200 miles long where no rivers naturally flowed. Reservoirs to supply water to the upland segments needed to be built. Bridges, tunnels, towpaths, and more needed to be constructed.

To accomplish this astounding task, surveyors and engineers of all kinds were needed. The initial route work, back in 1817-1818 had been the surveyors' time. Then came the era of the civil engineers who would take wisdom dating back to ancient China for the shape of the canal, to ancient Rome for the design of aqueducts and feeds, and to DaVinci to build locks and bridges.

It was toward the end of this process that Jebediah Smith arrived in Perryburg, recruited to be a construction engineer in the final phases of the construction. He had previously worked in Pawtucket, Rhode Island, on the power canal projects there on the Blackstone River.

Jebediah was a tall, upright man, with a pale complexion. He was also a loner, who found himself his own best company. He loved his work because much of it could be carried on alone. Just give him the maps and charts of the surveyors, the drawings of the marine architects, and the preliminary plans of the design engineers, and he would gladly and easily transform concept into working reality.

He found the Perryburg of 1824 a place he could do without. Its commercial and residential growth, coupled with its civic vision for a greater future, had no appeal. Yes, his work would take him right through the heart of the growing community, be he wanted no part of it.

That distaste for society and his own desire for solitude led him out, away from town. Especially as summer commenced its season of warmth and with it its season of stench, while he might be required to work in those conditions, in his personal hours he wanted something other, something better.

Most the canal workers were more drawn to company and to socializing. Hard work in the pre-mechanized era during the day was matched with exuberance of "letting off steam" in the evenings. Night was for sleeping it off before beginning again. This cycle was what had allowed the canal to be nearly ready by 1824, but it was also a cycle foreign, to the point of abhorrence, to Jebediah.

His ideal day began at sunrise, with fresh air to breathe and the quiet of nature. It progressed through hours of hard work strictly applying the principles of construction to the plans. It ended with a return to time among the trees, the evening song of birds, and the last glints of a day well spent.

He knew he could not find this in Perryburg. But could he find it near enough to Perryburg that an hour's ride each morning and another hour's ride each evening could separate him from all he did not desire?

Jebediah was a patient man. Like many an engineer, he did not make hasty decisions. Boarding in Perryburg to begin with, he spent his days at work but devoted his evenings to listening, listening to the stories people told about Perryburg and about the area.

After a month he had heard enough. The folk wisdom, or what passed as wisdom among the folk in town, was that they were all better off than the people who lived out by Tinsdale's and Wainright's. "Those people" were eccentric, not given to conviviality, not likely to be found in church, more sober, less fun. He figured he had found his people.

On the following Sunday, which would have been July 4th, while all the hoopla in town was winding up to its drunken evening conclusion (despite all the efforts of the clergy to entice piety in the morning that might infect the rest of the day [their terribly extended sermons did little to accomplish this]), Jebediah rode out toward the side of town he had heard mentioned.

After about 45 minutes on the relatively well-maintained road, he saw a signpost by a lane: "Wainright." Turning down the rutted, rural path, he eventually came to modest but well-kept farm, with fields judiciously tilled from forest. Yes, "modest" was the word that came to mind first, but then "prosperous" nudged it way into Jebediah's thoughts.

Here was a farm whose appearance said simplicity, but its care said sufficiency. There was a pride evident in each small detail, but no detail was overdone seeking to impress anyone.

Tying his horse to the front rail, he walked toward the house. Before he could reach the porch, a lone figure emerged. He was tall, taller than Jebediah. He was also darker and with more pronounced features. He was smiling, beaming a welcome that was uncommon in most solitary homesteads that Jebediah had encountered.

"Welcome," the tall one said. "If you are here, you must have sought us out. Again, welcome."

"Thank you, sir. I am Jebediah." Jebediah responded. "I don't know if I sought you out as much as sought out a place like this."

Pointing to one of the chairs on the porch, Andrew Wainwright said, "I'm Andrew. Please, let's sit a spell and get to know each other."

As he sat on the porch and surveyed the scene, talking with Andrew, Jebediah felt a calm he had not known since he had come to Perryburg. He also felt less like a loner, here on a porch with one other person, than he had ever felt in that busy, crowded, noisy, smelly town.

"So, Jebediah, tell me about yourself."

The invitation seemed so genuine, and his host seemed so caring, Jebediah surprised himself by pouring out his whole story.

"I never knew my parents," he began. "My father, I am told, was a merchant in Rhode Island, but not a very successful one. In the summer of 1801, he took sick (you know that was the summer when so many died of the paralytic fever). My poor mother, all alone then, felt the first stirrings of me inside her just after my father died, a bittersweet reminder of their love.

"Without his feeble but real income, my mother, I am told, was destitute. She relied on the kindness or the sympathy or the charity of the community, but that soon was worn out because apparently she was one of those for whom adversity wore thin quickly. She died in childbirth, and I am the only remnant of her life and her love.

261

"There was some kind of antipathy towards either my father or my mother or both and their names would never be spoken of again. Rhode Island had many people whose past or present left them less than mentionable.

"I, as a baby, was taken to an orphanage in Providence and I was named Smith. I have no idea what my real family name was. Life as an orphan was never pleasant but, luckily, it was never unkind. The Baptist were deeply into Christian charity.

"As a child, I quickly took to learning and the matron of the orphanage identified me as a 'shining light in the hellhole of darkness.' With her help, I mastered the usual subjects and was admitted to Brown University of Rhode Island and the Providence Plantations.

"Also, as a child in the circumstances of my youth, I learned to keep my own counsel and not seek love from others. I also, quietly, rejected the emphasis on sin and judgement so prevalent in the beliefs of my benefactors. This set me apart from most others, and it is still a core I do not share. I am surprised I speak of it now. You have brought a strange feeling over me, inviting me here to sit and share my life.

"But, back to my time at Brown. There I excelled in mathematics and the fundamentals of engineering. Brown was among the first of the colleges to see engineering as worthy of receiving a degree. After graduation, I was an assistant to the State Surveyor of Rhode Island, assigned to helping with the construction and maintenance of the new power canals in Pawtucket.

"When I heard of the plans of the great canal across New York, I was just beginning my studies. Every year I would hear more and more about the wild dream of Governor Clinton to build a waterway up and over his state. I would visit the library with hopes of seeing articles about the progress of the canal.

"When, at last, I had both the education and the experience to be worthy of participation in that dream, I sent a letter to the Governor, offering my services. I waited many weeks for a reply. At last, it came and I was invited to join the engineering staff assigned to the portion of work remaining in the area around Perryburg.

"I had not realized the great peril under which the canal was being constructed. Most of those who had initially designed and engineered the works had long since been tempted by either a return to real civilization or the promises of the west. When I arrived at Perryburg, I found a staff so depleted and so demoralized that progress seemed almost impossible.

"I poured myself into the work as much for the satisfaction of a job well done as for a way to avoid idle hours in a place that brought me no peace and comfort.

"I came out here today seeking a place to reside, a place where I might find a proper balance of work and renewal, of construction and nature. Your welcome has begun to restore my spirit. But, enough about me. Tell me about yourself, Andrew."

Just then, from inside the modest house, a small din arose, the sound of two children in some kind of tussle. That was followed by a strong, female voice, "All right, you two, now git outside and find out what your father is jabbering about, and with whom."

The door of the house swung abruptly open and two children, a girl and a younger boy, ran onto the porch. Standing at the doorway was a beautiful woman of moderate height, long black hair, and piercing eyes.

Jebediah stood to greet the newcomers.

"Mr. Smith, may I present my wife, Amanda," Jebediah gave a courteous bow as Amanda did the same.

"And my children, Prudence and Andrew the third." The children stopped their activity, stood before their visitor with calm and deference.

"Mister Smith, it is my pleasure to make your acquaintance," offered Prudence, who appeared to be about eleven years old. Andrew the younger simply bowed slightly and offered his hand. He appeared to be about seven.

Jebediah was immediately impressed by a family who had raised their children with such graces.

"My family has heard my story too many times, I am afraid," offered Andrew.

"No, Daddy, please, we love to hear it," pled Andrew the younger.

Prudence looked at her father and Jebediah could see Andrew soften as she said, "Please!"

"If you insist. Come, sit, listen, and don't interrupt."

"I'll bring us all some tea," Amanda offered.

"Mine with sugar and cream," Prudence requested.

"Yours will be with water, sugar, lemon, and no tea," Amanda responded.

"Aw!"

Andrew shot his children a look and Andrew the younger finally agreed, "Oh, OK."

"Actually," said Jebediah, "I think I would prefer that to tea myself," immediately making two young friends in the household,

When the lemonade had been prepared and served, Andrew began, reciting a story now so familiar to the family.

"About a century ago, my great great grandfather Ethan and his wife Sarah and their family came to this land. They had come from Massachusetts, the western part of the Commonwealth. The natives who lived here welcomed him and offered him a place to live and farm. They also set conditions on his time and place here. He eagerly accepted their terms.

"About half a mile west of here, in a small clearing, you will find the simple log cabin he erected, in the midst of the several small clearings he created. There they found sufficiency but never excess.

"In time, their son William grew to be a man, and he was my great grandfather. In his young adulthood he was much desired by the young ladies, especially those who lived in town, for he seemed exotic, living out here in what was considered native land.

"Many times, when he would take the wagon into town for supplies or to sell a few things the family had made, he would be approached by the bolder of the young women with invitations of all sorts, all very proper but all also a little flirtatious. The more blatant they were, the less interested was he.

"It became so annoying to him that he soon insisted that one of his sisters, Connie or Meg, accompany him. This ploy worked well for him, but then his sisters became objects of attention from the young men in town.

"When Connie began to look forward to the trips to town for this very reason, Wiiliam decided to leave the town to his sisters, and he retreated back to the original homestead. One day, out in his vegetable field, he was interrupted by a woman's voice, asking if she might have a drink of water from his bucket by the well pump. He did not look up and simply answered 'But course, I did not make the water, it belongs to the earth.' All he heard was 'thank you' and then a small splash.

"When he finished the row he was hoeing, he looked up, first to the sky's unclouded blue and then to a woman standing by the pump. Her face was partly shaded by leaves of the maple that stood beside the well, but what he could see took his breath away."

"This is the part we really like," Prudence proclaimed.

"Yes, I know. Now, let me tell the story. William looked at the woman who had the most beautiful skin he had ever seen, a tawny color akin to the core of a beechnut tree. Her eyes, slightly slanted, were framed by her dark, braided hair. He must have stared a moment too long because the woman said, 'I am sorry if I startled you. Thank you for the water. I am Wynnogene. My family lives about two hours from here, away from the white settlement. It was a hot, thirsty walk.'

"Let me condense the story a bit."

"Awww," was Prudence's response.

"Wynnogene caught William's eye, and William caught Wynnogene's eye, and they were both caught in love. By the next summer, William and Wynnogene were married, not by any preacher from town, but by the sachem of her tribe and Ethan, both of whom agreed that the Sacred Maker of all did not belong to, nor really reside in any church.

"The following summer, my grandfather was born, the first of what would become ten children, evenly divided between girls and boys. The children were all a wonderful mix of the two families, in looks as well as temperament. By the summer when the third child, a girl, arrived, grandfather bade his parents farewell from the original homestead and built this house, cleared these lands, called this home.

"But there is sadness in this story. Grandfather William and Grandmother Wynnogene were not welcome in the town, even as

266

they had little need or desire for its blessing. However, they had not expected the rejection they experienced from some of the native peoples. For a time, they were very much alone, supported only by their families. Slowly, a small circle of homesteads of acceptance and mutual support grew in this area. By the time my father was born, here in this house, the last of the children, our family was never alone.

"I, the last, remained in this house with my parents as their days on this earth grew short. I watched as my oldest brothers went south to the war, never to return. I watched as people who had never been in the country before acted like they knew more than I did about life and farming and God.

"When, following my father's death by only a month, my mother died, I was left with this place of peace and contentment. The old cabin in the woods, where my parents had happily lived out their last years away from the crowded reality of this house, is now my shrine to them. They are buried out there, but the house is always kept at the ready …"

At this point Amanda added, "so there is always a welcome should their spirits need a place to rest. And maybe kindred spirits as well."

"Sir," Andrew concluded, "I have known you for only a couple of hours, not as long as it takes for the sun to leave this porch for the cool shadow of evening, but I trust my feelings. If you are in need of lodging, and you are not encumbered by any notions of malevolence associated with the dearly departed, I, … er we offer you the little cabin as your home for as long as you wish to stay there."

And that was how Jebediah came to be in that cabin, his home in the summer of 1824. After his work on the canal each day, in the long evenings he would work to reclaim the old fields, repair the old fences, and even dream about some improvements to the old house. Out there, all alone, he felt less lonely than he ever had in the growing city. He felt like he had been gifted a heritage not of his lineage nor of his making but of his choosing and wise gifting of others.

That was the summer he finally came home.

Autumn

It was in the autumn of 1825 that the Great Canal was opened, and with it the opening of the west. As much as some people came to Perryburg, many times more simply passed through in search of their dreams.

Year after year they would come, first by canal boat, then by railway, to or through Perryburg. For some it was a journey of only a few miles along the river and canal. For others, it was from New York City, Boston, Portland, Providence, Philadelphia, Baltimore.

The longer journeys, however, were not labelled with such names. More likely were Dublin, or Killarney, or Belfast; Brandenburg, or Munich, or Wien; Palermo, or Napoli, or Milano.

One such journey started south of Napoli in early 1924. Pietro Domiano, known as Pepe, was a strange little man. The last of thirteen children to Angelo and Angelica (DeStefano) Domiano, he was short, only about five feet tall. He was strong, even from his time in the womb. Angelica swore he came out boxing.

What Pepe had in strength he had an equal measure of heart. He was always the one of the children who would rush to console one of the other children. When they played in the town square, he always tried to include the poor children who were lame, or otherwise handicapped.

Strength and heart were not, however, matched by intellect. Pepe was a slow learner. As each year went by, he saw his class moving ahead while he was kept behind. His slight stature meant he did not look outsized in the lower grades, but his strength would sometimes betray him.

At long last, his parents took him out of school and apprenticed him to a stone mason. Being an apprentice, the most menial and manual tasks fell to him. It seemed that most attempts to introduce him to the craft, much less the science, of the work were futile. Ask him to make a mortar of the right consistency or to tuckpoint the stones in an even manner and he would fail; ask him to dig the foundation or carry the stones and he excelled.

In October 1916, his father died in the war, a casualty to the greed of the world and the animosity between countries. His mother, still trying to keep house and home and family together, asked Pepe to contribute as he could. His earnings were small, the pittance usually given to manual laborers. There was no promise, much less a possibility, that he would ever advance from being a lowly apprentice into the craft.

In November 1921, his mother received a letter from her brother, Paolo, who had emigrated to the United States. It was full of new world bravado, with stories of New York, gangs, wealth beyond the wildest imagination of any southern Italian, and a money order for twenty United States dollars. Twenty dollars. Over 200 lira! A season of wealth.

She immediately wrote back, with many, many "Grazie, molto Grazie," and a simple inquiry about how anyone could make that much money. About three months later an answer came. "Work on the railroads."

With that response, Angelica began to make plans. All of her children were married, and all of them, as they could, were helping her out. Except for Pepe. None of her children wanted to leave her, leave Italy.

So, it was decided that Pietro Domiano would emigrate to the United States. He would sail from Napoli on the cheapest boat they could find, sailing to New York, where Uncle Paolo would meet him and introduce him around.

 Saving up the money for passage, even steerage passage, took time. Late summer in 1924, Pepe would wave goodbye to his Momma at the Ferrovia Benevento (the nearest station to their home) and, with tears in both their eyes, he boarded the train for Napoli. In that big, dirty, rough city, he had to more than once fight off some who would waylay this strange little man with the country accent. With only a few scars for his efforts, he found the ship on which he was to sail.

One look at the ship made him think about turning back. More rust than metal, from sometime in the prior century, it looked very unlikely to reach any new world. However, Momma had saved so hard, sacrificed so much for him, how could he turn back. He walked up the gangway ready to present his ticket when a gruff sailor asked him, "Perché ti trovi lì? Andare al lavoro!" Thinking that part of the deal of his ticket was work on the boat, Pepe set down his parcels and followed the man.

By the time Pepe had landed in New York, he was one of the favorites of the crew. They loved the little man with the strange accent who never took breaks, could do any hard work, and never complained. It was only on the last night, when Pepe had the nerve to ask the Captain what he should do with his ticket that his misconception was discovered. The Captain, with a roaring laugh, said, "Pepe, my boy, if could have a whole crew like you, I would be happy. But, you were to be a passenger on my ship. Here, let me take your ticket, and give you this."

Into Pepe's hand the Captain placed some funny money, all green with strange writing. "This is more than you paid for your ticket."

In broken English, some of what he had learned on the voyage, Pepe said, "I no-a pay for ticket."

"Oh," the Captain replied with raised eyebrows, now wondering if he was participating in some illegal international labor scheme.

"Momma Mia, she-a pay."

The Captain lit up with a smile and said, "Pepe, never forget your wonderful mother."

"No-a, I never-a forgetta."

At Ellis Island, he was ushered through the line of workers coming from the ship, a much easier path to immigration. Those in that line came with people who would vouch for them. Once ashore, he went to the address his mother had given him for Paolo. There he saw a black wreath on the door. Inside he found many people who spoke Italian, and they understood him even with his dialect. "He speaks just like Paolo," one said. At the mention of the name "Paolo," a women began sobbing.

Maria. Maria DeStefano, Paolo's widow. The kind soul that he was, Pepe sat down and sobbed with her. They held each other close for a long time. Finally, she told Pepe about Paolo's death, death at the hands of people from Sicilia. "Get away from this place, Pepe, get far away. I help you." Pepe understood only some of this. He totally understood her grief.

Two days later, a friend of Maria, Tomas, started walking north with Pepe, up the great canyons of New York. While Tomas kept his eyes on the pavement, and the cars, and the wagons, and the trolleys, Pepe could not help but look up. He had never seen anything like it. He had never heard anything so noisy. He had never smelled anything so like home and so foreign all in one breath.

At long last they arrived at a building bigger and grander than anything he had ever seen. Walking inside, on marble flooring, he passed through a room that was almost bigger than his whole town and then into another room even bigger, a room with a ceiling that looked like the night sky.

Here was a sea of humanity, rushing every which way. In the middle of the room sat a little house built with many sides, adorned on top with a clock. Along one wall it looked like this was a bank with many teller windows. At the ends of the room, marble staircases rose to great balconies while under the balconies arched tunnels led elsewhere, all labelled in English. The far wall was filled with many sliding doors with large numbers and great signboards to their sides.

"Wait here," Tomas said. And then he remembered and said "Aspetta qui."

Pepe waited. And waited. Finally, Tomas came back and said "rapido." The two of them then raced across the mighty concourse of Grand Central Terminal in search of Track 16. The sign by the door read, #39, North Shore Limited, and then a list of station names. All of them looked foreign to Pepe except two: Rome and Syracuse.

"Here," Tomas said, "rapido," pointing down the incline toward a waiting train while giving Pepe a paper ticket. Pepe gave Tomas a big hug, but Tomas interrupted him "rapido."

Pepe looked in the last car on the train, but it looked too fancy for him. Then another, too fancy. Then a ristorante car. "No." As he was looking into another car to see if he thought it was for him, a man in a uniform pushed past him, stood out on the platform, raised his hand, shouted (almost in Pepe's ear) "All Aboard," and almost shoved Pepe on board. The man pointed into the car and then to an empty seat. "Grazie," was all Pepe could say. The uniformed man looked at Pepe and smiled, then shook his head.

Pepe settled in a very comfortable seat, one he was sure was not for a person like he, Pepe Domiano, far from home, without his welcome in New York, now headed … headed where? However, when another man in a uniform pointed to his ticket, took it, punched it, and gave a small salute, no one tried to evict him. "Syracuse?" was all he said.

"No, No-a, No Siracusa!" Pepe knew he did not want to go to Sicily, especially after what had happened to Paolo.

"OK," the uniformed man said, "how about Rome, then?"

"No, No-a Roma!" Pepe was equally adamant about Rome. No one in his hometown trusted anyone or anything having to do with Rome.

"Ah, Perryburg?"

Now Pepe had never heard of Perryburg, which meant he had never heard anything bad about Perryburg. "Si, Si, Perryaburga."

The man wrote on another small tab of paper and stuck the tab into a slot in the luggage rack above Pepe. Pepe looked at it and it read "63," whatever that meant.

The train was moving faster now, smoother than any train he had ever ridden. They were in a tunnel, a long tunnel, but he could not smell any smoke from the locomotive. Then, suddenly, they burst out into the sunlight, and rose up onto a great causeway of steel. Here he was even with the third story of buildings, buildings with people inside, many people darker than the Sicilians. They crossed busy streets, made a stop at a place with the number 125. Everywhere buildings. Then over a small river and turning to follow the small river, the train twisted and turned until it made a big turn to the right and there, right in front of Pepe, was a river bigger than any he had ever seen. On the other shore, about a mile away, was a great wall of rock. Pepe was in awe. He glued his face to the window and looked, and looked.

At the next stop he felt the small shudder of a new engine being added, and he could see a whole yard of smoking locomotives plus a few, small black ones with no smoke. Then, with a slight lurch, his train started again, with the river outside his window. This continued for several hours until the train slowly crossed the river and entered a great station. By then, Pepe was hungry, and thankful Tomas had given him a bag with salami and cheese and an orange.

Soon his train was climbing a great hill, at the top of which they crossed a smaller river, and after a station stop they began to ride alongside that river. The sun was setting in the west when a different man in uniform took his little tab of paper with the "63" on it and said "Perryburg, five minutes."

"Grazie," was all Pepe could say, but he was startled when the uniformed man replied "Prego." It suddenly felt like home.

When he detrained in Perryburg he could see it was a very large station. He followed the crowd that took a stairway down, into a passenger subway under the railroad tracks, that led to a grand staircase up. At the top of that staircase was a lobby of glass doors. The crowd flowed through the swinging glass doors, and Pepe followed, but suddenly he just stopped.

He saw the interior of Perryburg Union Station, with its great marble pillars, its gold ceiling, its curved wooden benches. Except for the station in New York, this was the most magnificent space he had ever been in, even grander than a cathedral.

As he stood there stunned, something caught his ear – Italiano! But with a strange accent. But the words just the same as his. He went toward the group and said "Scusi."

"Paisano," an older man greeted him, with practically no accent.

Soon they were exchanging details of their lives. He had come from a town not more than eight kilometers from Pepe's. "Please, you come to my home for dinner. My family will welcome our language spoken properly."

And so, Pepe Domiano found dinner friends, housing, community, and even a job. The Italian partisans of Perryburg looked out for each other. "Look," Carlo said, "on Sunday you will make Mass at St. Anthony's and then on Monday, you will go with me down to the railroad and I tell them you are a good worker and they will hire you, on my say-so. Capiche?"

"Si, Si, Grazie"

November 3, 1924, would be Pepe's official sign-on day. He would work for the railroad for the next 50 years. He would always be a laborer, doing the hard and dirty work. He never sought nor was offered any promotion. However, because of the strong unions and various pieces of legislation protecting railroad workers and their retirement, he became better and better off.

He never married nor had any children. Living within the Italian community of Perryburg, his expenses were limited. But, he could send home what was a small amount in Perryburg but a godsend in the old country. After about twenty years, he sent for his Momma, the one who had sacrificed for him. Before she arrived, he bought a simple two-bedroom brick house on a quiet side street in an Italian neighborhood that had a corner store, a meat market, a coffee house, and more.

The yards of his house were his pride and joy. He turned them into great gardens, filled with seasonal and perennial flowers and shrubs. Until her last year, on a day with even a little warmth, Momma would sit out in the garden. When Pepe would come near, she would simply say, "Mio carissimo ragazzo, sei così gentile con tua madre," and he would simply look in her eyes and say, "No-a, Grazie a te."

About a year after his mother had died Pepe was working one day out on the tracks outside Perryburg when one of the bosses came up to him. "Pepe, Bill would like to talk with you."

Pepe knew Bill well. He was a Civil Engineer from the office in Union Station. Sometimes, on very hot days, Bill would bring Pepe and other members of the track gang a big bottle of cold water. In the winter, when the switches needed to be dug out from snow, Bill always made sure that he gave Pepe some of the work, always at double time.

"Signore Bill," Pepe said when he approached the man.

"Pepe, how are you today?" They exchanged pleasantries. Then Bill asked, "Would you like some extra work on the weekend?"

"Si, yes."

"I am helping a friend out by the Wainright Estates to build a home. I need a strong man to help me excavate for the foundation. Interested?"

Of course he was interested. He loved it out there, on the old farm, away from the city noise, with the trees and the meadows.

That Saturday morning, Bill picked Pepe up (Pepe never got a driver's license because he could not pass the written test. "It gives me a headache.") and then drove out to what everyone called the Wainwright Estates. It had been a century since any Wainwright had lived there. The old house had long since been razed for newer housing. However, the historical society had managed to save and preserve the older cabin, known as Smith's Retreat, named for the canal engineer who had lived there for so many years.

The spot they were heading for was across a field from Smith's Retreat. The disturbed earth of the proposed cellar hole stood where one could see the front of that old cabin. As Bill explained, one of the distant cousins of old Jebediah Smith had inherited this portion of the original land and now wished to build a replica of the old cabin. It would become her place of retreat from the world of Perryburg where she was the City Attorney for the city. Bill and Gladys had known Rosemary for decades and offered to help her achieve this dream of solitude.

Bill had begun the project but found the digging a long process. That day, Bill estimated that it would take three or four weekends to complete the work on the cellar hole. Almost immediately Pepe took off his shirt, stripping down to just an undershirt, grabbed his gloves and shovel, and went to work. Bill just watched in awe as this small, gentle man strongly attacked the earth filled with roots and rocks.

When the sun was setting on that Sunday, the earth had been hollowed, and it had been respected. No machinery, no noise, no fumes had fouled it. What had been taken out of the earth was distributed into a marshy area nearby that often bred mosquitoes in profusion. Gladys was already planting small shoots of myrtle in the newly moved soil.

Pepe was standing with Bill, and Bill said, "Pepe, I am amazed what you have done. Let me pay you for your work."

"No-a, Signore Bill. I do not need-a your money. These two days-a were like a vacation for me, outa here in the woods. But I hava one small aska."

"Yes, Pepe"

"Could-a your wife-a dig me up some little cedar trees I could-a plant in my-a yard?"

Bill readily agreed and went to help Gladys with this project. By the time they were all ready to return to the city, five little trees, about two feet tall, were all dug and bundled, along with ample supply of the soil they had always known.

On the ride back to the city, Pepe said, "I plant these-a trees for Momma Mia – my dear mother – they will make-a my garden complete and I always-a remember her."

Bill then told Pepe about the trees, the great great great grandchildren of trees that were there long before any white settlers. He told Pepe about how the historical society, doing digs in the area, had found traces of a dwelling in that area, a dwelling from hundreds of years before. "So," Bill continued, "you are taking with you a portion of the forest that is older than me, older than you, older than your mother, older than Perryburg." Pepe's eyes filled with tears.

Bill and Gladys helped Pepe carefully carry the trees into his back yard, and then Pepe hefted the bucket of dirt back there too. He pointed to where his mother had always sat and said, "I plant-a one a there."

Pepe retired after working fifty years at the railroad. He never received an award, he never got a promotion, he was never mentioned on a plaque. But, when death came for this simple, loving man, the calling hours, the Mass, and the wake were full, filled with other simple people who had received his love in so many ways.

And five big, strong trees graced his backyard.

Winter

Winter arrived in late 2023, coming on with a vengeance, more in spirit than in weather. A divided nation had chosen more division.

278

Many of the values of centuries in the land now called Perryburg seemed to be abandoned, or at least forgotten. Few, if any, recalled days when tribal elders would bless the earth in return for the earth's blessings. Few, if any, recalled days when differences between traditions and races were overcome with love and vision. Few, if any, recalled days when people would seek the quiet renewal of nature. Few, if any, recalled days when a person's character mattered most, when qualities of love and care mattered more than quickness of mind or power of deceit. Few, if any, recalled days when visible reminders of all that had been stood in stark contrast to desolation and destruction.

January 22, 2024 – the Winter's grasp on Perryburg was tight. The snow, not as deep as many years, was still deep enough. For the family of LuPway Doh, Karen refugees from persecution a world away in Asia, the hope was that 2024 would bring good things to their family, their community, and the city. That hope would be tested many times throughout the year.

The killing of a young teen, by the police, mid-year would seem to break the spirit of many people, not only among the Karen but also in many of Perryburg's long-term and more recent communities.

2024 proceeded like so many years. Winter tested the soul. Spring promised rebirth. Summer brought growth, only to be taken back by such losses in the Autumn. Now, in December, LuPway Doh stood with his family at the window of the small house he was able to buy. Home, after so long on the run, on the road, trying to make a home.

"But" he wondered, "with the changes of 2024, will we be welcome here in 2025? Will distrust of strangers, fear of changes, doubt about the future make others want to threaten us?"

As he stood by the window, looking out toward the distant, rolling hills, his gaze was attracted by a single bird, a single flit of bright red, like a glowing coal, landing in the dark green of the cedar trees in their backyard. In the midst of the seeming death of winter with the stark trees without leaves, his five trees, and especially the one in the center of his garden, promised something more, something better.

He called to his family, "Come here, see this."

When they had assembled, he told them, "To see signs of hope is always better than to find signs of despair. Today, I remind myself that I did not create that bird, but I can appreciate it and be inspired by it. I did not plant the trees, but they can be steadfast in my sight to encourage me. I am not the first one pass this way, but I can leave this world better than I found it."

Little did he realize how much history of the seasons of Perryburg he summed up. What will they create that will echo in 2124 in the never-ending cycling of seasons which is life?

Outside of Perryburg, through more than four hundred years, there is a small forest. Those are the trees that were here before Perryburg and will be here long after Perryburg is only a memory or a relic. And theirs are the more than 1600 seasons which have circled the sun, coming from untold seasons before and cycling into unimagined seasons ahead, seasons of this place, which, for now, is Perryburg.

13. MOHAWK STREET

Long before Perryburg was Perryburg, there had been a trail that led up from the river, up out of the valley, and off toward other native settlements. The First Nations' tales told of the paths of the deer, vast herds of them, who would travel from the low hills down to the river for the water, especially in time of drought when upland streams would dry up. The ancestors had been shown the paths of wildlife: some led to places to hide, some led to different types of food, some led to high places to survey the lowlands, some led to the water. The most evident ones led to water.

The First Nations followed those paths, slowly converting them to trails. Some of those trails led to the camps of other tribes, some led to the hunting grounds, some led to important natural features like rivers, some to trade with the slowly growing number of people from away. Many feet trod where once hooves left only little indents.

When the first settlers imposed themselves into the area they found these trails but at times were perplexed by them. Some made sense to the Europeans, but some did not make sense. In an attempt to bring their sense of order to this "new" world, they adopted some as their routes. Others were neglected into obscurity.

When the newcomers pointed to the river and said something which ended as if it were a question, the Indigenous would answer "Oneega" or "Ohneka," so the settlers called it the Oneika River. But their guttural German was softened by the English to give us the Oneida River we have today. Little did any of them know they were just being told it was water.

One of the first settlers to not just pass through but stop and stay where the Oneida River was fed by three substantial creeks was

Moses Backus. Establishing a store and a tavern and a very primitive inn, Backus soon encouraged a settlement, knowing steady business was much better than the sporadic fare of the travelers. Within a few years, the main non-river approach to his settlement was down the path from the low hillside to the river. As people would choose where to build, of course no one chose the swampy river side. For the sake of ease of travel, being along that growing path was beneficial.

It was just after the War of Independence that a surveying party arrived in town, full of chains and poles and sighting instruments. They came walking into the settlement down that path, measuring as they went. That the path was so straight by this time made their work easy.

As soon as word spread in the community that this band of surveyors was in town, many people gathered to greet them and quiz them. The big question was simple enough, "What are you doing here?"

"We have been sent by the governor to prepare a map for the Mohawk Turnpike."

"Mohawk Turnpike???"

Slowly the news came out. The governor had given a patent of the land and the rights of construction to a company from the Capital to build a turnpike from the Capital to other important settlements in the state. The new road would be cleared and surfaced by stone or logs, to the width of a standard wagon, with places for two to pass placed at convenient points. It was to be called the Mohawk Turnpike because a treaty had been made with the Mohawk tribe in exchange for rights across their lands for much of the route. It was one of the first examples of "naming rights."

The turnpike was partially built, especially the segment around Backus' settlement, and proved a great success. Where there was easy access to other modes of travel, such as navigable rivers or treeless, solid, level ground, the turnpike builders correctly reasoned that they would never earn their money back with so many options to avoid the tolls.

Mohawk Turnpike became the spine of the new community, still called Backus' Store. Just after the scares of the War of 1812, Colonel Marcellus Anthony Perry arrived on the scene, bringing with him a wife, six children, three servants, eight oxen, and a vast chest of wealth. In little more than two years, he had bought out the Backus family, erected a real Emporium, commissioned several buildings, and built the first impressive mansion, on but set well back from the Mohawk Turnpike.

In 1825, the whole region was transformed with the nearby arrival of the canal. The turnpike was deemed redundant, and its corporation dissolved, allowing the improvements to decline back into the earth. Colonel Perry quickly organized his own local improvement society to not only maintain but improve on the Turnpike, this time without tolls for the residents.

As a result of this change, Mohawk Turnpike became Mohawk Street. "No finer street can be seen in any of the great cities of Europe," Perry declared. In return for this vote of confidence in the future of the settlement, a citizens' committee proposed that the growing town be called Perryburg. The decision was by raucous acclamation from the land-owning men, and with equal affection by the women, children, indentures servants, and others that then called Perryburg home.

Perry, having set the example of building far back from the road ("less likely to endure the odors of the road"), encouraged others to do the same. Soon Mohawk Street became a broad swath of trees and green centered on the now-wide thoroughfare. Only closer to the river did it narrow a bit, but even there its width was enviable.

Down that great street passed so much of history. The arrival of the luminaries of the age, who came to speak and sing at the Lyceum. The troops marching off to the Civil War, and the survivors marching back. The arrival of the great Presidential candidates. The night the street was first lit by electric light.

By that time, the lower end of Mohawk Street was anchored by the railroad which now connected Perryburg in every direction for commerce and travel. Its upper end stretched further and further uptown as the community continued to grow.

While the Spanish-American War was raging far away, streetcars had begun to replace the horsedrawn conveyances on the great street. While the sparking trolley wire would frighten many a dog and not a few people, these new devices were infinitely cleaner and less odoriferous than their equine predecessors. Soon Mohawk Street, as well as the perpendicular Broad Street, would be filled with streetcars to and from diverse portions of the city and even into the surrounding communities. Especially down Mohawk Street the congestion and competition of streetcars, buggies, wagons, and horse riders became fierce.

To remediate this crush, city fathers proposed a daring plan. In the upper reaches, down to the circular square that was the upper limit of the business district, the trolley tracks would be given their own right-of-way. To accomplish this and provide for the same wide lanes for other travel as well as space for parked vehicles, each lot along that section of Mohawk Street would give up 15 feet of their land fronting the street, in exchange for being given a sewer system (storm and sewage), curbing, and sidewalks.

The sensitivities of the rich who had placed their homes so far back from the street now were swayed to the amenities they were to receive, and the project was universally blessed.

In two short summer work seasons, what had been a mighty street became an even mightier boulevard. When completed, two parallel streetcar tracks ran in their separate center area, with great shade trees planted between the tracks. Either side of that boulevard strip were two travel lanes for vehicles as well as a single lane where vehicles might lay by. The whole street was nicely curbed with slate, sewer lines were laid (running downhill into the Oneida River), sidewalks installed, and at regular intervals mighty elm trees planted on the grassy strip between sidewalk and street.

When one looks at postcards of Perryburg from 1900-1910, the most common picture was of Mohawk Street. Glorious elm trees lined both sides and the middle. Graceful streetlights of modern design accented the trees. The trolley right-of-way was immaculate. The mansions of Mohawk Street gleamed in the new framing of their location. Colonel Perry had been right. No city in the world could be said to have a more handsome main street than Perryburg.

At the same time as the work was being done on upper Mohawk Street, the street was extended across the railroad tracks, across the river flats and the river, and up onto the gentle sloping meadows on the far side. Here it was not as magnificent a street, having no streetcar tracks, nor boulevard effect, simply being 4 lanes of highway, little used for commerce, leading to the ambitions of housing for the less affluent. It would later be said that many of the later brick mansions of upper Mohawk Street were built on the profits of the cheap housing on the other side.

Perryburg had built a main street for the ages.

Time and circumstances, however, had other plans. The collapse of 1929, the end of the streetcars in Perryburg, the restrictions of materials in World War II, the exodus from Perryburg first to the suburbs and then away, the Dutch Elm Disease, and not a small amount of civic graft and corruption, left Perryburg with a desolate main street whose center strip, now unshaded, was haven to all manner of weeds. The great lawns, now encased by crumbling sidewalks and cracked curbs, fared no better without the shade. The river, from the outflow of the sewers, was foul. Only the scarcest maintenance was provided to the roadway and its supporting structures.

If one were to find a postcard of Perryburg from the late 1960s taken from the same point of view as the earlier ones, it would be hard to tell if one were looking at a barely recovered street in war-torn Europe or Perryburg. The only saving grace was that the cityscape of too many of America's great cities looked similar.

Down at its lowest point, down by where Backus' Tavern had been, Mohawk Street was an area to be avoided, or at least driven through quickly. The industrial buildings were now vacant lofts of uncertain future. The hotels were either boarded up or flophouses. Business after business in the business district had failed or fled.

That is where we first find three people in conversation: Roberto D'Angelo, Muriel Cummings, and Preston Walker. They are walking around the old tavern site, kicking through the detritus of urban decay, gazing at decaying buildings, smelling both the river and un-toileted human waste.

None of them had chosen to be there, but there they were.

Roberto had studied urban planning and ecology at the University of Chicago, a city setting not much different from Perryburg, just more so. He had arrived in Perryburg when his wife was offered a teaching position in nearby Adams College.

Muriel was an environmentalist and urban activist from the University of North Carolina. She had followed her husband when he became the regional administrator for the State Power Authority.

Preston had studied law at Yale, and then urban design at UCLA. He had been torn away from his life in Malibu to be with his husband, the new Director for the Perryburg Public Library.

The three had met at one of those newcomer events to which their spouses had been invited and they had dutifully been the plus-ones. While fuss was being made over their newly arrived partners, the three of them found themselves all in the same remote corner.

Muriel was the first to speak, "I keep asking myself, 'what have I gotten myself into?'"

"Tell me about it," Preston responded quickly. "I mean, I love my man and wither he goeth and all that, but Perryburg? At least on Long Island they call it Hicksville."

"Hey, not so harsh, man. It may not be paradise, but I keep getting the sense that something is happening around here," Roberto shot back. "Or might possibly happen."

"Or not."

Muriel looked at the two of them with a withering eye. "Come on. I made my choice. Actually, we made our choices. Not Perryburg's fault. I've seen worse."

"OK," Preston, said a little belligerently, "name one, just one place, with less to offer. We aren't even being offered good drinks and decent snacks."

"If you are complaining about these drinks and snacks, I could tell you about some of the interview weekends we had. Snacks from bags and beverages in cans," Roberto said.

"I just wonder," Muriel mused, "where the old Perryburg of the postcards and the history books has gone."

"Me, too," was Roberto's quick response. "The urban planner in me makes me want to dig deep and then dream high about any city, especially one as depressed and depressing as this one."

"Wait, did you say you are an urban planner?"

And so, three people trained in and dedicated to the vitality of cities met. Remember, I said that the real story of communities is played out more in the people than in the events. This meeting is a perfect example of that maxim.

Before long, the three were meeting regularly for what they termed "field trips:" treks around the city, library searches for maps, scrolls through the newspaper archives.

After about three months of such research, they met again over lunch, this time at the remnant of what had been a glorious restaurant and lunch counter in Union Station.

Muriel, the first to speak up, set the tone. "I think we have been going about this all wrong."

Roberto quickly chimed in, "I agree, but I am not sure why you are saying what you are saying."

Preston looked at the two of them with a curious grin. "Did you discover," he asked, "that all that looks old, worn-out, discarded is that way for a reason, not just neglect?"

"I wouldn't put it that way," Roberto said, "but for every piece of grandeur of the past I have found a piece of circumstance that ended that grandeur."

Muriel added, "It is like we are looking at postcards that made sense in 1890 or 1920, when the city looked bright and promising, and we are mourning the passing of those things. We are asking how to reclaim those things, but, to me, the larger question is, how do we reclaim those qualities."

Preston and Roberto looked at her with a look of "aha" on their faces.

At about the same time, over a much more ethnic lunch at the Europa, out on Albany Street, four older Italian-American gentlemen sat at a corner table. Tony, Sal, Vinnie, and "Quiet Man" Manny. The antipasti had been delicious, the minestrone had been rich and warming, the pasta was coming soon with red gravy, long simmered. Later, a whole branzino with lemon and capers would be shared around the table before some pastry from Café del Rossi and an espresso (or two). It would be a long lunch, the kind these four enjoyed once a week, every week, for over 30 years.

Of course, there would be much reminiscing.

"Remember Fat Tony, the guy with the candy store, who would run us kids off when we said we were 'just looking' at his candy."

"That Carmelita, she was one sweet woman."

"I just thought of Konrad Avenue, how that was like a wall. You didn't go to the other side if you wanted to come home in one piece. But then my mother, she sent me over to Dorffler's Meat Market to get some sausages, I don't know why, and I had to cross the street. My mother was surprised how fast I was back but I didn't tell her I had to run the whole way, over and back, just to return in one piece."

The pasta arrived, and while savoring it, Tony got a strange look on his face. "I was just thinking."

"Oh, no, here it comes," Sal said. "What now?"

"I was thinking about how we sit here, in this same place we have sat since we were old enough to eat out alone, and nothing much changes, but at the same time everything changes. That candy store is long gone, and it is just an abandoned building. Old man Dorffler

289

is long dead, and his namesake store is out towards Hurtzboro. Konrad Avenue no longer divides anything."

"And Carmelita?"

"Ah, Carmelita. Still beautiful, but she doesn't remember who you are even if you introduced yourself to her five minutes ago. It is all slipping away."

"So," interrupted Manny.

"So, this," continued Tony, "I think we four, you (pointing to Manny), and you Sal, and you Vinnie, have got to make a big decision unless we want to end up like Fat Tony, or Dorffler, or Konrad Avenue, or Carmelita."

"Hey, what do you mean?" Manny snapped.

"I mean we can either keep spending every week thinking about how our neighborhood, or all of Perryburg, used to be, or we can talk about what might make it a place like we remember it. Alive. With new stories to tell. With memories for our great great grandchildren to share around a table like this. I am getting tired of all this 'remember' talk. I would love to, for once, have one of us dream of the future. Better we all do it."

It was then that the self-proclaimed "Eastside Improvement Society" was formed. Four old guys, fed up with being fed up with how things had changed for the worse, decided to become just four guys seeking a better future for their community.

Their strategy was to continue to meet weekly but ban any talk of the past that did not lead to ideas of the future. Dreams, even outlandish ones, were shared, discussed, expanded, or dropped.

Once they had practiced their model for a few months, they decided it was time to "take it on the road." First stop, the St. Agnes Senior Center.

They were a tough crowd, not willing at first to forsake their daily dose of nostalgia. However, wearing them down over three weeks, they began to hear some simple ideas that were more about the future than the past. Of course, there were challenges.

"I remember how Mohawk Street would look come spring, with all the flowers planted and then the trees leafing out. We need some more of those elm trees."

"This city will never get anywhere until we bring back streetcars."

But then Agatha spoke up, "I am picturing Mohawk Street, not as it was when I was a girl, but what it would look like to a stranger today if it looked like a street they wanted to walk along."

"And," Sal asked, "what would it look like?"

Soon, nearly everyone was sharing their thoughts more about what the street might look like than what the street once looked like.

The tide had turned. Soon the "Eastside Improvement Society" was splitting into sub-groups to engage more people in the community. Elks, Knights of Columbus, and Masons, to name a few. The people came, the people shared, some of the people even joined the EIS.

It was in October 2001, while the country was still in shock over the events of September 11th, that a small notice appeared in the *Perryburg Gazette*: "Public Hearing to consider ideas for infrastructure improvements to the central business district of Perryburg."

Roberto spotted it. Manny spotted it. Each shared it with their own group. Plans were made to attend.

On Wednesday, November 14, 2001, at 7pm, what was planned was a very routine meeting of the Common Council with two public hearings, one on replacing sewer grates with bicycle-friendly ones and the other to consider ideas for projects in the business district. After the two hearings, scheduled to be brief, the regular monthly business was on the agenda.

Just before 7pm, people began to arrive. Those planning to speak started to sign in. The Clerk was surprised that the sign-in list was suddenly filled up. Almost all of those signing up to speak indicated they were there for the second public hearing.

Now, if you have been in the Council chambers, you know that the Council sits on an elevated platform at the front, all behind a continuous desk. Various city officials have tables on the platform either side of the main desk. Other officials, summoned witnesses, and the like join the general public in chairs on the floor. Those chairs are in two sections, either side of a center aisle.

That night, on the left side, you would see Manny, Sal, Tony, and Vinnie. Around them was a group of older people, most from the east side.

On the right side you would see Preston, Muriel, and Roberto. They had no one with them, but they had what appeared to be charts and pictures mounted on Styrofoam, reams of printed material, and clipboards.

"Uh, oh," Muriel said when she looked to the other side of the room. "That doesn't look good. A whole bunch of old-timers, dressed like it is still the 80s, and I don't think they are here about the sewer grates."

Roberto looked over and added, "Yeah, those four guys, I know them. I've seen them outside that old restaurant on Albany Street, looking like they are the kings of the community. I've been told that nothing happens over there without their OK, and they don't like change."

"Look," Muriel responded, "let's just focus on our presentations. We can't let a group of Luddites get to us."

Preston, looking more serious, said, "Did we do any reach out to that part of town?"

"No, but nothing we are proposing will have an effect on them," was Roberto's reply.

Muriel added, "And what if we did? Think they care about anything other than keeping their neighborhood the same it was when their parents got here?"

The three of them huddled, looking over the planned presentations.

On the left side of the room, the four eastsiders spotted the three on the right side, but not before one of the ladies from St. Agatha's did. "Are those three from the city?"

Tony shot a glance, and then moaned. "Oh, God. The city has brought in what they call 'experts'."

Sal immediately tried to calm him, "Do you know that for sure?"

"I've never seen them around City Hall, and look at them, all college like, and with papers and charts. Bet they are some of those historic preservation types. Give us the past over again because it was so good back then. I tell you, the fix is in.

The usually quiet Manny was quick to join in, "They look like the newcomer crowd, the ones who have been here a year at most and know what Perryburg needs to be."

Vinnie had had enough. "I'm going over there and find out who they are."

"No, no. Vinnie, just go up to the sign-in sheet and see who they are. Better to know your enemies than to tip your hand that you don't know them."

Vinnie stood, stretched, and sauntered up to the sign-in sheet. He looked, looked back at the guys, shrugged, and slowly walked back.

"They all live in town."

"Our part of town?"

"No, but not the fancy part either. Two Uptown just off Mohawk, the other over the river."

"Strange. We better keep an eye on them. Vinnie, were they signed up to speak three in a row?"

"No, looks like one of them signed up first, then you, Tony, then another of them, then me, then the third one, then Sal."

"Good, they can't control the discussion. But we have to listen carefully and plan on how to respond to what they are suggesting. And Manny, whatever you do, don't get all angry and shit."

"Who, me?"

"I remember when we were in third grade at Harper School, and that Sally D'Ambrosia said that the Dodgers were a better team, and you went ape about the Yankees. Remember?"

"So what – I mean she had it coming. The eraser didn't even hit her."

"That's what I mean – we are here on serious business and don't need any distractions."

Across the aisle, the three had watched the fuss on the other side. They saw four old guys talking and gesturing among themselves, one of them going up and looking at the speaker list, coming back, and then more gesturing.

"I don't like the looks of this," Muriel said. "Perryburg has been run like some old-world town for decades, and the power is never on the dais, it is with reputational leaders. I think we have now found the people who will make trouble for us."

"I agree," Roberto said. "Maybe we should have done a bit more outreach to the east side. Maybe we should have tried to figure out who thinks they hold power there. Did we blow this whole thing by not doing that?"

Muriel thought for a moment and then said, "Look, it is what it is. We have strong presentations, we have done our research, we have data to cite. Not like the stories of 'the good old days' we are likely to hear from them. And, Preston, whatever you do, don't get all upset and pissy over some little thing they say."

Preston pulled himself up into his formal pose. "Moi? I only get perturbed when people try to foist off opinions as facts, and history as controlling."

"Just behave, OK?"

"If you insist."

Together the other two said, "We do."

The Clerk tried to alert the Council President to the lengthy public comment list on the two, presumed routine, hearings, but Madame President was running late, striding onto the dais just as the tower clock struck 7. At the final clock chime, she gaveled the meeting to order.

The agenda started with the Pledge of Allegiance, followed by approval of the agenda and approval of the consent agenda. Only one item was taken off consent and added back onto the discussion agenda.

She then announced the hearing on the replacement of the sewer grates and asked if there were any who signed up to speak.

"Yes, Madame President," the Clerk responded, carefully using the title requested by the President. "One, Robert Comstock." The Clerk could see the President roll her eyes just a bit.

Mr. Comstock, the president of a local cycling group, slowly made his way to the lectern set up for speakers. He began a lengthy commentary (Madame President was already thinking, "This is going to be a longer meeting than I anticipated.") which could have been boiled down to three simple sentences.

"It's about time."

"We are grateful for the new grates."

"More needs to be done for bike lanes."

"Thank you Mr. Comstock. Any questions from the Council? No, do I have any objection to approval by consensus? No, motion passed.

"Next on the agenda, the public hearing about capital improvements. Do we have any speakers signed up?

"Yes, Madame President, fourteen."

"Did you say 'fourteen'?" with a look somewhere between bewildered and frustrated.

"No, I was wrong."

"Oh, good,"

"Fifteen."

There was a long pause, and then the President, with a sigh, said, "OK, let's get on with it." Those in the audience could see her look down for about 20 seconds but could not see that she was texting her husband "have dinner without me, again."

"Mr. Preston Walker."

Preston walked to the lectern carrying a large notebook in one hand and a large map in the other.

"Here it comes, boys," Sal whispered to the others, "better get your feet off the ground before the bullshit flows."

After the usual opening – "My name is Preston Walker, I live at 232 Hudson Street, Perryburg. I have a law degree from Yale and a master's in urban planning from UCLA."

"Yeah, here it comes," muttered Tony. The others murmured with him.

Preston then began a presentation about what had made Perryburg great in the past. He painted a wonderful picture of how it had been in the heyday of the city. By this point, the four men from the east side along with their cadre were all shaking their heads, grumbling, and passing notes like "What a pile of crap," and "Next, they'll want us to reinstall outhouses."

Preston paused, and then said, "that is what made Perryburg great then, but it is not what can make a better Perryburg for our future."

"Did I just hear that?" Vinnie asked, a little more aloud than he had planned. He got looks from the other side of the aisle.

Preston then shared that his colleagues would be soon offering presentations about how a new Perryburg could grow out of the past but not by returning to it or duplicating it. He then thanked the Council for their time and attention.

"Mr. Salvatore Mauro."

Sal stood and walked to the lectern. "I'm Sal Mauro, and several of you already know me. You probably brought your shoes to my family's repair shop when people had their shoes repaired. I live at 2337 Louisa Street and have from when I was born there 78 years ago."

He paused.

"I am at a loss for words, which is rare for me, as many of you know. I had come up here ready to argue about some proposals brought to you by some so-called experts who don't really know our city. But all I've got to say is, 'Yes' to everything Mr. Comstock just said.

"I represent a new group in town, the Eastside Improvement Society. Our focus is on how to create the Perryburg of the future, not duplicate the Perryburg of the past. Heaven knows Perryburg has much to be proud of and quite a lot better left to the past. Now, this is our question: what kind of city can we create that will, as people see it for the first time, make people and businesses want to move here? Thank you."

As he turned to return to his seat, he could see his group doing a series of 'thumbs-up' gestures but then he looked at the other side of the aisle and saw the other three giving him silent applause.

The comments then continued, with a strong synergy occurring linking the two groups into one vision. By the middle of the time, Madame President was not just enduring, not just listening, but was engaging. She asked questions and encouraged other Council members to do the same.

Once everyone had spoken a motion was made, seconded, and unanimously approved to create a new Task Force on the Civic Future, to be co-chaired by Sal Mauro and Muriel Cummings.

Then the two groups, together as one group, went over to the Europa for some coffee and pastries. New friendships were formed, and the really serious work began.

If one looks at the Perryburg.gov website in the 2020s, one sees many images of Mohawk Street. It looks much like the Mohawk Street of 1920 and also nothing like the Mohawk Street of 1920.

The dimensions of the street have not changed, but with the interstate and the eastside expressway siphoning off traffic that once flowed down Mohawk Street, the travel lanes have been reduced and bicycle paths have been added. The very wide sidewalks necessitated by the large pedestrian crowds have been narrowed to meet current demands, with the excess transformed into a combination of benches and plantings. The benches, with a gentle swell to them express motion, invite sitting, but not lying down.

At what had been major signaled intersections, rotaries have been built, so traffic slow-downs for traffic lights have been eliminated. The stately elms of memory have been replaced with disease resistant hedge maples, whose shade changes the desolate heat of a barren street into a shady retreat in the summer and bathes it with vivid color in the fall. Looking down Mohawk Street for its highest point, what one sees is a true boulevard with those trees planted on both sides and down the middle, with the middle accented by seasonal and perennial growth.

Towards downtown, where street parking has been replaced by bike lanes, one can find parking lots within a block off Mohawk Street on every side street. These smaller lots, on sites of decaying buildings now razed, are also tree shaded. The revealed sides of the neighboring buildings have been artfully given large murals of the city's history.

The old street lighting system which turned the barren downtown into a light-polluting zone has been replaced with a European system of suspended, down-facing lights that only illumine sidewalks and roadways.

The wayfaring signage has all been standardized. The old clutter of signs has been reduced. Informational electronic kiosks are on nearly every block.

The emphasis on commercial space has been to encourage local, small entrepreneurs to open store front businesses. As opposed to the national chains of shopping center row out in Hurtzboro, the intent is to create a walkable area for window shopping as well as entertainment. Where the Backus Tavern area was once sketchy in the day and avoided after dark, now the streets are busy almost every evening.

The biggest change happens between Main Street and Acorn Avenue, two parallel streets four blocks apart, both intersecting Mohawk Street. These secondary streets, one passing Union Station and one further uptown, had not been major streets for years. Coming downhill on Mohawk, all traffic now flows right onto Acorn for a large block, then left onto Comstock until Main, where a left turn takes one back to a right turn on Mohawk, up and over the train tracks and the river. In the other direction, traffic circles right onto Main, left onto Marshall, left then onto Acorn, and then right onto Mohawk. Each of those turns is without any intersecting traffic or traffic light so everything just flows. Inside the large box of streets formed by this pattern is a pedestrian zone with a central fountain, an outside venue that becomes skating rink in the winter.

Up and over the bridge over the train tracks and the river, the once stark roadway has been modified to resemble the other portion of Mohawk Street with a boulevard effect, bike lanes, and good lighting, and accessible sidewalks. There, between the railroad tracks and the interstate, where gas storage and junk yards once stood, several motel and hotel chains have brought lodging to the city.

Most visitors to Perryburg say it reminds them of a visit to a theme park. Everything labelled, everything accessible. As one person wrote on the city website, "It feels like what every city should hope to be."

Sure, there are those who like to remember a better time, but if asked when that was they become vague about a date. They just know they ought to complain about something because their own lives haven't moved on in decades.

Perryburg, and especially Mohawk Street, had moved on without them.

However, Sal and Tony and Roberto and Muriel and Manny and Vinnie and Preston are not among those stuck in the past or in prejudices. Now they alternate their weekly meetings between the Europa, which is enjoying its own renaissance, and the Thistle and Crown down on the newly created downtown fountain square. But not ones to rest on any laurels, the team, regularly enhanced by anyone with an idea or a suggestion for improvement, continues to dream the future into being.

Out by the interstate the old sign, "Perryburg – The Place To Do Business," has been long gone. Now, not only by the interstate but at every entrance to the city new signs simply proclaim "Perryburg – A Place You Want to Visit."

14. THE RIVER

The canoe, having drifted with the current, turns south and eases into the soft mud which is the summer bank of the river. She steps from the canoe and then helps her two children to reach slightly higher and drier ground. Together, they walk toward the trading area, with things to sell and needing to get other things. When the trades are over, and the conversations bringing news from elsewhere are completed, the three will return to the canoe. The river is not so fierce during the summer, so going upstream will not be so hard.

He steers his small boat out from the concrete wall below the floodgate, his small electric motor all that is needed in this lazy stretch of the river. About a quarter mile upstream, he anchors and casts his line into the murky water. In about ten minutes, the slightest tug on his line tells him to set the hook. The struggle of fish against man is relatively short and his net is soon filled with a midsize bass. He will spend a total of an hour on the river, rewarded with another bass and a walleye. Like those before him who, coming north from Alabama to work in Perryburg's factories, the river will help him feed his family.

The engineers, preceded by surveyors, are staking out the best outflow of the city's new storm sewer system into the river. Of course, they want it downstream, so the water in the city can remain clean. By their calculations, the river is healthy enough to absorb what little may come its way compared to its habitual flow.

Another set of engineers, preparing for the expansion of the railway through Perryburg, find the river to be a great nuisance, flowing by the edge of the prosperous downtown, flooding a great plain every spring. With the help of the state legislature, they proceed with a plan to move the river a quarter mile north and straighten its course. What was once river then can become the mucky foundation for four tracks of modern commerce.

Her kayak is colored what is called "water blue," but against the perennial brown of the river, it stands in stark contrast. She has made her way from the boat launch site by Mohawk Street, following the straight course set by the railway's planners, and now returns to the old, serpentine meander that was the river long, long ago. She will soon drift into little bays along the shores, bays where wildflowers are abloom. The air will fill with dragonflies. It is like she has passed through a time portal and been transported to the early Holocene river.

The whole family is working together to avoid disaster. The river, which annually gifts them with the loamy afterbirth of the spring floods, seems to have grown angry at their taking her for granted. The waters are rising like they have never done before since the homestead was chosen and the log house erected. Working without rest, they struggle to create a berm high enough to keep the farm from becoming part of the flow. In these river bottom locales, even a barrier a foot high can make all the difference. As she works beside her husband, she remembers a comment from one of the natives who walked by before the cabin was even conceived. Looking at the river and then where these newcomers were camped, the passerby used gestures to ask a simple question, "Why here?" She was beginning to understand the genesis of that question.

All the industries of Perryburg benefited from the river. Its waters provided power for the earliest mills, captured into races that fed waterwheels then turned grindstones and saws. Later, the water provided the source of steam to power even more. But, in turn, those industries were not kind to the river. Some years they taxed its water so hard that the riverbed became exposed. Every year they dumped their sludge, slurry, byproducts, chemicals, and more into it.

After the Great Canal had been superseded by the iron horse and the maintenance of the artificial waterway became too much of a burden for the State, plans had been announced to abandon the option of water transport of bulk goods from tidewater to the Great Lakes. The uproar that ensued resulted in plans to widen portions of the canal and to commandeer the river for about half of its route. This meant taming a force of nature that had never consented to that domestication. Dams, water gates, sluices, locks, and fortified banks are all enlisted to that cause. But every so often the river rises up against its servitude; great ice dams form on the gates, rushing waters scour under bridge abutments, and whole sections of towns become the river again.

The river has its friends – "Friends of the River." They began with one person trying to fish in the river and pulling out great clumps of sewage rather than fish. She announced a meeting in the basement of the old Episcopal church downtown, to which seven other people came. Those seven, from various neighborhoods, agreed to host meetings in each of their neighborhoods. Those eight neighborhood meetings attracted 106 people. That was enough to attract the attention of the newspaper and the TV station. The following month over 400 people attended a rally on the banks of the river. By the following spring, Friends of the River had been founded, incorporated as a non-profit, received its first grant, had over 5,000 members, and was a motivating force at the city, county, and state level. Now, celebrating their 25th anniversary, FOTR has spearheaded the cleanup of the river, now reclaimed to such a degree that the founder was able to healthfully swim in the river for the first time in the memory of anyone.

Beneath a weeping willow on the north bank of the river, a willow he was told his father planted on the day his father's girlfriend had said "yes" to his offer of marriage, the boy stands awkwardly hand-in-hand with his beloved. There is a gentle summer evening breeze flowing down on top of the waters. Slowly, the boy reaches into his pocket and then equally slowly lowers to a knee and, in age-old tradition, reveals a ring and asks a question. The answer again is, "Yes." Rising up from his knee, the young man takes his lover into his arms and the two men kiss beside the river, which has seen it all before.

The river. The River.

When the first European settlers arrived in the area, they used gestures to seek out the name of the river. Where they came from, back in the Old World, every body of water had a name and they could not fathom that this one did not also. They just didn't know it yet.

People had lived in the area for countless generations, from soon after the great ice had fled north after changing the landscape forever. That ice shield had brought with it the detritus of the lands north, a burden the retreating glacier left behind. In some places, those moraines blocked older waterways. In the great valley they were but remnants, and the river soon flowed as it had long before, now digging a deeper course, fed in different ways.

Over time the river aged, cutting its own easier channels. Strong currents found ways to become slower ones. The river meandered where it had once roared.

Through all its changes, those who lived in its vicinity knew it only by its essence.

So it was, when questioned by the strangers, the locals were taken aback. One could see for oneself what it was. Were these newcomers daft? OK, they ask, we will tell them.

"Ohneka."

"O, neck, ah?"

"Ohneka."

"Ona ka?"

"Ohneka."

"O nye da?"

The natives realized this could go on forever. So, after looking at each other, they turned to the newcomers and said, "O Nye da."

"Ah," said one of the settlers from the Netherlands, and he wrote it for the others. "Oneida."

"Ah," they said as a group. "Oneida."

And so, the river which was water was named water as a river. "Ohneka" was the Iroquois word for water. Plus, it was elevated to being the "Water River," one of the first of many redundancies of naming by the European settlers.

The Oneida River.

I could tell you how it was the backbone of the cultural development of First Nations' settlement. I could tell you how it was the obvious route for westward expansion of European colonization. I could tell you how it became part of the gateway to the great American west. I could tell you how it was vital to the second phase of the great American industrialization. I could tell you how it was used and misused by many of those same forces. I could tell you how it became one of the most polluted rivers in North America. I could tell you how some summers it stank so badly that people moved away from it. I could tell you how you can still catch a wisp of its aroma seeping up from its ancestral bed beneath the train tracks at Union Station. I could tell you how, through collective effort, the river is slowly but surely returning to its glory, before all that destruction and decay.

I was taught in graduate school that better than talking about something or someone is to let them do the talking. So, I let them talk. You have read vignettes of their stories, from the native canoe through to the riverside proposal in 2024.

Now it is time for the river itself to speak.

But, how?

The next time you are in Perryburg, go down by the river. It doesn't matter where. It doesn't matter if it shaded or not. It doesn't matter if it is sunny or not. It doesn't matter if it is summer, fall, winter, or spring. It doesn't matter if you will stand or sit. It doesn't matter if you sit on a mossy bank, or a fallen log, or a concrete wall, or even a chair you have brought along.

Just go down to the river as generations have done before you. Have nothing else on your agenda for an extended time. Give unmeasured time to the river, to listen for what it has to say. Leave your watch and cellphone at home. Let time be its own measure and know that all the pictures you might take are being gathered by your mind. There is nothing that needs urgent attention.

(If you can't get to Perryburg, find a river near where you are, a river that has been used and even abused over its years. A river that has known abandon and redemption. All rivers are part of the same ecosystem of precipitation, runoff, earth, and stone, repeated continually in cycle of growth, flow, and ebb. Find a river where you can stand, or sit. A river to which you will listen, to hear it speak its story. No river has ever been without its aqueous language ready on its crests and deep in its troughs.)

There, on the banks of the ohneka, on the banks of the Oneida, there on the banks of the Oneida filled with ohneka, become still. Let the river do the talking.

Let its voice tell you tales of many generations, tell you stories of long before you and stories of you, tell you wisdom it has shared with the wind and the seasons, tell you of struggles with the cycles of its being.

Hear, in chorus with the river soloist, the voices of the leaves and branches, the lichen and the bushes. Hear, also, the hums and tweets and rustles of other living things that call the river home.

Let your breathing gather together the words the river says in its bouquet, its redolence containing all of its history even if in the faint measure. Discover what it is saying in both freshness and acrid sharpness.

Let your eyes behold the words that are being rippled downstream and the couplets contained in the flotsam and jetsam that ride the river. "The leaves have fallen another year." "Spring blossoms bedeck me in whites and yellows." "My raging flood brings you word of a barn destroyed, and of mud from somewhere far upstream." "In the languid heat of summer, my seemingly tranquil surface hides all kinds of motions."

As you are beside the Oneida (or whatever river you choose), feel how your breathing is quieting. How peace is taking hold of you. How your thoughts stop racing and pace themselves to the waters. "I have been here for so long, and I shall be here for longer." "There is more depth to be seen than my surface." "I have strength even when I appear to be at my weakest."

Sense what the river is inviting you to say to yourself.

. . .

In interviewing people in Perryburg about their present realities and their family histories, I found the river was a recurring theme. It echoed entries into diaries and news accounts that mentioned the river. Most of these were ways in which people listened to the river.

From the diary of Elisabetta von Slyke, May 10, 1779 (as translated by Constance Bergman):

> *Today it has been a month since my second child, a son, was born, too soon, weak, small. He lived only three days before the good Lord took his spirit and left us with only his withered body. My confinement was more a refuge for the first two weeks. Thereafter, I lived as in a haze, barely tending to my tasks as wife and mother. Our three year old daughter asked much but received little from me.*
>
> *I am often absorbed by tears. They feel like my life is draining out of me. I have not started the garden yet, and the sun is eager for seeds to warm, but I have sown none.*
>
> *For reasons I know not, today I found myself down beside the river. I had not been there since the first bite of winter and my expectancy kept me closer to home. Along the bank bright green shoots of new life were showing themselves. I sat on the old mossy log that had been my home when I first detected signs of my impending pregnancy. I looked out at the river, and I looked down into its little inlet at my feet.*
>
> *I had so wanted to show the river to my child. He will never see it. The tears came again. But, suddenly, I notice that the placid pool at my feet was disturbed into a pattern of circles, little wavelets reaching from the center to the shore and out into the stream. At first I did not recognize what was happening. Then, with my breath stopping, I realized those waves were the result of my tears dropping into the water. I was feeding the river out of my sorrow, and the river was taking my sorrow with it.*

I suddenly had a vision of another mother upstream weeping into the river, her tears now among the water at my feet, and my tears becoming the water at the feet another bereaved mother. I saw the earth dropping her own tears into the waters, bereaved over all the loss of winter's death but resilient in preparing for the spring.

Suddenly with this vision of the river as the river of all life, I stood and walked back to our house. I looked in my daughter's eyes as I had not been able to do for weeks. When my husband embraced me, as I know he has done every day since that awful one, I returned his embrace for the first time in those same weeks. I would go on.

From my interview with Kyeesha Quinton (July 17, 2023):

Grandaddy always told me to go down to the river when life gets to be too much. "But, Grandaddy, why should I do that?" I would ask.

"Let me tell you a story," he would say. And this is the story he would tell me.

"When I first came to Perryburg from Mississippi, after that long train ride with nothing but clothes on my back and a good measure of gumption, I was not welcomed. No sir.

"Not by the white folk who saw me as either some dumb fool they would have to take care of or as competition for their miserable jobs. Not by them colored already here, who thought they was better than me because they had never seen the land of cotton where old times are not forgotten.

"No, not welcome. Signs on some doors said, "No Coloreds," and others, down here by the tracks, were just shut in my face. They said I talked funny, I dressed poorly, I ate strangely, and I prayed all wrong.

"You know what it feels like not to be welcomed by anyone, anywhere? No, I bet you don't, or maybe you do and just don't talk about it. You young people like to pretend that you have the world on a string, but I know when I was your age that string was pretty thin.

"Anyway, about a week after I got here, after a week without a roof over my head, I started walking up past them tracks, to see what was over there. I found a swampy patch, got my shoes all good and muddy. But then I came to the river. Oh, my. It was summer and the river was low, low enough to allow some wading in the water. That sure felt good on my feet – yes, I took off those muddy shoes and gave them a bath too.

"And I looked up to see I was not alone. No, not alone. Scattered along the river bottom were many people, all enjoying the cool comfort of the river. Lots of different people. I saw them all, looking very different, speaking all kinds of languages. But if you caught the eye of someone else, they didn't look away – they nodded a greeting.

"That's when I knew that the river didn't do no discriminating. No. It was a river for anyone who came to her. And we all sort of knew that when we were there. No fences, no gates, no doors, no sign. Just a river and all of us.

"When I was a little kid, that old preacher from down Goodwin had thrown a white sheet over me and dunked me three times in a muddy brook, saying I was cleansed by it. It never felt like I was cleansed of anything. But wading in the river here that night, I felt like everything that was troubling me, everything that was keeping me alone, was washing away.

"Now, not saying, everything magically got OK. I had to put my energy AND my attitude into it too. But that night, at the river, I was given a new start. You see, everyone was equal down in the river.

"So that's why I tell you, when life is getting you down, go see that old river. It has seen it all, it has borne it all, it has cleansed it all, and it is still there."

"I know," Kyeesha added, "that story is true. How do I know? Because when life has had by the collar and shaken me, I have gone and stood by the river and it has restored me."

From a letter, sent by Jeremiah Smith of Hurtzboro to his brother, Corporal Robert Smith October 6, 1862:

Dear Brother —

We have heard about the horrendous losses at Antietam, and I am sorrowfully distressed to think you may have been there. Your absence from us weighs heavily on my mind and spirit.

Yesterday, in church, Pastor Barnes had the presumption to preach to those of us men who are still here and not with you in the great cause. He excoriated any not offering up his life and went on to say "I see too many able-bodied men still among us here in Hurtzboro, and the too many more over in Perryburg, who carry on all manner of affairs as if no conflict was raging, as if no lives were being lost, as if the Divine call had not been heard. I ask, Jesus asks, the Lord God asks, 'Who shall I send?' and a deaf ear is turned to that plea, and so I ask it again to those who claim to be in worship here — WHO?"

I came home from Church in the most foul mood, that question echoing in my mind. Were I not crippled so badly, did I not rely on a crutch for any movement, I would surely answer "Here I am, take me." But I was not born to answer in that way. I feel a loss to the greater cause, especially knowing you are in the midst of battle for the union and the rights of all.

Last evening, in a fitful sleep, I heard over and over again the cry of the owl that calls our barn home: "who, who?" It tore at my soul and dispirited me beyond all measure.

This afternoon I took myself down to the river. It had been my intent, God forgive me, to end my misery and rid this world of one so dependent on the sacrifices of others. But my intent was thwarted, for there was no path that would allow my crutch passage to guide me to the waters' ultimate claim. Exhausted in all ways, I slumped upon that old stump, you know the one from the tree which had fallen in the storm of '59 blocking passage in the river. You and father had spent much of a week sawing that giant apart and making the river safely navigable again.

As I sat on that stump in thorough despair, on a small limb of the willow just beyond there, a small bird took roost. Not so much as a feather or two with legs of twigs. But then it opened its beak and out came a single call, and I swear to all that is holy, it said "why? why?"

Why indeed, I thought. But then it repeated its question. Again, and again. And it looked squarely at me. At first I felt accused, but with each repeated refrain I found new questions entering my mind.

"Why, why?" "Why do we fight?" An answer came almost immediately: "For the dignity of man, and the common purpose of our union."

"Why, why?" "Why do you not fight?" Again, an answer seemed to ripple off the river: "Just as the river cannot do what an ocean can does not mean the river is not carrying its share of the burden."

"Why, why?" "Why am I being told this, by this strange little bird?" On the wind that blew down the river, I heard my answer: "Because maybe you are not being called to fight, but to do something different."

Brother Robert, I was called back to life by that bird and the river. I may not wear the blue coat that you do, and I may not tamp the charge into the cannon as you do, and I may not reverse the charge of the enemy as you are called to do, but there is work I can do.

My dear brother, know that I returned home filled full of life and spirit, ready now to undertake any task which this wretched body will allow that might aid this war to its rightful conclusion. I start with my prayer for you and all those in arms with you. Tomorrow I will search out other ways to be of support of our shared cause. I may not be beside you, but know I am with you.

(Contemporaneous news accounts for the months that followed often mentioned Jeremiah Smith for his heroic actions on the home front, raising funds, gathering supplies, and otherwise supporting the Union effort.

Out in Noble Hill Cemetery a headstone slowly mosses its way into history, the etchings still visible: Jeremiah Smith, 1835-1885; Robert Smith, 1833 – 1897. Beneath the names is a simple inscription: "They Preserved the Union."

A 2003 newspaper story about the Memorial Day practice of the Scouts placing flags on the graves of veterans highlighted how two flags annually appear at this grave although only one of those interred there wore a uniform. Scout leaders interviewed said they did it because "it was always done that way." Further research found evidence that the Grand Army of the Republic, the fraternal order of those who served in the Civil War on the Union side, had also followed this practice after their records claimed President Grant had "commissioned Jeremiah Smith" as "an officer of the Nation" in recognition of his service in the cause of the war effort. No such Presidential Order can be found in the National Archives, but the flags continue to appear.)

From an interview with Kazimir Kapsinki in August 2022:

I came to the US in 1935, a teenager. I had been apprenticed to a blacksmith, so I put down "metal worker" on my entry form. Even though the country was still recovering from the Great Depression, apparently some industries could not find skilled workers and would interview people at the docks. Somehow they had access to the immigration forms and knew who to look for.

As I first set foot in New York, a voice called out to me, "Kazmir." I never have seen this man in my life, and I am frightened that he is one of the New York sharpies who will try to sell me something or rent me an over-priced room. I just walk away. But he walks too. He says, "So, you are a metal worker." I nod. "I have a job for you, and a place to stay." I nod again. "Are you interested?" I nod again. "Do you talk?"

"Look, Mister," I say, "I don't know you from Pulaski, I never see you before. Now you try to tell me where to go and what to do. I thought America was land of freedom."

"Sorry," he says to me, and presses a business card, a thick, embossed business card, not like those cheap ones you might fake, into my hand, and it says Perryburg Drop Forge. His name is Syzmon Kowalski. He is a Pole, like me. I decide to talk with him. He tells me where his family is from. It is not far from my home. I say I have a cousin who married a Kowalski. Turns out my cousin married his cousin. Small world.

He tells me about Perryburg, city of opportunity (boy, could he lie), where there was a place for a young, experienced metal worker like me. "But," I ask, "how do I get there?" He then presses a railway ticket into my hand and tells me if I am able to be on the 1pm train, I can be in Perryburg before dark. What did I have to lose?

And that is how I got to Perryburg. I was met at Union Station by another Pole, Jo Bukowski. He took me home and gave me the couch to sleep on. In the morning, he got me over to the PDF plant and I signed on as a forge operator. Mind you, I had never operated a forge, but I soon realized it was like blacksmithing but without having to do the hammering. I was up to speed in no time.

By the end of the week, I had found a room in a boarding house filled with other Poles and Czechs. Life was very good, but not perfect.

Back home, as bad as life had been, there was always the little stream that ran through town, ran right behind the smith's workshop. I could hear it talking to itself, I could smell its freshness, I could go and watch its flow. But in Perryburg, around the foundries and forges, there were only stagnant water pools.

On my second weekend in Perryburg, Jo says, "Come with me. I show you something." What he showed me was how, walking up to Mohawk Street and then up Mohawk Street itself, you could walk to a river. He and I sat on the edge of the bridge, a giant concrete step, and just watched the river. "Jo," I said, "I miss seeing my creek back home." And Jo said, "This river is a cousin to your creek." Cousin to my creek. I still remember that. Thousands of miles apart but cousins.

Now I live at one of the retirement homes in Perryburg. Not the big, fancy Wisteria Gardens, but a smaller, simpler one. Here has something the Gardens don't have. It has a view of the river. From my room I can see the water. And when the years get long, or my mind gets tired, or my heart yearns for my homeland, I can see the water, and everything seems better. I am "at home."

From an interview with Christine Walker, October 12, 2023:

I was the quintessential nerd in high school (probably still am). I really liked math and science, and one of my dreams was of winning the regional Science Fair. In my first two years of high school, I created projects about theoretical things: math proofs and extensions of already known scientific theories. I received Honorable Mentions in both years.

Going into Junior Year, my Chemistry teacher at Perryburg High School, Ms. Schodack, asked me to come see her after school in late September. When I arrived at her room, she invited me to sit down, and she moved from behind her lab desk and came to sit in a student desk. "Christine," she began, "you have been in my class now for about three weeks, and you remind me very much of myself at your age. You are a very good student and if I am not mistaken you are an overachiever. I also suspect you are intimidating to other

318

students so you are not invited onto many social events. Am I right?"

I remember blushing because someone knew me so well. I stammered, "Yes, you are."

"Well then," she said, "I want to help you with your assets and see if we can fill in some of those deficits. I like to see strong, intelligent women succeed."

If there were ever music to my ears, those words would have been the libretto.

"I want to suggest," Ms. Schodack continued, "that you start thinking about a project for the Science Fair this year that is different from the last two." (How did she know what I had done previously?).

"And I think you should work as a team with another student." (Oh, no! – I hate group projects because I always do all the work, and they all get the same credit.) I tried not to let my disappointment show.

"Do you know Kasheem Ali?" (Of course, I know Kasheem. He and I have been "rivals" since grade school. His is the other hand that is raised when tough questions are asked. His math work is almost as quick as mine ... sometimes even quicker. He is also such a ... was I about to think "nerd?")

"Yes, I know Kasheem. Why?" I already knew the answer, one I had avoided for many years.

"I think he and you are very alike. If you remember his work on Fibonacci's Number also got him an Honorable Mention last year." (I do remember because I was glad he had not gotten anything more than I.) "Can I arrange a meeting of the two of you with me and Mr. Briggs, the Earth Science teacher? Briggs and I have something in mind."

319

Let me cut to the chase. Kasheem and I met with the two teachers the following afternoon and it was evident that Kasheem was as nervous as I was.

"Kasheem and Christine," Mr. Briggs began, "I loved having you two in my Earth Science class two years ago. You challenged me to teach better." I looked over at Kasheem and found he was looking at me as we were both beet red.

"You have both produced quality Science Fair projects, but you did nothing to break any new ground. If you don't mind my saying so, you played it safe. We want to challenge to the two of you to think outside your safety zones." What was Ms. Schodack suggesting? I was relieved our biology teacher was not part of this discussion!

Kasheem broke the tension with a simple question, "What are you suggesting?"

"We are suggesting to you that the two of you look both closer to home and out onto the research edges of science. Make your project both local and universal."

I had to say something. "What are you talking about? Something in Perryburg?"

"Yes," Mr. Briggs responded. "But we are not going to do your work for you. We will point you in a direction and you need to take it from there. Are you game?"

I looked at Kasheem with a shrug, and he matched my shrug with his. In unison we replied, "why not?"

"That's great," was an immediate response from Ms. Schodack. "And I suspect, based on the books you both seem to be reading," (Had she noticed the scientific mystery books I loved?) "that all you need is a hint, a clue if you will."

Again, I looked at Kasheem and noticed he was trying to hide his copy of "The Andromeda Strain." I blurted out, "That's a great book. Have you gotten to the part where …" but he jumped in, "No spoilers!" A smile and a quick nod from each of us to the other sealed a truce, and the deal, and the partnership, and project.

"What's the hint?" I asked.

"What is the most neglected, under-studied part of Perryburg? Go there and the answer will become clear, we hope."

With that, hint in hand, the two of us were sent on our way. We began to meet daily at lunch to suss out the hint. For two weeks, nothing came to us. Finally, we agreed that we would meet up on the weekend and walk around Perryburg and see if the hint grew into an answer.

That weekend we clocked 11.3 miles of walking (we know because both of us logged it with our pedometers … a fact we kept hidden from the other for a long time). The old foundries, the rayon mill, the electronics factories, the old mansions, Mohawk Street, Union Station, the many neighborhoods. We saw them all. It was late Sunday afternoon, coming back from the north, that we fell into an exhaustion. Actually, it was I who fell and it was into a small sinkhole by the river. Kasheem, trying to help me out, pulled himself in. Then, as each of us tried to claw our way out we just made the opening bigger.

At that point, as tired as we were, we started laughing. I can't remember ever laughing so hard with another student. Here we were, the two smartest kids in the Junior Class, and we couldn't get out of that hole.

It was in the midst of that struggle and that laughter that one of us said "Nobody ever expected this along the river." (we both take credit for saying it) And then one of us said, "nobody ever says anything about the river." We looked at each other. The hint. The clue. Finally, our answer.

Now I could keep you here hearing my stories all day, but it was that simple. We chose to look more closely at the river. It was at a time when all sorts of micro-biology and genetics were exponentially striding into uncharted territory. We decided our project would be to ask, and answer, a simple yet complex question: "What makes up the Oneida River in Perryburg." Local! Cutting-edge! Wham!

In the end we, using samples of the river's water, traced its origin at the microscopic and genetic levels. We showed, to the best of two high school juniors' abilities and resources, what each sample contained and where it came from.

We swept the school's Science Fair, won the Regional one, and ended up on top of the national science talent search. We were courted by federal officials and many universities.

And what became of us? Kasheem was my date to Junior Prom (yes, I asked!), and I was his date for Senior Prom (yes, he did ask in a very Kasheemesque manner involving many hot air balloons in the gym), we were co-Valedictorians, and we both went to University in the Boston area. Our two kids, twins, a girl and a boy, are like little Christeems.

I know, more story than you wanted, but here is what I really wanted you to know. That day, out in that hole by the river, when we stopped thinking and started just sensing where we were, the river told us the answer we had been seeking. I know, for two science nerds to acknowledge the ineffable call of the river is unimaginable. But, then everything in my life after Ms. Schodack called me in was unimaginable at that time.

Oh, you probably are wondering how did we get out of that hole by the river? At the same moment we each realized that while we couldn't claw our way up, out of that hole, we could claw enough dirt into the bottom of the hole that it slowly became less deep, until, at last, we were almost even with the top.

. . .

The river is there. It has been there as long as anyone has known. It will be there as long as there are people to know about it, and probably even longer. It has had names and had no name. It has flooded and it has ebbed, it has grown tranquil and it has roared, it has supported life and taken it away, it has threatened and it has consoled, it has frozen and it has warmed, it has been moved and it has reclaimed its natural course … and through it all it has spoken to those who will simply listen.

It is waiting for you.

15. RETURN

The house has been sitting there for more than a century and a half, right on the corner of Garland Avenue and Esther Street. (You do know, I hope, that Esther was Herbert Garland's second daughter. He, and Gertrude Hayes Garland, had three daughters – Sara, Esther, and Ruth – which explains the names of three parallel streets that intersect with Garland Avenue. That we have neither a Herbert nor a Gertrude Street is just an unbidden blessing.)

You probably know the house. It was once a deep gray with green trim, a four-square with a three-quarters wrap-around porch which on the front had a balcony level. Inside, originally, had been a front parlor, a living room, a dining room, and a kitchen (with large pantry!) on the first floor and four bedrooms and a bathroom on the second floor. The attic was a large, unfinished area with dormer windows in all four directions, rough-hewn wood flooring, and a high ceiling of rafters in the middle that rose to a peak.

But, if you have driven by the house in the last decade you might wonder which word to apply: vacant, abandoned, derelict?

It was first built, not to speculation but to design, by the Howard family: Jason and wife Mildred, daughters Cynthia and Elise, sons Issac and Alfred. Three generations of the Howards lived there, with Alfred and his wife Suzanna (nee Knowlington), introducing daughter Molly to the world in the front parlor.

However, by the time that Molly was ready for school, her parents decided that the neighborhood school (old Latham Elementary) was neither ready nor capable of dealing with a child like Molly, who was clearly exceptional. Just ask her parents. In order for the parental estimation of Molly to be fulfilled, a new house uptown was purchased and the old house on Garland (or was it on Esther? The house strangely had two doors that faced streets, both of them

325

under the ample porch, and from outside one could not immediately tell which led to the entry hallway by the Parlor and which led to the kitchen pantry. Only the balcony facing Garland sealed the address as 1501 Garland Avenue.)

The Immolito family bought the house and called it home for many years. Not having been in on the initial design of the house, they felt free to modify it to suit their wishes. From the outside nothing seemed to change other than the addition of a free-standing garage.

On the inside, the pantry was modified to make room for a "powder room," sufficient to help people relieve or freshen themselves without going upstairs. Above, two of the bedrooms were merged into one large bedroom with space for an adjoining bathroom all its own. And to top it all off, the attic was insulated and paneled with pine. The rough boards were sanded to their natural wide beauty. Heat was provided up there by simply leaving the attic door open to let the hot air rise (which also meant that any sounds in the attic could infect the whole house, a reality realized when rock music, live rock music, became a passion of one of the Immolito boys.

The heating arrangement, while a boon in the winter, meant that summers up there were tropical. About the same time as the attic band was formed, a large, whole-window exhaust fan was installed in the back dormer. At least, if the attic door had to be open, it could serve as a duct to remove the stifling heat of the stories below.

By the time the Immolitos sold the house the only person to offer full price was an investor, a rental agent, a landlord. OK, let's call him what he was, a slumlord. I won't mention his name so as to slur an entire ethnicity, but if you have lived long in Perryburg, you will surely have heard his name, usually with some less-than-complimentary words attached.

The new owner then embarked on a reliable campaign to maximize profit and minimize expenses. New paint? Ha! New roof? Ha! New boiler? Ha! Air-conditioning? Ha! Ha! Ha!

He found willing renters for almost 20 years, but in a downward spiral. Because of his lack of care for the house, each re-rental meant a lower rent. But that lower rent meant his level of profit could only be maintained by even less maintenance.

Now, one might be quick to presume that as Perryburg became a nationally recognized port of welcome for refugees from around the world, such an increasingly inexpensive rental house would be a hot property. The adage, "compared to what they had come from it would seem like a palace" did not prove true for 1501 Garland.

The truth was that the house sat in no-one's land, the area of the city which had become home to no one ethnic group. As the modern settlers arrived from foreign lands, they sought out others of their heritage. Making a home in a new country, and especially in Perryburg, meant finding others who spoke the same, cooked the same, yelled at their kids the same, and worshipped the same. No one wanted to live where no one like them was within earshot or stone's-throw.

1501 became an albatross. The owner was more likely to stop three in three to complain about its burden. He once tried to divide up the house into apartments. He even spent some money (not a lot) to make that happen. Unfortunately, he did it before he had any permits. And, he planned to make it three apartments. That was his mistake. Zoning in that area allowed no more than two residential units on any given lot.

So, he walked away. When the most recent tenants disappeared a month before the lease was up, leaving their security deposit as last month's rent, he turned off the utilities and locked the door. For some unknown but fortunate reason, the water system was drained. (Rumor had it that he had already turned off the water because of a leak in the basement while the tenants were still there.)

As a matter of civic pride, he also stopped paying taxes. Actually, he was about a year delinquent already. After another year, the property appeared on the Tax Auction list. Now, remember this was during the great exodus when Perryburg shrank toward oblivion. The problem was not having too few housing units, it was having too few people. Even the growing number of immigrants did not match the departing natives. Stores closed, service stations closed, schools closed, roads became more pot-holed, and 1501 Garland was part of that. It was closed.

When the auctioneer's gavel fell on 1501, there had been no bids. The house was then, officially, city property. The property of a city with dwindling resources. If it had been leaning, if it had become a crack den, if it had posed a vermin problem, if it had … the list is too long to complete … it would have been demolished.

How well it had been built initially tells you why it did not appear to fall into ruin immediately. How ill-placed it was tells you why it had never been a place for squatters, for druggies, or even for arsonists. It was out in the open, on a corner, on a busy avenue, looking semi-well-kept. That the former owner had not wanted to spend any money for boarding it up meant it sat there, looking almost occupied. City maintenance staff would, at a minimum, make sure the sidewalks were cleared in the (long) winters and the grass somewhat mowed in the summer.

It sat there. Neither improving itself nor declining into oblivion for several years. You know what I mean if you ever drove past it. It looked like it was waiting for something, like an old person who sits on a porch looking down the street for the car that will bring their child back for a visit.

Then, about two months ago, Ruggiero and Sons' trucks pulled into the sublimating driveway. Something was happening. The few cars that came down Esther and stopped at the Stop sign at Garland would pause a bit longer so the occupants could see what was happening. Cars on Garland would slow down to see what was happening. One of them slowed so abruptly that it was rear-ended by the following city bus. The police, attending to the accident (thank goodness there were no injuries as almost everything in Perryburg, even accidents, happens in slow motion) took their time, most of that time to inspect what was going on at 1501.

While the patrol officers were working the scene, Sgt. Callahan went to talk with Phil Ruggiero. They had been in school together at PHS. Phil told him the house had been sold, and they were the first of many workers who would be showing up in the coming month. Livingston Plumbing had their work cut out for them. Alejandro Electric too. The Sargeant promised to keep an eye on the place.

By Thursday, Grover's Mowers were on the scene, not just mowing the grass but also reclaiming the flower beds, planting, and mulching. On Friday, Matera's concrete crew was tearing up concrete and even some slate sidewalks and placing the forms for new concrete.

Was this renovation? Restoration? Reclamation? Redemption? Insanity?

On Saturday, the corner was busy with a growing crowd of dignitaries, members of the press, and more than a few nosy neighbors. It was all about a sign.

Suddenly the neighbors remembered a notice in the newspaper, on TV, and on the city's website a year ago about a new program that would encourage people to move to Perryburg and restore a single-family home. Reading that announcement the universal response had been, "Yeah, right."

(Before I go on, I need to note that most of the neighbors also made comments about the names on the sign. President Biden came in for mixed praise and blame. But, what's with this "pro tem" thing? Apparently the whole community, during the local high school baseball playoffs, had failed to notice that the elected mayor had resigned amid sexual harassment charges.)

Speeches were made and photos taken. Round after round of applause, with each round getting softer, as various officials responsible for this all were introduced. The community was then invited to welcome the new owners of the house, Mr. and Mrs. Theodore Stone. Everyone looked around for someone they did not know. "Oh," Shakia O'Neal, house director for Perryburg said, "they are not here yet. But keep an eye out for them coming soon."

"Awww," was the disappointed community response.

I was hard to tell whether it was an "awww" of disappointment or an "awww" of sympathy for the poor Stones who had fallen for what was obviously a great urban hoax. They had bought the house for one dollar (as was explained somewhere in the many, lengthy speeches) but the title would not pass to them until they had lived in the house for five years. At that time, the house and all the improvements they made would be theirs, totally theirs. Anything less than five years and the city would reclaim the house, its improvements, and seek any unpaid taxes.

For the first week after the sign went up, neighbors and drivers-by alike would look to see if the Stones were there. All they saw were the vans and trucks of various workers.

In the second week, those who continued to look saw the concrete truck making several runs.

In the third week, the handful still interested observed the roofers and painters.

By the fourth week, the number of primary workers had diminished but now various supplier of cabinets, flooring, and the like could be seen, but few neighbors looked.

In the middle of the fifth week, the new blacktop driveway was installed. Nobody dared to drive on it. A scattering of light duty trucks came and went, usually spending an hour or two involving one or at most two workers, always parking on Esther Street, No one noticed except the neighborhood kids who eyed up the new driveway and thought about how nice a basketball hoop would look on the garage face.

It was a little more than six weeks from when the sign went up that a large, gray, unmarked van pulled into the driveway. A tall Black man got out of the driver's seat and walked up onto the front porch. He took out a large ring of keys, tried several, and finally found one that opened the front door. Satisfied, he left the front door open and went back to the van. He was about to open the rear doors of the van when Mr. Riley, from down at 2325 Esther Street, walking his dog Buster, came along.

"Say," Riley said, "what all are you putting into that house now? Can't be much more that needs doing."

"I surely hope not. Nope, just putting a few of these things in there." He opened the van and took out a large baby carriage, wheeling it up and in the front door. Then he was back, this time for pieces of a crib.

Riley observed all this and said, "you work local for these new folks, or are you delivering from some stores."

"Nope, don't work for them, and I'm not delivering for anyone."

Riley looked perplexed.

"Hi, I should introduce myself. I'm Ted Stone, your new neighbor. And you are?"

"Ah, er, I'm David Riley, 2325 Esther. Been here 76 years."

"Well then, you can help me know more about my new neighborhood."

Riley just let that hang there.

At that moment, a nice BMW, one of those new EV models pulled up behind the van. Out of the backseat popped a mocha skinned ball of energy, who rushed Ted and engulfed his knees in a hug.

"Ophelia," Ted said, "this is Mr. Riley, one of our neighbors. Mr. Riley, this is my daughter Ophelia, all three years of her."

"Three years and 10 months! I am pleased to meet you Mr. Riley." Ophelia reached out her hand to Mr. Riley who, never having been so nicely greeted by a child, reached his hand out to hers. As he gently shook her little hand he felt a small bead forming in his right

332

eye. It had been so long since he had touched such a young and such a precious child. Not since his own Cecelia had died fifty years before when she was four, not when she was four years and 10 months old.

The front door of the car opened, and a woman emerged. It took her some time to get out of the car and it soon became evident why. She looked about 10 months pregnant. And she was white, very white.

"Barbara, dear," Ted called, "we have met our first neighbor, Mr. Riley, and …"

"Oh, this is Buster."

"Can I pet Buster."

"Only if you don't come up on him too fast."

Soon Ophelia and Buster were becoming old friends while Barbara walked, or more waddled from the car up to the van.

"Mr. Riley, I am most honored to meet you. And what a wonderful canine companion you have."

Riley was a bit surprised by this couple and their child, by the way they talked, by their friendliness. He decided he needed to respond in kind, not his usual grumpy old man approach to life. "It is my pleasure to meet you, Barbara, and you Ophelia, and you too Ted."

"Ted, would you do us a favor and an honor?" Barbara said.

"What?" a startled David responded.

"Come inside for a few minutes, bring Buster too. You can be our first guest in our new house. I had the crew set up a card table and some chairs last week. Honey, will you get that basket out of the backseat?"

With that, a procession of Barbara, David, Buster, and Ophelia made their way to the open front door of the house. With Barbara's slow progress, Ted was easily able to get the basket from the car and catch up with them.

Inside the front hall, once his cataracted eyes adjusted to the low light, David Riley gave out a long whistle. "This place …. I can't in all my life remember when it looked this good."

The woodwork had all been restored, the floor sanded and sealed, the stairs carpeted with runners, the wall painted a warm blue, the ceilings with their ornate plastering restored, and the original archways to other rooms revealed from under faux doorways.

In the middle of what had been the dining room, and was again with its glass-fronted china cabinet in its original glory, stood an incongruous card table and four folding chairs. Otherwise, except for the baby carriage that was still in the entry, the house stood empty. Or at least it did until it filled with its first visitor.

"Here, please sit here," Ophelia invited, "with Buster between us." Riley did as he was invited. Buster too.

Out of the basket, Barbara pulled several containers which, when opened, revealed some sandwiches. Then she produced several plastic plates and four plastic glasses. Next there appeared two bottles, one of Prosecco and one of sparkling apple juice. Ted busied himself with distributing things, including napkins and utensils.

He took up the apple juice first and opened it with a "Pop." He poured two glasses and set one in front of Ophelia and one in front of Barbara, who received hers and pointed toward the growing presence of new life inside of her. Riley nodded.

Then Ted took the Prosecco and open it with a softer "pop." He poured two other glasses and set one in front of Riley, and he held the other in his hand.

"I would like to make a toast."

"Please," David Riley said, "may I make one first."

Barbara looked lovingly at Ted, and then gave a nod to David.

"To my new friends, Barbara, and Ted, and Ophelia, and a fourth to be named later." They all laughed. "It has been too many years since I have been invited into a newcomer's home, it has been too many years since I have shaken the hand of a charming young lady," looking right at Ophelia, "and it has been too many years since we welcomed any newcomers to the neighborhood. So, I raise this toast, a simple prayer: may you live here as long as I have and my you always welcome new neighbors."

"Amen," shouted Ted. Glasses clinked, or rather plastic glasses clunked.

"Mr. Riley," Barbara asked quietly, "I have a question, if you don't mind."

"Ask away."

"Are you related to Peter Riley over on Ridge Drive?"

David looked startled. "Why, yes, he's my kid brother. Why?"

"Well, his youngest daughter, Regina, was in school with me."

Everyone at the table looked at Barbara with surprised looks.

"Mommy," Ophelia asked, "where did you go to school? How old were you?"

"I knew her from the time I was in Kindergarten through High School."

"You went to Perryburg High School?" an incredulous Riley said.

"Yes, and that is a story for another time. But if you ever talk to Regina, tell her Barbara Bartles says hello."

"Are Ken Bartles daughter?"

"Guilty as charged."

"Well, I'll be."

Later, walking home with Buster, David Riley thought about the day. It had started out like too many of his day had since his wife had died, how many years ago was that, nine, ten? He had walked down the street he had known all his life, a walk which usually depressed him because it reminded him of so much loss. So many people had left Perryburg, never to return. He had brought with him a load of sorrow, and prejudice, and even not a little anger about all the changes he had seen.

But now this day felt different. His street held promise as well as loss. He had made new friends. He had met a charming little girl. Buster had made a new friend as well. He had had a toast of prosecco, his first in several decades.

"Life is beautiful," he said to himself.

Back at 1501, a similar glow filled the house. Ted continued to bring things in from the van while Barbara slowly tried to direct where things should go. The moving van was somewhere on the Interstate, claiming to be there in an hour or two. Ophelia was already chattering about how she hoped she could walk Buster sometimes.

But, who were these three newcomers? Ted's family came from Georgia. He often said that he is glad his ancestors, who were enslaved on a plantation east of Atlanta, had not been given the last name of Stone Mountain as their "owners" threatened upon hearing of the Emancipation Proclamation. "I am fine with Stone, but Georgia can keep its damned Mountain."

He had grown up as the only child of a couple of lawyers in Charlotte, North Carolina. He was bound and determined not to be a lawyer. Instead, he went to UNC undergrad, earning a degree in economics. He had been recruited by the federal government right out of college to work in the Bureau of Labor Statistics.

That is where he met Barbara. She had, indeed, grown up in Perryburg. The day after her high school graduation, she had packed her bags and was off as counselor in a gifted program for middle school students in Pennsylvania. That fall, she started at University of Pennsylvania, also in economics. There she was Phi Beta Kappa and became another recruit for BLS.

Back in the day, as they say, when office work was done in office, the break room was the social hub. The story differs based on which one of them is telling it. Each says they noticed the other in their first week there. Let's just agree to say it was sudden, mutual, and powerful attraction.

Just one problem. Ted was sort of engaged to Rachel and Barbara was seeing Kenneth. So, a friendship developed, nothing more. Or at least they say nothing more. Talk with their co-workers and you hear nothing of nothing-more and lots about dodging the sparks.

In time, the relationships from college, as many college romances do, fell away. But, for a long time, neither knew about the changed relationship status of the other. Remember, this was before either of them was on Facebook. No public announcements of relation changes in those days.

It was at an office party in the December holidays that each arrived alone to a party with a stated "plus one" expectation. "You mean you're not …" was met with a "You mean you're not?!"

Courtship, marriage, get settled in careers, life in DC as young adults. Finally, thinking about children (they both wanted several), trying (such a nice term for such pleasure), failing, trying (now not as pleasurable), failing, getting help in trying (down right not as pleasurable), success. Ophelia!

All this time they were living in a one-bedroom apartment in the District. As a young couple, more space than needed. Even with Ophelia there was enough room. But then, without trying (ah, pleasurable again), Barbara one day announced to Ted, "If I didn't know better, I would say I am pregnant."

This was during the pandemic, and the two of them had been working from home. Little Ophelia was there for some of that, but then began daycare when her growing propensity to join work discussions (and often making more sense than others on the Zoom calls) became too much.

As they say, necessity is the mother of compromises, or something like that. With an offer of permanent remote work dangled before them, a too-small apartment which cost way too much, the need for more space where any option of house owning meant indebtedness until forever even if a house could be found, one night Barbara turned to Ted (after Ophelia had consented to sleep after only five readings of Curious George), "I can't believe I am saying this, but what if we thought about moving to Perryburg?"

"What," Ted said, suddenly sitting up in bed.

"I know, I know. I said I would never go back. I left as soon as I could so I could get out of that dying city. I ran away fast, and I thought forever."

"I know," Ted responded, wisely not adding more.

"But recently I have been thinking back to growing up there. It was good. No, it was great. As I grew up, I could go where I wanted. The schools were good and not a matter of lotteries or who knows who."

"I understand."

"And then I saw this notice in the Federal Register about Urban Homestead programs under the IIJA. Since I work on employment and housing figures, I read through. And one of the cities with such a program is Perryburg."

"And."

"I looked it up. They have about a dozen properties listed, all city owned, in various states of disrepair. Here's the deal. Houses cost one dollar, and you get to own them if you live in them for five years."

"Let me get this right. One dollar, live in it for five years and it's ours?"

"Did you say 'ours'?"

"I did. Think about this. If we were to take even half of what we are spending on rent here, which is nothing compared to what we would need to spend once the new baby arrives, we could rehab almost anything, even a pile of bricks, into a nice house. But, do you want to live for five years in Perryburg?"

"I know this will sound strange, but I do. I think of Ophelia growing up there, seeing things I knew as a kid. I think of undesignated asset number 2 growing up there from the start. I picture a big, old house, with woodwork, and a formal dining room."

"I call that 'Blue Bloods' envy."

"And a yard, and maybe a dog, and garage."

"Ooooo, a garage!"

About a month after that, Ted made the drive up to Perryburg to look at properties. Between work, Ophelia, and the pregnancy, Barbara decided not to go. "I trust you. You know us."

One of the things Ted had learned in his life was that if he were to dress like a worker, put on a hardhat, wear an ID badge, and carry a clipboard, as a Black man he could become invisible, fade into the background.

In Perryburg, he met with the coordinator of the Urban Homestead program. They toured the five houses that had any possibility of being right for them. When he saw 1501 Garland Avenue (he had always wanted to have an Avenue as part of his address), he knew it was the place for them. Using less than half of the money they had saved for purchasing a house in DC, they could renovate beyond belief. He snapped and emailed loads of pictures to Barbara. Her only response was "Oh, please. YES!"

While he was in Perryburg, a place he had only visited in the stories of his wife, he looked around. Sure, it was a rust-belt city with some glory in its past. It was also a city with great diversity. He also saw it was a city on the way up, not the way down. How could he tell? He saw many local start-up businesses. He saw a local entrepreneurial incubator, a partnership between the city, local business, and the college. He found he could eat, and eat well, without ever needing to go to a chain restaurant. He could also eat in those local places without a hint of racism. He was becoming transformed from a willing but skeptical supportive spouse to an eager advocate.

The paperwork was approved, and the house became their responsibility and their possibility. The two of them worked in shifts to get plans drawn, permits pulled (the Urban Homestead program greased the way on many of those), estimates given, and contractors hired. More than one contractor, when told the house that was being worked on became eager at the prospect of working there. They knew the company's restoration reputation could be made with such a project.

Yes, theirs was Urban Homestead, House #1. By the end of the year, six of the properties were either owner-occupied or in the process of renovation. Six families were part of a renewal of Perryburg.

The homesteading program had collateral consequences. About ten families had, at first, looked at the Urban Homestead properties but found nothing to their liking. However, they were so taken with Perryburg's attitude, potential, and promise, they bought other properties in the city.

Now, it may be too soon to speak of a renaissance for Perryburg, so let's just say it is a return. "Return" in many senses of that word. For over half of the households relocating to Perryburg in the last year, it was a return to the city where one or both adults lived as children, or youth, or attended college nearby. For others, it was a return to a city after living in suburbs in other areas.

Perryburg was beginning to understand itself as attractive again. And as one of those returning said, "You know, when someone say to you, 'Hey, you're looking good,' you pick up a little bit and you soon are looking better."

This all is not to say that Perryburg is on a recovery curve that will take it back to when mansions lined Mohawk Street, and streetcars ran down its tree-lined boulevard. Rather it is on its own discovery curve of what it will become, but with a confidence that the future can be good.

. . .

Before we leave Perryburg, we need to make our own return, a return to 1501 Garland Avenue. The house will soon be featured in a "Parade of Homes" to benefit the Perryburg Public Library. People go out of their way to drive by, and many say something like "I just can't believe it! You remember when …"

But let's go on inside 1501. Walk up that new concrete sidewalk to the broad front porch. The hanging porch swing might tempt you to stop there and admire the blooming annuals and the supportive perennials. You might revel in the delightful shade from the restored trees out front. But don't stop there.

Ophelia will open the door to your knock, and invite you in. You will move through the front entry into the parlor where you will find you are one of about a dozen people, all of them neighbors from the street, now considered more friends than neighbors. Over there is Mr. Riley, sitting in the big, overstuffed easy chair. He looks about ten years younger than his age. At his feet is Buster, and beside Buster is a younger, equally black dog, lovingly known as Little Buster. Little Buster belongs to Ophelia. The two dogs are allowing three children, all playmates to Ophelia, to give them all the attention in the world.

Barbara walks into the room from what is now the family room that was created from combining the old living room and kitchen. She is holding her baby, who is now almost a year old.

Everyone oohs and ahhs over the baby.

Ted, with a gentle clap of hands, calls for the attention of everyone. Even Buster and Little Buster look up. Everyone has the beverage of their choice.

"My friends," Ted says, "A year ago Barbara and Ophelia and I were welcomed into your community. We have never looked back. You have made us feel at home, in this house, on this street, in this city. So, a toast to you all, and to us for deciding to make Perryburg home."

Barbara then continued the toast, "And to the one who was our first visitor, and now is a regular presence in our lives – Mr. David Riley." She bends down to place the baby in Mr. Riley's outstretched arms. "Little David needs you as a grandfather in his life." Riley gently gathers up his namesake and raises his glass, "To Perryburg," as the tears flow freely."

EPILOGUE

In the spring of 2023, the first chapter of this book, Exodus, was published as a stand-alone story in the print and e-journal of *The Rust Belt Quarterly*, that fine publication of Mohawk University. In the aftermath of its circulation, many people shared their thoughts.

Some wrote to ask why it was claimed to be about Perryburg when it was clearly about their city of origin, memory, or residence. To them, the story must have been located somewhere else, in New York, Pennsylvania, West Virginia, southern Ohio, or a smattering of other places. Something about Perryburg was emblematic of so many other small cities and towns.

Others wrote in to tell me of their relation to the story. Lisa Mitchell Purcell wrote to say she was the great-granddaughter of the Mitchells. She remembered pictures of the house taken by her great-grandparents, now in albums she inherited from her grandparents. For some reason, she still had a doorknob from the house, one that had been swapped out for a replacement on the day they moved out. On the doorknob was a tag, "Sarah's room." Until she read the story she never knew what that meant; no one in the family talked about it.

Lou Reznick said he had been a manager with the truck rental company back in the day. He remembers well how busy they were, and how the lot was always full except on weekends when nearly every truck was rented to those moving around town. If he were out in Perryburg on a Saturday or Sunday, he would see his trucks either being loaded or unloaded in nearly every neighborhood.

More than one person who had grown up in the neighborhood vouched for the warm cookies that Róża would give to them as children. They remembered her warm smile and broken English.

Others from the neighborhood wrote to remember the house and its decline, coupling it with the decline of the whole city. As their poignant nostalgia poured out, it was evident that a fuller story of Perryburg was needed.

Some offered tidbits of history. Others offered longer narratives, hints of resources, and more. By the time their offers were received, the other chapters about Perryburg had already taken shape, but it was reassuring to know that the new information only served to confirm the validity of the stories as they were being told.

At the same time, other responses suggested new stories needing their own telling. Perryburg was too big to fit into just fifteen chapters. And its story is still being written. This Autobiography of a City is neither an exhaustive nor a posthumous work.

ACKNOWLEDGEMENTS

Fact is always harder than fiction. To create fiction, one needs only oneself, sometimes aided by an editor, maybe an agent, and a willing publisher. To create a biography, one also needs access to others who have known the person. But, in the case of an autobiography of a whole community, a whole community is needed.

To all the people of Perryburg – past and present – I offer my deepest thanks. When I left you years ago to find my way in other worlds, you wished me well. When I returned to live among you again, you welcomed me back.

You invited me into your homes, showed me keepsakes of your families, and shared photo albums on cardboard, thumb drives, and virtual sites. You let yourselves be interviewed and I am deeply indebted to your willingness to ramble on, even when the others in the room thought you had said enough. It was often at the tail end of a tale from your memories that we hit paydirt together.

To Sylvia Maguire, Shawn MacNeil, Lou Perillo, and Stan Hapawicz, custodians of the oral history of Perryburg held by the many civic groups, deep appreciation for connecting me to members of the community you thought would add to my research.

Invaluable assistance was given by the Mohawk County Historical Society and the Office of the Mayor of Perryburg. Perryburg Public Library and Perryburg Public Schools opened their archives without limit or hesitation. The *Times-Dispatch's* extensive records of not only their daily newspapers but also of their commercial printing were indispensable to getting the dates and names correct.

Without the aid of Baxter and Sidney, LLC, and all their efforts to obtain any needed permissions or clearances, much of this story would have gone untold.

My deepest thanks to Della Vale of Vale Transcriptions for the meticulous work to transform the many interview tapes into transcripts.

My two editors, Betty Crawford in Perryburg and Hans Forst in Boston, made sure that the accuracy, the tone, the vernacular of Perryburg, and the common grammar were protected.

I also want to thank my parents, Bill and Gladys, who brought me into this world in Perryburg and instilled in me a respect for the diverse people who made and make it a community. I hope my brothers will not feel I have revealed too much or too little when our lives became part of the story.

And last, but not least, to you, the reader, deep appreciation. When you read about Perryburg and connected its story with your own story, wherever that story played out, you created an amalgam that is the story of Everytown. In doing so, you lived out the call to focus on connections, not on differences, a maxim that will always serve the world well.

DISCUSSION GUIDE
Dorothy Sprague, MRE
Robert Knowles, MEd

For an Urban Mosaic History work such as *Perryburg*, the usual discussion guides provided for book discussion groups will not suffice. Unlike most fiction and non-fiction, in which there is a single narrative or research thread and a continuum of characters, *Perryburg* presents us with multiple themes and a moving cast of characters.

To engage this community of events, ideas, and people, we will use the Shared Praxis model of Tom Groome (Boston College), which invites us to engaging process more than a series of questions. In that process there are six movements:

I. Initiating event or question (see the prompts below for each chapter)

II. Naming our own knowing – given the initiating event or question, what has been our experience around the topic. (see the second question for each chapter)

III. Connections – how do our individual stories (what we have named as knowing) find common ground. If done in a group, this is where the members of the group name those elements which appear in multiple participant's personal stories. Sometimes these might be evident activities or events, other times it might be threads or themes which are common.

IV. Sharing the story – in each case, this would be one of the chapters from *Perryburg*. Re-read the chapter with movements I-III in mind.

V. Dialogue and dialectic – in what ways do our personal and collective experiences around the theme match or diverge from what is shared in the chapter. How does our re-reading it in light of our initiating considerations change our perception of both our own stories and the chapter's narrative.

VI.   Now what, so what? – what new questions arise about our individual, our collective, and the Perryburg stories that might invite us to further inquiry or action.

As you might not, that sixth step could propel the individual or group back into the whole process again.

If engaged as an individual, we strongly recommend the use of journaling to process the material; as a group, it may be helpful to have newsprint and markers available for movements III, V, and V so no element of the collective process is lost.

For each chapter in *Perryburg*, we offer up one or more initiating questions or activities and then propose the prompt for your Naming Your Own Knowing.

Then follow through the other movements, using the first two movements as a foundation.

1.   Exodus

Perryburg appears to be a dying city. What are the hallmarks of a city in decline, as revealed in this chapter?

Have you ever lived in a dying city or town? What was that like? Did you stay or leave?

2.   The Reunion

What do you expect to have at a high school reunion?

Have you ever been to a high school reunion? What was that like.

3.	Union Station

Find a picture of Grand Central Terminal's (New York) main concourse. Looking at it, what is going on?

Was there a place of arrival and departure in the city of our childhood? What was it? How did it feel to be there?

4.	Wisteria Gardens

If I say, "Retirement home?" what is your first reaction?

Have you ever visited a retirement home or community? If so, share your experience.

5.	Emmett's

To start, Google some piece of hardware you would like to buy. Then, think of a question about that product. Who would you ask?

Remember a time when you visited any old-fashioned store – how was it different from modern stores?

6.	Tip-Top House

Find a picture of an old-fashioned lunch counter. See how many things in the picture would not be familiar to a teenager today.

Tip-Top house was about people who went unnoticed in their community, but who added much to it. Can you remember any such people in your own experience?

7.	Neighborhoods

Take a look at the images that come up from a search for "neighborhood."

With those images in mind, remember the various neighborhoods you have lived in. What made it a neighborhood?

8.   Matters of Faith

Go to https://www.pewresearch.org/religion/quiz/religious-typology/ and discover your religious type.

Then, share how what it discloses compares to your experience of religion. What is your own history of religious involvement?

9.   Suburbs

Think about where you live now – what are the suburbs of that place?

What has your experience of suburbs – did you ever live in one? What did you think of other suburbs?

10.   Log Cabin Motel

Look at images from a search for "Seedy motels nearby"

Does this remind you of any stays in any motels?

11.   The Ablatate

The story is about a hidden secret in an old building. So, let's talk about secrets, old secrets.

What is the biggest secret you found out about long after the fact?

12.   Seasons of Perryburg

On a calendar, for each month, write a word that expresses how you feel about that month.

Then, share your own story/stories of how you feel about each season of the year.

13.   Mohawk Street

Find pictures, both old and now, of main streets of several communities – what similarities and differences do you see.

Remembering where you grew up, what did it mean to be on the "Main Street" in the community?

14. The River

The chapter contains suggested activities around a river near you. Follow them.

What did the river of your choice tell you?

15.   Return

Read the first three paragraphs of this chapter.

Then, share what experiences you have had in returning to various places in your life.

And an activity for you to do during the reading of this work:

- Get a large piece of paper and pencils (colored pencils would work well)
- With the first chapter, start to create a map of Perryburg
- With each new chapter, amend your map as new information is shared
    - If you are using colored pencils, you might color code the changes to the chapters
- As the map gets closer to completion, ask yourself some questions:
    - If you lived in Perryburg now, where would you live? 1950? 1920? 1850? 1700?
    - What part of Perryburg still remains mysterious, unknown?
    - If you were making changes to the city you have mapped, what would they be?